Gazing at the Distant Lights

By

Doug Margeson

W & B Book Publishers
USA

Gazing at the Distant Lights © 2019. All rights reserved by Doug Margeson.

No part of this book may be reproduced or transmitted in any form or by any means, graphic, electronic, or mechanical, including photocopying, recording, taping, or by any informational storage retrieval system without prior permission in writing from the publisher.

W & B Book Publishers

For information:
W & B Book Publishers
9001 Ridge Hill Street
Kernersville, NC 27284

www.a-argusbooks.com

ISBN: 9781635541625

This is a work of *fiction*. All of the characters, organizations and events portrayed in this novel are either products of the author's imagination or used fictitiously.

Book Cover designed by Dubya

Printed in the United States of America

Prologue

Speak to me of wondrous things
Of autumn mists on robins' wings
In young girls' eyes such magic sings
Speak to me of wondrous things
And I will speak to you
Of the ordinary.

They arrived in the hushed mauve of a December morning. No one invited them. No one needed to. They owed him this. They owed him more, so much more, and they knew it and the knowledge ached and left an emptiness in them.

On Dec. 14, 1980, they gathered to say good bye to John Lennon; ten thousand of them, the newspapers would say, if numbers mattered.

She told her husband she would go and he nodded as if he understood. But he did not understand. He had not been part of it, not in the way she had. He had invested less, engaged less, felt less. But he had lost less, too. Maybe he was better for it. Who could say?

As she dressed, it mocked her: Nostalgia for the sixties, the Great Never Was, a half-light of impressions and illusions gleaned from a past that was, in truth, far from the stuff of idyllic reminiscence.

Well, you had to be there, she thought. Then she shook her head and chuckled. Already she was starting to sound like an old woman; one of the legions in their sensible shoes and makeup that never quite hides the advancing wrinkles.

The crowd gathered at the Seattle Center. It had been the place of a world's fair in the year 1962 and even now, as the wind whistled between buildings coarse with the peeling paint of decline, its modernist cambers and contours still managed to evoke phantoms of bright-eyed optimism, a certainty in the future, hope. Once people believed in such things, once upon a time before disappointment and perfidy and loss, such great loss.

The death of a Beatle; who'd have ever thought it. She inhaled deeply and let the reality settle. They had been young, so achingly, fiercely young. I thought we had more time. . .

Now, in mourning, they huddled in small groups, holding their hands over candles to keep the drizzle from the flames. It was what they had left.

A woman came out of the stillness and embraced her. "Peace and love," the woman said; a small middle-aged woman, her face puffy with spent tears, but with deep young girl's eyes.

She embraced the sad little woman lightly, surprised at the naturalness of such intimacy with a stranger.

"You too," she said, and then the little woman was gone. Peace and love; how long since she had heard it. For a moment, she felt again the world painted in magenta and orange, strung out on the long, extended twang of an electric guitar, a thick haze of scents and sensations– or so it seemed. Could you tell now, twelve years later, thirteen years later, a century later?

A small group started singing quietly: "All we are saaaying is give peace a chance." They sang it over and over, a familiar chant, appropriate, the sort of thing you were supposed to sing at gatherings like this.

But then, someone started singing another song.

If there's anything that you want
If there's anything I can doooo

Others picked it up. And soon they all were singing it, the early stuff, the simple stuff, the joyful stuff. They wanted to feel the spontaneity, the gaiety, just one more time.

She was thirty five-years-old now, an age when one gives over to practicalities, to the rote of the day-to-day. Her life had the sad sense of anti-climax reserved for old men. And she didn't like to admit it, but the last year she remembered as a year, as a set piece of time, was 1968.

Wow, browsing old bookstores and finding you spend all your time looking at back issues of *Life,* a dead magazine with pictures of Bobby Kennedy and Tet and Hendrix; time frozen on 12-year-old paper that doesn't matter anymore.

Who understood the years, if they were meant to be understood. Perhaps they were meant only to be felt; their white heat dwindled to an umber glow, cold and dark, but still there, always in the mental recesses of the old young.

On some nights, when she drank martinis and made the mistake of listening to music from 1968 in a dark room, she even found herself missing the war, for god's sake. It made her angry. Is there anything more pathetic than people who reminisce while managing to forget what actually happened? But Tolstoy found nobility in the retreat from Moscow, which sounds absurd until you read it. From the outside, it all was so brutal and wasteful and sad. From the inside. . . well, it was those things, too. But there was something else and she couldn't get it out of her mind, something in a quality of light, in a song...

She missed it. Oh, how she did miss it so.

Someone released balloons. They drifted white against the flat pewter sky, blending with it as they rose into one last infinity.

And so it was over. The current had taken her as far as it would go and now it had run out into the vague estuaries of long-ago perceptions. She remembered the beginning and she remembered the end. But mostly, she remembered the beginning.

****

Chapter 1

It began with fire.

The line for freshman registration stretched down Nickerson Street like a thin, cold string of beads. The only light came from a lamp pole across the street and the only heat came from the students themselves. It wasn't freezing, but it was cold enough, and it was one a.m., September 23, 1964 and the 18-year-olds in the line wished they were somewhere else.

But the doors to registration opened at 8 a.m. and signups for classes were on a first come-first served basis. There was no point in complaining about it. It would do no good. So no one did. They tried to endure the bleak ordeal with as much good humor as they could muster.

That's why someone had started a fire in the yard in front of Brougham Pavilion, about half way back in the line – that and the fact that everyone was desperate for a touch of heat, no matter how small.

The fire illuminated those around it, coating their features with in liquid amber. It made them anonymous, in a way, for it cast shadows upward, streaking them with splashes of black. Some were smiling. Some were talking. But most merely stared into the flames, enduring what they had to endure, hoping for better times.

****

Tom Brewer made sure he wore his new coat to registration. To him, it marked his passage into the world of college. He had bought it at Martin and Eckmann, one of the most prestigious stores in town, and it cost thirty dollars, which made the salesman whistle with satisfaction as he took it to be wrapped. It was a new vinyl material that looked like suede and it was long, reaching to about mid-thigh. That made it a coat, not one of the many kinds of jackets Brewer had worn all through school. His parents had chosen those and he rarely had a say in the matter. The suede coat he bought for himself, with money from a summer job bagging groceries. With four leather buttons and a lapel-like collar, Brewer thought it looked collegiate.

He had all his registration materials; a thick packet that included the fall quarter catalog, the freshman handbook and a dozen or so official forms that he barely understood. He also had a cashier's check for three hundred four dollars, made out to Seattle Pacific College.

As he waited in the front seat of his father's 1960 Buick, Brewer felt uneasy. College was irrevocable. He would succeed or fail based on. . . based on what? He didn't know. Intelligence and self-discipline, presumably, and he wasn't sure how much of either he actually had. If he didn't have enough, he would find out soon and that discovery, he knew, would be painful.

But college also would be something new and he wanted something new. For eighteen years, his life had been dictated to him in one form or another, and while that dictatorship offered security, the price for it was too high for him to bear indefinitely. For deep inside Brewer there was a voice, his voice, that wanted to be heard and a life, his life, that wanted to be lived ~ lived for itself, rather than as an element of someone else's equation.

His father opened the car door and got in. His father was silent with resentment. The college was across town and no buses ran at this hour so, in his mind, he was being burdened with yet another parental responsibility. He was tired of them, in all their embodiments.

"No other way to do this, huh?" he grumbled as the car crossed the old concrete bridge on Princeton Street and turned on to Sand Point Way. At any hour, the road was a soulless canyon of blind turns, cracked concrete and unwalkable shoulders of crudely broken basalt. At 1:30 a.m., it was even more desolate and dead, twisting and fading in the dark, past places where people slept behind locked doors, comatose in blackness.

There was no other way to do this and the father knew it. Doors opened at 8 a.m. and that was that. Therefore, the earlier you got in line, the better. Tom had explained it all, but his father was still convinced his son must have botched some step in the process and that was why he was on the road at such an ungodly hour. Tom could feel his father's contempt. He was used to it.

****

Marilyn Pennell had been trained in how to behave for as long as she could remember and this, she reasoned, would be no different. Be poised. Use proper diction. Make sure you have good posture. Choose the people you associate with carefully. You will be judged by your association with them. If need be, put others in their place.

Exercise those rules and the situation, almost any situation, will take care of itself. Or so she had been taught from the time she was five years old until now, four months after her eighteenth birthday. Her mother had instilled them in her knowingly, patiently and every day. The rules certainly worked well for her mother: Married to one of the most prominent contractors in the county, a two-story house in the best part of town, a country club membership, an excellent wardrobe, the respect of all who knew her – or, more accurately, all with whom she associated. For she did not associate with just anyone.

The rules worked for Marilyn, too: Honor Roll, Girls Club vice president, cheerleader, editor of the year book. Pity Wenatchee didn't have debutante balls, her mother said, for Marilyn would have been first on the list.

Marilyn was wrapped in a well-constructed shield. You could almost see it, like a plastic cylinder protecting her as she walked by; back straight, head erect, eyes focused forward, a clear awareness of the world around her and a clear mastery of it.

Nothing wrong with that, she thought. It was useful on a practical level. She had none of the social insecurities she saw in so many other girls.

But lately she began having doubts. From time to time, she liked to talk as if she had a wilder side, disclosing, in a knowing way, that she liked a good whiskey sour – which she never actually had tried – and, through the use of winks and a raised eyebrow, hints that she might have a taste for other revelries. It was all an act, of course . . . or was it?

****

Marilyn Pennell was a striking figure, tall, slender, with long auburn hair, cameo-like skin and rather aristocratic features – or maybe they merely seemed aristocratic because of her demeanor.

Yes, the shield did indeed work well, even at 1 a.m., even as she walked alone across the darkened campus toward the registration line.

No one would have guessed that inside her simmered a gnawing disquiet. She didn't like to admit it, but her future Junior Leaguer mien was becoming tiresome, enough she wondered if it was worth it. Boys didn't seem particularly impressed with it. But then, most of the boys in her town were oily-haired oafs self-absorbed with macho poses that involved a Lucky Strike dangling for one's lower lip. Or so it appeared to her.

And that was the problem. Was she seeing things as they really were or was she filtering them through her carefully constructed view of how the universe should work? A high school English class in the last quarter of her senior year had cemented that doubt. They had studied Hawthorne, who wrote about life as an illusion. To Hawthorne, the quantifiable features of a thing were not necessarily its essence. Essence was trickier, involving abstraction, distillation, and, most disturbing for Marilyn, intuition.

The concept of intuition, up to then, was something people like her mother used to keep witty repartee moving along, as in referring to feminine intuition when they couldn't cite any actual facts to back up whatever point they were trying to make. A knowing roll of the eyes concluded the process and, as with most of the behaviors Marilyn had been taught, it usually worked. It made you seem worldly and wise. It made you seem witty. Above all, it protected you from any exposure of weakness.

But intuition as a way of understanding a thing? That had never occurred to her until the class on Hawthorne and until she turned in a paper on the subject, complete with all the carefully calculated concepts and phrases that teachers seemed to like - and got back a C.

The teacher was one Miss Ferch. She was thin and stringy, with short-cropped hair, thick glasses and a perpetual scowl. Not yet thirty, she already had permanent frown lines on her forehead and at the corners of her mouth. She smelled of stale cigarette smoke. It was rumored that she liked to take casual strolls through the girls locker room just as the assembled were toweling off.

Just who does she think she is, giving *me* a C, Marilyn thought. It had never happened to her before. She asked Miss Ferch about it. Without looking up for the pile of paperwork that permanently blanketed her desk, Miss Ferch said, "I see no originality here. You really don't understand what Hawthorne is saying. I thought you were smarter than that."

Marilyn was dumbstruck. No teacher had ever criticized her work before, and certainly not with the cold bluntness she had just heard. People did not talk to Marilyn Pennell like that. Her reputation, her demeanor, her well-established prestige would not allow it.

Well, what would you expect. Miss Ferch was neurotic. Miss Ferch was a lezzie. Miss Ferch was. . . Marilyn could not get around the fact that for all her brittle enmity, Miss Ferch knew her stuff. Her class was the first English course that actually made Marilyn think. Sometimes, she even found it interesting.

Once her indignation died down, some cold, Miss Ferch-like realities started to settle in Marilyn's mind. It was true; she really did not understand what Hawthorne meant. She didn't understand because she wasn't trying to understand. She was, as always, trying to find the right collection of details, the right combination of safe, convincing phrases and the right neat conclusions that would impress a teacher, get her a good grade, make her parents happy and ensure she would continue on the path to the bright, successful life for which she was destined.

But now here was something else, another reality, and it actually might be her reality. Illusion, essence, distillation, intuition; Hawthorne was on to something. But what? She couldn't put it into words, but she knew it involved more than turning in neatly-typed papers and getting a good grade.

Doubt was a new experience for Marilyn, an unsettling experience, but one she found she rather liked. Uncertainty may have been a bit scary, but it also was exciting. Fear and excitement; maybe they were the same thing.

Or course, one could not ignore practicalities. Marilyn still managed to pull a B from Miss Ferch's class and still managed to stay on the Honor Roll. She managed to march down the aisle at graduation with a gold cord draped around her shoulders, the badge of a student in the top ten percent. Her parents were delighted. All was well.

But Marilyn continued to wonder if her carefully-constructed, well-disciplined approach to life might have flaws. No, not just flaws. Maybe it was missing the point entirely. Was her reality a facade, a mere imitation of life?

She didn't know what to do about it. There was no one she could talk to. And even if there was, what would she say? She could think of no words or phrases that expressed her doubt. Doubt for its own sake was a foreign concept in her world.

Fortunately, she knew to mask her confusion. Be poised. Use proper diction. Make sure you have good posture. Choose the people you associate with carefully.

And now here she was, doing just that as she walked past the giant glass cube of Moyer Hall on her way to freshman registration. She had done a lot of the paper work earlier. Her parents contributed properly comfortable amounts to SPC and it was easy to pull strings. But she would still have to wait in the line. And she still had to get up at 1 a.m. to do it. All the poise in the world could not ameliorate that.

Marilyn Pennell refused to wear a beanie. Some freshman did wear them; maroon and white skull caps with a bold 68 on them. Rumor was that if upper classmen saw you without one, they could razz you. Marilyn was willing to take the risk. She had spent a lifetime learning how to dress for effect, and beanies certainly were not part of that construct. If beanies were the accepted fad, well, she was above the fad. Choose the people you associate with carefully. If need be, put others in their place.

She walked by The Loop, the semi-circular road that constituted the main entrance to the lower campus, and then past the Student Union Building. She came to the crosswalk at Bertona Street and Third Avenue West. That's when she got her first good look at the line of students waiting for freshman registration. They were silhouetted by the light from a small bonfire.

****

The Brewer family Buick turned off Northeast 45th and passed alone through the gothic arched canyons of 15th Northeast. It turned on Campus Parkway, stopped briefly at the tangle of streets converging at Seventh Northeast and Northeast 40th and then continued on. The lights from the power station at Sixth

Northeast sparkled like icy fireflies as the car passed. Then it turned on to Northeast Pacific Street, the route to SPC. Brewer looked out the widow, toward Lake Union, its shore lined with lumber yards and boat yards and shipwrights and welding shops and warehouses filled with nets and buoys and cleats and chains and pulleys; the stuff of the sea; a place of purpose, always in motion – always except for now, in the India ink of night.

It was his parents' idea that Brewer attend SPC. The reasons for their insistence involved his older brother Orrin. From his early childhood, Orrin had been a sullen, bad-tempered kid, an extreme version of his father, perhaps. Orrin Brewer's response to the universe was a grunt.

The family dynamic came to revolve around him: The father habitually haranguing him to quit being so goddamned lazy and Orrin slouching, moping and mumbling, if he spoke at all.

The mother fretted. A normally proper and decorous woman, news of Orrin's various misdeeds and failures would put her in paroxysms of either wide-eyed helplessness or burned-out resignation. At those times, she reminded Tom of women from 1930s movie melodramas; slumped listlessly in a chair, cigarette drooping from the lips, her haggard expression of defeat and world-weariness lovingly rehearsed and perfected.

Somehow, Tom could never understand how, Orrin got accepted to the University of Washington. After two quarters, one on probation, he flunked out.

What followed was a time of great trauma in the Brewer household. The father ranted endlessly that the education system was a fraud manipulated by elitists and fops and the mother openly discussed suicide. Orrin either stayed locked in his room or went for long drives in his rusty, 1953 DeSoto.

Tom did his best to become invisible. But the fact that he was the one in the family who continued a normal rhythm of life seemed to aggravate his parents.

"Oh, off to high school again, eh?" his father would say. "Just our own little version of Archie, aren't we."

In his sophomore year, Brewer turned out for football and made the junior varsity team. His father, who usually was obsessed with manly pursuits, sneered.

"Look at your forearms," he would say and point at the bruises, the badge of high school football players. "You're too damn skinny. Why don't you just stay home and help out around here for a change."

His father's pronouncements became reality, after a sorts, in the third quarter of the fourth game of the season. Brewer picked up a fumble, took two steps and was promptly hit by three tacklers all at once. He came down hard on the point of his shoulder, the collarbone snapped with a sound like kindling and he felt himself enveloped in a lightning bolt of pain. Between his teeth a "gggggggg" sound emerged and purple dots danced before his eyes. The dots grew bigger and bigger and then he saw nothing until he woke up.

When his father arrived, he shook his head resignedly.

"Well, I told you," his father sighed. "I hope you understand how much this will cost me."

When the doctor told Tom he was done with football, he felt desperate. Football was his escape. He hadn't played enough basketball to be especially good at it and, despite hours and hours of boyhood practice, he had no particular knack for baseball. So he decided to try distance running. At that, he found he had the least talent of all. But everyone in the sport, both coaches and his fellow runners, assured him that if you simply disciplined yourself to run, run, run, day after day, week after week, you would become good at it. So he ran day after day, week after week, firm in the belief that a will of iron could conquer all.

It did not. The best he ever did was an occasional third place, and then he would stagger across the line on the ragged edge of unconsciousness.

He blamed himself, specifically his weak will. So after school, while others walked home, hung around with their friends or tentatively developed their skills at approaching the opposite sex, he would be out running; in the sun, in the rain, in the hot, in the cold; a gaunt, lonely figure in blue trunks and gray sweatshirt loping arduously through Woodland Park, or Ravenna Park or around Green Lake or along the sidewalks of the back streets leading between the parks and the school; always the same back streets because they were obscure and he did not like to be seen. Sometimes, he would round a corner and a classmate would come into view and he would be embarrassed. If he was a champion and known for it, that would be one thing. But he was not. He merely looked peculiar.

But he persevered. Every afternoon at 3:10 p.m., his daily ritual of pain would be waiting for him. It weighed on him, turning him more and more somber with apprehension as the day wore on. The fear made him austere and aloof, and so he was judged by others; a strange, lonely kid, and yet, in the minds of some, oddly attractive in the way of the eccentric.

He came to believe in that image himself, to a point. Mostly, though, he wanted to win a race. But he never did, not in three years. If only he had more discipline, more will, he told himself. The fact that he simply was not cut out to be a long distance runner, the way that some are not cut out to be jugglers or trumpet players or tightrope walkers, never occurred to him.

In his parents' minds, his lack of success was a symptom of the same sort of unfathomable woes that caused Orrin to flunk out. Accept the safe and the secure, they told him. Anything that involved a risk was fraught with nameless perils.

"A high school guidance counselor, that's the sort of thing for you," his father said. "They don't really do anything and once you get a job, they can never fire you. Or maybe a good desk job at a big insurance company. Yessir, keep your nose clean and your mouth shut and you've got a job for life. Just ask Mr. Poscowicz."

Mr. Poscowicz was their next door neighbor. Every weekday morning, Mr. Poscowicz would pass the Brewer house at 7:42 a.m. on his way to the bus stop a block away; never at 7:41, never at 7:43, and if he missed a day, Brewer never saw it.

Mr. Poscowicz trod his daily odyssey with a distinctive, robot-like plop, plop, plop of fallen arches. He did not move his arms. He did not look left or right.

Mr. Poscowicz always wore the same nondescript baggy overcoat and the same tan felt hat with the brim turned up all around. He always carried a sack lunch.

He always wore the same expression: No expression, his face a gray blank, for Mr. Poscowicz had no discernible personality, none Brewer had ever seen, at least. He caught the same bus at the same time and travelled the same route, day after day, year after year, to a big insurance company in a big building that resembled, more than anything, a tombstone. There, Mr. Poscowicz he joined a torpid stream of his own kind shuffling insensate through the maw of the corporate necropolis.

The company ran on bells: A bell for starting time, a bell for lunch, a bell for quitting time. The times never varied, not for as long as anyone could remember and many had worked there for twenty years or more. All men were required to wear white shirts – no other color – solid colored ties and suit jackets they never took off. All women wore long sleeved dresses with hems six inches below the knee. No smoking. No eating or drinking at one's desk, not even coffee. Conversation about anything other than business was strongly discouraged. Managers watched closely to make sure.

At 5:37 p.m. every weekday, Mr. Poscowicz caught the bus home. At 6:02, it stopped at the same stop where he waited in the morning. Baggy raincoat and tan hat properly affixed to his substructure, Mr. Poscowicz would plod his flat-footed plod past the Brewer home, disappear into his gray house and not be seen until 7:42 a.m. the next day, when the grand adventure that was his life began all over again.

Brewer swore he would never let himself end up like Mr. Poscowicz. But how? The world that he lived in offered few models for anything else. It made Brewer shudder.

As for becoming a high school guidance counselor: Another shudder. To Brewer, school was a prison. Within its walls, it was ruled by spoken and unspoken strictures designed to focus on the irrelevance of the individual and the authority of the group.

Some of the rules were simple rote; the hours of the class periods, the bells, the schedules, the overdue library book fines and the like. Others were idiosyncratic exercises in whim that came out of nowhere and exhibited no visible rationale. One teacher would not let boys in her class if they did not button the cuffs of their shirts. Once, Brewer had a music class in which the teacher insisted the students sing Negro spirituals, replete with Al Jolsen-style hand gestures. Brewer found it embarrassing and tried to hide. But she spotted him and threw him out of class because, in her words, "You are not having enough fun!"

Another time, a friend of his, a member of the golf team, came back from practice wearing a pork pie rain hat, his good luck charm. He had to meet his girlfriend, which required a walk past the main office. The principal spotted him, demanded to know what this sartorial subversion was all about, confiscated the hat and put a note in the kid's file marking him as a known troublemaker.

And so it went. You never knew when such things would occur and you never knew why. You only knew that you had to suffer it silently, betraying no hint of response. Otherwise, even worse would happen.

The other strictures were the societal rules the students developed themselves. Their most obvious manifestation was the lunchroom crew. Their job was to make sure the lunchroom was kept clean - trays were returned, garbage thrown away and the like. It looked good on paper, the sort of Responsible Young People Contributing to Their Community that impressed the people back at district headquarters. In reality, the crew was made up of members of the bruised knuckle and heavy-browed set who discovered that lunchroom duty gave them license to push people around. So they wandered about the room, slapping and bullying anyone who spilled milk or left their tray behind, all under the approving gaze of the administration, which concluded it gave it one less problem to worry about.

More subtly, student subculture conceived scores of status systems - who knew who, who looked right, who best reflected the mores of the society - and they were constantly fluctuating.

Brewer was aware of them and kept abreast of them enough to get by undisturbed. But he couldn't outmaneuver School Spirit. Bands, cheerleaders and pep clubs were formed to encourage it, but Brewer never understood why because he never understood what it was. He felt no kinship to the school and, while he was glad when its teams won, he couldn't see why it was cause for the feverish delirium many seemed determined to evoke.

At one basketball game, a cheerleader, a tiny, hyperactive girl who liked to call attention to herself, stood with her hands on her hips and glowered at Brewer because he didn't rise with the others in a unison clapping. She was going to see to it that there would be School Spirit or else. Everyone turned their gaze toward Brewer. As he squirmed, he could hear titters of laughter. The crowd was enjoying the scene.

Then, one day, it was all over. Brewer graduated. As he walked down the aisle with diploma in hand, it was all behind him;

the stuff of misty, nostalgic memories, if one chose to see it that way – which Brewer did not.

On to the future. So, what exactly did Brewer envision for that future?

He did not know.

He did know, or at least sensed, that this moment in history, this 1964, was a singular time, something special, a pivotal moment in generational history. Maybe it was just Beatlemania. Or maybe it was something more. He sensed more; something unpredictable and dangerous and grand. Or maybe it was just a combination of youthful longing and the vivid imagination of the inexperienced.

****

Marilyn crossed Nickerson Street, turned and walked down the line toward the far end. As she walked, she made sure she smiled, as if she were enjoying some festive gathering; a homecoming dance, the line to a new movie, whatever.

. . . play the role, play the role, play the role . . .

Sometimes, she saw a familiar face framed in the silvery mist of a street lamp and she would nod pleasantly and say hi; a small thing to set her apart from the legion of the cold and the sleepless who huddled in thick coats, apathetic and anonymous.

. . . play the role, play the role, play the role. . .

Marilyn reached the end of the line and took her place. She found she didn't know any of the people around her. They didn't seem to know one another. No one spoke. No one tried to make eye contact. Their faces were slate.

She looked ahead. The campfire by Brougham was at least fifty yards away. Nothing to do but endure. At such times, Marilyn turned inward; her thoughts, her senses, her consciousness folding into a cocoon, detaching herself from the rest of the world. She did that now. Then, like the others, she settled down to wait in silence.

****

Brewer grew up four miles from the University of Washington. Like everyone else in Seattle, he followed its football team and, since he was a child, had heard of the university's lore. Above all, he heard that it was hard to get in it and harder still to stay. To Brewer, the university represented an extension of the monolith that seemed to hover over much of his young life. We are the power, you are not. We can accept you or reject you as we see fit. We control your future.

The perception was sealed when he attended a UW admissions conference. The university's registrar – its admissions director – conducted it. He was a big, red-faced, rumpled man who prided himself in blunt, straight talk; a self-appointed civic raconteur who knew how to put freeloaders, lefties, pinkos, percy-boys and other forms of malcontents in their place. "Down to earth," "plain-spoken" and "no-nonsense" were among the terms the local press used to describe him. The town's babbitry canonized him. He was one of their own, their resident delegate to the feather-brained ivory towers of higher education.

When he spoke to a room full of high school seniors, he knew just what to say.

"So go ahead, goof off, hang around the coffee shops, play the bongo drums. Then when your grades fall below a two point, out you go, down to get a job at the dump." He gave a contemptuous, dismissive wave of his hand when he said it. Clearly, he relished the image of once bright-eyed young hopefuls, thrashed and broken, shuffling up to the gates of the garbage dump – which, as luck would have it, was just down the hill from the university so all could view their disgrace.

It was the registrar's hand gesture that got to Brewer, the almost superfluous dismissal it personified, the connotation that human beings who didn't measure up to his standards barely existed at all.

Brewer remembered a high school English class where the teacher asked the students what they meant by "they." Who was this "they," this anonymous authority the students were always referring to, as in "They won't let us?" No one had an answer. But now Brewer realized there actually was a They. He was watching Their embodiment.

The registrar could be as insulting, vulgar and officious as he liked. No one dared challenge him, no one in this room, certainly. They wanted to get into college, he *was* college and they would have to endure his condescension. He knew they would.

They always did. Some, the future Rotarians in the crowd, even laughed at his wit.

Yes, there is a They, Brewer thought. They were the well-entrenched and the well-practiced; so accustomed to wielding Their power that a skinny kid from Seattle, Washington mattered no more than a gnat. Well, maybe you have the power, he thought, but you don't have the right, you arrogant old bastard. Oh, I have to put up with it, and I will. But I never will bow to it. Never.

The thought was still on his mind when he arrived home. His parents were waiting for him in the living room.

"Tommy, your father and I would like to have a little talk with you," his mother said solemnly. She was sitting on the couch; a prim, white-starched personification of a proper suburban matron. His father was, as always, sunk in his leather easy chair. That left a straight-backed wooden chair against the far wall, placing Brewer at the converging azimuths of his parents' very serious eyes.

"Tommy, we've been talking and we've decided the UW is not the best place for you," his mother said.

"What?" Brewer asked, surprised.

"Don't interrupt your mother," the father said.

"I've done some calling around," his mother said. "Seattle Pacific said it will provide you with a good Christian education. That's what the lady said, 'A good Christian education.' So you won't get into any trouble there. And it's small, so you won't have all those problems Orrin had."

Brewer tried to take it all in. He wouldn't get into trouble? Like what? Except for once being thrown out of that music class in eighth grade, he had never been in trouble of any kind in his entire life.

Those problems Orrin had? Brewer's grades were good. Orrin had never read a complete book in his life, certainly never a complete textbook. Did they actually think Orrin would succeed in college?

Before he could complete the thought, his father took something from his breast pocket and flipped it across the room. It landed at Brewer's feet. It was a condom, its foil package creased and worn but unopened and still unmistakably a condom.

"You want to tell me what that is?" his father said.

Brewer could think of nothing to say.

"One day, I was searching your room for . . . for the newspaper and I accidentally bumped your wallet and that fell out," his father said.

It was a lie, of course. Brewer kept his wallet in his dresser drawer and he kept the condom tucked deep inside its card pocket.

"It's pretty clear we can't trust you," his father said. "You're headed for trouble, mister."

They had him.

A Good Christian Education? What did that mean? Church every day? Chanting prayers in class? Cadaverous, frock-coated missionaries marching around campus with bulletproof Bibles clutched to their chests? And the girls; he remembered the sort of girls who enjoyed Sunday school. They were a sterile lot, always with their hands properly folded, always with their ankles properly crossed and never, from what he saw, with a single original thought in their demure little heads. He also remembered that their knees were always tightly clamped together, including when they slept, presumably. Just how did these people reproduce? He started to smile.

Then he remembered where he was. If he dared to appear even the slightest bit amused, his parents would jump on it.

A Good Christian Education? It sounded like even more forced conformity than he was enduring already. Since his parents liked the idea, it probably was. And where was this place? He had heard the name, but that was all. He had never even been to that part of the city.

"Hey you, pay attention when your mother is talking," his father said.

His mother was smiling at him with oversaturated sincerity.

"We really think it would be the best thing for you," she said. "I'm sure you will make a lot of nice friends there."

Nice? *Nice?* Brewer had been force-fed nice for as long as he could remember – by teachers who in the name of nice, would throw you out of class because you weren't having enough fun, for one example. He'd had enough nice, enough of pasted-on smiles and vapid conversations, enough of bloodless, meaningless, strangling Nice.

He quickly tried to review his options. He had earned enough money bagging groceries to pay for textbooks and part of tuition at the university, but not enough for anything more, and certainly not enough for a place of his own. So he couldn't stand his ground and defiantly announce he was going to do what he damned well pleased whether they liked it or not.

But still, A *Good Christian Education?* As opposed to what? A good Hindu education? A good Druid education? The family only went to church on Easter and then not every year. His parents would sit in the pew, expressionless as lignite and Orrin would pick his nose and sneer. Brewer tried to listen to the sermons and sometimes he found the ideas interesting. But since he heard them only once a year, they left no particular impression.

A Good Christian Education? What was good about it? He tried to think of something to say. But his mother was already ahead of him.

"I sent them your transcripts and you've been accepted," she said. "Here's the catalogue and the registration forms."

"But I've already been accepted at the U-Dub."

"Well, we hadn't sent them the confirmation check yet. We sent it to SPC instead."

"What?!"

"Don't use that tone of voice with your mother, young man," his father said.

"Now, registration is September 23 and classes begin September 28," his mother said. "That gives you two whole months to get ready!"

He thought. Maybe he should go enlist. He would have to get it over with some day anyway. Everybody had to. The draft was a net, omnipresent and poised, always there, always ready to snare you. He had heard a radio ad for the Marines, where a baritone chorus sang something about "The eagle, globe and anchor of the Corrrrps" and it touched him on a testosteronal level: Something far from home, a place for real men and crisp, direct discipline. These guys were tough, really tough. And, of course, there were uniforms. No doubt about it, the Marines had the best uniforms.

But, rationally, he knew college was a more sensible choice, even if it wasn't the college he wanted. SPC would, if nothing else, be something new. And he was ready for something new, anything new.

So quietly, without complaint, Brewer took the envelope from his mother's hand. He accepted his fate.

Chapter 2

When Marilyn Pennell first saw Tom Brewer, he was crossing the street; a tall figure striding through the mist. For reasons she did not understand, reasons she later would contemplate many times, she could not take her eyes off him. He had the lean, loose-limbed look many tall boys had, their arms and legs seemingly too long for their clothes, their clothes seemingly too large for the rest of their bodies. But he moved with none of their awkwardness. His bearing was erect, his stride long and confident. It was as if he owned the space around him and he knew it and he didn't care.

And so it began. For in that moment, something shifted within Marilyn Pennell; something she could not identify, something she found both exhilarating and discomforting. She could not take her eyes off him. She didn't know why. Her confidence, her arrogance, her command of her environment left her for a moment, only a moment, but the vacuum it created struck to her core; a heart-stopping chasm that nearly staggered her. All she could see was him and him and him and him and all she could think was yes and yes and yes and yes. The rest of the world dissolved into the night mist.

It wasn't supposed to happen like this. It was . . . it was . . . inappropriate. It was, it was, it was. . .

It would not go away.

As Brewer got closer, he passed under a street lamp and she saw that, unlike the majority of SPC males, he was well-dressed: A long suede coat, pressed dark slacks and, from what she could make out, shined shoes.

She continued to be lost in him until she remembered she was the last person in line. She looked away quickly. A moment later, he was standing behind her. His presence pulled at her. She didn't understand it and it left her, Marilyn Pennell, the girl with the unshakable poise, confused and unable to concentrate.

She had to get a look at him. How? Well, just look at him, how else? People do it all the time and she knew that and she knew she shouldn't feel so confused. This was ridiculous. He was just another boy in the registration line. There were hundreds just like him. Except they weren't just like him . . .

Time passed; a not a long time, although it seemed like it. Finally, she forced herself to turn her head.

He had an intelligent, open face, mitigated somewhat by deep-set, rather penetrating eyes. His hair was blond, short and neatly combed. He gave her a small, affable half-smile and nodded his head. She smiled in return and turned back around as fast as she could.

Now what? She had to meet him. It didn't matter if she understood why or not. She had to meet him.

Find some excuse, any excuse. Ah! Twist and search for something in your coat pocket.

"Darn," she said, as she fumbled and probed. "I know it's here somewhere."

"Lose something?" His voice was low, with an undercurrent of confidence; assumed, unconscious confidence.

"My watch," she said. "The band broke. I have to keep it in my pocket."

"Will it make this line move?" he said.

"I wish," she said with a slight laugh. *For god's sake, don't let it sound like a nervous laugh.*

He looked at his watch.

"Can't read it anyway. Not in this light. Should have brought my Buck Rogers Glow-in-the-Dark Special."

He stretched to look down the line.

"So this is college registration," he said. "Any idea what we are getting into?"

"Well, the gym will be filled with tables. Each one has a blackboard listing the classes you can sign up for at that table. When a class fills, they erase it. That's about all I know, really."

"And we have to get a lot of signatures," he said, holding up the registration packet. "Sounds like a barrel of laughs."

Enough.

"I'm Marilyn Pennell," she said.

His smile broadened slightly.

"I'm Tom Brewer. Pleasure to meet you."

Suddenly, Marilyn felt frightened and excited and intensely, achingly alive. This boy, this time, this place, this small, moving fragment of history, it was all so unexplainable and luminous. She had spent her life learning how to master moments and now she saw how wrong she had been. Moments define themselves . . .

Hold on, kiddo. Get back on task. You still have to register for classes.

She tried. Then she remembered he had introduced himself.

"I, I, I'm Marilyn Pennell."

You already said that, dummy. And a stutter? You've never stuttered in your life!

"Sorry, it must be the cold," she said. "What dorm are you in?"

"I'm not," he said. "Have to live at home."

"Near campus?"

"No, other side of town, north of the U Dub, near Sand Point, if you know where that is."

She did not. She searched for something to say.

"That's a long way."

"My parents believe I should pay my own way," he said. "Builds character and all that. I can't afford to move out. And you?"

"Oh. I live in Hill, the one. . . "

"The one up the hill. Must make it easy to remember."

"The walk up there does that," she said. "Can't imagine what it will be like in the snow."

"You're from around here?" he said.

"No. Wenatchee."

Just then, a large truck sped by, skimming along the curb only inches from them. The icy blast of its backwash buffeted the students in line.

"Welcome to Seattle," Brewer said.

Marilyn paused.

Keep him engaged. You can't let him drift away. Think of something, anything.

Then she said, "What's your major?"

Okay it's trite and unoriginal. But it will keep his attention.

"Nothing yet. For the first year, I think I'll take all the required classes. See where things lead. And you?"

"I'm uncertain," she said.

"Aren't we all, aren't we all."

He looked around, scanning the line, the street, the dark houses, everything in range. His eyes seemed to study things, as if he were memorizing them. Then his eyes locked on hers.

"Tell me your life story," he said.

Marilyn was unable to speak. Tell me your life story? It was the sort of thing Bogart would say to Lauren Bacall over bourbon in a smoke-filled room. A freshman in the registration line at SPC?

Brewer's affable half-smile came back. It all seemed to come so naturally to him. She found herself smiling the same smile in response.

"Oh, the usual," she said. "Small town high school, couldn't wait to get out. And you?"

"Big town high school, couldn't wait to get out."

Without thinking, she reached out and touched his coat. It felt like velvet as she ran her fingers down its lapel toward his chest. Maybe she should just forget it no, maybe this was merely a flight of imagination no, that can happen when it is dark and cold no and you are far from home no and you are alone within yourself no.

"That's really nice," she said, drawing her hand away as inconspicuously as possible.

"Thanks. I just got it."

"You can afford that and not a dorm?"

"I think I prefer the coat," he said. "Can't imagine what I'd get for a roommate."

Marilyn thought about her own roommate, Janet Small, a sweet, dewy-eyed girl from Prineville, Oregon. Janet wanted to be a nurse. Or a missionary. Or a teacher who worked with handicapped children. After less than a week, Janet's oft-expressed nobility was already starting to wear thin.

Across the street, from a radio somewhere, came the first chord of "Hard Day's Night." Everyone had heard that song that summer, so many times that they barely heard it at all. But now, in this cold, dark place, the voices were sharp and bright and the rhythms seemed the stuff of life itself. It felt good, very good; at least to Marilyn Pennell. At that moment, everything felt good to her.

"You're a Beatles fan?" Brewer said.

"I never thought so until now," she said. "There's something there, but I'm not sure what. Reminds me of summer sunsets."

Brewer nodded.

"Like nothing I ever heard," he said. "I wonder how long they'll last."

A long time, I hope. I hope this all lasts a long time.

Marilyn found herself looking directly into Brewer's eyes. A moment of understanding passed between them. Nineteen sixty four would not last and they knew it. But it was here now.

There was some kind of commotion up ahead. Marilyn saw a figure pouring water on the fire. The thick, wet smoke blew back her way, its grit and stink enveloping the line.

"Ahhh, now why'd they have to do that?" someone moaned. Others coughed. Marilyn fanned the smoke away from her face. Brewer did nothing. He didn't seem to notice.

Marilyn and Brewer talked some more, and some more after that. They talked about The Beatles and the upcoming election, and the classes they were hoping to get, and hometown memories, and then about The Beatles some more. Marilyn liked The Beach Boys, too, although she conceded their music seemed a little bubble-gummy, and Brewer liked a new group called The Rolling Stones. Marilyn had seen them on The Hollywood Palace. "They look like they need to take a walk through a car wash," she said and Brewer laughed. Maybe that's part of what they are trying to project, he said. Marilyn was not convinced.

They both liked a song called "We'll Sing in the Sunshine" by Gail Garnett; Marilyn because it sounded poignant and romantic, Brewer because it spoke of freedom; specifically the freedom to choose your own rules. Marilyn found that a bit unsettling. Love and marriage, love and marriage: There was no other method for such things in her world; the proper world, the genteel world – and as she thought about it, the smug and narrow world, too. But Brewer's observation still made her uncomfortable.

As they talked, conversation became easier and easier and, in a way, that felt odd.

It felt odd to Brewer because he rarely talked at length with anybody, particularly a girl. He was used to choosing his words carefully, lest he sound off-key and nerdy.

It felt odd to Marilyn because after a few minutes she wasn't calculating what she said or how she said it or the effect it would have but, rather, was simply saying whatever was on her mind. And the more she talked with Brewer, the more there was on her mind. She wanted to share it, not just state it, and it seemed he wanted it shared.

She couldn't understand it. In many ways, he was so dissimilar to her. He had no apparent interest in status symbols - country clubs, student body offices and the like - nor in the assiduously-defined codes of etiquette and propriety in which she has been drilled for as long as she could remember. But he wasn't coarse or oafish ~ anything but, actually ~ and spoke with a sort of unconscious politeness that could not be taught. He simply was that way.

His range of interests were broad, she found. He knew a lot about the forest, its trees and plants and animals, although, oddly, he did not hunt or fish. Couldn't stand killing anything, even an insect, he told her. They did him no harm, after all.

He had no particular interest in cars, which astounded her. Back home, the local boys seemed interested in little else. The louder, smokier and more obnoxious the car the better.

He didn't drink, or at least he said he didn't - this was SPC, after all - and found the subculture of teen drinking, with all it knowing nudges, in-jokes and public vomiting, rather childish.

But he liked to have a good time. Once, he told her, he and some other students put folded-up squares of cardboard under the legs on one side of a teacher's desk. The teacher's pencil rolled off and he stopped his lecture to put it back on the desk. It rolled off again. And he put it back again. And it rolled off again. And he put it back again. And so it went for the entire period, everyone wondering when he would catch on. He never did and for all Brewer knew, that pencil was still rolling off that desk.

For his part, Brewer found Marilyn interesting, for lack of a more specific word. The way she stood, the way she held her head; if gave the impression that she was on the reticent side, and at first he concluded he may as well forget about talking to her. But somehow, they started talking anyway. She wasn't dumb, thank god, and he enjoyed the experience of sharing ideas with a girl who didn't respond with blank stares of incomprehension. There was nothing wrong with the way she looked, either: Clear skin; big, dark eyes and a distinctively feminine bearing.

She was confident, which, after knowing more girls of the lip-biting, hand-fidgeting variety than he cared to remember, Brewer found particularly refreshing.

But she also seemed conventional, determinedly conventional. But this was SPC, so what would you expect. Besides, the unconventional girls he knew - if unconventional was the right word - usually left a lot to be desired, with their black stockings, oversized sweaters, burnt cork eye makeup, coffee-saturated breath and demeanors that indicated they were very angry about something, even if they couldn't quite say what. At least that was one version of the breed. Not much fun to be around, in any case, and Brewer decided his world was serious enough. He didn't need more.

So, he didn't like dumb, he didn't like self-conscious, he didn't like pretentious and he didn't like terminally serious. Well, what do you like, Brewer wondered to himself. How about good legs? Yes, that certainly was a plus. Unfortunately, they were standing too close for him to give Marilyn's a proper check-out. But she appeared otherwise trim and healthy, so the prospects were favorable.

He wondered if he should ask her out. No, it would be too sudden. Maybe the next time he saw her. But how would he find her on campus? Go to Hill and ask for her? Too direct. Just wait to spot her walking around campus? Yes, that probably was the best way, but it was iffy. His schedule and hers could be different. Still, it seemed as unforced and natural as such things can be.

But was it worth it? Was she really so important, this one girl? There were lots of other girls on campus. He was bound to meet some of them and some of them he would like, maybe more than he liked her. But he had met her first and for now, this moment, she was in his life, if only to a small and possibly fleeting degree. And remember, he told himself, you do like her.

Don't you?

Yes, he did. How much was another question. And the direction things might lead was another question still.

He looked at her. Her eyes caught his and stayed there, unwavering, for a full, distinct measure. Then, self-consciously, they both looked away.

****

When Chester Dalrymple arrived at 3 a.m., the line was a quarter-mile long. It was very cold and very dark. Maybe that's why someone had started a small fire between the sidewalk and the south wall of the building. Or maybe, as Dalrymple had concluded about the young men who had camped on the front steps in sleeping bags, it was to impress girls in the crowd. Freshman boys were predictable.

Chester Dalrymple was a short man with a bulbous nose, receding chin and the sort of dark, bumpy complexion that had a blue tinge even when shaved twice a day. He was nearly bald and the few black hairs he had he combed over a perpetually oily scalp. He rarely smiled – except, of course, when the president of the college said something that might be construed as witty.

He wasn't smiling now. A night watchman had spotted the fire and called Oscar Thorkelson, the head of grounds maintenance. Thorkelson called Dalrymple. Dalrymple should do something about it. After all, he was director of public relations and, by Thorkelson's reasoning, this was a public, not a maintenance, matter. Besides, Thorkelson never, ever, came to campus except during his regular work hours. And then, from what Dalrymple observed, he spent most of his day drinking coffee in the Student Union Building and whining about how short-staffed and overworked he was.

How does he get away with it? Dalrymple wondered. He's a lifelong church member, of course, so he knows a lot of the right people. And he's a longtime Kiwanian, so he knows a lot more. He also is dull-witted, sullen and a constant, tireless complainer.

Yes, that's it, Dalrymple decided. Complain all the time about all the same people and eventually you will be believed. Especially here. Such was the nature of small, isolated, insular Seattle Pacific College, a place where you ignored people like Oscar Thorkelson and their silly, trivial games at your peril.

Occasionally, Dalrymple used the complaint tactic himself. It was a good way to put assistants on the skids and, therefore, draw attention away from his mistakes. Now Thorkelson was using it on him. That rankled. Blame Dalrymple for the fire and it becomes his responsibility. At least it was now that Thorkelson had beaten him to the initiative.

In reality, of course, it was all the fault of the dean of students, Layton Fleming, who came up with this first-come, first-served registration system because it meant less work for his office. He was a loud man who wore loud shirts and loud neckties. He laughed loudly, particularly at the president's witty remarks, drowning out everyone else. That is how he became the president's favorite and that was why he was warm at home in a comfortable bed while the director of public relations was here.

Chester Dalrymple tried to drive the thought from his mind. He had a situation to deal with. If the fire department or the police showed up, it would get back to the president and the blame would fall on his, Dalrymple's, shoulders. The fire itself wasn't important, of course. It was the blame that mattered.

He could go tell the kids himself, but they might not want to put it out and that would mean confrontation. If Chester Dalrymple had learned anything in his ten years at SPC, it was that confrontation was dangerous. It forced you to think on your feet and that might cause you to make a mistake, out in the open where you couldn't dodge responsibility for it.

And, it might make your face familiar to students. Again, not a good idea. The more distance between you and them, the less they knew about what you actually did and, therefore, the more they were awed by your appearance of authority.

So, Dalrymple had called Greg Lammermuir, the student body president. Lammermuir was an acquiescent young man, eager for the references from teachers and administrators that would get him into a properly prestigious graduate school.

Dalrymple knew the type well; all the student body presidents he could remember, as a matter of fact. That's why they ran for the office and that's why they were such dependable flunkies.

When Lammermuir heard Dalrymple on the phone, he cheerfully barked "Yes, sir!" and promised he would be there in fifteen minutes. Dalrymple checked his watch. The ninny was ten minutes late.

Dalrymple caught himself. A flunky? A ninny? No, no, no. He is an exemplary young man, a spokesman for today's youth, a campus leader at a school dedicated to the finest in Christian education. That's what Dalrymple told the various churches around town when he booked Lammermuir as a guest speaker. And they believed it because, of course, that is what they wanted to believe.

Dalrymple caught himself again. Careful, Chester, careful. Thoughts like this can have a ripple effect. They may lead to doubt. Doubt is weakness and weakness can put you at the mercy of people like Oscar Thorkelson.

The thought made Dalrymple feel small, cold and alone. He shook his head. Think, think.

Those kids on the front porch. He studied them. They were gaping, guffawing apes of the fraternity genus, the kind who goosed each other, told unfunny jokes and laughed loudly, even at 3 a.m. Perfect. They would gladly pose for the camera when the photographer from the Post-Intelligencer arrived at 7 a.m. Old-fashioned college boy buffoonery; readers never got tired of it. Pity they weren't more the kind of kids SPC liked to put in the publicity pieces it sent to alumni: Devoted little church elders-to-be, preferably from families long affiliated with the school, the sort of kids you saw at Billy Graham crusades, singing hymns from memory, scowling earnestly during prayers and all but racing up the aisles when it came time for the alter call.

Such kids were easy to pick out in the crowd. Something about their posture. They didn't look as bored, cold and resentful as the others. Dalrymple spotted a group of them and studied them, registering their faces in his memory. They would be useful too, although not like Lammermuir. You won't have to ask them for favors. Just call it "service" and they'd volunteer. They may amount to only ten percent of the kids in line, and, like the rest, only about half of them would be back for their sophomore year. No matter, no matter. They represented what the college wanted people to believe and they were more than happy to play that role, whether they knew it or not.

Unfortunately, Chester couldn't control all the kids the reporter would interview and that was a risk. But the whole situation was a risk. If you don't get that fire out soon and if you don't put a good spin on the long line and the cold and the fact that five hundred eighteen-year-old kids are suffering through it because some dunderhead hadn't considered what any of that might mean, and if the rest of the town heard about it in those terms, well then, the president might frown. A frown is all it takes. It is a seed of disapproval. Thorkelson and the dean of students would make sure the seed grew.

Well, the best defense is a good offense. Dalrymple had a neatly-typed news release in his pocket detailing how this is the largest freshman class ever. It also had demographics about numbers of students from each state, grade point averages and the like. Give that to the reporter, smile, be helpful, make sure those idiots on the porch act like the college boys of the unwashed public's fantasies and this could work out. At the cabinet meeting, you plop a copy of the paper on the table, chuckle about the photo, act like you are master of the moment and you will have the upper hand. Make sure to mention that Lammermuir asked the kids to put out the fire and that they cheerfully complied. Student government is in good hands. The president loved it when he heard such things.

Maybe it was the hour and the cold, but suddenly Dalrymple felt another twinge of doubt. The reality is, most of the kids in the line don't care about the school's goals, or its long-term vision or its role in the community or all the rest of the things you are paid to promote. They just want to go to college. Most don't know why, other than it is better than not going to college. Few have any idea what they want to study.

They are just kids: Young and cold and tired and uncertain and vulnerable.

Hmmm.

Vulnerability in others can be used to one's advantage.

Chester Dalrymple smiled ever so slightly.

****

Up ahead, there was movement in the line. The lights had switched on in Brougham, which meant the doors would open soon. The students were stirring, checking their packets, making sure they had a pen ready, preparing themselves for what they assumed would be the ordeal of freshman registration.

"Looks like we're about ready," Brewer said.

"I'm glad I pre-registered," Marilyn said. "I hope it makes things easier."

Brewer had not pre-registered. Up until this moment, he had never even heard of preregistration. It made him feel ignorant and clumsy, like he was wearing a sweatshirt and dirty Levi's and accidentally wandered into a posh restaurant. He was an outsider, and despite what western movies said about the strong silent type who rides alone and makes his own rules, being an outsider had its disadvantages – not knowing what the hell was going on at freshman registration, for one.

A few minutes later, the doors opened. A sound of relief went up from the crowd and slowly, in fits and starts, the line began to move. As it moved, Marilyn found herself being jostled from behind and to the left. The jostling moved her along against her will. She turned to spot Brewer and saw him about eight feet behind her. He too was being jostled and it looked like he was moving to the right. Then a fat boy with thick glasses too small for his face and a moronic, leering grin, moved in front of him. Brewer tried to look past him but the fat boy was being jostled too and kept getting shoved in front of Brewer's field of vision.

As Brewer and Marilyn tried to find one another, the crowd moved them along with a current of its own, bearing them, inexorably, toward the open doors. Marilyn saw Brewer one more time. His eyes were darting about, searching, but not in her direction and he did not see her. Then a tall girl moved in behind Marilyn, blocking her view and she saw him no more.

Chapter 3

The doors open and the crowd of eighteen-year-olds, cold and tired, file in, past the trophy cases with their tarnished cups and plaques and shadowy black and white photographs of basketball players and baseball players and track stars from years past, not very far past, actually, but already awkward and dated and a little embarrassing, whatever life once in them gone now, never coming back; the sad melancholy of forgotten glory.

Through the next set of doors and into the huge, gaping gym with its glaring lights and hard, hard, yellow-varnished maple floor.

Tables arranged there, dozens of tables, some with signs on poles, some with signs on the table tops.

There is no order to the tables, or if there is it is not discernible to the students. Political Science, Sociology, Biology, Math. English, Chemistry, Psychology, Music. Economics, Physics, Nursing. Anthropology, Philosophy, Zoology. History (American), History (Ancient), History (European). Religion (Bible Studies), Religion (History), Art.

The polyphony goes on and on. Table after table, subject after subject, class after class.

Then there are Parking Permits. Yearbook photo. Meal Tickets. Chapel Registration. ASSPC cards. And Cashier. That's the biggest sign of all, the letters in bright red ink.

Advisors, two to a table, their names on little placards. A few instructors, mostly part-time instructors. Bored. Hostile. Assigned. Most have never met the students they supposedly will advise. Take a look at the applications. Make sure the right boxes are filled in. Move the kid along. Next. What did you say your name was? Not on my list. What? How would I know where to send you. Look around. Geeze. How'd I ever get stuck doing this? It's early. Any coffee around? No, of course not. It figures.

Upper division students at some of the tables, seniors, earning fifteen dollars for a day's work, smug and cool, enjoying their superior knowledge. Hey, look at that one. Fresh off the farm. Lost. Big eyes. Big tits. Get her name. Offer to help her move in. Show her the ropes. The ropes, heh-heh-heh. Act like you care.

And look at that guy, the dork with pimples on top of pimples. Those shoes, they must be ten-years-old. And what did he use to cut his hair, garden shears? Freshmen, where do they find them. Half of them will be gone by the end of the year. Wonder what happens to them. Who cares. Losers.

The students mill, the students wander, the students talk among themselves, sometimes comparing notes on classes, sometimes trying to figure out where to go; each alone, alone as a human being can be, alone in the big room with the glaring lights and hard, hard floors, trying to navigate the future.

English 101. All's that left is 8:30 a.m. with Rolstad, or Frazier at 2:30 p.m. Any suggestions?

Frazier is a bitch, from what I hear. Doesn't believe in giving As to freshmen, dings you a grade for a misplaced comma, tests you on the footnotes, for god's sake. Don't know anything about Rolstad. Must be a TA.

But 8:30? I'm hardly awake at 8:30.

Yeah, well. Welcome to it.

The lines are long. The lines are slow. Fatigue. Resentment. Resignation.

Behind the tables, any vestige of geniality gone after the first half-hour. Cold courtesy. Officiousness. Condescension.

You haven't been assigned a chapel seat yet? I can't issue you a student body card until you've been assigned a chapel seat. Oh, you say you have been assigned one? Well, not according to this form. You need a signature. See, it says so right there. When all else fails, read the instructions. Next!

So you are from Dillard, Oregon. How nice. What's that near? Roseburg? Golly gee, your mother must be so proud. Next!

You completed this form in blue ink. As you know, as it says in your packet, we prefer black ink. Maybe you should redo it. Now, now, no need to get upset. We'll send it through. Of course, filled out this way, with all this blue ink, you increase your chances of things being misinterpreted, maybe even lost. You know. Then you'll have to register all over again and all the classes you want will be gone. End up taking seventeenth century Estonian history in the basement of Marston at 6 a.m. But if you insist . . . Next!

You again? Finally got that chapel assignment, huh? How about your yearbook photo? See, it says so right here. You did read this, didn't you? When all else fails, read the instructions.

Forms and forms and boxes to check and carbon copies and signatures, so many signatures, so many signatures. A purpose to be served, no other way to do it, probably, but that does not make the lines shorter, the passage of time less tedious.

The upper classmen are enjoying themselves.

Hey, look at that one, the one with the crossed eyes. Wanna ask her out?

No way, I'm not that hard up.

A four-year virgin, there's always a few.

Come on, man, she can't help it.

Yeah, yeah, but she's still a four-year-virgin. Well, there she goes. Let's see if she walks into a wall.

You actually think you'll score on any freshmen girls this way?

Sure, why else would I be here? It's easier than you think. Smile at them. Act like you care. They're desperate for that. Then catch 'em at dinner, act like you're happy to see them again, like you know your way around. Act like you care. Then you're half-way there.

You talk a good fight.

Don't believe me? Wait for them to come to you and you're gonna wait a long time, my man. Hey, here comes cross-eye. Try it out on her. Tell her she messed up some form, but you'll help her out. Smile. Act like you care.

At the far end of the room, near the entrance doors, the Cashier. She takes checks, cashier's checks preferred. Most are filled out and signed by parents, in any case. Many saved for eighteen years, some even more so their children could go to college, their beloved ones, their magic ones. Their signatures on checks from banks in small towns and big towns, important, so painfully important to them, their signatures saying so much that they cannot say themselves. Farewell, my little one, the one I sired, the one I bore, the one who raced to me every night when I got home, who hugged my leg, who showed me your color crayon drawings, so proud, who laughed when I read to you and made funny voices, such a pure laugh, such pure happiness.

Farewell, farewell. I love you more than you can imagine. This I can give you, this way to a future and, oh, how I pray it will be a good future. I have done all I can, for better or worse. I tried, I tried so much, so desperately and now I am done. My love for you is an ache, my breath stops, tears come to my eyes. Your teddy bear, your little coat, your little mittens.

Farewell, my little one, my everything. Farewell, farewell.

****

Chester Dalrymple trudged across campus, a stooped, shabby figure, his face lumpy and sagging, like a basset hound with a head cold.

He was oblivious to the campus's giant elms and maples and oaks, their autumn leaves an incandescent canopy of reds and yellows in the crystalline morning air. He was oblivious to the people he passed, even the pretty girls, crisp and fresh, on their way to the breakfast line. He was oblivious to everything except what was on his mind at the moment.

What was on his mind was freshman registration. He ticked it off, incident by incident.

He had managed to convince the student body president to persuade the baboons in the line to put the bonfire out before the police arrived. That was good.

But when they poured water on it, it sent out billows of smoke, particularly thick and smelly smoke for some reason, and the more water they poured, the more smoke they made; a nightmarish scenario if, like Chester Dalrymple, you were the school's director of public relations.

Dalrymple frowned. What if the smell had drifted up to Hillford House, the president's home? Was the wind blowing in that direction? Dalrymple hadn't thought to check. He mentally kicked himself.

And even if it hadn't, what if people in the neighborhood complained and it got back to the president? Couldn't have that. The school was fastidious when it came to brown-nosing every malcontent, neurotic and crank in a half-mile radius, particularly if they were active church members, which most were. Keep them happy, keep them docile, reassure them, frequently, that SPC students were not among the sinister hordes of Hugh Hefner disciples and fledgling communists infesting other college campuses, and you could push through every rezone, every building code appeal, every traffic regulation variance you filed. And the school filed a lot.

If there was a complaint, how would he frame his explanation? Dalrymple considered. He would have to word it in a way that would reflect favorably on him, and, if possible, cast suspicion on someone else. Maybe Oscar Thorkelson. Well, there were all these twigs lying around, perfect for a fire. I guess the maintenance staff missed them. Well, no harm done – except for all that smoke, of course. But what would you expect from a fire that big. All those twigs, you know.

Yes, that might work. Maybe he should call Thorkelson. Take the initiative, throw him off-balance, make him sputter and puff like the incompetent dim bulb he was. Or maybe he should call the president and complain to him. Maybe, maybe. Might be too obvious. Have to think about it. But don't take too long.

The photo shoot with the students on the front porch had gone a lot better. The reporter and photographer from Post-Intelligencer showed up around 7:30 a.m., a good two hours after the fire had been extinguished, so there was no smoky smell, no telltale pile of ashes (Dalrymple had personally kicked them into the uncut grass), nothing that would arouse interest.

And, by that time, the students in line were starting to perk up. Their long wait in the cold was nearly over and the sun had risen to reveal a bright, clear morning.

Dalrymple made sure he personally handed two copies of the news release to the reporter; a lot of pointless trivia, actually, but it's what newspapers liked – and he even offered to introduce him to some of the students in line, students Dalrymple had carefully chosen himself, the sons and daughters of properly pious, properly conservative, properly wealthy alumni.

The reporter, a late-middle-aged man with the downtrodden expression of a newsroom drone habitually assigned to pointless space-fillers, didn't care. The news release, which he stuffed in his pocket without reading, was enough.

The photographer found four clean-cut looking freshmen who were more than happy to smile, mug for the camera and jump up and down like the initiation ceremony for the Benevolent and Protective Order of Village Idiots.

All was well with the world.

At least all was reasonably well for that one small part of Dalrymple's world. But he had learned from experience never to trust good fortune, no matter how minor it might be. Chester Dalrymple was an inherent, habitual worrier and it served him well. He wasn't personable, he wasn't even very bright, but he worried, and his constant anxiety over details that others might ignore had helped him maneuver the labyrinthine rocks and shoals of small college politics with a success few could match.

The actual responsibilities of his job - the news bureau, publications, church relations, fund-raising and the like - he left to his subordinates, always carefully positioning himself so that if anything went wrong, it would be entirely their fault. For, he had learned, and learned well, that the less one actually does, the less chance there is that one will make a mistake. Ergo, he did as little actual work and made as few actual decisions as possible.

Which is why, after five hours of standing in the cold and dark trying to prevent a public relations fiasco - a fiasco caused by someone else - of being forced to do something where he had to think on his feet, something for which he could actually be held accountable, Chester Dalrymple was in a distinctly displeased frame of mind when he reached his office. Where was a news bureau director when he actually needed one? Well, not in this year's budget, for one thing. Fortunately, he needed to hire a new publications director. All he had to do was combine the two jobs and gloss over the fact it was impossible to do both within the confines of time and motion physics. A lack of clear-cut job description usually accomplished that. A vague job title. Communications Coordinator was good - was frosting on the cake.

Any number of unemployed journalism majors and public relations agency cast-offs had applications on file. All were desperate. All would work for a year or two until they got fed up and quit. That was the typical pattern for staff jobs at SPC anyway and Dalrymple found it a good one. It created instability and instability drew attention away from him.

The secretaries had not arrived and would not for another half-hour. Dalrymple was desperate for coffee. He went to the closet where the coffee-maker was kept and looked at it for a long time. He had no idea how the thing worked. Something involving a specific measure of coffee - he rummaged around until he found the can - a certain amount of water and then you press the ON button. When the red light came on, it was done.

Dalrymple poured what he thought was a reasonable amount of coffee into the percolator, then added water to the top and pressed the button. After a minute or so, it began to burble. He noticed that the water erupting up into the small glass regulator was full of coffee grounds. He had never noticed that before. He shrugged. It's probably supposed to be that way.

A few minutes later, the red light came on. He found his cup, the one emblazoned with "World's Greatest Boss" - he bought it himself - and poured the brew in.

It turned out to be a gritty slurry of grounds and water, about half of each. What had happened here? Dalrymple had no idea. What to do about it? He had even less of an idea. He did know he would have to face the day without his morning coffee, at least until the secretaries arrived and, at this moment, that was much too long. He went to his office - where was that light switch? - where he waited, dark and coffeeless, for the day, the official 8:30 a.m. to 6:30 p.m. school day, to begin.

****

Tom Brewer emerged from Brougham and into the bright daylight. Registration, for him, had lasted eight hours: Five hours in the line and three hours navigating the purgatory of shifting schedules, signatures, petty bureaucrats, more signatures, nine different Official Forms, each of which had to be filled out perfectly, and more signatures still.

Before registration actually began, Brewer was convinced that he was singularly ill-prepared for the whole business, that everybody else had it meticulously pre-planned and would coast through it on a wave of flawless poise. Then, after about two hours, he looked around and found that everyone was still in the gym, marching resignedly from table to table and then back again, all with the same frustrated expression as him.

Many were still there when he finally left, the big door to the gym closing behind him with a resonant boom. It reminded him of a movie he once saw where a British ship got torpedoed and a deck officer was ordered to close the hatch to a flooding compartment. Men were still left below and he drowned out their screams by slamming the hatch shut and then locking it to make sure.

Well, not as dramatic as that of course, but Brewer did feel a palpable sense of finality when the door closed and he no longer had to listen to the grating chorus of people with their nerves on edge or feel the residue of dried morning sweat sticking to the back of his neck.

He actually got the classes he wanted: English 101 (required), History 142 (Pre-Twentieth Century America), Physics 114 (well, physics) and a P.E. class, (also required) in body-building. He had been assigned a chapel seat in the balcony, front row, corner; obscure enough that, he hoped, he would be left alone, maybe even catch some sleep.

It was done. He was outside.

He was thirsty. There was a small cafe in the old grime-blackened brick building at Third and Bertona. It was a place straight out of an Edward Hopper painting; a sour muse of badly-painted fiberboard and cracked linoleum the color of aged urine. The woman behind the counter matched the decor, with thin, unnaturally black hair and a mouth turned down permanently at the corners, the effect accentuated by too much lipstick and too many wrinkles.

"I'd like a Coke, please," Brewer said.

"We only have Pepsi."

"That's fine."

"And only in the bottle."

"Yeah, okay."

"And it isn't chilled."

"I don't care, just so long as it's wet."

The woman shrugged indifferently, reached under the counter, pulled out a dusty bottle, uncapped it and set it down in front of Brewer.

"Fifty cents."

Brewer paid. The Pepsi was indeed unchilled, which made it taste even more like mothballs than Pepsi usually did. Brewer was a Coca Cola man himself. Now he remembered why.

He turned on the counter stool so he could look out the window. So this was Seattle Pacific College. So far, he was less than impressed. Of course, to be fair, registration, like any type of bureaucratic herding, was hardly a reasonable criterion.

He gazed at the campus. It was small, to be sure, but the buildings were not unattractive and the grounds, with big trees in their autumn colors, were actually quite pretty.

Brewer forced himself to finish the Pepsi. Despite its camphor-like aftertaste, it did quench his thirst. He smiled at the counter woman ~ who didn't smile back ~ then headed out to explore his alma mater-to-be. It didn't take long.

Lower campus was shaped like a horseshoe, open end to the east, closed end to the west. The Student Union Building anchored the northeast corner. Heading west, there was Tiffany Hall, a big mock-Tudor office building, followed by the Health Center, then Watson Hall, a women's dorm. Another women's dorm, Marston Hall, AKA The Cell Block, formed the north-south arch of the horseshoe. A huge glass cube constituting the entrance to Moyer Hall, a men's dorm, started the horseshoe east again. Behind Moyer, parenthetically, almost hidden, was Adelaide Hall, a wooden structure hurriedly thrown up during the Second World War, the plan being to tear it down once victory was achieved. But it was still there, its clapboards constantly pulling loose, its floors creaky, its stairs disconcertingly wobbly. Not far from it was Beegle Hall, an applied sciences building that, accordingly, resembled a New Jersey truss factory.

In front of Beegle and continuing the eastward leg of the horseshoe was the spired and turreted Victorian edifice of Alexander Hall, the school's first building, circa 1892. In contrast, next door was the determinedly nondescript McKinley Auditorium, where the college held mandatory chapel every weekday. The horseshoe ended with Crawford music building, best known for its private practice rooms where, after dinner and on weekends, students could lock the doors, hang a coat over the small window and copulate in something akin to privacy - cramped quarters and hard, angular surfaces notwithstanding.

Peterson Hall, a classroom and admin building, was in the middle of the horseshoe, rather like a large ink blot, if viewed from above. It had been built about the same times as Alexander and, to Brewer's eyes, had the same sort of earnest Victorian charm.

So much for lower campus. Brewer's walking tour took him all of twelve minutes.

Upper campus was well-named, being built on one of the idiosyncratic small hills that pop up here and there throughout Seattle. The hill was steep and the students who climbed it daily cursed it daily. Its best feature was Weter Library, a concrete, glass and stainless steel structure which proved that modern architecture could, on rare occasions, actually look good. Brewer went inside and found the place bright and airy. Good. If the academic demands of college were what he was told, he would be spending a lot of time in Weter.

As he continued up the hill, he passed Gwinn Commons, the school dining hall, although Brewer did not know that. He did know that students were lined up at its door for some reason or another, and they were chatting and laughing like whatever it was they were doing was all old hat to them.

Brewer's original fear came back, that everyone else knew what was going on, that they all had mastered the rules of this new game and he had not. It didn't help that, as he walked on, he passed students in groups of twos and threes, none of whom he had ever seen before and none of whom paid him the least attention. It was as if he was an invisible man in a foreign land.

At the top of the hill was Hill Hall, the college's only coed dorm; men on one side, women on the other, with a large, glass-walled lounge in the middle, so any comingling could be closely monitored.

Brewer stood outside the front door and looked in. He could not make himself enter. He was an outsider in a tight little society that disdained outsiders, the way any in-group disdains those not in the know. And he was convinced his uncertainty and discomfort showed; which, at age eighteen, is probably the most degrading demeanor one can project.

Back on lower campus, on his way to the bus stop on Nickerson, Brewer smelled coffee wafting from the SUB. It reminded him that he had not eaten since midnight. He followed his nose and found himself in the coffee shop. A counter with a menu board constituted one wall. Brewer studied it for a minute or two but had no idea how to actually place and order. He could ask the cashier, but he was afraid that, again, it would make him look like some lummox from the foothills. So he picked up a piece of apple pie and a carton of milk from the glass shelf, paid, found a table next to a window and ate quietly, wondering if he would spend the next four years feeling as awkward and out of place as he did on his first day.

****

Marilyn Pennell lay on her bed and stared at the ceiling. She was still wearing the skirt, blouse, sweater and shoes she had worn for registration, and that was unusual. Lying in them like this would set the wrinkles, an unthinkable thing- until today.

For it had been an unusual day. Registration had gone not at all as she had planned. Her careful pre-registration turned out to be worthless once she entered the muddled maze of registration forms and class lists and, above all, other freshmen, whose very confusion took on a life of its own, clogging lines, interrupting conversations and tripping over everything in sight. She thought about her roommate, Janet, whom she had last seen desperately grasping a sheaf of papers and looking about in wide-eyed, open-mouthed bewilderment. Janet had yet to return to the dorm and probably wouldn't for quite some time. Marilyn wondered if perhaps she had gotten trapped in the gym, her mummified remains showing up in a year or two when a janitor spotted a suspicious-looking shoe sticking out from some out of the way crevice.

But, in the end, Marilyn had managed her way through registration, all the while keeping her poise and calm - at least on the outside. Inside, she was angry, mostly angry with herself for not realizing it all would probably happen the way it did. Naiveté is the domain of the weak. How could you have been caught so off-guard, so . . .

No, that wasn't it, she thought, not really. It was Tom Brewer. Admit it. Why had he unsettled her so? She couldn't understand it. But he did and Marilyn found herself governed by feelings she could not articulate. He was good-looking, but not exceptionally good-looking. He was intelligent, but not exceptionally intelligent. He was charming, but not . . . No, charming was not the word. Charming connotes he had tried to charm her, which he had not. He simply was what he was. Why did that leave her so disconcerted?

Physically, there was a grace about him, an economy of motion. She envisioned him naked, as best she could, and she conjured a body like a prowling lion's, cord-like muscles coiling and flexing, latent power, beautiful and a bit dangerous. Don't be silly, she thought. He's actually on the slender side. But the image remained, refusing to leave her consciousness.

Marilyn's fingertips brushed across the tips of her breasts and she felt her hands drifting downward, lightly, as if they had a will of their own.

When she had discovered it at age fourteen, it distressed her. Surely, she was the only girl who knew of it. She could tell no one else. She thought it was an admission of loneliness, of failure, and she despised herself for it. But when it came upon her, as it had now, she would find herself inexorably giving over to it and, for a time, for such a exquisitely brief time, her world would be one within her, a vortex of infinite depth; unrestrained, indefinable and wondrous.

Chapter 4

Paul Trimble was fresh out of the Air Force, he needed a job and he was rapidly approaching desperation.

He had a journalism degree, which he thought would land him work at a newspaper. But that was proving difficult. There was only one large newspaper in his native Portland, The Oregonian, and it rarely hired anyone unless a member of its staff died. After reading a few issues of the paper, Trimble concluded some of them already had. They just didn't know it.

Anyway, Trimble interviewed there. A pasty-faced man in a rayon shirt and stained necktie told him he needed more experience. Trimble responded that he had worked two years on the student newspaper at the University of Oregon - sports and general assignment. Toward the end, he also wrote editorials because the editor, who got the job by assiduously sucking up to the advisor for three years, was incapable of writing an intelligible English sentence. Trimble left that part out. He didn't want to frighten the man in the rayon shirt. Unvarnished truth can have that effect.

Then he spent two years writing for the base newspaper at Kunsun, Korea, where, and he didn't tell the man in the rayon shirt this part either, he nearly went batshit crazy. Stories about training schedules, safety reminders and the latest doings of the supply depot did not for challenging journalism make, and for a newspaperman, nothing is more soul-killing than trying to glorify boring subject matter.

He also avoided talking about Kunsun itself - a military backwater used to temporarily house units on their way somewhere else. It was built on a reclaimed river delta tide flat and it smelled like it, particularly in hot weather. There was a lot of hot weather in Kunsun - except when there was cold weather; very cold weather, numbing, paralyzing, excruciating cold weather. There was no in-between weather.

Nearby were rice fields, which the locals fertilized with human waste. In the summer, it dried to powder. From time to time, the hot wind blew it toward the base, where it formed a thin but discernible film on buildings, cars and anything else out in the open, thus adding to the picturesque ambiance of USAFB, Kunsun ROK.

Then there was the town of Kunsun itself. Like most towns attached to American military bases, it consisted of three streets of ramshackle laundries, pawn shops and bars ~ and strip clubs staffed by girls with bow legs and missing teeth.

Kunsun's only saving grace was that the beer was cheap - Hite Prime from Korea and, much better and for a dime more, Kirin from Japan. Trimble usually spent about a quarter of his paycheck on Kirin - and another quarter or so on the bowlegged girls, although he didn't like to admit it. Hell, he was desperate. What was he supposed to do?

Well, it was all behind him now. He was a PFC - a Proud Fucking Civilian - and he was eager for what the civilian world had to offer.

It didn't offer much for a journalism grad from Oregon. The man in the rayon shirt was a prototype for others who interviewed him; insular, hidebound and condescending. None ever looked at the resume and clips Trimble sent them. He knew because he paper-clipped them top and bottom and always in the exact same spot; one inch from the left on top, dead center at the bottom. He also pressed the paper clips in hard, to leave an impression. They always came back the same, the impressions undisturbed, not a sixteenth of an inch movement.

He decided to give Seattle a try because it had four good-sized newspapers in a fifty-mile radius. After meeting with their versions of the man in the rayon shirt, Trimble applied at smaller papers in Bellingham, Bremerton, Lynnwood, Bellevue, Kent - and on and on and on. Some actually showed interest and said they would call him when a job opened up. But none did, at least not fast enough for Trimble and his inexorably diminishing bank account.

So, he started looking for jobs in public relations. He had no idea what public relations was, other than it involved writing, graphic design and photography. He knew how to do all three. A job was a job. It had to be better than Kunsun.

And so it was that Paul Trimble's two-toned VW beetle smoked and rattled itself to a stop on Third Avenue West in front of the SPC campus. The car was two-toned because the door on the passenger side was tomato red, the result of an attempted repair by the previous owner. The rest of the bug was light blue, oxidized to a flat pearlescence accented by random groupings of rust spots. Trimble couldn't afford a paint job. He couldn't afford a new muffler, either, and it was becoming increasingly evident, on a daily basis, that he would need one soon.

Trimble scanned the campus looking for Peterson Hall. It turned out to be dead ahead, across an expanse of lawn and trees. He tucked the envelope containing his resume and clips under his arm and began his introduction to Seattle Pacific College.

It looked like a lot of college campuses – a hodgepodge of buildings in unrelated styles depending on when they were built – only smaller. Quite a bit smaller, actually; distinctly compact, rather like an architectural model on a display table. It had lots of big trees. Trimble noticed that none of them were native to the Northwest. Maybe that was good. Most Northwest trees did not change color in the fall. These did. For now, the sun probed through them, forming yellow and white dapples on the ground. A pretty enough place, Trimble decided; unremarkable but pretty.

He climbed the stairs to the third floor of Peterson and found the Public Relations office at the end of a long, dark hall. Before he went in, Trimble brushed off his blue blazer, the only sports coat he owned, and tried to smooth the wrinkles from his gray slacks, the only pair of dress pants he owned. His white button down wasn't the only dress shirt he owned. He had one other. He had two ties, too; the solid maroon one he was wearing and a solid dark blue one, courtesy of the United States Air Force. Trimble hated being broke.

A fiftyish woman with the look of a church secretary was manning the reception desk. She smiled politely

"Good morning," Trimble said. "I'm Paul Trimble. I have an appointment with Mr. Dalrymple."

"He's tied up for a few minutes. Have a seat and I'll tell him you are here." She disappeared through a nearby door.

Trimble looked around. Three other secretaries were at work in the office. All were young, perhaps not yet out of their teens. Two were quite pretty. He caught one of them glancing at him furtively from the corner of her eye.

"Would you like some tea?" the other pretty girl said. She was tall, with lovely long legs. She had perfect white teeth.

"Yes, thank you," Trimble said.

He had one sip before the older woman returned.

"Mr. Dalrymple will see you now."

Chester Dalrymple's office was dominated by an oversized desk, painted black but done in such a way that the wood grain still showed. It was big, expensive, and awful. On it was a pen and pencil set with a polished alabaster base and a desk ornament that consisted of a large Lucite cube encasing floating pennies, dimes and quarters. On the wall were two framed signs. One read, "I am having a nervous breakdown. I've worked for it, I've earned it and it is mine." The other read, "You Don't Have To Be Crazy To Work Here, But It Sure Helps!"

The curtains were heavy, gray and shut. No daylight peeped through them.

Chester Dalrymple was hunched over his large, prestigious desk, the top of his greasy bald head mucous-like in the dim light. He was signing a stack of brochures, mechanically, one after the other. It was a big stack.

"Good morn. . ." Trimble started to say.

"We have a position opening up for someone with your qualifications," Dalrymple said, without breaking the rhythm of his signing.

Trimble opened his mouth to speak. Dalrymple didn't notice.

"Someone who isn't afraid of a little hard work, someone who'll put in the extra time because he believes in what we do here."

There was a pause. Trimble concluded he was supposed to respond.

"Yes," he said, for lack of anything better.

Dalrymple gathered up a bunch of brochures and headed for the door. Trimble deduced that he was supposed to follow.

Dalrymple dropped the brochures on the older woman's desk.

"Helen, I want these in the mail by eleven." His voice was flat and rushed. "Have the alumni mailing ready by four. Cancel my breakfast meeting for tomorrow. I'll be at the coffee shop for the next twenty minutes."

As Dalrymple and Trimble went out the door, one of the secretaries laughed, apparently at something one of the others had said. Dalrymple stopped, turned and walked to her desk.

"Don't you have enough to do?" he said accusingly.

"I. . ." the girl began, fright in her voice.

"Because if you don't have anything better to do than giggle and carry on, we can find more work for you."

The girl couldn't speak.

"Well?" Dalrymple demanded.

The girl's eyes grew wide with hurt and fear. Dalrymple stood over her menacingly for a moment more. Then he left.

As they walked across the campus, Dalrymple kept his head down, as if deep in thought. He had been talking steadily since they left the office. He had yet to look Paul Trimble in the eye.

"The newsletter comes out every month," he was saying, his voice still flat and rushed. "The annual catalog is published in June, freshman bulletin is printed in April, we've budgeted for sixteen publicity brochures a year, news bureau's goal is seven hundred inches coverage in the local press, six hundred in the Christian press, and a major profile on the president. . ."

It all blended into a monotone. Trimble tried to listen but could not keep up. As they entered the Student Union Building coffee shop, Dalrymple was still talking.

". . . personal evangelism week and, of course, the Tony Fontaine concert in February. . ."

They stopped at a table where two men sat. One was middle-aged and round-faced with longish hair lacquered into a semi-pompadour. He was wearing a maroon and blue plaid suit two sizes too small; a variant of the uniform sported by used car salesmen the world over.

The other was an older man, smallish, with the thin, chinless face and the slightly protruding buck teeth of a kid who was the last chosen in sides-up for a baseball game. He was telling a joke.

". . . if little Izzy takes the toro, he'll be a rabbi. If he takes the bottle, he'll be a drunkard. If he takes the money, he'll be a thief. So what does little Izzy do? He takes all three and Mrs. Mrs. Goldblatt, she says, "Oy, oy, such a terrible thing this is. Little Izzy's gonna be a Catholic priest!"

He and plaid suit laughed heartily. Then he spotted Dalrymple.

"Hello, boss!" the small man boomed enthusiastically. "You look like you've been working hard! Let me tell you the latest!"

He exuded the sort of vim, vigor and pep that made Trimble want to run from the room.

"This is Paul. . ." Dalrymple began to say.

"This morning I went over to see Agnes Gutormsen, the poor old soul," the small man exclaimed with a TV pitch man's assurance. "She's an inspiration, let me tell you. An inspiration!"

"This is Paul. . ." Dalrymple started to say again.

"She can hardly see at all. And most of her hearing's gone," the small man said. "But I convinced her to sign her will over to the school. Eighty thousand! How about that?! Eighty thousand!"

"That's what Christian stewardship is all about," plaid suit said. He was not being sarcastic.

"We're interviewing Paul for the publications position, "Dalrymple said. He gestured at plaid suit. "Paul, this is Bud Gafney." Then he gestured at the small man. "And this is Skip Reinhardt."

Trimble held out his hand to the small man, who squinted at him with suspicious, ferret-like eyes. His hands stayed firmly wrapped around his coffee cup. Trimble felt embarrassed and angry. Then Bud Gafney said, "Chet, what have you heard about this granola business?"

"What?" Dalrymple said, his face assuming the expression of a sheep.

"I heard some students talking about it," Gafney said. "They eat it."

"What is this?" Reinhardt said suspiciously.

"That's all I heard," Gafney said. "One of them had a beard."

"Uh, Paul here graduated from. . ." Dalrymple said.

"Bean salad," Gafney said.

"Bean salad?" Dalrymple said.

"Maxine makes it by the gallon!" Gafney said. "Bean salad. Can't keep enough of it in the house! Darndest thing you ever saw."

"Bean salad?" Dalrymple said again.

"Yes?" Gafney said.

"Apple sale this weekend," Reinhardt crowed in his best Rotary club tenor. "Yes sir, got a quota of six crates, but I won't settle for less than eight. Why, I can sell three or four all by myself. By myself! And Gafney is good for a couple."

He gestured at Trimble.

"And Dumbo over here can probably sell one or two."

Dumbo? Trimble had a sudden urge to punch Skip Reinhardt square his go-getter mouth. He swallowed the urge, and did his best to keep a poker face.

"What did you say your name is anyway, fella?" Reinhardt said. He was smiling. But behind the hardy fellow well-met grin, carefully camouflaged, but never completely hidden, were eyes with the knife-edged glint of the practiced sadist. Through years of practice, Reinhardt had learned to mask his malignity, to unsheathe it out only at certain, risk-free times, times when he could camouflage it with humor, or bullying or toadying or any number of other smooth defenses. And he had learned to spot the people he could use it on. Skip Reinhardt was a connoisseur of human vulnerability. He could see in Trimble a lamb waiting for the knife.

If Trimble had been able to read Reinhardt's eyes, he might have understood some of that. But he could not read them. He was twenty five-years-old.

"My name is Paul Trimble," he said.

"What's that, fella?" Reinhardt said. "Speak up, I can't hear you." A faint smile was forming on his lips.

"Trimble. Paul Trimble."

"Thimble? Thimble, you say? What kind of a name is that?"

Reinhardt's grin was spreading. Bud Gafney was smiling too, the smile of one who enjoyed being in on a good evisceration.

Trimble didn't know what to do. He wanted the job because he needed the job. But did he actually have the job? He thought he did, but Dalrymple was so fey he couldn't be sure. Besides, even if he had the job, what would happen if he told

Reinhardt to go to hell? Nothing good, certainly. But he had to do something.

"The name is American," he said, looking Reinhardt straight in the eye. "And it's spelled T-R-I-M-B-L-E."

Reinhardt did not flinch. He had been challenged before. Just who the hell did this punk think he was?

"Don't raise your voice, Tinkerbell, we can hear you," Reinhardt said with practiced menace. The don't-raise-your-voice maneuver was one of his favorites.

As usual, it worked. Trimble's anger turned to confusion. What was going on? He had done nothing to this man. With confusion came paralysis. Gafney broke the moment with a chortling belly laugh.

"Man oh man, Skip, you really had him going." He slapped Trimble on the shoulder. "We like to have fun around here."

I need a job, Trimble kept saying to himself. I need a job; it's the one irrefutable necessity of the universe, of this universe in any case; the one reality you ultimately must accept, whatever your opinions about it. Queer how all the high-minded moralists, all the great thinkers, all the distinguished intellectuals always manage to neatly dodge that reality. Too mundane for their lofty ideals, apparently. Or, more likely, they never had to schlep themselves around town in a rusty VW, hoping something, anything, would come their way. Unemployment is the loneliest, most helpless state of being in existence. And if existence had any particular meaning, Trimble had never seen it. Henry David Thoreau and Ayn Rand, go fuck yourselves.

Trimble and Dalrymple marched back to Peterson, Dalrymple droning on his flat monotone about alumni newsletters and summer school catalogs and on and on. Trimble tried to listen, but it became a blur.

The secretaries were chatting quietly when they arrived. The chatting promptly stopped. They young women stared at Trimble warily. Dalrymple walked past them as if they were lumps of concrete. He went straight to his desk, sat down and began signing brochures again. After a few minutes, he looked up, starting a little in surprise to see Trimble still there.

"We have some administrative shuffling to do, so it will be about a week. Say, the twenty first," he said.

Trimble waited. "A week or so before what?" he finally asked.

"Before you start." Dalrymple went back to signing brochures; brochure after brochure, like an automaton.

Am I supposed to leave now? Trimble thought. Apparently. But there is one other minor matter.

"Excuse me," he said. "What does the job pay?"

Dalrymple did not look up.

" What? Oh. Hmm. Standard rate," he muttered.

Trimble waited for another few seconds. Then, as politely as he could, he said, "And what's that."

Dalrymple suddenly became befuddled. Again the sheep-like expression.

"What?" he said.

Trimble waited a few seconds more. It was clear he was not going to get an answer. A job is a job, it's better than Kunsun. . .

On his way out, he noticed the secretaries were busy, very busy. None looked at him.

Chapter 5

On Marilyn Pennell's third day at Seattle Pacific, a notice appeared on the bulletin board. Hazel Rexler, the dorm's resident director – its house mother – wanted all freshmen coeds to report to big lounge on the first floor at 3 p.m. It was time for a little chat.

Marilyn Pennell had seen Hazel Rexler only once before, on the day she had moved into Hill. To Marilyn, she resembled nothing so much as a scarecrow; gray-haired, pencil thin, with an oddly flat sort of body. The skin of her face was wrinkled into a furrowed quilt. One eye was cast askew and the corners of her mouth turned down in what appeared to be a permanent scowl.

On that first day, Rexler stood very still as she watched the parade of eager young women rushing back and forth with bundles of clothing and bedding, her face frozen in an expression of disapproval. Or maybe that was merely because of her eye, Marilyn thought. She had grown up among sour-faced old women. They seemed to gravitate to churches. Marilyn shrugged Hazel Rexler off.

When the freshmen girls were all present in the lounge, Rexler gestured for them to gather around in a semi circle. Some found chairs and couches. The rest ended up sitting on the floor.

Rexler placed a chair in the middle of the semicircle, carefully arranging it until it was just so. She sat down and then silently scanned the crowd as if she was conducting an inspection. Finally, she leaned forward attempting, apparently, to create some kind of just-us-girls intimacy. She smiled, although it looked more like a baring of teeth; crooked, gray teeth, one of them dark gray.

"Welcome to SPC and to Hill Hall," she said, in a voice that attempted to be friendly, but ended up sounding brittle and worn-out. "Now, each of you has a copy of the student handbook, so you should know all our rules by now. But I want to remind you of a few just the same. On weeknights, you are to be in by 10 p.m. On Fridays, Saturdays and Sundays, we lock the doors at 12:30 a.m. After 6 p.m. and on weekends, you are required to sign out at the front desk. You are required to wear skirts or dresses to all meals and all classes."

Marilyn looked around the room. Some girls were picking lint off their clothes. Some were checking their nails. Some, most, were staring ahead blankly, their faces masks of boredom and resignation.

Rexler tried smiling again. "Well, enough of that." she said. Then she hunched forward further. Her wrinkled face distorted into foreboding Gordian knot. Marilyn noticed that her lips disappeared in determined compression.

"There's something else you need to know about," Hazel Rexler said in a near whisper, as if discussing something dark and secretive. "There are boys on this campus, in this very building."

There certainly are, Marilyn thought. But from what she had seen, most of them were nothing much to pay attention to.

"And boys want things from girls," Rexler said, her eyes flashing briefly. She let the words sink in. "Boys have urges, animal urges."

She shuddered in disgust.

"You are special. God has blessed you with purity. And, in His name, you must be living examples of that purity."

Marilyn had heard similar lectures before, always steeped in fear, fear epitomized in the most horrific images the tellers could conjure. And they were good conjurers: Rags and gutters and filth and degradation and oozing sores, among other things.

It had the desired effect. Whenever Marilyn felt attracted to a member of the opposite sex, the deep, visceral fears of rags and gutters and filth rose in her.

But lately, for the past year or so, rational thought had been gaining some agency in the battleground of ideas that was the mind of Marilyn Pennell. She liked young men. She liked their company. She liked the look of their bodies, lean and hard, form and function.

But there was something else – what was it? She wasn't sure. She couldn't define it. But she knew it when she saw it: Maleness, an unconscious, unapologetic confidence in what they were. It drew her.

As she thought about it, a vision of Tom Brewer took form in her mind. She let it settle and it stayed, deep, and it would not go away.

For now, Hazel Rexler's talk had piqued her curiosity. Just where was she going with all this?

Rexler was bent so far forward that her posture resembled a jackknife. Her eyes were squinted nearly shut with intensity and her voice was hushed and throaty, so low everyone in the room had to concentrate to hear it.

"Girls, have you ever seen a white rose? So beautiful, so pure, so perfect. And do you know what happens if someone touches that rose? It forms brown spots and those spots spread and grow and putrefy. They can't be stopped. And the beautiful white rose decays, petal by precious petal, until it dies, brown and defiled.

"Girls, you are God's white roses. A boy's touch will create brown spots on your soul and they will spread and grow and putrefy."

It was clear Rexler had given this speech before. Some of the girls looked like they couldn't believe the nonsense they were hearing. A few had turned their heads away to stifle giggles. One fiendishly poked the bare arm of the girl next to her with her finger and then withdrew in mock horror.

But others, not many but enough that they constituted an identifiable body, looked like they were taking the whole business seriously, their heads nodding, their attention rapt.

For her part, Marilyn concluded the obvious: Hazel Rexler was just another neurotic old bat and her speech was just another in the endless litany of pointless talking-tos she had been hearing all her life. But Hazel Rexler was bad at it, so bad she was pathetic and laughable. At least get a better act, Marilyn thought.

Marilyn despised the girls who seemed to take Rexler's gibberish to heart. Brainless losers. And the gigglers – well, on one hand, she couldn't blame them. The whole business was so ludicrous it tempted you to laugh. But giggling was silly and childish. Grow up.

So Marilyn concentrated on remaining poised and in control. It was not difficult. She was Marilyn Pennell. She was superior to the rest of these girls and she must maintain a demeanor that expressed it.

Hazel Rexler was done. She let her words hang in the air, trying to created aura of awe and portent. But the gigglers were having a hard time with their stifles. Rexler shot them a ferocious glance verging on the homicidal. She stared the gigglers down until they stopped.

Rexler slowly rose from her chair, angrily eying the crowd the whole time. She continued to glower at them for a full minute. The silence in the room became palpable.

Finally, she said, "All right, now go to your rooms."

The girls filed out. Marilyn stopped just outside the door and looked back. Hazel Rexler was putting the chairs back in their places. She threw them around angrily, her mouth still set, her eyes still blazing.

****

Tom Brewer's first college class was Physics 114 in the second floor auditorium of Beegle Hall at 8:30 a.m.

The first thing Brewer noticed was that the hall was nothing like the oak-paneled college classrooms of popular imagination.

The lectern was on a small stage backed by windows with the sort of wire-meshed textured glass they use in factories and men's rooms. Seating consisted of concentric rows of counters that rose upward like a miniature amphitheater. They were made of unpainted plywood. The walls were perfunctorily painted plaster board and the ceiling was paneled with cheap acoustic tiles. The effect was one of a place the Navy would build in the Aleutians. So much for the hallowed halls of academia.

The teacher was one Mr. Van Holder, a young man and nervous. He fidgeted and stuttered through the first lecture – on heat transfer in a fluid solution – and seemed relieved when the 9:30 bell rang. Brewer concluded – correctly he would later find – that Mr. Van Holder was fresh out of graduate school and this was his first teaching assignment.

Fine with Brewer. The material was a more detailed version of stuff he'd already studied in high school. Would he actually learn anything? Probably not much, but if this was its level of difficulty, he was on track for a passing grade without too much work.

He seemed to be the only one. Everyone else in the class hurriedly took notes and wore the big-eyed expression of those struggling to keep up. Maybe I just went to a better high school, Brewer thought. If that's the case, I'm in a puzzling environment, perhaps one with more opportunity than I thought.

English 101, Expository Writing, was held in small room at the top of the balcony in McKinley, another picturesque exemplar of academic interior design. It was originally designed as a practice room for the choir and here too the rows were arranged amphitheater style. This time, they were occupied by portable semi-desks – wooden chairs with armrests that served as writing surfaces – and they were packed very close together. The result was that students awkwardly tripped and collided with one another as they took their seats.

English 101 was taught by Miss Habib, a small, soft-spoken woman not much older than the students she taught; another recent grad school alumnae, apparently. Brewer quickly learned not to underestimate Miss Habib. She was a lot smarter than she appeared. English 101 was going to be a challenge. The idea made Brewer nervous. The word challenge, in his experience, usually meant a great deal of work with assurances of rewards that rarely materialized.

Miss Habib was sharp, obviously, but was she interested in teaching her students effectively, or in merely using their sweat to enhance her own academic stature? And that raised the question that would dominate Brewer's approach to school that quarter: Which was more important, learning something or surviving? Learning something meant risk; the disquieting risk of reaching beyond your intellectual comfort zone. Surviving meant doing the required work, to be sure, but always with the caveat of not doing too much lest you reach too far and fall. Freshmen could not afford to fall. Brewer would observe Miss Habib closely, watching for clues that would help him survive English 101.

History 142, Nineteenth Century American history, was taught by a Dr. Schnieder, a formal, rather wooden man who addressed his students as Miss this and Mr. that and spoke in distinctly formal academese.

But he knew his stuff, too; really knew it. As Brewer took notes during one of Dr. Schnieder's lectures, he found that things were fell into the form of a precise, detailed outline – with main point I, secondary point A, supporting information 1 and 2 and so forth.

Dr. Schnieder spoke without notes. His knowledge was so complete and his mind so lucid, he didn't need them. As much as anything, he understood, almost intuitively, the people and the times he described - to the point, Brewer concluded, it almost seemed like he had actually been there.

"Prudent" was one of his favorite terms. Nineteenth Century America was full of people who were anything but. Rash, sometimes reckless decisions characterized the times, until a cool-headed logistician named Lincoln showed up at just the right moment and brought clarity to the pandemonium. And somehow, perhaps because God reached down and touched this brilliant, enigmatic backwoodsman, Abraham Lincoln gave a nation direction, a direction it was still following. Dr. Schneider had a moment of something approaching emotion.

"We were lucky," he said reverently and then, without missing a beat, moved on to his next point with flawless scholarly precision.

What would Brewer learn from this class? Well, a lot about American history if he paid attention. And perhaps he might learn something about clear, systematic thinking, for Dr. Schneider was a very clear and very systematic thinker.

Brewer's final subject was a required two-hour P.E. class. The only one available at a time he could fit in was Bodybuilding, which Brewer dreaded, assuming he would end up in a room full of Charles Atlas clones. Instead, he found most of his bodybuilding classmates were no more muscley than him. The one exception was a short, rather shy young man named O'Connor; a spectacular figure of masculine pulchritude the other students nicknamed Tarzan. He had begun lifting weights in eighth grade and continued to do so for ninety minutes a day, every day, ever since. He only broke his routine once, when he came down with the flu for three days in 1962.

Brewer watched him do curls one time, his muscles pulsing, the serrations on his deltoids deep and rippling. O'Connor saw the admiration in Brewer's eyes and smiled.

"Hey, it's not that big a deal," he said. "Anybody can do it. You just have to get in the habit."

"I'm not so sure," Brewer said. "I doubt if I could look like you if I worked out for the next ten years."

O'Connor shrugged. "Then you wouldn't. I've been doing this so long, I couldn't live any other way. Do what's right for you, I guess." Then we went to the leg press where, again, veins popped and muscles surged and flexed.

Brewer thought, okay, I never will look like that, but I can sweat and grunt and maybe I'll get somewhere with it. It can certainly do me no harm. But what kind of grade will I get? Ultimately, that's the most important thing. That made him nervous.

Chapter 6

SPC's mandatory student chapel was convened at McKinley Auditorium, 10:30 a.m. every day, Monday through Friday, and every day, Monday through Friday, students did their best to weasel out of it.

There were various methods. The easiest was to make friends with one of the checkers, students who were paid ten dollars a week to roam the aisles with practiced earnestness, clipboards at the ready, diligently jotting down the numbers of empty chairs. They didn't check every day and if one of them was an amenable sort, he might tell you that today they wouldn't be taking roll.

Another way was to stand at the door in the back of the auditorium and wait for the checkers to appear. They usually showed up two or three minutes after things started. If so, you rushed to your seat. If not, you merrily skipped away. There was a risk to the method. Occasionally the checkers showed up, left and then came back later. Then your name went on the list of the missing. Three times and you were sent to the dean for a little "talk." Usually, miscreants pleaded a case of the flu or some such thing and usually they got away with it. If, however, you were absent three times in a quarter, for two quarters in a year with no convincing excuses, you were looking at possible expulsion. That was rare. But it did happen.

Students who truly detested chapel, and there were many, usually ended up simply sleeping through it. Indeed, the phenomenon of snores punctuating the proceedings at inopportune moments was one of the more notable features of the liturgical observance.

Other students mastered the tricky art of reading while being preached at loudly. Somehow, they could turn off their ears, concentrate on a printed page and come away prepped for their next class. It took practice. They had a lot of opportunity.

Chapel shirkers were particularly prevalent among the junior and senior classes. The progression went like this: Most freshmen paid attention in chapel and tried to get something out of it – at least for their first quarter. Then reality set in. One of the drawbacks of mandatory religion is repetition. There are only so many ways you can say do what I tell you or burn in hell, and after hearing them all – there are about six variations on the theme – even the most devout start to yawn. So by Spring Quarter, the freshmen were getting restless and bored.

They were, without knowing it, evolving. Next came a combination of resignation and ennui that characterized the sophomore chapel experience. By junior year, actual hostility began to infiltrate. Seniors were desperate to get out – of both school and chapel. Sometimes, the urge to flee nearly overwhelmed them and they stayed in their seats only through exceptional acts of will.

Mind you, these were broad trends and not true of all students. Some – a very few – actually liked chapel. Brewer sat next to one such during fall quarter.

Originally, Brewer nearly ended up sitting next to no one. On the first day of classes, he dutifully went to his assigned chapel seat and found it occupied by someone else, a pasty-faced, square-jawed young man who eyed Brewer suspiciously.

"Hi, I think you are sitting in my seat, AA4?" Brewer said.

"My name is Norbert Verbles," the young man said, his expression becoming even more suspicious.

"No, I mean I think I was assigned this seat," Brewer said patiently. He held out the paper with Tom Brewer, AA4 printed on it in large, block letters.

"My name is Norbert Verbles," the young man said, his eyes darting about in confusion. There was a mix of fear and anger in his voice.

Brewer looked at him. He thought he had made himself clear. Norbert Verbles continued to stare at him, his face hostile with incomprehension. Brewer started to explain again, but then chapel started, so he left.

He went to the chapel office and reported the error. It was only later that he realized he'd blown it. He had the right seat. Norbert Verbles did not. So, as long as Norbert Verbles occupied it, Brewer was marked present. Then he could go to SUB, drink coffee and check out girls.

Instead, he did the right thing, the responsible thing, the conscientious thing - in short, the dumbshit thing - and ended up stuck next to an individual who actually liked chapel.

He was, in many ways, a familiar SPC type; small-town church nerd, hopelessly lost at sea in the big city, with the social graces of a hyena. He was chronically cheerful and chummy, enthusiastically greeting Brewer with a loud "Hi! How are ya?!" every morning. At first, he would punctuate his greeting with a manly slap on the shoulder, until one day Brewer politely informed him that if he did it again, he'd get his fucking nose broken.

He took that as a challenge. His pet project for the quarter would be to make Brewer just as gosh-darned chipper as he was.

"Don't you ever smile?" he would say. "Look at it, it's another beautiful day!" It was autumn in Seattle: A world slowly turning the color of lead.

"Don't ya just love this guy?" he would say to no one in particular while gesturing at Brewer. "Just gotta pep up a little, that's all!"

Brewer would grunt and try to sleep. The small town boy would shake his head in amusement and then, with the boundless enthusiasm of the terminally clueless, commence to drink in the wonders of student chapel.

It followed a routine. Students would file in and sit down. Then they would sing a hymn, sometimes accompanied by a music major on the organ or piano. Then came the day's announcements, usually read by Dr. Mendal Miller, professor of business and chapel programs director. A big, good-natured man, utterly devoid of dishonesty or meanness, Miller was beloved by all, even by the chapel-fatigued seniors longingly eying the exit doors.

After announcements, Miller would introduce the day's speaker or program. That's when things could get peculiar.

Once, in an interview in the student newspaper, Miller freely admitted it was impossible to get first-rate speakers or programs every day, five days a week all year. He and his staff did the best they could. Sometimes their best was pretty good: An appearance by the governor of the state; a report on daily life in Vietnam by a New York Times reporter recently returned; a presentation on linguistics in which a Bible translator showed, through pantomime and repetition, how the vocabulary and grammar of an unknown language eventually revealed itself.

Other times, there could be, shall we say, problems. Usually, they involved preachers with an evangelistic bent, passionate orators determined to move their audience to some sort of spiritual paroxysm. They alternately made Brewer squirm in embarrassment or gape in disbelief.

His first major squirm came during Spiritual Emphasis Week, which was held once a quarter and usually featured a pulpit-pounder of the especially vociferous sort. This particular one was the director of evangelism for some branch of the Methodist church; a skeletal, hunch-backed old man with deep-set eyes, bushy eyebrows and claw-like hands. He dropped his chin, glowered out through his hedge-like brows, pointed a crooked talon at the audience accusatorily and snarled:

"Breaaaad!"

Pause for emphasis. Voice raised a note.

"*Breaaaad!*"

More glowering. Then, "Boys in Rhodesia walk thirty miles to a mission no shoes only the clothes on their back danger at every turn sleeping in the open rain and wind and mud and mosquitoes."

Another pause.

"*Breaaaad!* For a slice of **BREAAAAD!**"

Another pause, another glower. Grinding jaw for further emphasis.

"Thirty miles through jungle and swamp mountains and chasms no friends no family only a hunger for the word of God only hoping for a slice of. . ." Longest pause yet. Wait for it.

"*Breaaaad!*"

From there he quickly dissected society as undergraduates understood it and showed that most of its elements – financial success, popularity with the opposite sex, professional achievement – were empty and meaningless. Worldly success and rewards were shallow and selfish and shame on you, the soft, spoiled progeny of a decadent materialist culture for embracing them.

Or words to that effect; enough well-rehearsed dialectic and polemic delivered fast enough and with enough fervor that it left some of the listeners feeling confused and hopeless. It made them forget that ten minutes later they would walk out to a college campus, and a college education, which they were earning by sweating their way through difficult classes every day without letup for four years. Or that they lived in a prosperous city, in the freest, most progressive nation in the history of the world – which was free because hundreds of thousands had fought and died to make it that way. Or that they were twenty years old, in astonishingly good health, with sixty more years of life stretching out before them; with time, blessed time, on their side and the opportunity to make of things whatever they wished.

No, thanks to the practiced manipulation of a malcontent with a fixation for baked goods, they should be ashamed of their very existence. That's when he made an altar call.

Brewer had never seen an altar call, or even heard of one, before he set foot on the SPC campus. They usually went like this: As all in the room stood, heads bowed, the preacher would say something along the lines of, "Do *you* feel the need to turn your life over to God? Do *you* want to accept Jesus Christ, the son of God as *your* personal lord and savior? Then come forward now and kneel before the altar of redemption!"

And then it would happen. People would squeeze their way to the aisle and with heads bowed and hands clasped at their chests, shuffle solemnly forward to the front of the church. Many were misty-eyed or visibly weeping as they kneeled and waited for the preacher to place his hand on their shoulder and say something along the lines of, "Oh, Lord, help this, thy servant, in this moment of turmoil. Help him (or her) to find peace in thy loving kindness, help him (or her). . ."

And blah blah blah. Brewer watched in amazement. From what he could discern, the message, whatever it was, was mostly in the preacher's tone of voice, not his words, for they rarely said anything that chapel-goers hadn't been hearing on a daily basis for months. Apparently, its effect was from the spirit of the moment, or a sense of group identity, or too little sleep and no breakfast – or something. But not from any particularly astute logic.

What amazed Brewer the most is that people would fall for it, that they would expose their emotional state in a big auditorium full of people, mostly strangers; that they would, in Brewer's evaluation, make blubbering fools of themselves in public.

He felt embarrassed for them even if they didn't feel embarrassed for themselves. No, that wasn't it. He felt embarrassed that he was even there, like walking through the woods and suddenly coming upon two people fucking doggy-style.

As the deformed old man scowled and roared about breaaaad, Brewer looked around to see if anyone else felt the same kind of discomfort. All were motionless, with their heads down. Was he the lone doubter? Was he swimming in an ocean of people who believed it perfectly normal to make an ass of one's self in the name of religion? The idea disconcerted him. Where had such people been before in his life? Hiding? Were they like the pod people from *Invasion of the Body Snatchers*, a secret army of zombie-like spacemen waiting for a command from their supreme leader to rise up and annihilate the unaware?

Brewer had to wonder. Surely no one would fall for The Breadman. Then came the altar call ("Come, accept the breaaaad of salvation!") and sure enough, the penitent started trickling down the aisles. Among them, Brewer noted, was a girl known colloquially around campus as Handjob Ferguson. How regrettable to see such an admirable talent extinguished, Brewer thought.

Then the guy next to him sniffled, a good, long, trying-to-control-himself-during- a-deeply-spiritual-moment kind of sniffle.

Good god, Brewer thought, there's been a pod person next to me all quarter! Has he been sending out tendrils to slowly creep under my skin and make their way to my brain? Will I get a bad haircut, worse clothes and begin walking around campus prattling platitudes with a sappy look on my face?

Then he looked at Handjob Ferguson again, or at least the back of her as she walked up the aisle. It was a pleasant view. No, Brewer thought; some may find enlightenment in whatever it was that made them answer altar calls, but he preferred more tangible epiphanies. Of course, his preferred kind required the participation of the opposite sex. And, viewed in actuarial terms, its frequency tended to be unpredictable and, therefore, its per unit expense high. (Love that Economics class in high school.) But it was worth it. Well, most of the time, Brewer thought. At least I don't do it in front of a gallery of gawking nitwits.

Chapter 7

Brewer wanted to meet Marilyn again, but he didn't know how.

He would see her walking through campus, or waiting in line at Gwinn, or in chapel, but she was always too far away or going the wrong direction or . . .

Cut the crap, he thought. Call it shyness, call it uncertainty – *Call it what it is: You're a pussy!* – but he could not bring himself to simply go over and say hello.

What to do, what to do. . .

Call her on the phone? Why? You don't just call someone for the heck of it. Casual chitchat in the registration line was one thing; it was merely passing the time. Expressions of interest were quite another. The thought of it made Brewer's stomach knot up. He could no more call her up than he could sing opera in a jockstrap on the Freeway Bridge at rush hour.

Maybe he would run across her at the SUB. Unlikely. He had never seen her there. Like a lot of people who lived on-campus, she probably spent most of her off-hours in the dorm lounges. Brewer had never been to the lounge in Hill. Lurking there when he didn't even live in the dorm, hoping on hope to bump into her; it struck him as distinctly pathetic and a little creepy.

He wondered what he would say if he finally did connect with her – not that it really mattered. He just wanted to see her again, to be in her presence, to feel the reality of her. That would be enough, more than enough.

But would she want to see him? He had no idea what kind of an impression he'd made in the registration line. Favorable, he thought, but how could he be sure? Maybe she was only being polite. It reminded him of a cartoon he'd seen in one of Orrin's Playboys stashed under the workbench in the garage. A curvy blond is telling a nebbishy young man, "Of course I love you. I love everybody!"

But... but.... Whatever his inexperience and insecurities, somehow Brewer had to see her again. You only appreciate water through thirst, he had read in a poem required for an English 101 assignment. Odd how it came back to him now in perfect, word-for-word clarity.

... beauty through longing, poppies in November through lips at night ...

He had noticed that after chapel, Marilyn often walked back to Hill by taking the gravel path behind Moyer. An unusual route that, one few people used. Maybe that's why she took it; to avoid crowds, to find a few moments of silence on a small, crowded campus, to be apart from the shabby routine of day-to-day college life ...

... except it is not shabby or routine, not when she was in it...

Brewer shook his head to clear his thoughts. But there Marilyn Pennell remained, winsome, ethereal and distant.

What he decided to do was sneak out of chapel a minute or so early. Usually, they had everyone stand to sing one last hymn. If he moved slowly and steadily, no one would notice him heading for the door. And even if they did, as long as he didn't leave more than a minute or two early, they likely wouldn't care: He probably had his reasons, a doctor's appointment or some such thing.

Once out of McKinley, he would hurry along the front of Moyer to the far end of the gravel path, then double back. That way, he could meet her face to face – if he could get out of chapel, if she showed up, if she remembered him, if, if, if...

Jesus, can you make things any more convoluted?

No, but no other worthwhile ideas were presenting themselves at the moment.

So Brewer tried it. When all rose for a rather bleary rendition of "How Great Thou Art" (Bleary was about as good as one could muster at 10:30 a.m.), Brewer rose too. But his books were under his arm and he stood two feet forward of his chair. In the middle of the first verse, he began sidling toward the aisle. Only two people stood between him and it and they were juniors. Two-plus years of rigorously-applied institutional piety had mutated them into totems of apathetic protoplasm. One held the hymnal but did not sing. The other stared blankly into space with dead eyes, his mouth slightly ajar.

In any case, if they noticed Brewer they didn't acknowledge it. The small town hick who occupied the seat next to Brewer's did look over to watch him moving toward the aisle and his expression indicated he found it suspicious. Brewer shot him a look, using the same glower he had used some two weeks before when he had informed the youthful rustic that if he didn't leave him alone he would rearrange his facial bone structure. The hick had been wary of Brewer ever since. He quickly buried his nose, so far unbroken, in the hymnal.

Brewer rushed silently down the stairs from the balcony, then out the door, down the front steps and over to Moyer. He waited by the corner of the building, where he had a view of the steps to McKinley. He didn't have a complete view. That was a risk. Well, all plans involved some kind of risk, no point in worrying about it. He pictured himself in a James Bond movie, coolly studying the situation, calculating the odds, moving with grace and economy, smooth as silk, mission accomplished.

Then reality set in.

He spotted Marilyn when she was about half-way down the steps.

. . . she moves like the scent of irises . . .

Jesus, get a grip. You're going to blow it.

She reached the sidewalk and began toward Moyer. She was walking fast, which meant Brewer didn't have time to get to the far end of the path and start back. He hadn't counted on that. He would have to walk from the near end of Moyer and hope she caught up with him.

But how would he do it? How long would it take her to reach the path? Thirty seconds? A minute? Who knows? But she was getting closer every second. He began to panic.

Well, you can't just stand here, leaning against the wall like some hood from a George Raft movie. Make a decision, dipshit!

Brew started walking up the path very slowly. He counted as he walked. At thirty - it seemed as good a number as any - he quickened his pace a little; still slow but close enough to normal that no one would notice.

Wait a minute. Won't she notice you hadn't been walking on the sidewalk to the path? And, therefore, wouldn't she conclude you had been lying in wait? Hell, you'll look like some kind of pervert.

Maybe, Brewer thought, maybe. But probably not; not unless she had some reason to pay attention to those kinds of details – which she did not. The odds were on his side. Or so he reasoned. But, of course, reason and calculation were not the answer to all things...

Then, ten counts later, he heard footsteps hit the gravel behind him.

Wait for it, wait for it...

"Tom!" Marilyn called out.

Today I'm lucky.

Brewer turned. There she was, framed in gold by the morning sun, looking like all things fresh and young and alive. And that wasn't a fragment of half-remembered poetry or some harebrained mental meandering. It was the reality; the solid, true reality Tom Brewer experienced in that moment.

He took a quick deep breath to calm himself.

"Enjoy chapel?" he said.

Hoo-boy, are you the suave one, a regular Cary Grant – or is it Mortimer Snerd?

"Only the parts I slept through," Marilyn said with a smile. She hurried her pace a little to catch up with him.

Holy crap, she actually wants to walk with me...

"A lot of that going around," Brewer said. "Funny they don't notice."

She drew along side of him, walking close to his arm, brushing against it occasionally.

Hmmmm!

"Oh, they probably do," Marilyn said. "That's why they have so much music. Hard to sleep through that, especially when they have all the stand up and sit down."

"I always wait to have my morning coffee until after chapel," Brewer said. "No point in wasting the caffeine."

Marilyn laughed.

"So," she said with crisp good cheer, "I haven't seen you in a while. How go the classes and all that?"

"They're hard," Brewer said.

"So I've noticed," she nodded. "I'm wondering if it will be like this for all four years."

"If it is, only ten percent of us will make it to graduation," Brewer said. "I'm told that at the UW, professors are expected to flunk a certain percentage of freshmen every quarter. I wonder if it's that way here."

"Could be," Marilyn said. "But enough doom and gloom. It's good to see you!"

"Good to see you?" She said that? She actually said that?

No one had ever told Brewer they were glad to see him, not once in his entire life. He found himself enfolded in her brightness.

Marilyn kept on talking; about her classes, about the dorm, about college life in general. She was surprised that she did not miss home. Even the cooking at Gwinn didn't bother her. And the classes; challenging, to put it mildly, but after only a month, she was amazed at how much she had learned.

As she talked, she gradually spoke faster and faster and her voice rose note by note as she continued.

Then she went silent. He looked at her. Her lips were pursed, her head down.

Finally, Marilyn said, "Do you have a bank around here somewhere?"

What an odd thing to ask at a moment like this, Brewer thought. Maybe she was as desperate to fill the silence as he had been and she had run out of things to say.

"Washington Federal over in the U District," he said.

"Is it reliable?"

Brewer's account was so miniscule that he didn't think much about the qualities of the bank itself. No need.

"I suppose," he said.

Well, at least it was a conversation, Brewer thought. Any conversation with Marilyn Pennell was a worthwhile conversation. But the fact she was as nervous as he was gave him a sudden shot of confidence. He decided to make things challenging.

"Why so interested in banks?" he said. "There's plenty of fun to be had in this world."

That seemed to make Marilyn even more nervous than before.

"It's, well, it's just that, uh. . . some things must be saved for the future," she stammered.

If that wasn't a Freudian slip, I don't know what is, Brewer thought. His hesitancy and doubt disappeared.

"But they also are meant to be enjoyed," he said. "Surely what belongs to you is yours to do with as you please."

Marilyn's demeanor suddenly changed. She looked at him with sharp, analytical eyes.

"To use however I please, whenever I please?" she said. "Wouldn't that just be self-indulgent?"

"Only if you do not recognize value," Brewer said.

Marilyn stopped walking.

"Wait a minute. Value? But what is value?" she said.

"What we determine it to be. No thing has value except what we assign it."

Marilyn studied him a bit more, turning over her thoughts in her mind. Finally, she said "Doesn't inaction have value then?"

"Inaction is negation," Brewer said. "Negation is denial. Denial is the acceptance of unreality. By definition, unreality has no value."

That stopped Marilyn cold. She started walking again, her head down in thought. Finally, she said, "But do all things have to have value?"

"Without it, what purpose do they serve?" Brewer said.

"Must all things have a purpose?"

Brewer laughed.

"You have found the flaw in my argument," he said. "There are things you do just for the hel. . . just for the heck of it."

"Why?"

"Because you feel like it."

"Not much of a reason."

"Well, some say that to be human is to initiate action," Brewer said. "To be free is to act without having to justify it to anyone but yourself. What could be a better exercise of freedom than simple enjoyment?"

"Sounds like you've thought a lot about this," Marilyn said.

"Actually, I haven't," Brewer said. "It's all from an essay we read in 101 last week. Impressed?"

Marilyn choked on a spasm of laughter. Eventually, she regained her composure, more or less, and said, "Do you do this all the time?"

"Only when I can get away with it," Brewer said. He smiled at her. She smiled back. They reached the door to Hill. Marilyn stopped outside the door. She was still a little flushed.

"It's a beautiful morning," she said.

Brewer looked at Marilyn with calm, unwavering eyes. She met Brewer's gaze. They looked at one another for what seemed like a long time. Finally, Brewer said, "Would you like to go see Carlos Montoya with me Friday night? He's playing at the Moore Theatre downtown."

Carlos Montoya? Marilyn had heard the name, but she wasn't clear on details. He was a musician of some kind, that she knew. She tried to remember. Then she remembered Brewer was expecting an answer.

"Oh. Yes. Yes, of course," she stammered "I love his music."

She tried to think of something else to say. But she was frozen.

"Curtain is at eight," Brewer said. "May I pick you up at seven?"

Marilyn was speechless for another moment. Finally, she said, "Yes. Yes, seven would be wonderful." Again the stammer.

Brewer smiled, clearly happy with her answer.

"Looks like you have a lot to do," he said, nodding at the stack of books she was carrying.

She recovered her poise.

"A test in Psych and a term paper for English," she said "Too much to do, when you think about it."

" I'll leave you to it," Brewer said. "See you tomorrow after chapel?"

"That would be great."

Brewer turned to walk away and Marilyn turned to enter the dorm. Once through the doors, she glanced quickly over her shoulder. Tom Brewer was walking into the morning light. His back was very straight.

Chapter 8

Layton Fleming, SPC's dean of students, was on his way home after a morning of tennis with the president. He had let the president win one game each set. He even let him come close on one other. Then he won the rest easily; although not so easily that it showed. Sometimes Fleming wondered if he really fooled the president by allowing him to win from time to time. The poor man was hopeless; tripping and stumbling around the court on his pasty, stick-like legs, feverishly slapping and flailing at the ball, utterly bereft of coordination or timing.

But then, when they finished, the president would be flushed and panting, his eyes lively, laughing and joking with the enthusiasm of a competitor who had enjoyed a hard-fought contest.

So Fleming's carefully-orchestrated tennis matches had the desired effect: The president enjoyed them. The president enjoyed Fleming. He enjoyed hanging out with him. He enjoyed taking him into his confidence. Through unspoken consent, he had invited Fleming into his inner circle. A very hard circle to join, that, and Fleming worked assiduously to make sure he was ensconced in it beyond question. He had become the president's right hand man.

Fleming smiled at the thought. Of course he was the president's right hand man. He was Layton Fleming. Layton Fleming was a winner.

He looked like a winner, he sounded like a winner, he moved like a winner. He relished it; walking down a hall and having people step out of the way for him, or entering a room and knowing that he was smartest, hippest, most on-the-ball guy there, the center of attention.

Fleming had perfected the look of a winner; the most stylish suits, the sharpest shoes. He worked on his hair for a half hour every morning so it would look exactly like Craig Stevens's in *Peter Gunn*. He was a winner right down to what he wore when he played tennis: Pressed percale whites, spotless Converse Net Stars and socks that matched a pair he saw JFK wearing in a *Life* photo spread; one black stripe and one red stripe around the ankle. Nobody did it better than Layton Fleming.

He had been cultivating his winner's persona for some ten years, ever since he was named a college All-American in lacrosse. When the trophy was placed in his hand and the audience applauded and flashbulbs flashed, he had an epiphany and in a moment of clarity understood, in his bones, in the very core of his being, that he was inherently better than other people – and that those other people needed to be reminded of it.

He had a carefully-honed winner's demeanor: Cocky verging on overbearing, but done in such a way that it came across as good-natured, the sort of macho banter you hear from test pilots, race car drivers or All-American lacrosse players; edgy, vaguely rude, even mildly insulting so to remind people of their place in the pecking order.

He was always one step ahead in a conversation thanks to a seemingly endless supply of jokes, barbs, pat sayings, adages, witty clichés and, of course, the latest buzz words. Buzz words were important at a place like SPC, or any college or university, for that matter. "Viable" and "emblematic" were making the rounds just then, with "cachet" and "paradigm" showing up more and more. Fleming had started inserting them into conversations, albeit carefully. A winner had to be cautious about which fads he embraced, lest he appear overeager.

Fleming was the master of it all, a virtuoso. When he thought about it, and he thought about it several times a day, he took great satisfaction in knowing that no one got the best of M. Layton Fleming. (The M, incidentally, stood for Marvin. It made Fleming wince; the antithesis of a winner's name if ever there was one. He had trained himself to force it from his mind.)

He turned his Lincoln Continental into the driveway. He had special-ordered the car. It had to be black on the outside, red on the inside, the ultimate color combination for a winner's car. It was worth the two months he had to wait for delivery. The Continental exuded all that was power and prestige. When Fleming drove it, the rest of the world receded into the shabbiness and mediocrity it deserved.

There was a note on the kitchen table: "Lunch in the refrigerator." So she was not home. She hardly ever was home during the day anymore and when she was, she was moody and distant. She didn't laugh at his jokes. She didn't nod adoringly when he enthused about his latest triumph.

She cooked meals mechanically and served them without a word. In bed, well, she never said no, but more often than not, she lay on her back with her head turned to the side, her expression blank, her eyes focused on something far away.

Fleming noticed. But then he reminded himself that he had the quintessential winner's wife; blond and pretty, with the faintly aristocratic air a winner's wife should have, a bit like Grace Kelly, Fleming liked to think. She was poised. She had exceptionally good taste in clothing. She had a degree in English lit; the ideal area of study for a winner's wife, the sort of thing candidates for Miss America majored in. It gave her cachet. Few men could lay claim to better. It all made Layton Fleming feel very good about himself.

****

Brewer's date with Marilyn went the way dates should go. Brewer arrived promptly at seven and was standing, not sitting, by the front desk when Marilyn came down from her room. He was wearing a black and gray herringbone sports jacket, blue Oxford cloth button-down shirt, red and navy regimental stripe tie and pressed charcoal slacks. His shoes were shined. Marilyn noticed he did not use any hair oil, which some boys did, particularly the dirty t-shirt and acne set back home.

Brewer held the car door for her. The car itself was clean inside and out. He drove well, with grace and economy. He did not hot rod or otherwise seem interested in impressing her with his vehicular skill.

He went straight to a parking lot a block from the theater. No searching around; he knew exactly where it was. Again, he held the car door. As they walked to the theater, he was careful to stay on the street side of the sidewalk.

These all were things Marilyn had been taught to expect from a boy, but had rarely actually experienced. Most boys simply didn't know about etiquette. Others seemed to sneer at it as unmanly. Brewer? Odd, she thought; for Brewer it seemed natural, all but seamless. He wasn't stuffy, he wasn't fussy. Good manners were simply an inherent part of him.

She was disappointed with the theater. The Moore was old, even a little dingy, with steep aisles and rather cramped seats. She had expected better. Seattle was supposed to be a sophisticated city, the home of a world's fair, after all.

Carlos Montoya was a small, balding man who sat on a simple wooden chair in the middle of an unadorned stage. There was no printed program. A tall, dark woman, apparently Montoya's wife, came out to announce the first piece and explain a little about its history. The overall effect was simple verging on dull.

Marilyn was beginning to wonder if the evening would be a bust. And then Don Carlos Garcia Montoya de Madrid, maestro del flamenco, began to play. And all the sets and lighting and staging in the world became unnecessary.

The music enveloped Marilyn, carried her, sent her mind floating along a river of fluid sound. It was unlike anything she had ever experienced. Oh, she had heard music on records and on the radio. She even had attended a concert or two of the local philharmonic. Her aunt played flute in it. But nothing had prepared her for this one man, this one guitar, this one moment.

After the second song, she found herself holding Brewer's hand; grasping it, clenching it for safety, for surely she would drift away on a note. The music and the presence of this calm, gentlemanly boy put Marilyn in a place she had never been before, a place of grace and nuance, a reality which spoke for itself without explanation. It was not the forced gentility of her mother's country club teas or the self-congratulatory affectations of the artsy posers she had known in high school. Carlos Montoya's music, live and in person, was something beyond all.

And Tom Brewer; what to make of him? He sat throughout the concert with a pensive expression, occasionally tilting his head to one side or leaning forward slightly as if he was mentally exploring what he heard. Once, she looked over at him and her eyes stayed there. He looked back briefly, nodded, smiled affably and then returned to listening.

Does he feel what I'm feeling in this moment? Marilyn wondered. She couldn't tell. But he clearly was paying attention, drinking in the moment as she was.

When the concert ended, Marilyn's senses were alive. The evening air was warm and soft. The city was alive. She couldn't stop smiling. She felt like dancing along the sidewalk.

They went to European Café on University Avenue. A half-block away, on their route to the café, was The Wall, which was indeed a concrete retaining wall to a parking lot. Beatniks and fringies sat on the wall and gathered around it.

Normally, Marilyn would have been vaguely disgusted with the beatniks and fringies. They were, by any standard, slovenly and boorish. But tonight, as she and Brewer walked past them, her arm linked in his, she actually found their flaunting of convention evocative of the moment. They all were searching for. . . for what? Something was in the air. Life seemed a breath of pure oxygen deep in your lungs, filling you with its warm, pulsing euphoria. Simply to be there, in 1964, to be eighteen years old in that fleeting flick of a frame; the moment-to-moment exhilaration of it was something onto itself. Marilyn would never forget it, not for the rest of her life.

The European Cafe was low-ceilinged, its small tables lit by candles. Classical music, mostly string quartets, played quietly over the speakers. Mozart, perhaps. Maybe Haydn. The waitress brought a tray filled with pastries, the like of which Marilyn had never seen. They were sculptures, layered color by color, bedecked with delicate ribbons of frosting, like the friezes on Greco-Roman temples; glowing with glazes of ruby and amber. They had names like Kaiserschmarron and Ischletorten and Rigo Jancsi. Marilyn had no idea what any of it meant. But neither did Brewer, apparently, because he asked what a number of them were.

Marilyn chose something that looked like chocolate cake, but coated with a crystalline glaze. Her first bite told her it was flavored with rum; strong rum and a lot of it. She nearly winced, then caught herself. She didn't want to look unsophisticated. The harsh sting of the rum intrigued her, as so much of this night had intrigued her.

She and Brewer lightly nibbled at the pastries with the names they could not pronounce, drank tea and talked. They talked about school, they talked about politics, they talked about movies. They talked about the concert. Brewer was particularly impressed with the third piece in the program, a heavy, strumming and thumping canción; fierce, intense and very Spanish. Marilyn liked it too, but her favorite was actually just the opposite; a light, ethereal piece that, from time to time, seemed on the verge of evaporating into nothingness. Brewer nodded thoughtfully, turning it over in his mind.

"It was like someone weeping in the wind," he said. Then he colored slightly and looked down in embarrassment. Real Men didn't say such things. But Marilyn realized that's exactly how it sounded. How did he know?

As they drove back to the SPC campus, neither spoke. Marilyn was content to sit close against Brewer, luxuriating in his warmth.

He did not try to kiss her good night, nor did anything in his demeanor indicate that he planned to, which surprised her - and, she had to admit, disappointed her a little, too. He walked her to the Hill lobby, cheerfully bid her good night, smiled at her one more time, then left.

That night, as Marilyn lied in bed and stared at the ceiling, she reflected on the evening. On one hand, it was a date; a pleasant date, perhaps, but no more than that. On the other hand, it had been a singular mixture of heightened perception and gaiety and elegance; none of it expected, all of it in a city she barely knew. What else lay out there, waiting to be experienced, she wondered.

And then there was Tom Brewer, her guide, her muse through it all. Did he plan it to happen the way it did? She doubted it. He had moved and acted with unconscious ease. Manipulation was not in him.

But there was more; something beneath his veneer of courteous, good-natured intelligence, something beyond the ordinary and it was part of what she had experienced that night, too. She remembered a fragment of a poem she had read somewhere.

he glides through grove and moor
the hinterland
for it is his
this mortal sand . . .

****

Elizabeth Fleming looked in the mirror. She did not like what she saw.

She was tired at the moment and when blondes get tired, their rosy skin turns gray and their supposedly golden hair hangs lank and stringy.

Beyond that, she wondered who, or what, she actually was looking at. The Dean's wife? Pleasant to look at, poised, well-spoken, the perfect hostess? It was the role she was playing these days, the role she had been playing since childhood.

It was an accident as much as anything else. Her parents had never sent her to charm school or any such thing and she had never belonged to a sorority, much less a prestigious one. Her parents had, however, taught her to always stand up straight, always look people in the eye when they were speaking to her, always choose her words carefully, and, if in doubt, to keep her mouth shut. All of that or, more likely, a lot of preconceived stereotypes involving her looks, the sound of her voice and so forth seemed to make people conclude she was charming and polished and eminent.

Eminent? She had no idea what the word meant, although she had heard it used to describe her. In any case, she made the best of it. Among other things, it helped her land Layton, who was considered quite the catch on the Wesleyan campus. She smiled ruefully. Well, wait until you get to know him, she thought. BMOC luster wears off fast. What's left can be banal and foolish and you end up stuck with it and no idea what to do.

She sighed and looked in the mirror again.

Was she pretty? Men certainly seemed to think so. Layton said she looked like Grace Kelly. She couldn't see the resemblance herself. She was not tall - five foot three - and with a maiden name like Klopflugle, she definitely lacked aristocratic pedigree.

She did have the blue eyes and blonde hair, but having grown up with it - her entire family and the most of people in her small Wisconsin hometown were blue-eyed blondes - she didn't see the attraction.

For Layton, her looks made her the ideal accessory for a Young Man on the Way Up. But was it her? She liked to think otherwise, but when she forced herself to be honest, as she was doing now, she had to admit she was not sure. Status may have come easily for her, but that didn't mean she underestimated its importance. The idea of being looked down upon, particularly by the schemers and status-seekers of the world, made her shudder.

But clearly something was missing in her life. What? She wondered. And even if she indentified it, what could she do?

The sad face in the mirror offered no answers. In two hours Layton would come home; long enough for cosmetics to work their deceptions. He would be pleased. Only she would know the truth, although she wasn't quite sure what the truth was beyond the fact she was unhappy, so very unhappy.

Lately, he had taken to calling her Betts. She went by Elizabeth or, occasionally, Liz. But never Betts. She asked him to stop. That amused him. He made sure to introduce her as his wife Betts. Or he would say things like, "I'm going out for a moment, Bet. . . oh, I mean *Ee-lizzz-a-beth.*"

Then he would stand with his arms folded and smirk at her impotent rage. Once he even said, "You look so cute when you're mad." That made her all the madder and made him smirk all the more.

Charm, reason and friendly persuasion did no good. The idea of shouting and throwing things had been programmed out of her years ago. She felt cowardly and weak and she was coming to hate herself for it.

Layton either didn't notice or didn't care. He had more important things on his mind than her childish pique. A couple of months ago, he read about a dean in the Midwest who had taken to holding something called rap sessions in his home. The magazine article went on to say how he typified the new generation of deans: "Modern young men who knew how to talk with the kids."

Layton had to get on that train right away. So he decided that every Wednesday night, he would hold a rap session. Elizabeth, of course, would clean and prepare the house, order the pizza, make sure the cokes were iced and all the rest. Then she would clean up the greasy mess afterward. It never occurred to him to ask her opinion on the matter.

Layton selected the kids he invited carefully: All male, all upper classmen, most from appropriate evangelical backgrounds and none known for their incisive intellects. A jock or two gave the gathering status and a student body officer gave it legitimacy – but never more than one student body officer, for such individuals sometimes thought their offices gave them license to express original ideas. And, of course, Layton Fleming could not permit ideas more original than his own.

To her surprise, Elizabeth found she liked most of the boys; the ones who were good-natured and well-mannered. Some were even passably bright. Not that it mattered. Layton made sure they never talked about anything substantive. She had seen him do it so many times: A constant patter of jokes, sports references and macho bluster that effectively gave him mastery of the moment.

Sometimes, one of the boys would bring up the civil rights movement, or the war in Vietnam or other serious topics, but Layton was too smart for them and the conversation, such as it was, fell back into chortles, jibes and generic male prattle.

Inexplicably, to Elizabeth, an invitation to the dean's rap sessions became the hottest ticket on campus. Dr. Donald A. Fotheringham Ph.D. made a special effort to compliment Layton on it at the weekly cabinet meeting.

God, how she hated it; the phoniness, the manipulation, the pointless absurdity of if all.

For the past few months, even the feel of him had come to revolt her. In bed, after he had used her body, he liked to lay his head against her chest; his head with its Brylcreemed hair, warm and oily and rank, oozing its slime across her, mixing with his sweat and slithering worm-like rivulets down her ribs, soaking into the sheets, where it stayed and where she had to sleep in it. She couldn't feel it, really. It was only a few drops after all. But she knew it was there and it made her gag.

Layton's latest affectation was English Leather aftershave lotion. Time magazine had run a story saying it was the latest hip thing on college campuses so, of course, Layton immediately went out and bought the biggest bottle he could find.

Now, every morning, he slathered it on in handfuls after his shower. Sometimes, he skipped the shower altogether and slathered on even more. It smelled like a mixture of cough syrup and insecticide and its stench saturated the bathroom, where it seeped into every nook and cranny and where it settled for the rest of the day. Elizabeth opened the windows, turned on a fan and even tried spraying the room with a diluted bleach solution, but it did no good. The stink remained, permeating her consciousness, a constant, nagging reminder of her entombment.

Chapter 9

After morning coffee, after lunch and between classes, Brewer studied.

Usually, he went to one of the corner desks by the windows on the second floor of Weter. They offered a view to the north. On clear days, Brewer could see the docks and warehouses and shingle mills of Ballard; busy places, always in motion; a clamorous contrast to the enforced hush of the library. The combination of the two environs created a tonal median Brewer found useful for the wearing grind of college study.

Sometimes, he would study assigned readings. It was just plain hard. The subjects were more sophisticated than in high school and the texts were dense – dense to the point of impenetrable, in some cases.

He tried forcing himself to plow through them line by line, pushing the arcane knowledge into his brain by force of will. It worked, but it was like slogging uphill in soft sand. Once he finished an assignment, he felt too bleary to begin the next one. And there was always a next one.

So he tried reading the assigned text twice; the first time to get a general sense of it, the second time to pick out its specifics.

That worked, but again, it was slow, much too slow. For the first time in his life, Brewer faced the predicament of too much to do and too little time to do it. It frightened him: The fear of failure, a cold, empty sense of vulnerability like no other lodged deep in him. Brewer visualized himself walking along First Avenue South, amid the shabby, rundown buildings of fly-by-night schlock. It was a dirty place, with litter blowing along the sidewalk and a film of road grime coating the store front windows. In Brewer's vision, he was walking in the wind and the rain, a hole in his shoe, nowhere to go, consigned to squalor forever.

It could happen, figuratively if not literally. Such was the fate of those who failed. The vision made at Brewer's throat squeeze shut. The feeling never completely went away.

Then one day, he noticed that a group of jocks made a point of sitting next to him in lectures. One, a basketball named Rothman, was copping furtive glances at Brewer's notes and then hurriedly scribbling in his own notebook. Brewer caught up with him after class.

"Hey, were you copying my notes?" Brewer said.

Rothman looked down at the ground, embarrassed.

"Uh, yeah. Sorry," he said.

"No, it's okay, I don't mind." Brewer said. "I just want to know why, that's all."

"Oh. Well, you're the one guy in class who seems to know what's going on," Rothman said. "You're really organized."

Who me? Brewer thought. Well, looks can be deceiving. But then again, maybe he was really organized. Brewer had been taught how to take notes way back in seventh grade at Nathan Eckstein Junior High - thank you, Mr. Moylan - and over the years, the practice became an unconscious habit.

He decided to start taking notes as he studied assigned reading. Soon he learned to spot the main points and supporting points and began writing them in an outline. Then he found that the outline formed a reasonably clear train of logic. He actually understood what the writer was trying to say.

It all seemed so simple, and often was - but not always. Many of the learned scholars, philosophers and scientists he studied had a chaotic organization style and wrote in prose which could best be described, kindly, as obtuse. It led Brewer to conclude that a large part of being an eminent intellectual involved creating convincing appearances. If people had trouble following you, it simply was because they were too damn dumb to comprehend your manifest brilliance. That realization explained a lot of things: Modern architecture, Eric Sevareid and the music of Philip Glass.

Lectures from bad teachers were a different matter. Good teachers usually arranged their lectures in an outline style of some kind. So, Brewer tried to go over his notes as soon as he could after a lecture. When he did, he often was surprised at how clear it all seemed. He could actually learn things on his own terms.

Lectures from bad teachers were another matter. How such individuals ended up teaching colleges classes was a bit of a mystery. The often didn't seem to know their subjects well had trouble stringing together intelligible English sentences. Some were just plain strange. A psychology instructor was noted for picking her nose as she lectured. A chemistry professor was rumored to be senile and when asked what nitric acid was, could not remember. Then there was the female phys ed instructor, a campus legend, who imploded into paroxysms of giggling whenever anything involving the groin and its nether regions were mentioned. And so it went. But they were the teachers and students had to keep up with the muddle as best they could.

Over coffee one afternoon, a classmate mentioned to Brewer that he managed to make sense of a particularly unintelligible lecture by structuring his notes in a system of questions and answers. On the left side of the page, he put questions -"What are the elements of the Socratic method?" for example - and then on the right side, he would write the answer, usually in the form of a numbered list. It meant he often had to search his notes - bad teachers were, by nature, adverse to a systematic approach - but eventually he could figure the mess out.

Brewer tried it. It worked.

Brewer came to realize that, without meaning to, he had developed effective study skills.

Effective Study Skills? He recoiled at the thought. Good God, it was only one step from Good Study Habits. Back in junior high school, honor students, those with Good Study Habits, were held up as models for the rest of knuckle-dragging rabble. Brewer found them a preening, smug lot, hopelessly square, their badges of prestige the little fabric rings they glued over the holes in their notebook paper. Worst of all, they were precious in the eyes of teachers and principals. Brewer, at age twelve, could think of no worse fate.

But, well, now it was true. Through necessity of survival, he had developed effective study skills. What was hopelessly square in junior high was a life or death requirement in college.

And Brewer was mastering it. As long as he was reasonably diligent, he could use his skills to pass the challenges academia threw at him. Would he be a brilliant student, a Summa Cum Laude? Brewer chuckled at the thought. No, he knew himself better than that. But he would pass, and many, very many, would not. Or they simply would get discouraged, quit and end up with lives dictated by the nagging knowledge of their deficiencies; a life you put up with but did not really live; a long, pointless journey along a dirty street in the rain.

It was all very unfair, Brewer knew. The line between success and failure in college was a tenuous one, only partially related to intelligence and talent. Learning to navigate the maze was the key to surviving and Brewer had learned it. Who'd have ever thought...

He didn't think about it long. A truism of college life is that every professor believes his class is the only one you are taking. The workload can be killing, even after you get used to it. Hence Brewer's trips to Weter, then evenings locked in his room until 11 p.m. and then Sundays spent all day in studies. Friday night and most of Saturday, he took off.

His English 101 textbook was The World of Ideas, a collection of essays by everyone from Socrates, Martin Buber and Carl Jung to H.L. Mencken and Mark Twain. Most were hard reads, but after the first two or three - and the grueling labor of having to write weekly themes about them - Brewer started to understand why. They were tough because they had a lot to say, much of it thought-provoking, even profound - except for one essay by George Bernard Shaw, which Brewer thought was a lot of vainglorious crap. He had to read it a couple of times before he identified its bombast - love those good study habits - but once he did, he concluded it was the self-indulgent hogwash that it was.

Then Brewer took an extra step, something he had never done before. In his weekly essay, he said Shaw was full of baloney. He wanted to say full of crap, but he knew that would never go over at SPC. Even baloney was a bit of a risk, but Brewer was feeling bold.

He picked apart Shaw's arguments point by point. It didn't take long. Beneath all the highfalutin jargon, the great mind didn't really have much to say. His conclusion: What Shaw called deep thought, Brewer called masturbatory egotism. He left the word masturbatory in. Damnit, that's what he honestly thought!

On Friday, he handed the paper in. Then, twenty minutes later the magnitude of his mistake hit him. You don't attack one of the great minds of the twentieth century, not if you are a freshman at an obscure college in an obscure corner of the continent. But

Shaw was not a great mind. He was just very good at slinging highfalutin bullshit, if this essay was any indication. And that was rather the point: In Brewer's experience, even if you were right, you didn't contravene the intelligencia's conventional wisdom, not if you wanted a good grade.

He sweated out the weekend, picturing the moment when he got his paper back marked with a D, or lower, and notes to the effect that how dare he suggest such sacrilege.

Then, on Monday, he actually did get the paper back – marked with a large, red B-plus a scribbled note, "Good analysis."

For a brief moment, something shifted in Brewer. Do you mean my opinion actually counts for something? That I can think and analyze? That inside me, there is intelligence; not just the kind that can figure out problems involving one train leaving New York at 2 p.m. and another leaving Chicago at 4 p.m., but the kind capable of original thought, *worthwhile* original thought.

Brewer had turned a corner, although he didn't realize it. He also didn't realize that once he turned it, he wasn't going back.

****

Among the things that were going well in his life, Brewer was making friends. He found it surprisingly easy. Unlike high school, with all its cliques and strata of status and unspoken rules, college was an open environment. All you had to do was get some coffee at the SUB and sooner or later someone would pull up a chair and within a few minutes you would be talking.

It was even easier if you knew people from a class. So it was with Brian McLean and Dale Griffiths. They sat near Brewer in English 101, they knew each other and they were outgoing. So when they sat down for lunch at the SUB, Brewer joined them. He had a hunch they were worth knowing.

They were. Dale was easygoing, quick with a smile and blessed with the ability a few people have of finding humor in almost anything.

McLean was like a coiled snake; intense, opinionated, full of ideas he could barely contain.

"Johnson's an idiot," he declared. "Just another Texas grit who's bullshitted people so long they've come to accept it."

"Goldwater's better?" Dale said with a slight grin.

"Fuck no. Why is it we get stuck with two rotten choices? Something's wrong."

"And what would that be?" Dale said, the grin growing.

"The system! Damnit, the system!"

"Whose system?"

"Fuck, I don't know. I'm hungry. How are the burgers today?"

"The toasted cheese is better," Brewer said. He hoped it would help him to be accepted.

"The smart guy votes for toasted cheese," Dale said.

"Vote? Vote?! Why vote? It's all fixed," McLean said.

"And how would they go about corrupting the process of grilling cheddar?" Dale said.

"White bread."

"Do go on."

"It's all processed and diluted. I suspect they put chalk dust in it."

"That's milk," Brewer said. "They put chalk dust in milk. Arsenic too, sometimes. Improves the color."

"Right, right!" McLean said. "But cereally, folks, is the grilled cheese any good?"

"Try it on whole wheat," Dale said. "No chalk dust in that."

"Just bugs and twigs," Brewer said.

"Taste is largely a matter of texture," Dale said

"Hmmm. All right," McLean said. "Better than chalk dust, I suppose. What kind of bugs do they have on the menu today?"

Just then a young woman in a short skirt and tight sweater walked by. Conversation stopped. The young men had found a mutual subject of compatibility.

Chapter 10

Brewer didn't know anyone in the crowd milling about the foyer of Hill. It reminded him of registration, when everyone else seemed to know what was going on and he did not; a stranger, an outsider, an interloper in a world where he did not belong.

He found a dark nook near the door to the parking lot and stayed there. No one so much as looked his way.

When Marilyn entered, Brewer's breath stopped. Rarely had simplicity so elegantly epitomized beauty; a plain silk long-sleeved rose-pink top and a long, burgundy velvet skirt reaching nearly to the floor. No jewelry, save small, one-diamond earrings which radiated needles of light through wine-dark auburn hair. She gathered all the light in the room like a soft halo.

She stood for a moment, searching, her chin high and regal, her eyes crystalline, and in that moment, solitary in an aura of her own making, time shifted on itself and dissolved into mist and Marilyn Pennell was, to Brewer, all things beautiful.

He slowly emerged from the dark and walked toward her, not speaking, not wanting to break the spell. For him, the milling crowd, the room the time, the place, the world itself were no longer there. Only Marilyn was there, only the wonder that was Marilyn.

She spotted him and broke into a smile, her teeth, like the rest of her, perfect, her expression warm and welcoming.

"For a minute, I thought you'd stood me up," she said brightly.

"Wouldn't think of it."

She cheerfully linked her arm in his.

"Where's the car?" she said.

"Out front. The back lot was full." Brewer was embarrassed. The street in front of Hill was steep. You weren't supposed to discomfort girls on a date, particularly when they were wearing formals, particularly when every time she brushed against you, you felt yourself go dizzy.

"Oh, don't worry about it," Marilyn said. She reached over with her free hand and gave his bicep a quick squeeze.

"So, how have you been?"

"Busy," Brewer said. "Do these people ever get tired of piling on more work?"

"It doesn't seem like it," Marilyn said. "I don't know how anybody is supposed to get an A. Just keeping up is an achievement."

Brewer knew what she meant.

They reached the car. Brewer held the door for her. If ever there was a night to be a perfect gentleman, this was it. If ever there was a girl that deserved a perfect gentleman, it was her.

When he got in, she already was on his side of the seat. As he settled in to start the car, she burrowed even closer.

The banquet was a unique feature of schools like SPC. Since the college forbade dancing, students had to organize banquets for large gatherings. Banquets had their advantages and disadvantages - mostly disadvantages when it came to socializing. Without cocktails, there was little if any mingling beforehand and once seated, you were limited to the company at your table. The entertainment could be good or bad. On one hand, the student entertainment budget was limited. On the other hand, there were a number of starving performers in town, some of them talented. The worst problem was the masters of ceremonies, usually the students who organized the whole thing and usually Rotarian wannabes who fancied themselves, mistakenly, as quite the witty raconteurs.

Brewer found himself at a table of six. Marilyn knew both the other girls: A tall, bespectacled blonde named Sharon and a nervous-eyed, almost silent dark-haired girl named Carla. Both were accompanied by boyfriends from home, in this case rural Oregon, who had driven up for the weekend. Carla and her boyfriend, Fred, an entomology major, had spent the day cruising electronics shops for parts for his ham radio and the hi-fi stereo he was building. Brewer had no idea what they were talking about - when they talked. Which was rarely.

Sharon's boyfriend Steve, on the other hand, was a sports fan, specifically football, and he and Brewer hit it off immediately. A junior at Oregon State, he had spent two years watching Terry Baker earn the Heisman trophy. He was worried the Beavers were having trouble replacing him. Paul Brothers was good, but no Terry Baker. And nobody could really replace Verne Burke at split end. On the plus side, Mad Dog O'Billovich was probably the best linebacker in the league. Brewer disagreed. The Washington Huskies' Rick Redman was better.

They good-naturedly argued back and forth until Brewer became worried he was ignoring his date. Then he saw Marilyn was happily chatting with Sharon. But he still felt compelled to engage her more. How? You didn't break into girls' conversations. Fortunately, just then, the program began. Marilyn moved her chair so she was touching him.

The student emcee was predictably amateurish but blessedly brief. The evening's entertainment was a young standup comedian who made jokes about current events. Some of them were pretty funny. Then came a men's quartet; part singers, part comedians, who also were reasonably entertaining. When it was all over, Brewer was feeling good.

Where to go next? Brewer had no idea. Where do you take a girl in a formal dress? He tried to think, but the presence of Marilyn, her touch, her warm laugh, her wonderful smell, the fragrance of irises, kept disconcerting him. So he offered to drive her around to some of the prettiest views in Seattle. Since the town had a lot of hills and was surrounded by mountains and water, there were plenty to visit. Marilyn said that sounded like a fine idea and away they went.

Marilyn was impressed by the Boren lookout at 15th East and Garfield. On a the edge of a cliff nearly four hundred feet straight up, its view included all twenty two miles of Lake Washington north to south and the area east of it out to the Cascade Mountains. From Boren's height, the hills and bays of the lake's basin took on a primeval glacial ruggedness.

"How in the world did people get around when they first settled here?" Marilyn wondered aloud, shivering slightly in the cold night air and nuzzling closer to Brewer.

There were more stops: The small park at the foot of Boyer Street which from an elevation of more than three hundred offered the sight of the University of Washington's gothic towers and spires and buttresses rising from the light as if emerging from hot coals, taking one's mind to places and times far, far away; then Kerry Park lookout, which made the Space Needle seem close enough to touch. Hamilton View Park in West Seattle had a unimpaired view of downtown Seattle, which on this night, was a chalky pastel cityscape of art deco imaginings.

Throughout it all, Marilyn talked. She wanted to talk and she was very good at it. For all of her aristocratic bearing, Marilyn was plain spoken. And she was bright, Brewer found; even brighter than the first time they dated. Her literature class had opened her mind, she said. Suddenly, language was more than just a functional implement for making oneself heard. It had a life of its own, an ability to express more than the person using it. It revealed truths of its own making.

Brewer had similar experiences in his English class. They were reading essays by various philosophers. The different systems philosophers came up with were, often as not, essentially just different forms of thinking. As such, their intellectual value varied.

"I think Plato was full of it with his talk of an ideal republic," Brewer said, and then he regretted it; not the idea, but the phrase, "full of it." Marilyn might find it vulgar.

She did not and they talked on. Both liked SPC well enough; Marilyn because it was small and quiet and free of the drinking and wild parties she heard about at other campuses, Brewer because it was small – smaller than his high school – and it was relatively easy to meet people. Both were lying. Marilyn found the state university culture of drinking and carousing tantalizing, at least from a distance, and Brewer often found himself isolated, even on a campus of only thirty acres and two thousand students. Both kept such thoughts to themselves.

Neither liked chapel; Marilyn because it was badly done, Brewer because its daily routine was becoming wearing and monotonous, even after less than one quarter. He left out that he'd come up with a way to skip it. That was best kept secret, even from people he trusted.

They continued to drive and talk until Brewer reached the lookout park on the south crest of Magnolia Bluff. It offered a breathtaking view of downtown Seattle, especially when the liquid pinks and purples of a Pacific sunset bathed the city in an ethereal chroma.

But it wasn't sunset. The parking lot was full of cars, some of them rocking, all of them with windows coated in the thick, sticky steam of carnality.

When Marilyn realized it, her body stiffened. She jerked away from Brewer. After a long moment, she said coldly, "Tom why did you bring me here?"

Her words hung in the air, destitute.

"I thought, maybe you would want to. . ." Brewer's voice trailed off, an admission of failure, as sad a failure as a man can effect.

There was another long, cold moment. Much too long. Brewer wanted to die. All that was Marilyn, her beauty, her warmth, her transcendent presence, all that mesmerized him was now gone. Had he misread the signs? Or were there no signs, only hope, hope for the experience of true beauty? What a foolish hope, he thought, and he hated himself even more.

"I think you had better take me back to the dorm," Marilyn said with icy, controlled anger.

Brewer reached for the ignition key. Then he paused. Without really thinking about it, he said, "Okay, I understand. I'm sorry if I upset you. Can we just stay here for a while and talk? I genuinely like talking with you."

Marilyn seemed momentarily confused. She continued to move away, but her body relaxed. She looked out the window for a long time, gazing at the distant lights. Finally, she said, "All right. What do you want to talk about?"

****

Brewer asked Marilyn about her classes. He asked her about her home. Tom Brewer and his questions; they should be merely irritating, she thought, the meanderings of a self-important wiseass. Yes, she could take them that way. She probably should take them that way. But she could not. Why did he have such a hold on her?

They talked some more, about school, about popular music, about current events. Marilyn found herself relaxing, then enjoying herself. Eventually, Brewer looked at his watch.

"About time to get you home," he said and without missing a beat, started the car.

They drove back to campus in silence. Marilyn was perplexed. She should be outraged. Or insulted. Or something. But she was not and it gnawed at her.

They reached the parking lot at Hill. Brewer thanked her for the evening and then, like a gentleman, opened the door for her and walked her to the lounge, where, again, he opened the door and held it for her. He smiled politely and wished her a good night. She did not wish him a good night. She tried to look angry and hurt. She wondered if it was convincing.

As Brewer drove home, he thought about her. What a girl; so beautiful, so smart, so poised. Did he love her? He couldn't decide. He didn't know how love was supposed to feel. But whenever he thought of the sound of her voice, he felt transported to another world.

You shouldn't have taken her to Magnolia bluff, that's for sure. At least not on the second date. You're supposed to wait to the third. Now he would have to wait until the fourth of fifth - if there will be a fourth of fifth. She seemed upset, but then she calmed down and they actually had a nice time. He thoroughly enjoyed talking to her.

Should he call her? Probably not. It would seem pushy. Besides, Sunday was always a busy day. Professors made Monday the deadline for papers. Others scheduled their tests for Monday. So much for all the b.s. about a day of rest. Brewer smiled. Ah, SPC. There was the appearance, the upright, pious, façade the school liked to advertise, with photos of extraordinarily clean-cut young Anglo-Saxons; happiness and wholesomeness incarnate. Then there was the reality: The college grind; chronic overwork, unrelenting pressure, the constant feeling that you were skating on ice that could crack at any moment. No sentimental nonsense about a Christian Community or The Rewards of Serving Others in that world.

And in that thought, his mind drifted away from Marilyn Pennell. He had an English paper due Monday morning and he hadn't even started it yet. Sunday would be a long, tedious haul as he struggled to compare Spinoza's principles of imperfect virtue with his conclusions on the value of intuitive knowledge. Brewer would get it done, of course, but for now, he needed some sleep.

****

Marilyn spent the rest of the weekend turning her date with Brewer over in her mind. The more she thought about it, the more frustrating it became. She still wanted to see him, but to do so would be to forgive his slight. That she could not do; not if she wanted to maintain her stature. She was special, a cut above others and as she thought about that, she felt slightly ashamed. All you are is a snob, she thought. She shook her head dismissively. Call it what you want, she could not settle for the average, for the ordinary. She had worked her entire life to be better than... than... than what?

Did any of it really matter? Was it not just a way of closing herself off from reality? Yes, probably. But it worked. It kept her focused, and freshman year, perhaps more than any other time in one's life, was certainly a time to remain focused.

Her thoughts went back to Brewer. He didn't seem to care about status, hers or anyone else's. He did not pose. He showed no interest in belonging to the right cliques. He seemed to accept her as she was at the moment she was with him; no more, no less. It was maddening. She couldn't get him out of her mind.

Marilyn went through the motions of her studies, but very little from the ponderous prose of her psychology book, or the arcane symbols of her statistics book penetrated her brain. So she wrote down notes as she read. That way, she could memorize, even if she didn't understand.

As always, Janet Small fussed and fidgeted and whined rather than actually study. For once, Marilyn didn't mind. It was like the music from KJR that played constantly throughout the dorm all day and most of the night; after a while she didn't notice it and it became a low hum that muffled other sounds like a thick blanket, sending her deep into her thoughts.

Chapter 11

That Monday, Marilyn received back her essay for English 101 and the results of her first math test. The math test was marked with a C-minus. The English paper bore a D. The teacher had been especially brutal, all but covering the paper with red marks and comments like "Trite," Redundant" and "Where are your facts?"

Marilyn's eyes blurred and her hands went cold. It was like standing at the mouth of a cave, a deep, desolate cave, windy and rank. Failure: She had never faced it before and the sense of its reality elicited a kind of fear she had never felt, a cold, hollow fear of the irrevocable. Her best efforts, her hardest work might not be enough to prevent her failure. And then what? A wasted life, a pointless life. You accept your own mediocrity and live out a banal, second-best existence until you die. The world will not remember you.

All because of one English paper and one math test? Well, yes, actually. Each paper and each test was a percentage of your grade. Each grade was a percentage of your success of failure in that class - and that was a percentage of your success of failure in school. Once failure began, it built upon itself; an ever-steepening mountain that, try as you may, you could never surmount.

Marilyn went to morning chapel. The speaker was a minor league evangelist recently returned from a tour of military bases in California and the Southwest. He had found them to the citadels of depravity, overflowing with Marlboros, Schlitz and Playboy magazines; in short, Sodom and Gomorrah incarnate. Eyes bulging, a vein throbbing on his forehead, he finished his fulminations with the thundering exclamation, "You stink, G.I.!"

Marilyn couldn't help herself and fought to stifle a giggle. Others in the crowd were struggling to do the same thing, with greater or lesser degrees of success. Well, he had the effect of making me forget my troubles for a few minutes, Marilyn thought. Take you comforts where you find them.

But then it ended and she was back in the real world, thoughts of inadequacy tumbling through her mind. Why is this happening to me? I've done all that's expected of me. It doesn't make any sense.

As she walked down McKinley's stairs, she spotted Tom Brewer from the corner of her eye. She found herself resenting him. All that's happening in my life and now I have to deal with some guy who just wants to get his hand up my skirt. Okay, he's cute and kind of interesting, but he's also complicated. I don't need any more complications.

For a moment, a fraction of a second, a part of her said, "But he is *The One* and you know it!"

And then the thought was gone, drowned in a stream of fear and anger and resentment. She had to survive. The country club princess emerged from the recesses of Marilyn's personality and snapped into place like the cylinder of a revolver. She knew what to do.

"Good morning," Brewer said, drawing up beside her.

"Good morning," Marilyn replied in an icy monotone without looking his way.

"How are you today?" Brewer said in a friendly voice, clearly trying to warm her up.

"I am fine, thank you," Marilyn said, raising her chin in a gesture of caste superiority.

Brewer understood. The silence between them was palpable as they passed Moyer and started up the hill to Weter. Finally, Brewer said, "Look, if you want to say good bye, just say it."

"Good bye."

Brewer nodded thoughtfully. It made Marilyn even angrier. Did he have to analyze *everything*?

"It wasn't my fault," she said.

" No, I suppose it wasn't," Brewer said. "Well, good bye, then. Best of luck."

Did he have to be so calm about it? Did he have to be so reasonable, so civil, so courteous? It made her all the more angry, so angry she couldn't think of anything to say.

Brewer stopped. Marilyn kept walking. She didn't look back, but she could hear him turn around and start in the other direction, probably to the SUB for coffee with that herd of baboons he hung out with. She wondered if he would tell them about her. No, probably not. He's too thoughtful and polite for such things. He really is quite nice. . .

No. No one makes a pass at me. No one makes me uncomfortable and gets away with it. I am better than that. I am above that and don't you forget it.

She walked on, her jaw set, her mind gradually narrowing and focusing on what she must do. She must survive, she must survive.

****

Brewer had just finished the bench press but he wasn't tired enough.

The body building class was a P.E. credit and P.E. credits were required. But to Brewer it had become something more. Always slender, he hoped the class's weight lifting would bulk him up. Broad shoulders and short, thick necks were the norm for male beauty just then.

At the moment, however, he didn't care. He came to class that morning hoping to vent all his anger and shame about Marilyn on the weights. He tried to attack the weights, to jerk and heave with a loud growl, attacking them as savagely as he could, ferocious in his intensity. Only then, when his muscles convulsed with pain and the blood rushed to his head with such force he saw spots; only then could he forget her. Enough pain, enough exhaustion and his mind would go blank. That was the plan.

It wasn't working.

He couldn't summon up enthusiasm, little less ferocity. Instead, he went through the motions, and went through them badly, the picture of lethargy and ennui. It made him hate himself all the more.

You dumb shit! You could have waited to the third date. You could have waited until she put out some kind of vibe. But noooo. You, the great ladies man, you didn't need any of that.

With that thought, Brewer finished his eighth rep on the bench press. He could have gone for nine. He could have gone for ten. He could have poured it on and sweated blood and all the rest. He could have purged his soul through pain. But he preferred to be depressed and wallow in it. He let the barbell drop onto the brackets. He stared up at it. The motionless piece of metal mocked him. It sneered silently. You should have done better. But your delicate little feelings have been hurt. Pansy.

"You seem a bit preoccupied."

It was Dale.

Brewer caught his breath and wiped his forehead with his wrist.

"Just trying to clear my head," he said. "Bad weekend."

"Ah yes, bad weekends. I know them well," Dale said, taking a seat next to Brewer on the bench. "Women or alcohol, if you don't mind me asking?"

"Women."

Jesus, Brewer thought, how could I have been so fucking dumb? She isn't like the others. She . . .

"Ah, yes, yes," Dale said. "Alcohol's cheaper and generally easier to justify, headaches and vomiting aside. But women; no trouble quite like woman trouble. Is she worth tearing your limbs off trying to propel heavy weights through the ceiling? Wait, don't answer that."

"Can't make up my mind," Brewer said. "Why can't getting along with women be simple, like getting along with guys?"

"Wonder about that myself, from time to time," Dale said.

"What do you do?"

"Nothing very effective," Dale said. "I don't know there's anything you can do – except remind yourself that there's more than one girl in this world."

Brewer inwardly nodded. Good point. But if you'd seen the way she looked that night, as if she was dressed in a mystery she had stolen from the rest . . .

"I don't think I'm getting through to you very well," Dale said.

"Oh, that's okay," Brewer said. "Maybe I just enjoy being miserable. It has to run its course, I guess."

"Yes, yes, my friend," Dale said. "Done your leg presses yet? Vent your spleen on them and they could consign you to crawling for the rest of the day."

"Goddamn right," Brewer said. The goddamn caused some of the church nerds in the room to glower at him. Fuck 'em. Brewer sat on the small metal stool of the leg press machine, put his feet on the pedals and with a loud snarl stomped down with all he had.

The weights on the guide rails jumped off the floor with a noisy clang. Take that, motherfuckers! Urrrrgh! Again! Again! Urrrrgh!

Dale watched with studied curiosity. Brewer decided to go for fourteen reps. On the last one, his legs would barely move, pushing out inch by trembling inch, sweat pouring down his forehead. Finally, he extended fully. Then he let the weights drop with a loud crash. He slumped for a few seconds on the stool, panting.

He got up. More accurately, he tried to get up. It was like the cliché said: His legs had turned to rubber, bowing and bending under him in ways he couldn't control. He grabbed the frame of the machine for support, hoping no one had noticed.

"A new dance step?" Dale inquired with exaggerated politeness.

Brewer smiled and nearly laughed.

The class ended and the Charles Atlas wannabes headed for the locker room.

Brewer greeted the hot blast of the shower, welcomed it, lost himself in it. Wash off the sweat, wash off the memories. Damnit, if nothing else, he would go through the rest of the day clean.

He dried off and dressed quickly. Lunch, that would help. He had been thinking about the toasted cheese sandwiches he had seen in the SUB. And the biggest, iciest Coke they had. Yes, time to taste things, to smell things, to *feel* things. Maybe he could forget her after all.

Dale caught up with him as he was going out the door to Nickerson.

"More classes today?" Dale said.

"Two more, history then English."

"You're in Schnieder's American history class, right?"

"Yeah."

"I've heard good things about it. Do you like it?"

Brewer thought for a moment.

"Yeah, I do," he said. "Actually, I like all my classes. They're so different than high school. No busy work, no b.s. Learn it or leave it; it's up to you."

"Wish I was so enthusiastic," Dale said. "I'm pretty much in the survival mode."

"Aren't we all," Brewer said.

"True, true," Dale said. "But I'm having trouble seeing beyond it. I may not be what they call 'college material.'"

"Come on, everybody feels that way sometimes," Brewer said.

They reached the SUB.

"You don't eat at Gwinn?" Dale said.

"I live off-campus," Brewer said.

"Ah, me too," Dale said. "Aren't we supposed to be seditious trouble makers or some such thing?"

"I wish."

Brewer ordered his toasted cheese sandwich and Coke from the bad-tempered, toad-like woman behind the counter. He joined Dale at a table by the glass-paneled wall that looked into the SUB's big meeting room. Dale was drinking coffee and checking out girls. He tried to be subtle. He failed.

Brewer was beginning to like Dale. He wanted Dale for a friend. Making friends took effort. Brewer decided it was worth it.

"You're from Seattle?" Brewer said.

"Vancouver. I wanted to go to Oregon State, but my parents insisted I go here. Thought it would be good for me."

"I've heard that before," Brewer said.

"Yeah, I think half the people at SPC are here because somebody else thought it would be good for them."

"Got a major yet?" Brewer asked.

"Anthropology!" Dale proclaimed with a proud flourish. "No practical value, whatsoever! I'll probably end up working in an insurance office or some such thing anyway, so I figured I should at least study something stimulating before I molder. How about you?"

"No major yet," Brewer said. "No idea where I'll go, really."

"Yes, yes," Dale said. "You know, I've always wondered about individuals who are absolutely certain what they want to be from their very first day of college. They seem unaware of the world beyond their immediate perception."

Brewer enjoyed the way Dale talked; his mock formality, his detachment, his gift of laughter and a sense that the world was mad.

"Maybe they're better off for it," Brewer said. "Uncertainty can be a real pain in the ass."

"True, true, but at least it shows you are thinking," Dale said. "People who have no doubts have no thoughts; no original thoughts, in any case."

"Around here, original thinking can get you in trouble," Brewer said.

"Really? I haven't noticed that so much," Dale said. "I mean, there are all those religion majors and preachers' kids and other tight-assed idiots, but they're a minority. If you go over to the UW, you'll find that liberals and radicals are just as closed-minded. Different side of the same coin."

Brewer remembered the outspoken liberals and self-appointed intellectuals he knew in high school; how smug they were in their inherent superiority to the unenlightened.

"TOASTED CHEESE SANDWICH." The toadwoman behind the counter had a voice to match her looks. Now the whole room knew what Brewer was having for lunch. He paid and hurried back to the table.

"So you have girl trouble," Dale said.

Brewer took a bite of the cheese sandwich. It was hot and rich and gooey and good; all that he had hoped for.

"Yeah, but I don't want to talk about it," Brewer said, lightly wiping his chin.

Dale nodded sympathetically.

"Well, let me ask you this. Is she an SPC girl?" he said.

"Yeah," Brewer grunted, taking another bite.

"There's your first mistake," Dale said.

Brewer grinned.

"Who else am I supposed to meet?" he said. "Besides, like you said, it's not fair to assume everybody here is some out-of-it church nerd. Most aren't."

"But they are encouraged to be," Dale said.

Indeed they are, Brewer thought. The cultural conditioning was relentless. The school seemed determined to inculcate, to saturate, to permeate every single student with unquestioning devotion to organized religion and its machinations. Guilt appeared to be one of its favorite tools. And, as he thought about it, Brewer decided there is no guilt quite as effective as sexual guilt. SPC girls looked it.

God, would he ever get laid at this place?

Two other boys sat down at the table. Brewer knew them, or at least knew their names, from English 101. Paul Meadows was blond, round-shouldered and chubby. Jerry Naylor was short, compact and athletic, a gymnast or wrestler perhaps. Neither introduced themselves. Introductions were considered uncool.

"Hey, dirty old man," Meadows said to Dale.

"Good afternoon, good afternoon," Dale said. "Deflowered any virgins today?"

"I would if I could find one," Meadows said.

I wish that were true, Brewer thought. The cult of virginity, with all its smugness and narcissism, seemed alive and thriving at SPC. They think it's soooo special . . .

Good grief, get her off your mind!

Naylor smiled conspiratorially.

"Wanna see what I just learned?" he said.

The rest nodded.

He took a half-empty water glass in his left hand, dipped the fingers of his right hand in the water and then started rubbing his index and middle finger around the rim. The rest watched, wondering where this was going. After a few seconds, the glass started to ring; a low, musical sound.

"How do you do that?" Dale asked.

"It's all in the touch," Naylor said. "You use the bottom of your first knuckle. Do it for a while and you'll pick it up."

The rest found water glasses, put some water in them and started rubbing.

Brewer found it frustrating. He tried rubbing softly, he tried rubbing hard. He got either a soft scraping sound or no sound at all. The others were getting more or less the same results.

"There must be a trick to this," Brewer said.

"No trick," Naylor said. "When you get the touch, you'll know it."

Brewer was dubious. But he kept rubbing. Finally, after what seemed like a very long time, he got a squeak.

The others stopped and watched.

The squeak extended into a steady, quiet squeal. Then, for no reason Brewer could discern, it lowered and became a clear, distinctive tone.

The others nodded appreciatively and redoubled their own efforts. Soon, Dale got a squeak, then a squeal, then a tone. A couple of minutes later, Meadows got the same.

Brewer found that the faster he rubbed, the louder the tone. He stopped and looked at his fingers. Had the skin changed somehow, maybe puckered from the water? No, it looked just the same. He looked at the rim of the glass. Nothing changed there, either. He rubbed the rim again. He got a tone instantly.

This made no sense. What, exactly, was this touch thing? With no evidence to analyze, how could it be explained?

Naylor smiled his knowing smile again. Then he pulled his finger across the rim in short perpendicular jerks, creating a series of staccato tones.

"Any more tricks?" Dale said.

"No, that's about it," Naylor said, "other than you get different tones depending on what kind of glass you use and how much water you have in it. Now, follow my lead: Put your glasses under the table so they don't show."

The others obeyed.

"Now, everybody else stop," Naylor said.

He began ringing his glass under the table, gradually making the sound louder.

At first, no one noticed. But as the sound filled the room, a few people started looking around, as if searching for whatever was causing the ringing. When Naylor lowered the volume, they squinted and cocked their heads, straining to pick it up. Then he stopped.

The people looked perplexed. The boys at the table laughed.

"Okay. Brewer, drink up your water until there is only a half-inch left. Then you do it," Naylor said.

Brewer did as directed. The tone was low and mellow, quite different than the one Naylor had produced. He too built up the volume and soon people were looking around again, more perplexed than ever. One student, a handsome young man with chiseled, angular features, a supercilious sneer and a tan that looked suspiciously like it came from a bottle, seemed particularly bothered He shook his head as if to clear it. Then he looked around angrily. Brewer lowered the volume. Right on cue, bottle tan squinted and strained. Brewer slowed his rubbing until the tone was barely audible. Bottle tan strained all the more. Then, with a burst, Brewer rubbed fast until the sound nearly filled the room. Bottle tan was visibly agitated now, squirming in his seat and jerking his head around accusingly.

Brewer stopped.

That seemed to upset bottle tan most of all. He huffed and puffed in anger and searched the room. Meadows started to laugh, couldn't control it and turned his head to the wall so bottle tan couldn't see it. The others were barely containing hiccups of laughter.

After a minute or two, bottle tan calmed down. Then Dale began ringing his glass. The tone was high-pitched and grating, a squeal.

Bottle tan started searching the room again. His jaw was set, his eyes were dark and indignant. He would fix whoever was doing this. But he couldn't find anyone. Eventually, he looked at the ceiling. Yes, that must be where the sound was coming from; a glitch in the PA system or some such thing.

By now, other people in the room were likewise distracted, to one degree or another. Some stuck their fingers in their ears or shook their heads trying to stop the irritating wail.

The boys at the table acted as if nothing untoward was going on – all except for Meadows, who occasionally spasmed in snorts.

Finally, bottle tan went to the counter and demanded to see Toadwoman. She eyed him with rheumy disinterest as he shouted and gesticulated. Right in the middle of his rant, Dale stopped.

Bottle tan looked around in confusion. Toadwoman smacked her gelatinous lips loudly and turned to go back to work. Then Naylor started ringing his glass.

Bottle tan spun around and faced the room, beside himself with frustration. Toadwoman stopped in mid-waddle. Her turgid thought process was starting to actuate, and although it was incapable of advancing beyond first gear, it sensed that something was amiss in her private little fiefdom.

Meadows began to choke and Brewer couldn't hold it in much longer.

Toadwoman galumphed over to the microphone she used to announce orders.

"WHOEVER IS MAKING THAT NOISE, STOP," she wheezed.

Naylor stopped.

Toadwoman looked around the room with a menacing expression. Finally, satisfied that her august authority had quashed the insurgency, she put the microphone down and started to locomote back to her duties.

Naylor began ringing again.

Toadwoman stopped, and for one astonishing moment, actually displayed an emotion other than her standard dyspepsia. Her eyes widened and her jaw went slack; a portrait of complete bewilderment.

Brewer doubled over in laughter, Dale was giggling like a demented hyena and Meadows, by now, could only gasp for breath.

Naylor stopped.

Most of the people in the room looked about, trying to figure out what happened. Others were laughing, enough of them that the boys went unnoticed. Bottle tan tromped out of the room, his face a maroon storm of rage. Toadwoman disappeared behind the stainless steel ramparts of pop machines and coffee urns. Some say she was never seen again.

****

Brewer's good mood didn't last. He had two more classes for the day. There was a test in his history class - a hard test, as it turned out - and the lecture in English was tough, with Miss Habib conducting a question and answer session about the required reading. She would ask a question and then point to a student to answer it. It quickly became obvious who didn't do the reading, or who didn't understand it. Brewer had read it, thought he understood it, and fielded his question successfully. But it made him sweat. He was relieved when the bell finally rang.

He needed a moment before catching his bus home and stopped by the SUB. It was 4 p.m. The narrow sunbeams slanting over the campus were becoming darker and darker shades of amber. Brewer felt awful. *You blew it and she's gone*, he thought. *Even worse, you made a fool of yourself doing it. Is there anything more* pathetic than some clown with a hard-on getting turned down by a beautiful girl in a formal? What were you thinking?

On the other hand, if you don't try, you don't succeed. If you don't ask, you don't get. Surely, reality teaches us that. You have to take risks in this world. Sometimes you will succeed, sometimes you won't. It's not all that different than missing a free throw or swinging on an inside curve. Nothing to get upset about, right?

Bullshit, Brewer thought. Logic and reason don't explain everything. If they did, I wouldn't feel like such a loser. Damnit, I actually *care* about her. I don't know why, it doesn't matter why, but I do.

So this is what girl trouble is about, he thought. They write songs about this sort of thing. But none he could think of captured it.

Shit!

Shit, shit, shit!

Now what do I do?

Well, obviously, find another girl, the voice said.

Again, the logical, rational thing to do. But Brewer didn't want another girl. Marilyn Pennell, she of the pearlescent glow; no other girl really compared.

Well, she's gone now, dipshit, the voice said. And, of course, the voice was quite right.

He stopped at the counter in the SUB's lounge and ordered black coffee.

"You chose a good time," the girl behind the counter said with a smile. "I just made a fresh pot."

Thank you, Brewer thought. Thank you very much. That actually means a lot right now.

He found an empty table by the back door. The first sip of the coffee was wonder, its vapor penetrating his senses with dark, ruby richness. Ahhh. Thank you again, he thought. The first cup of coffee from a new pot was a small kindness, probably unintentional, but it brought me comfort when I needed it.

Brewer had been so wrapped up in his gloom that until now it hadn't registered on him that the girl behind the counter was exceptionally pretty; tiny and delicate with huge green eyes and long, black hair, Italian or Greek or some such thing. And she had smiled at him.

He looked up, searching for her. Just then, Dale sat down.

"I got a soshe test tomorrow," Dale said. "I think it's going to be a bitch. We've been studying group dynamics. There was this test they did on telephone company workers back in the twenties, to see if bright lights or dim lights made for the most comfortable workplace. Turns out, the workers liked both equally. The researchers finally figured out it wasn't the lights that mattered, it was the attention the people were getting from being test subjects."

"That doesn't sound so complicated," Brewer said. He was still looking for the girl. He saw her back briefly was she walked behind a dishwasher.

"It isn't," Dale said. "It's the language they use to describe the project. Sociologists don't speak English as we know it."

"They do it to make themselves look smarter than they really are," Brewer said.

"Yeah, that. And to cover their tracks so no one can spot their mistakes," Dale said.

Brewer searched for the girl again. She was gone. He went back to the counter to order another cup of coffee. Toadwoman was at the counter. She stared into space as she poured the cup. It was as if Brewer wasn't there. He listened, hoping to hear the dark-haired girl. But there was nothing.

As he sat back down, McLean joined them.

"Oh, I'm hurtin', I'm hurtin'," he said shaking his head.

Dale raised an eyebrow in curiosity.

"It's my psych class. I'm hurtin', I'm hurtin'," McLean said.

"You flunk a test?" Dale said.

"Oh, yeah. And my paper is due tomorrow. And Pam is givin' me crap. I'm hurtin', I'm hurtin'."

The conversation irritated Brewer, but he listened out of politeness. All signs of the counter girl were gone. Maybe her shift was over and she left by the back door to return to Marston or Hill or wherever she lived. Maybe he should duck out and head up Bertona to catch up with her. No. You've seen how well that approach works, haven't you. Then how could he meet her? He didn't know her name. He didn't know who her friends were. He didn't remember seeing her in the Hustler's Handbook.

How do you introduce yourself to a total stranger? Hi there, I'm Tom Brewer and your green eyes and black hair really turn me on.

No. She was gone from him too.

Chapter 12

Paul Trimble had been on the job five months. He met his budget, he met his deadlines. His small corner of SPC ran like a reasonably efficient machine and he found satisfaction in that.

True, the things he wrote about often made whatever was left of the honest man in Trimble gag - "The Sixties, A Crossroads of Destiny in Christian Education!" - and the ways he wrote about them would challenge Baron Munchhausen, but Trimble had grown used it much more quickly than he ever imagined.

For, you see, the money was good.

Ah, the places journalism majors end up.

The bane of his existence was not the clichéd drek he had to grind out, nor was it the nagging reminders of his hypocrisy that ate at him late at night, when he was alone and couldn't dodge them.

No, it was the weekly staff meetings. Every Monday at 9:30 a.m. sharp, the public relations staff gathered in Chester Dalrymple's office for a half hour or so of, well, something. There was no agenda, no progress reports, no discussion of policies or strategies. Dalrymple would sit at his desk in silence, usually signing brochures to alumni, or letters to rich businessmen, or something or another - Trimble had never seen a human being sign so many things - and wait for someone else to get the ball rolling.

That someone was usually Skip Reinhardt, who believed a good joke was the best way to jump start the week's activities. A typical Reinhardt knee-slapper: "Seems they've chosen a Negro for an astronaut. Martin Luther Coon, he hears about it and he says, 'Well, the jig's up!'"

Hearty h-yuks and guffaws followed.

From there, the conversation would become fluid, flowing in directions even the most astute semanticist would find taxing to graph.

Bean salad was an ongoing topic of discussion. To vinegar or not to vinegar, that was the question. Bud Gafney, a vinegar proponent, even brought his mother's recipe - "From the Depression, when we had to make things stretch!"

And with that, the discussion was closed. The Great Depression gave him authoritative precedent in many such matters.

The latest news from the Chamber of Commerce and the Cascade Club could always be depended upon. Reinhardt told how the chamber invited the student body president from the University of Washington to speak at its monthly gathering.

"He starts his little talk - about 'college students today' or some such booshwa and Flashy Florence pipes up and says, 'Hey, the way I hear it, you just let all those fool beatniks wander around campus shooting off their mouths however they please, like a buncha bolsheviks. Just who's payin' you, anyway? That's what I want to know.' And Flashy, well he just owns this town, you know, and the kid, who thought he was such hot stuff, he starts to talk and Spuds Perry shouts, 'Ah, nuts to you. A hitch in the army would do you a lot of good!' And the whole room breaks up. You shoulda seen the look on that punk's face!"

Gafney occasionally shared his family news, including an account of the crisis that occurred when his son wanted to go to a Bob Newhart show at the Civic Arena. Bud refused.

"He's one of those, what do you call 'um, beat comics," Gafney exclaimed.

"Reds and troublemakers!" Reinhardt exclaimed. "This country is headed for socialism."

The assembled frowned and nodded weightily. Trimble shrugged. In the world of the mad, the sane man is the leper. Or so he had heard somewhere or another. Four days to Friday. The money was good, the money was good . . .

Now it was late October and the presidential election was the talk of the campus, with Young Republicans holding rallies for Barry Goldwater, Young Democrats holding rallies for Lyndon Johnson and everyone else - the majority - irritably pushing their way through the sign-wavers so they could get to their next class. They were too young to vote anyway.

Anyway, on this particular fair autumn morn - it actually had stopped raining for two whole days - the public relations staff meeting was being held in Skip Reinhardt's office. Chester

Dalrymple was away at a conference for the American Association of Alumni Association.

Notepad in hand - he used it to doodle - Trimble dutifully traipsed across the hall at 9:29 a.m.

When he arrived at Reinhardt's office, he was surprised to find it full. In addition to Gafney and Mildred Turbot, the department's director of church relations (of whom it was rumored had no red blood cells in her entire body), the secretarial staff was jammed in the room.

The hired help actually standing on the carpet of a second level administrator, on institutional hallowed ground? What the hell was going on? But practical matters first. Trimble found a comfortable chair - always a priority - and moved it close to the door so he could exit at the earliest available moment.

"All right everyone, sit, sit!" Reinhardt said, fluttering his hands in a dismissive gesture. The secretaries, giggling nervously, milled about in confusion, looking for a place. Eventually, they all found something. Trimble checked his watch. Nine thirty two. Twenty eight minutes to go.

"Good morning, everyone," Reinhart proclaimed crisply.

"Good morning, Mr. Reinhardt," the group replied in rote unison - except for Trimble. Reinhardt noticed and shot him a look, holding it for a moment to make Trimble uncomfortable. Trimble yawned, which seemed to irritate Reinhardt all the more.

"Well, now that we're all here, Helen, how about some refreshments?" Reinhardt said.

Helen Mueller dutifully bustled out of the room, returning a minute later with a large cake decorated like an American flag.

"Natasha, coffee!" Reinhardt snapped. Natasha's real name with Marie. But she was tall and thin with long dark hair, so it amused Reinhardt to call her Natasha. Trimble noticed that every time Reinhardt called her that, Natasha, or Marie, rather, would show an unmistakable hint of hurt in her eyes. She returned with a large pot and some cups and began serving it. Reinhardt watched her with expression of a prison guard who enjoyed his work. Meanwhile, Helen Mueller was cutting the cake and passing it out. People had to balance both cake and coffee on their laps. The atmosphere was forced.

Reinhardt got a piece of cake featuring Old Glory's blue field with stars. He ran his finger across the icing and popped a large blue blob into his mouth. Then he grinned with blue teeth, as if he had done something particularly witty.

A nervous titter ran through the room. Trimble ignored it, put his cake on the floor and began doodling.

Reinhardt took a pile of booklets from his desk, handed them to Helen and, with his mouth still stained with blue frosting, told her to pass them out.

"Everyone have a pencil?" Reinhardt said.

A few of the secretaries raised their hands. Helen gave them pencils.

"Well, looks like election time is coming around again," Reinhardt announced. "Time to see if those crooks are worth the money we pay them!"

He waited for a laugh. There wasn't one. Then some of the secretaries understood the moment and, again, a nervous titter went around the room.

"I know you all want to make the right decision," Reinhardt said weightily. "So, turn to page one."

Curious, Trimble looked down at the booklet. It was a voters pamphlet. Something inside him said wait a minute, this doesn't feel right. But what else was new. He went back to doodling. Everyone else dutifully turned to page one.

"Now, for governor, you all will be voting for Meckling, of course," Reinhardt said, as if it were a foregone conclusion, and an obvious one, at that. "For lieutenant governor, Shelton. State senator, third district, Foster . . ."

Trimble stopped his doodling. Did Reinhardt say you all *will be* voting for Meckling? Not you should or I recommend, but *will be*, as in an order? Yes, he did. Trimble looked around the room. Everyone was obediently marking their pamphlets as Reinhardt dictated.

". . . representative for the eighth district, you'll go for Welch," Reinhardt was saying.

"What about Ecklund? He's had the job for 12 years." That was Linda Green, the newest secretary on the staff and not yet properly conditioned to hierarchical veneration. Reinhardt's body went visibly rigid.

"Welch," he said. He gave Linda a hard look, his eyes boring in like gun sights. He held his gaze until her shoulders slumped, her chin dropped and she marked her pamphlet as she was told.

Trimble scanned the room. Everyone except him was doing exactly what they were told, with no sign of doubt or disagreement. Reinhardt rambled on confidently, the master of the moment.

". . . now this Referendum Eleven, the one about the rivers. Buncha eggheads want to shut down all the factories because they're worried about making the poor little fishies sick. Let's see. . . oh yes, President. Well, heh-heh, no need to even discuss that, is there?"

The rest chuckled knowingly. Trimble found himself frozen in disbelief. This clown is telling everyone how to vote and they are going along with it like so many lemmings? Suddenly, Trimble felt ashamed; very ashamed of his cynical dismissal of his three years in the Air Force. Whatever had happened, he had signed on the line and taken his chances, partly because he had to, but also because deep down he actually believed in freedom and democracy and the Bill of Rights and representative government and all the rest. And for that, he was sent to pound a typewriter and inhale powdered shit all day on a Korean mudflat . . .

Well, so be it. Against his nature, Trimble was feeling pangs of patriotism. Nobody, *nobody*, told him how to vote.

Not so the other people in the room. All were earnestly doing what they were told. Some even had eager, anxious expressions, like they couldn't wait for the Great Man's next pearl of wisdom.

Good god, didn't these people think? Didn't they understand the importance of making your own decisions? Didn't they care that brave men died - or that not-so-brave men spent two years inhaling powdered shit on a Korean mudflat - so they could have the right to vote?

Had they no souls?

Trimble found his hands grinding on the arms of the chair, grinding hard, as hard as he had ever squeezed anything in his life. He knew SPC was a world of its own, spinning in a universe of peculiar cultural rules and mores, many of which he was still learning, but was the right to vote different here, too? It certainly seemed so. No one thought to challenge Reinhardt and it never occurred to Reinhardt that anyone would. He was important, they were not. Their role was to obey.

And They All Accepted It.

"Everyone clear?" Reinhardt said. Everyone smiled and nodded - everyone except Trimble. Fortunately, Reinhardt was looking the other way.

"All right, then, everybody out, shoo, shoo, shoo," Reinhardt said, fluttering his hands. They all filed out. Trimble stayed for a moment, watching the parade of lobotomized drones leaving the hive. He looked at Reinhardt, who was standing over the cake, running his finger through the frosting in a big diagonal swath. Trimble thought, America, America; where goest thou, America mine?

Chapter 13

After a while, Brewer decided to follow Dale's advice and start dating again. There certainly were a lot of eligible prospects around campus. How tough could it be?

The first was a pleasant blond girl majoring in psychology. They went to a movie and then, assuming it would be a sure-fire winner, Brewer took her to the European Café. When the pastries arrived, her face took on an exaggerated, big-eyed look of perplexity.

"Mmmm," she said through tightly-pursed lips. "I just don't know, I just don't know. . ." She looked up at Brewer, pleading.

"Mmmm, should I? Oh, look at all that cream. Mmmm."

She carefully picked off a small speck of whipped cream with her fork and slowly, carefully, as if testing poison, touched it to the tip of her tongue.

"Ooooo!" she squealed, squinting her eyes and raising her hands to fan herself. "Ooooo, Tom, this is so naughty!"

She pushed the plate away and looked at Brewer coyly.

"Do you think I should?" she said, raising her eyebrows provocatively. "Maybe just a little wouldn't be so bad. Do you think I should?"

Brewer didn't care if she did or not. He tried to smile.

She started up again. "Oh, maybe just a little. Mmmm. Oh, it's so hard. . ."

And so it went for the next fifteen minutes or so. Brewer kept trying to smile, nodding occasionally as he nibbled at his cherry torte. As he ate, the girl watched him with an amused, scolding expression, as if he were a child who needed to be reproached. It made Brewer lose his appetite. He pushed the torte aside and poured himself a cup of tea.

The girl leaned forward with a conspiratorial gleam in her eye. She pointed her fork at Brewer's torte.

"Are you going to eat the rest of that?" she said with a knowing leer.

Well, the next girl he dated had to be better, Brewer decided. She was slender, with dark hair, glasses and a composed manner. He knew her from his American history class, where she seemed to be one of the brighter pupils.

When he picked her up, Brewer held the car door for her as he always had been trained and she responded with a thank you, as she always had been trained. As Brewer was starting the ignition, he remembered that he forgot to lock her door. He reached behind the seat to press the knob.

The dark-haired girl hurled herself against the door and cringed there, clutching her coat to her throat with both hands, her face a mask of terror.

"Oh, sorry," Brewer said. "Just locking the door."

The girl did not move. She did not speak. She continued to gape at him as if he were a python closing in on his next meal.

The ensuing date reflected her sensibility. When they arrived at theater, Brewer held the lobby door for her. She stood for a moment, her head down, apparently gasping for breath. Then, still clutching the neck of her coat, she rushed past as if crossing on stepping stones over a creek full of alligators. She sat with an empty seat between them. When Brewer held the popcorn over to her, she flinched. Brewer had her back to the dorm by 9:30. She thanked him for a lovely evening.

The next date, with a strapping P.E. major named Bonnie, actually went pretty well; a concert by Glenn Yarbrough, pizza at Harry's on University Way, pleasant conversation, a general sense of good times and good cheer.

Bonnie lived with her parents in Ballard. Brewer parked in front of the house, she leaned over, gave him a peck on the cheek, thanked him for a nice time, and all seemed well with the world.

Then Brewer noticed the curtains to the house's front window were parting. A head emerged from the side, the head of a young man, with dark hair, an unshaven face and a very angry scowl. The head, and the scowl, remained motionless, like a cardboard cutout on a stick.

"Oh, dear, I was afraid this would happen," Bonnie said.

"What?"

"Oh, that's Neil, my boyfriend. My parents must have told him I was going out with you."

"Your boyfriend?"

"Well, I guess you could call him that. We've been going together since seventh grade. My mother is very fond of him."

"He looks mad," Brewer said.

"Yes, he probably is. When I go in, there probably will be a big row; mom and Neil against me."

Brewer remained silent. What else could he do?

"Say, I don't suppose you'd like to come with me?" Bonnie said. "Take my side and all that? I could really use the support."

Brewer smiled weakly. Then he went around the back of the car and opened her door. As they walked toward the house, he quickly dodged away, got into the car and drove off as fast as he could.

The next girl was a chatty little thing, from a big family in Walla Walla, Washington; two sisters, two brothers and her. And of course, mom and dad who, if she was to be believed, were the most wondrous progenitors the human race had produced since Joseph and Mary. She offered ample evidence to that effect; talking about her family constantly throughout the evening. Oh, dad, he's so funny, always putting on funny hats and making jokes. I don't like it when he makes those jokes about Negroes and Jews, but, well, that's just dad. You know how it is! And mom; she bakes bread every day, can you believe it, every day! You always know where she is because she sings hymns all day long - all day! Except when dad gets home. He likes it quiet in the evenings. That makes Mom nervous, so she goes to her room, closes the door and knits for the rest of the night. All of us have closets full of sweaters. How about that!"

After a Drama Department performance of The Glass Menagerie at McKinley, she asked Brewer to drive her to her sister's.

"I promised her I would return that sweater she loaned me and she had some stuff she wants me to give to Linda, that's my other sister. And Linda has some things she wants me to give to. . ." And so on.

It turned out to be a long evening. The girl couldn't get the hang of the street grid system - the idea that Second Avenue came after First and before Third flummoxed her - and she didn't believe in maps. So, they wandered around the back roads of Lynnwood, a swampy, semi-rural area north of Seattle, looking for the big white rock by the side of the road or the green Royal Crown Cola sign – or maybe it was a 7-Up sign. Or maybe a Canada Dry sign. Oh foo! Even when they found such landmarks it didn't help much. Along with everything else, the girl had difficulty discerning left from right.

Finally, there was Sharon, ah, sweet Sharon. To get right to the point: The girl oozed carnality. She had a broad, rather girlish face offset by long, thick chestnut hair, which she was prone to sweeping off her face with languorous, feline grace. That, plus blue eye shadow and pink lipstick, gave her the look of Jacqueline Kennedy as envisioned by Russ Meyer. She also was prone to the shortest skirts she could get away with at SPC, along with lightweight blouses she wore a size too small. On cold winter days, she was wonderful to behold.

It turned out she delivered on the promise. She let Brewer finger her. However, when he took her hand and guided it toward him to indicate reciprocity, she jerked back as if she had just touched a live electrical wire. She gave him a reproachful glare. Brewer started to pull his hand away from her crotch.

"No, no," she said. "I'm not done yet."

So back his hand went, where it stayed, slowly cramping into a painful knot as she rocked and groaned and Brewer looked out the window, counted the stars and wondered what the hell he was doing there.

Chapter 14

Finals.

In the ninth week of Fall Quarter, the campus began to implode upon itself. Freshmen who had procrastinated for the past two months were suddenly gripped by throat-clutching fear. Their laziness, their weakness, their immaturity were things they no longer could dodge. They were about to suffer the consequences and they knew it and they felt shame and regret and desperation to degrees they had never imagined. This wasn't high school, where they wanted to pass you, where a bad test grade could be made up for a little later, where simply being reasonably intelligent would get you through most courses. No, no. This was a matter of survival, on the most primal of levels.

Finals.

Here no allowances were made: You failed and you were out; out to look for a job waiting tables or pumping gas, out to find a draft notice waiting in the mail box, out to go home and endure the devastated expressions of parents who had dreamed so much for you. You would run into kids who had stayed behind, the kids who had not gone to college and never would and you would make excuses to them. They wouldn't believe you, of course, and that, living a lie, a lie that fooled no one, would haunt you for the rest of your life. Now, as finals approached, that pitiless specter robbed you of all peace.

Finals.

Freshmen who had been diligent in their studies were scared too. Most had found college every bit as demanding, and more, than they had been led to believe. Work that got you an A in high school got you a C-plus here. You weren't as smart as you thought you were; a severe shock for those who had been at the head of the class their entire lives. Would finals complete the process? Would you be locked into mediocrity for the next four years, perhaps even beyond that?

Did you really Have What It Takes?

Upper classmen who had sweated through finals for three years, who knew their way around the academic world; they felt it too. Are you smarter than you were four years ago? Well, you know more, it was true, but finals were as hard as ever – hard and uncertain and unnerving. You could still fail, and that fear, that deepest of fears, nibbles and tunnels its way behind your carefully-constructed self-control and relentlessly picks at your consciousness with tiny, needle teeth.

You open a textbook and realize you barely understand the subject at all. So you try to force the words from the book into your brain, but they will not penetrate, no matter how hard you try. You memorize and hope for the best. So this is what education comes down to. You feel like a fool, a fraud. There is no escaping it. But here you are and finals begin Monday and you sure as hell had better be ready. That much you know. You know it so well, too well, and you try to cram on and try to repress your fear and find that you are not succeeding at either.

Finals.

Term papers and research projects were due too and students cursed themselves for not having put in an hour a day, every day for two months, the way they knew they were supposed to. You saw them at the library, a pack of refugees frantically scavenging for books, frantically poring through them, frantically writing down notes and then slamming the books back on the shelves and beginning the process all over again. Then, later, would you hear them typing at 3 a.m., banished to dorm lounges and basements by roommates who wanted only to sleep, oh blessed sleep, the only escape.

The fear was on them. There was no delusion. Not now, not with only a week left.

The campus had grown silent, as silent as a crypt at 4 a.m. No waves and shouts at friends, no jokes on the way to class, no chatty gossip as students wait for chapel to start. In the SUB, in the dining hall, the same groups of friends met, but they were rarely complete. At least one member, usually more, was gone; to the library, to some empty classroom, feverishly rereading books and reviewing notes, alone in cold sweat, alone in dread, the deepest dread they would ever know.

For Marilyn Pennell, preparing for finals was proving more aggravating than frightening. Her roommate, innocent, misty-eyed, oh-so-good Janet Small was panicking. Janet would paw through her binder, looking for class notes. She would ransack the room searching for misplaced textbooks, knocking things over and bumping into the wall loudly. She constantly ran her hands over her face and through her hair. She would huff. She would puff. And then she would cry.

Sometimes it was a sniffle. Sometimes it was a whimper. Sometimes it was a full-blown sob. Marilyn gritted her teeth and did her best to ignore it, but it wasn't easy. She thought she should feel sorry for Janet - so far from home, so unprepared, so lost - but after two nights of listening to her blubbering, Marilyn just wanted the whiney little twit to go away. Then one night, after about an hour of huffs and puffs and face pawings, Janet apparently broke down.

"Marilyn, what will I do?" she sobbed. "I just don't get this stuff. What will I *doooo?*"

Marilyn wanted to tell her to stop her theatrics, read the textbooks, study her notes and sweat it out, the same as everyone else - but above all, <u>Shut Up!</u> Instead, as always, Marilyn Pennell said what was expected of her.

"You'll do fine," she told Janet, not believing a word of it. "Everyone is stressed out. When it gets to be too much for me, I usually take a walk and clear my head."

Yes, take a walk, she thought. Please take a walk, a good long one.

"Oh. Will you go with me?" Janet said, in a plaintive tone.

"I'm really busy."

"But it's dark out there," Janet whined. "I'm not used to a big city like this. *Pleeease.*"

"No. Sorry."

"Then I guess I'll just stay here," Janet said. For a moment, her voice sounded calm and controlled. But the moment didn't last.

"Oh, Marilyn, what will I do?" Janet said, her whine building momentum like a fire siren. "What will I *doooo?*"

Marilyn clenched her jaw once more, this time so she wouldn't shriek out the longest and loudest stream of obscenities ever heard in the Western Hemisphere. Awkwardly, with movements labored by efforts to maintain her self-control, Marilyn scooped up her books and binders and bolted for the door. She turned briefly to see Janet staring at her in incomprehension.

Marilyn headed down the hill to the library. It closed at ten, but at least she would have two hours to herself. She needed it. English 101 was proving hard. Her math class, Introduction to Statistics was proving harder. Psychology 130 was proving hardest of all. She had attended every lecture. She had read every assignment. She took careful, detailed notes. She thought she understood the subject, but she wasn't sure. It felt like trying to swim in very cold water.

Concentration and self-discipline were on her side. Marilyn could study for two hours at a stretch without a break. Then after that break, she could study for two hours more. And so on. Her mind rarely wandered, her attention rarely lapsed.

Then Janet had to come along. Poor, poor Janet. But there was nothing she could do for Janet. College was not an exercise in lofty goals and noble intentions. Mostly, it was a matter of rote perseverance and dependable shoes. Even after less than a full quarter, Marilyn had figured that out. But Janet had not. It seemed to Marilyn that Janet never would figure it out because she didn't want to. Facing hard truths simply wasn't in her.

Well, it isn't that hard a truth, Marilyn thought as she walked down the steps to Weter. It's just the way of things. If you had given any thought to what college was likely to entail, you would have predicted at least some if it long before you ever set foot on campus. But, apparently, Janet had not given it any thought, and never would.

What did I ever do to deserve a roommate like this? Marilyn wondered.

Weter was nearly full. Bright and airy in the daytime, it was umber-tinged and murky at night, at least on this dark December night when clots and orts of dingy figures, their frayed nerves barely concealed or not concealed at all, raw and bare, hunched over every desk and every table, or slumped in every stray chair, or huddled in every dim nook, every grimy corner. Marilyn searched the first floor for an empty space and did not find one. Then she checked the second floor. No luck. On the third floor, she managed to find an empty study desk near a window.

She put down her things and set to work. After about a half-hour, she happened to glance out the window. There was Janet, walking across the plaza toward the library's front door, her arms wrapped around a disheveled buzzard's nest of papers and books, her face the expression of a shipwrecked raccoon.

"Shit!" Marilyn said it out loud, which surprised her. She looked around. No one seemed to notice.

Shit! SHIT! ***SHIT!*** I should feel sorry for her. She just needs a little love and compassion. I'm a decent person who tries to treat people with kindness and consideration. . .

Or maybe I am not. The thought settled on Marilyn for a moment. She had always tried to be kind and considerate, even when she didn't feel it. But aren't you supposed to feel it? she thought. Otherwise, it is just an act.

Well, maybe it's time to stop acting. Maybe I am cruel.

Funny, but I don't find that realization particularly disturbing.

Enough. I truly *need* to study. I can't waste my time and energy on the weak and foolish. Call it cruel. Call it heartless. Call it whatever you like.

I don't care!

I have to survive!

Now what?

Marilyn looked around quickly. There was no place to hide. Then she spotted the sign pointing to the women's restroom. She would have to move fast. She did, grabbing a chair along the way.

Inside, there was a sink and, next to it, a small counter. It would have to do. She set the chair in front of the counter, spread out her psychology notes and set to work. From time to time, someone would come in, glance at her with momentary curiosity and head for one of the stalls. Then Marilyn would be treated to the sounds and smells of a large, meat-eating mammal excreting its bodily wastes as forcefully and for as long as it took to achieve completion. It was often quite a long time indeed. Good god, what had they served at Gwinn tonight?

Marilyn found herself chuckling. After the first two sonorous declarations, she had gotten used to it. After the third, she didn't hear it at all. I suppose you can get used to almost anything, she thought. In any case, it was preferable to listening Janet all night long.

She got on with divining the intricacies of the ego, superego and id. Then a girl in one of the stalls let loose a particularly long, gurgling fart. Marilyn laughed out loud. My, my. What an appropriate environment for studying Freud.

****

The finals for English 101 were held in a large room in the music building. The big room was necessary because instructors from three classes were giving the same test at the same time.

The room had no windows and its walls were covered ceiling to floor with thick black soundproofing panels textured in a deep checkerboard pattern.

The result was a dark cavern with no echoes. The absence of echoes struck Brewer. You could hear everything, but that is all you heard; no reverberations, no extraneous noise to hide in. The people in the room seemed to sense it, too. No one spoke as they prepared themselves for the first college final exam of their lives.

Brewer looked around. He knew a few of the people from his class, but only a few and not well. The other fifty or so people he knew not at all. He found himself categorizing them, wondering how they would respond to the test, wondering what characteristics separated success from failure, wondering what would happen to them.

There was a curly-headed small town jock. He was from some nameless farm town in Kansas and with his mail order clothes, he looked it. He even wore his high school letterman's jacket around campus, a bush league affectation, even at SPC. Brewer remembered seeing him on the first day of English 101 class. He came in the room cheerful and confident. But after the first half-hour he looked wide-eyed and lost, clearly out of his element. And so he stayed for the rest of the quarter, never raising his and, if called upon, shrugging in embarrassment.

One afternoon, Brewer happened by the gym and saw the small town jock playing basketball. He was quick. He was graceful. His moves were practiced and confident. He had an excellent outside jump shot and could hit blind passes with dead accuracy. In short, once in his element, he was a different person.

But a final exam in English was not his element. It was cruel. Brewer felt sorry for him.

There was a Filipino girl, short, dumpy and with glasses so thick her eyes were barely visible. She was in his class and never spoke. Once, while studying in the library, Brewer found he wasn't sure if the assignment he was working on was due Wednesday or Friday. She was sitting nearby. He went and asked her.

She looked up at him through her glasses, her expression frozen in a blank mask. She looked for a long moment as if she didn't understand a word he said. Then, in a near whisper, she said, "Friday."

"Thanks," Brewer said. "I was getting worried."

She didn't say you're welcome, she didn't respond in any way. She just continued to stare at him blankly, her lips pursed tightly, her eyes imperceptible behind coke bottle glass. Brewer realized that was all the response she was going to give. He walked back to his table. When he looked over at her, she was once again bent over in study. Brewer noticed that her feet, primly crossed at the ankles, did not touch the floor.

He wondered what went on behind those thick glasses. Did she think like him? Did she perceive reality in ways they both would understand? Did she have hopes and dreams? He would never know. Maybe she would never know.

Then there was a girl with the look of a high school cheerleader; lovely, almost overly pretty. Brewer did not know her, but he had checked her out every time he saw her, as did every other male on campus, for she was worthy of a particularly thorough checking out. But Brewer noticed there was an air of fragility about her, a semi-sad, rather pained expression. She always was alone. Was she simply a snob or, like Brewer, was she unhappy about being at SPC because her parents forced her to go there? Or, like the small town jock, was she out of her element and miserable about it? Such things weren't supposed to happen to pretty girls, but perhaps they did. Or perhaps it was something else, something unique only to her. Brewer wondered.

A clean-cut young man sat in front and to the side of Brewer. He had bright, alert eyes and an open, friendly expression. Would he pass this test? Or would it erase his pleasant demeanor, would it destroy some element of his inherent good nature?

Others looked cool and prepared, deadly. Sharks. They had mastered the subject and they knew it and had no qualms about leaving lesser minds behind.

And Brewer? He had a lot on his mind this day, but mostly he found himself bemused with the idea that this was the proverbial It. They had endured the trials of applying for college, they had left their parents' homes (a bigger bereavement than they cared to admit,) they had suffered the dehumanization of registration. They were in. Now they would find if they would stay in. Smart or dumb, mature or foolish, succeed or fail; illusions were about to disappear. In the muffled hush of the big room, there were no distractions, no escapes.

The more Brewer looked around, the more he was struck by the scene. Everyone there had a story. Whatever they had once been, whatever potential their parents had told them they had, whatever they had achieved so far in their young lives, it stopped here. Brewer found the uncertainty exhilarating and bittersweet. Here the history of my generation is being lived. Where will it take us?

Then came the test, passed out by rigid, austere instructors, bloodless, walking row to row in mechanical choreography, no one speaking, no one needing to. The students scanned the first page and their ordeal began.

Brewer was surprised. The test proved easier than he thought. The first essay question was about a story by Henry James. Ah, Henry James, the most turgid of the turgid, a plower of prose so stultifying that even the class suckups, the habitual front row hand-raisers, could find in it nothing to fuel their never-ending campaigns of toadying.

But Brewer knew the story, titled *The Pupil*. In it, a young man is hired to tutor the son of impoverished, corrupt aristocrats. They take advantage of the tutor every chance they get and he puts up with because he feels affection for the boy. In short, he was a sucker, Brewer concluded, and said so in his essay, although he made sure that rather obvious conclusion was steeped in appropriately learned sounding terms, relating the whole business to the inherent venality of aristocracy and the self-delusion of the lower classes.

The other question was about a treatise by Paul Tillich, *Men and God*. Brewer had done a paper on it early in the quarter. During the course of writing the paper, he found himself reading and rereading Tillich's dense verbiage until, at last, he thought he actually understood it.

There was a key sentence that Brewer liked: "If God can be found within the whole of reality, then the whole of reality is the basic and dominant concept." When Brewer first read it, that sentence stopped him in his tracks. If God exists in reality, then which is predominant, God or reality? Which came first, and what created it?

Well, which and what indeed? Were God and reality merely constructs human beings invented to explain the world around them? Brewer suspected that was probably closer to the truth than all the tortuously-worded conclusions Tillich spent the rest of the essay pontificating. So Brewer said so, noting that the question was, ultimately, unanswerable and that Tillich, a Christian philosopher, did his best to dodge that discomforting reality by blathering on for the next five pages with what, when you saw past his learned locution, were the usual collection of foregone conclusions and churchy clichés you heard in chapel every day.

In a final at SPC you say <u>that?</u>

Well, yes, Brewer thought. To hell with it. It's the truth. Flunk me for the truth if you want to, but I don't think you will. Who knows, original thinking might even get me a better grade.

Then came the spelling. Brewer's optimism sank. If you missed four words, your grade for the quarter went down one whole point. Brewer had never been a good speller and made up for it by carrying a pocket dictionary. But memorizing spelling was a trial. The words usually looked more or less the same to him whether they were spelled correctly or not. Irrational spellings like rhythm, necessary and good bye (<u>always</u> an e at the end and <u>always</u> two words) were tricky and words that ended in ence or ance threw him off completely.

The test required him to find the misspelled words in a page of random words and then correct them. Brewer tied. He spotted a few right away, but he knew there were more and he knew he would miss some of them. Why was the spelling of the English language so devoted to chaos and illogic?

Brewer soldiered on, finding a word here, a word there; fewer and fewer words as the clock inexorably ticked away.

And then time was up. How did he do? Pretty well, Brewer thought - except for the spelling, of course. The reality was, he would never ace a spelling test. He could only hope he made up for it in the rest of the exam.

As Brewer put on his coat to leave, he looked around one more time. He couldn't see the small town jock. He did see the cheerleader girl. Her delicate features were set in the hard, brittle planes of resignation. The Filipino girl with the glasses was expressionless, almost wraithlike. She was enveloped by the sharks as they swept out the door. Brewer never saw her again.

The pleasant-looking young man was, like Brewer, perusing the room. His bearing was still open and friendly, but his eyes were cold as they scanned back and forth, back and forth.

****

It was 7 p.m. and it was raining. No one on the bus had thought to open a window except Brewer, and he could force his up only an inch before it jammed. As a result, the coach was fetid with the exhalations and evaporations of thirty wet, tired people. The windows were opaque with an oily layer of condensation. The poles were slippery with the stuff. Brewer's face felt slimy.

The ride from downtown had been uneventful, save for a woman in a dirty, frayed wool overcoat and greasy stocking cap who kept babbling about goddamned men and, as she put it, that stinking piece of meat swinging between their legs. She got off at Allison Street under the freeway bridge. Brewer wondered if she was going to hide there and wait for some unsuspecting billy goats. At least he would have twelve minutes of anonymity, peace and silence, blessed silence, before his stop.

Brewer had spent three hours studying at Weter before leaving for home. Now, as he resignedly trudged the three blocks to his parents' house, he was thinking about the long night ahead of him: In the morning, he had to turn in a History paper on the Buchanan administration. Fortunately, it was mostly done. But it would still require an hour or two.

Then, at 2:30 p.m., came his physics final. He was as prepared as he could be. He had reread every assignment, reviewed all his class notes and memorized as many of the formulas as he could.

With luck, Brewer would finish his toil by midnight. He wanted sleep. He knew he wouldn't get much. Fortunately, Dale had agreed to swing by at 9 a.m. and give him a ride to school. That might give him an extra half hour or so.

His parents were waiting in the living room. Both looked at him carefully when he entered, something they rarely did. Brewer felt wariness spreading coldly from his chest to his arms to his fingertips. His parents wanted to have a talk. That was never good.

His father raised his chin so he looked down his nose at Brewer; a supercilious expression he sometimes adopted when exercising parental authority.

"Tom, have a chair," he said in a tone of affected gravitas.

Brewer had not yet put down his books or taken off his coat. He did both, using the time to get a sense of the situation. His parents were solemn; solemn to the point bad overacting. Brewer tensed.

"This came for you today," his father said, handing him an envelope. The return address read, J.P. Addelton, Attorney at Law, 202 State Street, Albany, N.Y. 12210. The envelope had been torn open. Whatever it was, his parents already had read it.

Sticking out of the envelope was a single sheet of cream-colored paper. The paper had a heavy, expensive feel to it.

    Mr. Thomas J. Brewer
    6326 52nd Ave. N.E.
    Seattle, Wash. 98115

Dear Mr. Brewer;

Mr. Lee W. McEwen of Albany died Oct. 14 of this year. I am Mr. McEwen's attorney and executor of his estate.

In his will, Mr. McEwen left you a portfolio of stocks and bonds valued $30,406.27. I have enclosed documents transferring ownership of that portfolio to you, along with directions on how to fill them out.

You can either assume ownership if the portfolio, or you can liquidate its assets at their market value. You then would receive a one-time cash payment.

Please let me know what you wish to do.

Respectfully,

J.P. Addelton
Attorney at Law

Lee McEwen was Brewer's mother's cousin. Brewer had met him only once, when McEwen visited Seattle some ten years before. He remembered a rather moody old man who disliked the Republican Party and said so, which did not endear him to the assembled.

He did, however, like baseball, which young Tom discovered when McEwen came upon him looking over his baseball card collection.

"Who's your favorite player?" McEwen said, his voice uncharacteristically friendly.

"Willie Mays," Tom said.

"Not Mickey Mantle?" McEwen said. "He batted .353 last year."

"Yeah, he's great. But Willie Mays hit 36 home runs and stole 40 bases. And he's the best fielder anywhere. He's my favorite."

McEwen nodded.

"It's tough to choose between the two," he said. "You ever play catch?"

"Sure."

Tom got his mitt. He gave Orrin's to McEwen. They tossed the ball back and forth for about a half hour. McEwen urged Tom to throw hard and winced a couple of times when the ball hit his mitt. Then Brewer's mother called them in for dinner. It was the only time Tom Brewer ever saw Lee W. McEwen.

Brewer quickly thumbed through the other documents. They appeared to be just what Addelton said. He looked up. His parents were staring at him intently. He got the impression they expected him to speak. He had nothing to say. What do you say when you've just been given thirty thousand dollars?

His mother had a sad, big-eyed expression, as if she was about to cry.

"He didn't leave a single dime to the girls," she said with a sniffle. "When I saw it, I couldn't believe it."

The Girls were his mother's nieces; ages six, eight and ten. Brewer's mother doted on them. No, it was more than doting. It was more akin to worship. They were perfect, in her eyes; lovely little angels, beautiful, smart, multi-talented, flawlessly- behaved and cute. Above all, cute. Every pose they struck, every sound they uttered, no matter how trivial, was cause for Brewer's mother to clasp her hands to her chest, smile sappily and let out an adoring "Oooooh."

Brewer never understood it. Perhaps it was because she had no daughters of her own. Who knows. For his part, Brewer neither liked nor disliked his cousins. Because of their age difference, he had nothing in common with them and generally did his best to avoid them.

But that wasn't easy.

Every time one of them had a birthday, or appeared in a school play or did much of anything, the entire Brewer clan was packed in the family Buick and driven 58 miles to Mount Vernon, where they would spend the rest of the day, usually to 10 p.m. or later, in a small, overheated house – his aunt was convinced open windows caused tuberculosis – where one of the main challenges was finding a place to sit. Brewer usually ended up on the floor. His mother spent the entire time adoring The Girls' every delightful movement, every endearing remark.

There was nothing for the rest of the company to do. They ran out of conversation after about a half hour and his aunt kept the television set in the basement because she believed the entertainment industry was an organ of the communist party. No one got to watch TV without her approval and in all the years the Brewers visited, she never once granted it.

Sometimes, Brewer would suggest that it was getting late and perhaps they should go home. His mother would glower at him as if he was interrupting a holy observance.

Holidays revolved around the girls, either at their home – again the 116-mile roundtrip and 10-hour day – or at the Brewers'. When they arrived at the Brewers', usually just after breakfast, all other activity stopped so The Girls could tear around the house, make noise and do pretty much do whatever they pleased.

Interfering with them, in any way, was unwise. Once, one of them came out of Tom's bedroom waving one of his model airplanes around. It had taken him two weeks to build it, including trips to the library to find books that showed the color scheme. Gently, even smiling a little, he took the model from his cousin - who was preparing to slam it into the wall. She exploded with a shriek that drove ice picks into the eardrums of everyone in range. She continued to wail in a banshee-like din for a full fifteen minutes, bringing all other activity to a standstill. When she finally stopped, Brewer's mother commenced to shout at Tom, calling him a brute, a bully, an oaf and whatever else she could think up that reflected his incarnate male bestiality. The rest of the family watched. As near as Brewer could discern, they found his castigation very gratifying. You did not cross The Girls.

Whenever Brewer complained about long trips or The Girls' domination of family life, his father was quick to jump on it.

"Ooooo, little Tommy is jealous," his father would say, pursing his lips is a tsk-tsk expression. "Aren't we getting enough attention from mommy? Are little Tommy's feelings hurt?" Then he would chortle and nudge Uncle Walt in the ribs knowingly and they would chortle together. Whenever Brewer tried to respond, whenever he tried to explain that he had studying to do or that the trips were simply a wearying, monotonous burden, they would laugh all the more. So much for the value of reasoned discourse.

In quiet moments, when he reflected on the situation, Brewer came away ambivalent. He resented it and it aggravated him, to be sure, but there were more important things in the world. It wasn't like The Girls were the cause of famine, war and pestilence. Perhaps he was overreacting. It all weighed on him.

One thing he did know for sure was that if there was any way his mother could integrate The Girls into whatever the rest of the family was doing, she would find it.

Brewer suddenly understood that was what was happening now.

"Those poor little dears," his mother said, dabbing her eyes with a Kleenex. "What did they ever do to Lee that he would treat them like this?"

Brewer looked at the letter again. Then he thumbed through the papers again, anything to create a moment, to stall, to play for time.

Finally, his father said, "Tom, we've spent the last hour or so talking this over. He didn't leave anything to the girls. They're family, too. We want to be fair about this."

We?

Brewer waited for the next move.

"Now, the fair thing to do here is divide the money equally between the girls, Orrin and you. You each would receive twenty percent. We'll keep yours in a trust fund and turn it over to you when we think you are ready. Six thousand bucks! Pretty good deal, huh?"

Now the truth was on the table. Brewer took the papers from the envelope and looked them over. The girls were not mentioned. Orrin was not mentioned. Only he, Tomas J. Brewer was mentioned.

"It says here the money is mine," Brewer said.

"Well, technically," his father said. "But the State of Washington doesn't allow anyone under twenty one to keep an inheritance. You'll have to sign it over to a guardian, to us."

The State of Washington says what? Brewer knew there were all kinds of laws restricting what people under twenty one could and could not do. You could be drafted, but you couldn't vote. You had to pay income taxes, but you couldn't drink a beer. There was no discernible pattern of logic to it all. So maybe his father was telling the truth. Or maybe it was a trick. The Girls must have their way . . .

"Just give me all that stuff and I'll take care of it," his father said, as if it were a foregone conclusion.

The pause that then ensued lasted five seconds, maybe ten. But it seemed much longer. Then quietly, introvertedly, his head down as if he were talking only to himself, Tom Brewer said, "No."

"What?" his father said in disbelief.

"No," Brewer said.

His mother's eyes grew wide and tears started welling in them.

"Don't use that tone of voice with me!" his father said, his voice suddenly angry. "I'll take those papers now!"

"No."

And with that third No, something changed in Tom Brewer, something he couldn't articulate, but something he felt, something sure and true. He could say no. Whatever other people said or did or felt, whatever they tried to make him do, he could say no. It put him on a plane they could not touch. They could not take it from him.

His mother began to whimper.

"Oh great, now you've made your mother cry," his father said "I hope you're proud of yourself, mister."

Brewer picked up his coat and books.

"Don't you walk away on me, fella!" his father growled.

"Oh, Tommy, please," his mother whined.

Brewer wanted to run. He wanted to be someplace else. But he could not. The power to say no was all he had.

"So, you think you can just keep it all for yourself, huh? You really don't care about anybody but yourself, do you? I can't believe a son of mine is that selfish," his father said.

"Oh, Tommy," his mother wailed again, her voice even more melodramatic than before.

"Have you ever given any thought to your future?" his father said. "Just what would you do with that kind of money, blow it on some hot rod?"

"I have no idea."

"Ooooh, you have no idea, huh? Have you thought about inheritance taxes? How about liability insurance? How about escrow? Have you thought about escrow? Have you ever thought about that? Huh?"

Brewer had no idea what liability insurance and escrow were. He didn't care.

"Look, I have a lot of homework," he said.

"Oh, yeah, just you go do that. Big college man. Thinks he's so important. Doesn't give a damn about anybody else, not even his own mother."

Brewer did not answer.

Finally, after holding it in as best he could, anger rose in Brewer, anger hot and strong. He would not be pushed anymore. He would not allow himself to be manipulated for the benefit of others anymore. He had made his stand. He had said no.

"I'm done talking about this," he said. He started for his room.

"Well, you can't keep it, you know," his father said.

"Why not?" Brewer said.

"You're too young. Nobody eighteen-years-old can have that much money."

"It's mine," Brewer said.

"No it's not," his father said sternly. "You'll have to sign it over to us. May as well do it now. The sooner the better."

Brewer closed his bedroom door. He slipped the envelope into his notebook. Jesus, I have to prepare for that test. And how will I ever get that paper done with all this bullshit on my mind?

Outside, down the hall, he could hear his mother blubbering, "Oh Lloyd, oh Lloyd . . . "

It made Brewer feel all the more angry – but mostly it made him feel terribly, terribly alone. He took some deep breaths and tried to force it all from his mind. He got out his notes on Buchanan.

There was a knock on the door, a loud knock. Brewer opened it to find his father, his hands on his hips, his face dark.

"You're a real chump, Tom," his father said. "That's what you are, a real chump. That's what I think." Then he turned and stomped away.

A chump? Brewer wondered. What the hell's a chump? Something detestable to his father's generation, apparently. Brewer laughed softly. Of all the dumbshit things his father could have called him – some of which actually might have drawn blood – chump was the dumbest.

He laughed again and the anger and loneliness suddenly evaporated from him. Chump, huh? Well, dad, it isn't 1939 and this isn't second half of a double feature starring Leo Gorcey. Maybe I am a chump. But I don't really give a shit. Chump. You gotta be kidding me."

He went back to Buchanan. A really hip and far-out guy, old Jimbo, right up there with Warren G. Harding and Clem Kaddiddlehopper. Nothing like interpreting four years of indecision and ineptitude to take your mind off your troubles. Brewer tried to concentrate. But visions of money, $30,406.27 to be exact, kept wheedling their way into his consciousness, and with them, something even more insidious: a cool, breeze-like vision of living his life free of the domination of others; a vague feeling, elusive and hard to identify, but one that was there. It definitely was there.

Brewer forced it from his mind, too. Freedom would have to wait. Physics 114 and the fifteenth president of the United States would not. Wasn't higher education a thrill.

He finally finished at 1 a.m. At seven thirty, he got up, showered, and then went back to his room. Under his dresser, far under it where you couldn't find it unless you knew where to reach, was an envelope. In it was about thirty dollars, the accumulation of spare dimes and quarters and an occasional dollar bill that Brewer had carefully shepherded, hoping to spend it on some new clothes for spring quarter. He tucked it in his coat pocket.

Acting as if he were running late, he poured himself a glass of milk for breakfast. His parents glowered at him, but said nothing. Then Brewer was out the door. A couple of minutes later, Dale's rusty blue Chev drove up.

Dale looked rumpled and sleep-deprived, too. Or maybe he was hung over. With Dale you could never be sure.

"Thanks for the ride," Brewer said.

"You bet," Dale said neutrally, a cigarette dangling from his lip. As they pulled away, he reached for the lighter.

"You look like hell," Dale said.

"I've been better."

"Yeah," Dale said with a sigh, as if he understood how it felt.

They drove on in silence for a while. Dale turned on the radio. KJR was nothing but ads. KOL was playing a new song, "This Diamond Ring," by a group called Gary Lewis and the Playboys.

"I like that sound," Dale said.

"Me too," Brewer said. "I've never heard of these guys."

"They're new. Kind of unusual. Their harmonies. Interesting."

"Yeah."

They drove on, silent in the comfortable way of friends who trusted each other.

Dale parked behind Beegle Hall.

"I want to finish my cigarette," he said.

"Okay," Brewer said, opening the door. "Thanks again for the ride."

"Later."

****

Brewer walked down to the SUB. Rather than go to the coffee shop, which was his morning habit, he stopped at the front desk.

It was manned by a middle-aged woman trying to look twenty years younger and failing. The SUB was her turf, you better believe it, and nothing, *nothing*, went on its walls, windows or bulletin boards without her permission. No one used the desk phone except for official business, and she defined what official business was. And, certainly, no one dropped a wrapper on its floor. Brewer had recognized her as the sort of individual best avoided. But now he had no choice.

"I'm told there are lockers in the SUB basement," Brewer said, as affably as he could. "I'd like to rent one if there are any available."

"Oh, would you?" the SUB matron said, as if he was being terribly presumptuous. She stared at him for a long moment, her right eyebrow arched in disapproval.

"Yes, please," Brewer said.

She stared for another moment, sighed wearily and went to a small filing cabinet that resembled a library card catalogue. She looked through it languidly. Finally, she said, "Hm, here's one."

She tossed the card on the counter, nowhere near Brewer. Her expression was one of a person enduring some terrible imposition.

"How much does it cost?" Brewer said.

"The student handbook states clearly that they cost ten dollars a quarter. It's on page five."

Brewer stayed focused. Was he actually getting use to bureaucratic indignity? He was beginning to wonder.

"I'd like to rent it for this quarter and winter quarter," Brewer said.

"This quarter is almost over."

"I'd like to anyway."

The receptionist eyed him with world weary contempt.

"We've already processed the fees for this quarter," she said.

"I'd still like to rent one. I'll pay the full amount."

She sighed loudly. "There's always one like you. Now I'll have to enter a separate payment in the accounts. Then I'll get a call from the accounting department asking for an explanation. All because you couldn't get here in time like everybody else."

Brewer counted out twenty dollars. He had eight dollars left in change.

"Oh, and you want to pay cash," the receptionist said with feigned surprise. She scrutinized him with studied distaste. Brewer kept his gaze level, his expression neutral and non-threatening. He would wait her out.

Finally, she took the money.

"You have to supply your own lock," she said.

Brewer had a combination lock in his coat pocket. He filled out the card.

He found the lockers in the SUB basement. His, number 428, was in a far corner. That was good. He clamped his lock on it and made sure the lock was secure. He already had memorized the combination.

He went back upstairs, this time to the office of The Falcon, the school newspaper. It was closed. The door to the yearbook, The Tawahsi, was open.

The editor, whom Brewer had seen but never met, was lazily going through some back issues.

"Can I use one of your typewriters?" Brewer said.

"What? What for?" the editor said, his voice wary and hostile. He was a skinny young man with a flat-top crew cut and particularly vicious case of adolescent acne which had continued unabated into his twenties.

"I have to make some corrections to an assignment. My own typewriter is at home."

"These typewriters are for the Tawahsi staff," the editor said indignantly. "If we loaned them out, pretty soon everybody would be using them."

"Look, I'm in a real bind here." Brewer said. He tried to say it as if the editor was a friend and he was sharing a mutually-understood undergraduate dilemma.

The editor considered it for a moment. Then he said, "All right, but don't take too long. And don't make a habit of it."

Brewer began to type.

Mr. J.P. Addelton
Attorney at Law
202 State Street
Albany, N.Y. 12210
Dec. 12, 1964

Dear Mr. Addelton;
Yesterday I received your letter regarding my inheritance from the estate of Lee McEwen.
I have enclosed the necessary paper work you requested.
Your letter stated that I could liquidate the stocks and bonds in the inheritance for cash. That is what I would like to do.
I need to know if this inheritance is taxable and, if so, what that amount would be.
Please send all correspondence to me at the following address:

Thomas J. Brewer
Mail Box 72
Student Union Building
Seattle Pacific College
Seattle, Wash. 98119

Respectfully,
Tomas J. Brewer

Brewer couldn't think of anything else to say. He checked carefully for punctuation and misspelled words. Everything was proper.
"Thanks again," he said.
The editor grunted and glared suspiciously as Brewer walked out the door.
Brewer found an out-of-the-way table in the SUB coffee shop. There, he filled out the forms Addelton had sent. They turned out to be surprisingly straight-forward and simple.
He addressed an envelope to Addelton, put the forms and his letter in it and pasted on two stamps – one might not be enough

and he wanted to be certain. Then he went back to the basement, opened locker 428, put the rest of Addelton's documents in it and locked them up. He looked at the clock. Chapel would begin in ten minutes. He would not skip it this time. From now on, he would not make waves in the world that hovered around him. He would not attract attention. He would not stand out in a crowd. He would do nothing to upset anyone or anything until he heard from J.P. Addelton, Attorney at Law.

As he left for chapel, Brewer was the very picture of a proper SPC student; an appropriately nondescript little conformist who just happened to drop a letter in the mail box.

For the first time in his matriculation at Seattle Pacific College, Brewer found chapel helpful. The banality of the ritual – standing for the opening hymn (always some tome from the nineteenth century), bowing one's head for the opening prayer (always something involving being a Committed Christian) – Brewer found it all perversely soothing in its predictability.

The speaker was a missionary recently returned from Surinam. He told the usual stories about converting the quaint, simple-minded natives and then finished with the usual pitch for money ("One dollar will buy a hungry child milk for a week. . .") Brewer had heard it all before, many times, many versions. It was all part of the game, all part of the comforting daily institutional routine. As long as that routine rolled along, soothing, unchanging, benumbing, no one would notice him. No one would have a clue what he was up to. He would be safe.

Chapter 15

He was late.

He often was late, but this time it aggravated Elizabeth Fleming. One too many nights watching the hands of the clock, one too many nights putting his dinner in the refrigerator, one too many nights eating alone.

He never called. He was too important for that – and she was too unimportant for it to cross his mind. At least that's the way it seemed to Elizabeth Fleming as she thumbed through the newspaper on the kitchen table and wondered if this was how she was destined to spend the limited time she had left on this earth.

How had it come to this? She certainly didn't plan it. But she had done little to prevent it either, and her shame at being weak gnawed at her.

Finally, she heard the front doorknob turn.

"Hey, Betts, I'm home!"

He strode across the room and embraced her. He cupped his hand, pressed the tips of his fingers into the cleavage of her buttocks and ran them up and down, the way he liked and she hated. Then he gave her ass a squeeze, a hard one, painful, and leaned back and smiled.

Usually, she managed a smile in return. It was expected of her. But not tonight. He didn't notice.

"What's for dinner?" he said jauntily.

"It's in the fridge."

"Great!"

He bounced across the room, took the plate from the refrigerator and popped it in the oven. The oven was already heated. He set the timer and then he stood, tapping his foot as if he was listening to music. He smiled, but his eyes were those of a cobra perusing its prey.

It was often thus. But for some reason on this night she found his oh-so-smug arrogance too much to bear.

She looked down at his foot tapping on the linoleum floor.

"Please stop that," she said. She wanted to shout it, but it came out timidly, like an apology.

Layton looked confused. He gave his head a quick shake as if he hadn't heard her correctly.

"What?'

"Your foot. Please stop tapping it like that."

He chuckled as if she had just told a joke.

"Sure, whatever you say." Then he started drumming his fingers on the counter. His smirk remained unchanged.

"I spent an hour fixing you dinner," she said. "I've been waiting for you to come home for two hours." She wanted to say more. She wanted to shout, to rant at him, to rip off her apron and throw it on the floor in righteous rage. But the words didn't come. And she wasn't wearing an apron. It all made her feel impotent and silly; a squirming tangle of emotions that choked her thoughts and made her hate herself all the more.

He was looking at her quizzically, as if studying some charming diversion. She searched for words. He continued to smile. For a moment, she thought she might cry. Finally, she said, "I'd like you to listen to me."

"Hey, that's what I'm here for. I'm all ears."

"It's just that you never call. It's just that. . ." she stopped. Again words failed her. Again she felt like a fool.

"If it's because I was late tonight, hey, I'm sorry," he said. "The president wanted to see me. You know how it goes."

"It's not that. It's just. . . it's just. . ."

The timer to the oven went off, abrading the air with a buzz saw squawk. It shattered Elizabeth's train of thought. She tried to get past Layton to turn it off, but he wouldn't move. She twisted and squeezed until she finally got a hand on the knob that controlled the timer's hands. Frantically, she turned the knob until the racket stopped.

She took some deep breaths and tried again, but again her voice came out weak and reedy: "It's that it's just, I mean. . . I'm supposed to be the dean's wife, to make you look good, to advance your career and all that. It's like I'm an accessory. . ."

"Oh, come on," he said. "You know I care about you."

Actually, she knew nothing of the kind. He cared about the impression she made on others, others he wanted to impress. And he cared about her body - god, how she was coming to detest it - and he cared about having a neat home and meals cooked for him and all the rest. But her? Her instincts told her he did not. He could not. He wasn't made that way. But instincts were unreliable. Instincts were the prevue of the empty-headed and the childish, worthy only of ridicule - and he was the master of ridicule, the kind that went straight through you and lodged in your spine and stayed there. . .

"So you are unhappy," he said.

"Yes."

"But you can't say why."

She started to stammer a response, but he was ahead of her.

"Sounds to me like your real problem is yourself," he said. It was one of those statements that it is impossible to respond to effectively, one of the best ones. This was his territory. He was the smooth talker, the master of all moments.

She said the first thing that came into her mind.

"What am I to you?"

"What am I to *you?*" he said, his smile growing even more superior. He was enjoying himself.

Elizabeth could feel the veins at her temples throb.

"Please, just answer my question," she said. It came out in a near whisper, flat and totally without power.

"You are my wife until death do us part. I assumed you knew that. You were there when we took the vows."

"What if those vows were a mistake?" she said. Funny how easy it was to say. On one hand, it was an awful thing to admit out loud. On the other, a much more important other, she had known it was the truth for a long time.

Layton seemed taken aback. He had never heard her speak with resolve. He regained his composure quickly.

"A vow is a vow," he said with a self-righteous flourish. "It's in the Bible. . ."

"I know, I know. But so are a lot of things. . ."

"Now wait a minute, don't start taking scripture out of context," Layton said.

"I don't think you care about me as a person," Elizabeth said. "I don't think you know me as a person. . ."

The buzzer from the oven squawked again. Again Elizabeth squeezed past him and fumbled with the dial, her fingers slippery with sweat, her eyes unable to focus.

"Live with someone nine years and not know her?" he said "Come on. You're being ridiculous. I know you better than you know yourself."

Know you better than you know yourself? What in the world did that mean? Well, nothing, actually. It was just his way of turning the conversation back on her yet again. He was A Winner and she was not. More anger rose in her, anger at herself for not being more capable, for not standing up for herself, for not. . .

"Actions speak louder than words," she said weakly.

"Avoid clichés like the plague."

"Okay, okay. But, I mean, it's like. . ."

"So, you just want me to stand here and listen to whatever you have to say, no matter how pointless it is, and never respond?" he said.

She tried again. "I don't like it when you belittle me and think it's funny. I don't like it when you touch me. . ."

"Ah, the heart of the matter. You're frigid and you blame me for it."

The buzzer started rasping again. Its abrasive wail rendered Elizabeth speechless. This time, for some arcane mechanical reason, it turned itself off after a few seconds.

Layton strode across the room and embraced her.

"I love ya, baby," he said.

What? "I love ya, baby?" Like some Vaseline-haired moron in a B-grade private eye movie? "I love ya, baby?" That was supposed to solve everything?

He bent his head to kiss her.

"No," she murmured and tried to push him away. He didn't move. She felt feeble and alone.

"I like it when you get mad," he purred, bending his head again.

"I said no!" She braced her legs and gave him another push, as hard as she could. He stumbled away.

No one had ever said no to Layton Fleming like that. For a moment, his eyes went wide with surprise. Then he caught himself and they returned to their usual arrogance. But his mouth remained open.

"I'm going to bed," he said. "Looks to me like you've got a problem."

"I'm going to stay up for a while."

He nodded vaguely, as if she wasn't quite there. Then he turned and headed for the stairs. The timer to the oven buzzed again, mournfully.

Chapter 16

When Marilyn arrived at the white, two-story house on Columbine Avenue, the house with the pristine picket fences, arched trellises and meticulously-tended rose gardens, she felt relief flow over her, enfolding her in warmth and comfort. The knot twisting in her chest since finals unclenched. The scowl on her face relaxed.

Well, you made it through your first quarter of college, she thought. No honors, no Dean's List, no gold stars of any kind, not even close. So you aren't returning home in the glory that was expected of you. But you did survive, and considering how trying it had been, that's an achievement. Home looked very good indeed.

Her mother apparently had not heard the cab arrive because she was not at the door. All the better, Marilyn thought. The surprise will be fun. But when she opened the door, no one came. She put her bags down and stood alone in the hallway, waiting for some sign, listening carefully. After a few moments, she heard a sniff from the living room.

Her mother was seated on the big flowered couch she favored. Marilyn smiled.

"Hi, mom."

Her mother looked up but did not speak. Puzzled, Marilyn walked closer. Her mother's face was gaunt and slack, her eyes red from crying.

"Mom?"

Her mother stared at her blankly.

"Mom?" Marilyn said again. What in the world was going on?

"Have a chair, honey," her mother said.

Something was wrong. How bad, Marilyn wasn't sure . . . yes she was sure. It was bad.

"Marilyn, I, I . . ." her mother caught her breath and tried again. "I'll just tell you straight out. Your father's business has been going downhill for years. He hid it by taking out loans on everything, even the house. I didn't know. Last week, he filed for bankruptcy. Everything's gone. We're ruined. We've, we've . . ."

Her mother put her head back and inhaled a long sob. She caught her breath and continued.

"We've lost the house, we've lost everything. Our friends won't talk to us anymore."

For a moment, Marilyn thought she hadn't heard her mother correctly. Her hands went cold and numb. Her eyes blurred. Her father? The Chamber of Commerce's Man of the Year for 1959? The two-term city councilman? The man for whom success came so smoothly, so effortlessly? He had always seemed like a prince to her, her rock, the handsome, supremely confident master of all he surveyed.

Marilyn looked at her mother again. She had been all the things a rich society matron should be; president of the Municipal League, chair of all the right committees. Her poise was flawless, her taste impeccable.

That was not the woman staring back at Marilyn now. Instead she saw a woman with exhausted, empty eyes, a shrunken figure, small and lost.

"If you get a job, maybe you can continue at Wenatchee Valley JC," her mother said. Then her voice trailed off and her chin dropped to her chest. "I'm sorry, honey, I'm so sorry . . ."

Marilyn reached out and touched her mother's hand. What was she supposed to do? Ask about the details? Her mother had told her the details, at least the ones that mattered. What about the future? Ten minutes ago, she had been headed for a career in business or teaching or maybe even law if she could bring her grades up a little. Now? *Wenatchee Valley JC?* A two-year degree, if she was lucky, and then what? The rest of her life as a receptionist in an insurance office, with its cheap linoleum floors and cheap, loud men? A checker at the downtown Pay 'N Save, maybe marry the assistant manager and join the legion of women with sallow faces and varicose veins living out their shrieking desperation in two-bedroom cracker boxes with brown lawns?

Marilyn shuddered. She couldn't help it.

"Is he okay?" she said.

"What?" her mother seemed confused. "Oh. Yes . . . I mean . . . He . . ." She stopped for a moment to calm herself. "He's in his study."

Her father was looking out the widow, his back to her. The room was a retreat of elegance and understated good taste; walnut paneling, fox hunting prints, shelves of leather-bound books, a green lawyer's lamp on the expansive desk. Now it seemed all wrong, like a bad film print, scratchy and out of sync.

"Daddy. . ."

"I'm sorry," her father said without turning around.

"No need," Marilyn said. "I'll get by," Good god, what a dumb thing to say. Get by how? Doing what?

Her father turned his leather chair so he was facing her. He was, as always, calm, collected, elegant. Only the dark circles under his eyes gave him away.

"How was school?" he said.

"Fine. I mean, I did okay. Well, I survived."

He smiled slightly. It didn't last.

"I'll keep you there as long as I can," he said. "To the end of the school year, maybe. . ." His voice trailed off in uncertainty. He closed his eyes briefly, as if to collect his thoughts, and sighed deeply. "I'm trying to salvage what I can but I'm not having much luck. I'm sorry, love. "

"Why. . ." Marilyn began.

"Why didn't I tell you and your mother sooner? I didn't want to let you down. I wanted you to have it better than I did." He shook his head resignedly. "After a certain point, things were headed where they were headed. Talking about it wouldn't have made any difference. I wanted you to be happy for as long as you could."

There was a certain logic to it, Marilyn thought. Be shocked now, be shocked later. The shock is the same. Later is better.

"What will you do?" she said.

"I have no idea. I can probably get a job as an estimator somewhere, maybe even a project manager, but that's unlikely. The word is out on me. We'll have to move. My friends; now they're my creditors. Most of them won't get their money back."

"Did you break any laws?" Marilyn couldn't believe the words came out of her mouth.

Her father's face took on a hard expression. There was a long pause.

"I don't think so. I'm not sure." His voice flat, almost a monotone. "But I did tell a lot of lies, mostly to myself. I was so wrapped up in looking the part I came to believe that's what that mattered."

Marilyn looked at her father carefully. Something had left him, a vibrance, a life force, and it was not coming back.

There was a plaque on the wall, "World's Best Dad." She had made it in the third grade, walking home with it proudly, watching his eyes light up when she gave it to him, luxuriating in his hug. He was the man who took her sledding on the big hills west of town, the man who taught her to swim and ride a bike, the man who read her all the Wizard of Oz books and all the Raggedy Ann books. He had pushed her on swings and tucked her into bed every night and never missed any of her school plays or awards ceremonies, not one

She had loved him as only a little girl can love her daddy. But love can be taken from you. Joy can be taken from you. All things can be taken from you.

Marilyn Pennell wanted to cry, but she did not, she would not.

****

Marilyn spent the next two weeks disconnected from the world.

She was disconnected from her parents. They did their best to act normally. They went to the woods outside of town, cut down a tree, decorated it with the usual fanfare and invited her mother's brother and his family over for Christmas breakfast and gift-opening.

Their extended family did not know of their financial ruin and the Christmas celebration seemed perfectly conventional – until Marilyn reminded herself that whatever gifts her parents gave they bought with credit cards they would never pay off, and that their holiday good cheer was nothing more than a act; a convincing act (they'd had a lot of practice), but thin and grotesque. They were floating along on a filmy layer of wit and charm, fragile and hallucinatory, over a crater of lies and invention, creating reality as they went – except it wasn't real. Marilyn remained silent, considered it all and, in the end, drew no lasting conclusions. What was was, be it good, bad or otherwise.

"You seem awfully subdued," her aunt Kathy said and Marilyn answered that she was just a little tired out from finals, which as true enough and, more importantly, managed to change the subject.

When the festivities were over, Marilyn and her mother cleaned up the ribbon and wrapping paper on the floor, going through the motions silently, both aware of the fiction they had just played out. So this is what togetherness means, Marilyn thought: Keeping each other's secrets, covering each other's lies. Not exactly the sort of thing you see on Father Knows Best.

Once the cleanup was done, her parents disappeared; her mother to her bedroom - to weep, presumably - her father to his study.

Marilyn wandered the house for a while, hoping that familiar sights and sounds and smells would prompt memories of happier times. They did not. To her, the most evocative symbol of her home was the swimming pool. It had indeed brought the family happiness - and no small of amount of status - and was the scene of many wonderful childhood memories. With no money left to run the pumps and lights, it lay empty and dirty, with dried leaves littering the bottom, the sort of thing you see at deserted cheap motels. So ended her past.

Marilyn spent the next few days driving around town. The kids still cruised Wenatchee Avenue from the North Bridge to Stevens Street, then over to Chelan Avenue, past Memorial Park, where leather-jacketed greasers leaned against chromed and candy-colored rods, following the prowling steel with practiced eyes, studying, hunting. A car next to her beeped its horn and Marilyn turned to see a boy - not a young man, a boy - smiling at her with a hopeful expression. She sped away. At age 18, you are too old for this? she thought. And the answer was yes. She felt very alone.

She looked up some old friends. Dorrie Lehman, her friend since kindergarten, was home from Washington State University where, it seemed, the academics were every bit as tough as SPC. Dorrie doubted she would finish her freshman year. She could probably get a job as a bookkeeper at her dad's car lot, so all was not lost. But she had hoped to become a veterinarian.

Jeff Grinnell, Marilyn's lab partner in chemistry class, came from a poor family and couldn't afford college. So he waited around town until he got drafted. Now he was in Georgia, learning the intricacies of the M-60 machine gun. Jerry Osborne had been drafted, too. He and Marilyn used to walk to elementary school together. He liked to pet the dogs they met along the way.

Laura Houck had gotten pregnant and was living at home. Steve Chaffee was the father, apparently. Steve played baseball and, as Marilyn remembered him, always smiled. Now he pumped gas on the west side of town.

And so it went. The class of '64 seemed destined not for greatness promised in graduation speeches, but for disappointment; society's cannon fodder. It looked like Marilyn might become another of them, a lost statistic, a potential stillborn. So ended their future.

The present? If her father's predictions could be trusted – a big if – Marilyn might make it to the end of the school year. That was something to hold on to. A summer job might see her through another year, but a summer job doing what? She had spent high school taking college prep courses. She could type, but nothing like the girls who had taken secretarial classes. She knew nothing of accounting, she couldn't drive a stick shift and had never made a sale in her life. People a lot less intelligent than her did get jobs of one kind or another, of course, but how? She had never applied for one.

Her parents, to their credit, were trying to make the best of things, at least for her sake. Her mother regained her cheer, or the appearance of it, her father regained his confidence, or the appearance of it. No complaining, no bitterness. They never talked their financial ruin, and that was good. Instead, it was the usual dinner table chit chat about family and the weather and current events. They asked Marilyn about college and she told them. It was hard, the food was something the Army would throw out and her roommate was a pathetic nitwit. They gaped with momentary disbelief at their daughter's brutal honesty. Four months ago, she never would have said such things. Which brought up the second half of her answer: She was learning a lot. She was learning about a world of thought and experience far beyond her own, of ideas she had never heard and of answers to questions she had never thought to ask. She was learning to think critically. Yes, it was hard. But it was worth it.

Boys? her mother asked. For a moment, she could not speak. She could think only of a tall, lean figure parting the silver mist of a cold September morning, graceful and clean; fearless. Oh, god. . . She shook the thought from her mind. But the ache remained.

Chapter 17

Brewer finished his last final, for his American history class, at 3:30 p.m. on a Thursday. As he walked across campus toward the bus stop, he felt a weight being lifted from him. He had survived his first quarter. Now he knew he had the intelligence to succeed in college. The rest would be a matter of perseverance. Now he knew he had that, too. The self-doubt that had nagged him most of his life was gradually disappearing. Brewer wondered what would take its place.

Brewer caught the bus to downtown and, as he did every day, he waited by the Bon Marche on Third Avenue and Stewart Street for the bus home. He had always found the wait tedious and the place dreary. Worn-down, morose people huddled in heavy coats under awnings or in doorways, finding what shelter they could from the rain and the grit and the constant, ear-pounding racket of downtown traffic. Occasionally a bum or a loony or some greasy-haired punks would wander by, but for the most part the scene was a gray watercolor of the fatigued and the nameless, resigned to jobs they didn't like, waiting for a grimy bus ride to homes and families that had proven disappointments.

On this night, however, it seemed different. Brewer noticed the street lights and neon signs reflected on the wet pavement in shifting, glowing patterns and, although it had been playing for some days now, he heard, for the first time, Christmas carols rolling warmly from the stores.

He walked down to Pine Street. The Bon Marche's corner window display featured every kind of toy imaginable, set on tiers and jammed in corners and piled in stacks and arranged on the floor in gay patterns: Dolls and toy trucks and paint sets and stuffed animals and Lincoln Logs, sleds and footballs and miniature tea sets and mechanical devices that blinked lights and rang bells, toy soldiers and Mr. Potato Head and Etch-a-Sketches and silvery jet planes. And on and on, a cosmos of childhood fantasy, a glowing constellation of imagination and innocence and joy.

Brewer particularly liked the Aerial Daredevil. The Aerial Daredevil was a little toy man on a unicycle. He held a long horizontal pole with weights at each end. The unicycle's wheel was grooved. It fit on a string stretched between two small towers. One of the towers had an electric motor that raised and lowered the string. When the pole went up, the string went up and the little unicyclist peddled across the tight rope, his tiny legs pumping away diligently. When it went down, he went back the other way. Up and down it went, back and forth he went, hour after hour, day after day, always conscientious, always fun. Brewer envisioned the smile on a child's face as he watched it. He envisioned the child giving the Aerial Daredevil a name, assigning life to this little plastic man.

Imagination, such a wondrous thing. Brewer scanned the bus stop again. The street, the rain, the people; it all may not have been beautiful, but it was not ugly, either. Life was being lived there and it could be more than something one merely endured. It could be a child's imaginings.

But then that child would have to grow up. Did wonder cease with adulthood? Perhaps it did, Brewer thought, or perhaps you finish your first quarter of college and find that you are smarter than you thought you were, that you can become more than you are.

He had grown. The thought settled in him. It created no great epiphany, no magic moment, but he felt the truth of it; a deep, certain truth.

His bus came. The ride home was the ride home; monochromatic and featureless in the dim, greenish glow of the bus's fluorescent lights. Usually, Brewer slept through it, or at least tried to. But not tonight. A calm had come over him. The petty irritations of the world no longer had the hold on him they once did.

When he got home, he found that his parents had put up the Christmas tree. It was a plastic tree. The family used to buy real trees, with much ritual and debate and comparisons to trees from past years. Then, when Tom and Orrin hit their teen years, their parents decided it wasn't worth the trouble.

"I think it's delightful," his mother said of the artificial tree, which she bought on a close-out sale at K Mart. "It looks every bit as good as a real one and it will last year after year."

Brewer protested. It looked nothing like a real one, and from what he could see, it wasn't worth keeping five minutes.

"Then you go out and cut one yourself, mister," his father said. "And haul it home and trim it and set it up. Then take it down and haul it off to the dump. And while you're at it, spend ten hours a day breaking your back so your family can have food on the table. See how well you like that!"

That was five years ago. Ever since, Christmas spirit had been distinctly lacking in the Brewer abode. They still went through the motions of lights and gift-giving and the like, but whatever substance had been behind it was long since forgotten.

As with everything involving his family, Brewer resigned himself to it. Then a department store window full of toys had transformed him back into a sense of wonder. He could not change his family, but he could be different than them. He would not live his life enduring second best simply because the best required too much effort.

That was the thought on his mind as passed the plastic tree on the way to his room.

"Dinner in a half hour," his mother said in the flat, mechanical voice she had been using with him ever since the argument over the thirty thousand dollars. His father hadn't talked to him at all, except to order him to take out the garbage and sweep the garage. Orrin was rarely home and when he was, never came out of his room except to eat.

Brewer closed the door to his room, set down his books and hung up his coat. Maybe Orrin was on to something, he thought. When Brewer stayed in his room, they didn't bother him. It was lonely, to be sure, even a little depressing, but was better than being constantly glowered at and wheedled.

He thought about a dusty framed photograph on a shelf in the living room. It showed the Brewer family, circa 1951: A handsome young couple proudly holding their two small sons. Everyone was smiling. And now we've come to this, Brewer thought. How do such things happen?

Did his parents love him? They had loved him when he was small child. But then, it is easy to express love to a small child. The older you become, the less adorable you become. You become a human being, rather than a pet.

Jesus, listen to yourself, Brewer thought. Maybe you are completely off track. Maybe you are wrong and they are right.

Right about what?

The money? Well, it doesn't matter who is right or wrong, you are not giving up that money. It is yours. It is your freedom. Brewer had spent his life at the mercy of other people's meddling, other people's control. Oh, to be free of it. Money bought freedom. Nothing else did, that was for certain; not in this place, not in this century.

Were his parents right in forcing him to go to SPC? The place was proving a mixed bag, not all of it bad. It was small. You could meet people. The classes, at least the ones he'd had, were good. But it was pious and piety was weird. It's queer how angry people get, and how quickly, when you in any way challenge their piety, Brewer thought. It doesn't matter whether you mean to or not.

About life in general? His parents weren't bad people. They weren't drunks. They weren't criminals. They paid their bills. They paid their taxes. The family had enough to eat and the roof didn't leak. And, as they reminded him, frequently, they were paying for his college education.

But there was a darkness about them. His father constantly complained about his job, but he never tried to find another one. His mother had fears: Fears of electric fans (a blade might break off and hit you in the eye), fears of folding chairs (she had once heard that a child had gotten tangled up in one and suffocated), fears of space satellites (the Russians could use them to shoot ray guns at us), fears of almost anything, mostly imagined, that might threaten her security. They kept her in a continual state of worry. But that's all she ever did: Worry. She never confronted her fears or tried to do anything about them. She clung to them. They defined her.

Brewer's parents grew up in the Great Depression and came of age in the Second World War. It seemed to Brewer that for some people the Great Depression and the Second World War were the best things that ever happened to them. It gave them something to blame their own weaknesses and failures on. Any number of things in your life couldn't be your fault if, in some way, even distantly, they could be related to the Great Depression or the Second World

War. Or so the argument seemed to go. Brewer didn't buy it. But he had no worthwhile response to it, either.

Nor did he have a response to the second half of the syndrome: You kids today don't know what tough is. It was a proclamation of status Brewer had heard, regularly, throughout his childhood. Its proponents took great pride in their history of suffering, but it also made them angry and resentful; dark.

It seemed to vent itself in an especially virulent contempt of all things young. Was there any other time in American history when young people's clothing, their hair, their music, their dance, their vernacular, seemingly everything they said or did, was so roundly despised? The adult world even seemed to resent their very presence. When Brewer was in elementary school, Seattle had a curfew. Anyone under eighteen on the street after 10 p.m. was subject to arrest. The Seattle cops must have loved that, Brewer thought; a license to roust anyone they didn't like, and they most assuredly did not like teenagers.

How did it all explain his parents, or, more to the point, their insistence that he attend SPC and give them his thirty thousand dollars? The only answer Brewer could come up with was that they simply assumed it was their god-given right to do to him whatever they pleased. Whether or not it made any sense was not a significant factor. Brewer's opinion was not a factor at all.

Good god, you're whining, Brewer thought. My Parents Don't Understand Me. Boo-hoo. What a load. But, on the other hand, it must be admitted that his relationship with them was more than a little strained these days. He did not understand it. It simply was the way it was.

Brewer closed his eyes and took a deep breath to clear his mind. He decided to ponder some good things for a while. He was doing well in school. He was about to come into a lot of money. But the night with Marilyn still haunted him.

Then his mother called that dinner was ready.

Brewer hoped they would get through dinner without a scene. A scene usually involved one of two things. Number One: Brewer's father would start haranguing Orrin to quit being so goddamned lazy and get a job. Then Orrin would leave, his dinner uneaten.

Or Number Two: His mother would start talking about The Girls, waxing delightedly about the latest endearing thing one of them had said or done, extolling the incomparable wonder of their adorability. From there, she would carefully edge toward the subject of the thirty thousand dollars and how delighted The Girls would be when they received their share.

"I'll bet their little faces will just shine!" his mother would say - or she would try to say. Brewer would get up from is chair at the first mention of it and be in his room, with the door tightly closed, before she was in mid-sentence. His dinner would remain at the table, uneaten.

As it turned out, this particular dinner did not feature either Number One or Number Two. The Brewers were silent, the only noises the clack of tongs on the bowl full of chopped iceberg lettuce that served as salad and the frustrated sawing of dull knives on gristly cube steaks. Sharp knives made Brewer's mother nervous. The rank smell of overcooked canned green beans permeated the room.

Then Orrin said, "I think I got a job."

His father's fork froze in mid air. His mother's eyes widened in disbelief.

They waited for Orrin to expand on his announcement. But Orrin continued to eat, his head down, as always, his hand pushing green beans onto his fork. Finally, between mouthfuls, he said, "Bob Gilmore's uncle owns a tire shop. He got me a job there."

His mother smiled broadly, as if Orrin had announced he had received an acceptance letter from MIT.

"Why that's just wonderful, dear," she gushed. "And what will they have you doing at this, um, tire shop?"

"I dunno," Orrin mumbled. "Putting tires on cars, I guess."

"Sounds like a real challenge," his father said sarcastically, taking advantage of the opportunity to remind Orrin what a disappointment he was.

"Aw, quit buggin' me," Orrin muttered. He kept on eating.

"Where is the shop?" his mother said, trying to keep the conversation moving.

"In Ballard someplace," Orrin said. "He gave me the address."

He pulled a crumpled piece of paper from his pocket.

"Ballard. Well, isn't that nice. Maybe you'll be able to see the water from there," his mother said.

"Yeah, maybe. I start Monday. We got any more green beans?"

Orrin continued to eat mechanically, his head down, his face expressionless. It was clear he had nothing more to say.

"Well, I have some good news, too," his mother said, beaming even more widely than before. "The Nicklemans have invited us all up to Mount Vernon for Christmas dinner!"

The Nicklemans were The Girls' family. Brewer thought this might happen - it had happened before - but he still winced. No one noticed.

"And your aunt Edna tells me that little Amanda is learning to play the piano," his mother said. "I guess she can just make that keyboard sing!"

Amanda was a vacant-eyed child prone to tripping on carpets and knocking lamps off tables. Brewer doubted she could touch a keyboard without breaking it. No matter. The assembled would be treated to an evening of Amanda fumbling and pounding while Brewer's mother and aunt looked on rapturously and everyone else tried to find something, anything, to divert their senses. There would be no question of taking a walk or watching TV. Christmas was Family Time.

Another memorable Yuletide, Brewer mused. He would take a book. Since he was in college now, he had to study a great deal. The family actually respected that, to a degree. The fact that fall quarter was over and winter quarter didn't start for another week probably wouldn't occur to them. Brewer was far from the center of attention, and over the years he had learned to take advantage of it by rendering himself invisible at family gatherings. With a book and a little luck, he could blend into the wallpaper.

****

The trip to Mount Vernon was tedious and predictable. The long stretch out of Seattle crept for miles through nondescript scrub, broken by an occasional glimpse of moldering post-war pre fabs peeping through the slash.

A few miles further they came to Everett - or, more accurately, Everett came to them. Everett stank. You knew you were approaching it from ten miles out and when you got there, the rotten eggs/swamp scum stench of the paper mills overwhelmed all other senses.

"Well, here we are in Ever-rat," Brewer's father would say. It was as succinct a description of Everett as any.

After Everett were the polluted marshes and sewage lagoons at the mouth of the Snohomish River and, beyond that, rolling hills that eventually leveled out to farmland; dead flat and utterly featureless save for the occasional collapsing barn or, at one place, a crop duster someone parked near the road twenty years before and then abandoned. There it stood, year after year, the fabric on its wings rotting away panel by panel, its tires flat, then hubs, then nonexistent as the landing gear inexorably sunk deeper and deeper into the soft earth. Rarely was pointless existence epitomized better.

On this particular day, Brewer didn't mind the drive. Its predictability gave him time to think without distractions. Christmas dinner with the Nicklemans would be an ordeal, but he was prepared. With a little luck, and careful attention to the flow of events, he could disappear with his book and be left alone.

Christmas morning had been pleasant enough. The Brewers had scrambled eggs, sausages, sweet rolls and orange juice. Per tradition, the orange juice came in tiny glasses and there were no refills. Brewer once asked why and his mother replied that she didn't want it to go to waste. Wasteful orange juice usage? Brewer never could figure that one out.

Then came the gifts. Brewer had bought Orrin a blue Oxford cloth dress shirt and Orrin seemed genuinely grateful. Brewer bought his father a chrome cigarette case and his mother an art deco glass vase. They issued muttered monosyllabic grunts that passed for thank yous and shoved the gifts behind their chairs.

Brewer received a sweat shirt from Orrin, a tie tack from his father and three pairs of Argyle socks from his mother.

"The salesman told me they are the latest thing for boys your age," his mother said, while Brewer tried to think of inconspicuous ways to throw them away.

Oh well. If you don't have any expectations about such things, you won't be disappointed, Brewer thought. Now all he had to do was get through the rest of the day.

At Mount Vernon, the big Buick pulled off the freeway at Kincaid Street and labored its way up the long, curving road to Laventure Ridge. As they grew closer to the Nicklemans' house, Brewer felt his stomach tightening. Too late to do anything about it now. So no use worrying. But the knots drew tighter and tighter.

When they arrived at the Nicklemans', The Girls came hurtling out the front door, screeching and waving their arms like a gaggle of demented octopi. They jumped up and down, still screeching, next to the car's passenger side front door. Brewer's mother had to force it open to get out, accidentally knocking down little CeeCee in the process. CeeCee screamed as if she had just been bayoneted. When she realized no one could hear her above her sisters, she promptly stopped.

Eventually, the Brewers managed to make it to the front porch, where they were greeted by Uncle Walt. Uncle Walt owned a combination real estate office and insurance agency and he took great pride in his role as the foundation of Western civilization.

"Move the merchandise. Yessir! That's what makes the world go 'round. Yessir!" Uncle Walt was fond of saying.

He had other aphorisms. About the choking fumes that wafted up from the asphalt plant in the Skagit Valley: "Smells like money, to me." About the Black people who were consigned to rotting shacks on the west side of town, on a flood plain: "Nobody made 'em move here. If they just gave up their dice games and purple Cadillacs. . ." About building safety inspections, zoning laws, fire codes and the like: "It's gettin' so a man can't make an honest buck anymore. Government's tryin' to run our lives. Pretty soon they'll be tellin' you who can marry."

Uncle Walt's universe consisted of selling houses at inflated prices to families who couldn't afford them and scaring timid souls into buying insurance policies so indecipherable that the only people who understood them were the adjusters who turned down claims.

He rarely talked about current events because he didn't follow them. They were a foregone conclusion anyway.

"The government is infested with Jews and reds. It's a fact, look it up."

The last book Uncle Walt had read - he had been forced to read in high school - was The Grapes of Wrath.

"Steinbeck was a goddamned red! We had Okies work the fields up here. We made sure they kept their noses clean. Lucky to have jobs and they knew it!"

Truer to the essence of the American ethos, in Uncle Walt's opinion, was his favorite TV show, Petticoat Junction.

There was a tangle at the Nicklemans' front door as The Girls tried to go through all at once. Then they got in a fight over it. Finally, everyone managed to squeeze by, although it was unclear just how they did it. CeeCee was yowling about some terrible injury she had incurred and Amanda and Joanie were pawing at Brewer's mother like howler monkeys. She nearly fell down. Aunt Edna stuck her head out of the kitchen, scowling and glaring. Once she ascertained the racket was The Girls being The Girls, her head retracted, turtle-like, and she returned to banging pots and pans with manic ferocity.

Brewer watched it all with the cold squint of a combat veteran. 'Twas ever thus at the Nicklemans, and thus it ever would be.

Out in the living room, Brewer's mother finally made it to the couch, picked The Girls off her like cats whose claws got stuck on her coat and sat down. She was beaming, nearly radiant in her joy.

"Now, guess what Santa left at our house, this morning?" she said cloyingly.

"WHAAAAT?!!" The Girls screeched like banshees on caffeine, puncturing nearby eardrums.

"Welllll, " Brewer's mother grinned, stretching out the moment. The Girls' jaws were slack, their eyes wide and unblinking with anticipation.

"He left some presents. . . for . . . some. . . very. . . special. . . girls!"

The Girls squealed, The Girls screeched, The Girls howled. The Girls jumped up and down. The Girls, at least CeeCee, fell on the floor with a thud. Although Brewer had observed it all a number of times before, he was morbidly fascinated. He wondered when they would start foaming at the mouth and go into conniptions.

Alas, they did not. Instead, they managed to regain their composure, somewhat, as Brewer's mother resumed her ritual.

Moving ever so slowly, drawing out her words ever so carefully, she reached in the bag.

"Oh, what have we here?" she said, rummaging around, while exchanging knowing looks with her worshipers.

Lovingly, overacting with dewy-eyed affection, she carefully pulled the gift-wrapped box from the bag and held it out.

"It looks . . . like. . . a. . . present. . . forrrrr. . . Amanda!"

Amanda pounced forward, wrenched the box free with both hands and began tearing it apart like a refugee setting upon her first rice ration in two weeks.

Brewer's mother repeated the process with the other two girls who, like Amanda, attacked the packages in feral delirium, each more savage than the other, each possessed in her lust for lucre.

Actually, it was not that big a transition from their normal demeanors, Brewer mused. He turned away and found himself face to face with Uncle Walt.

"So Tom, hear you're a big college man these days," Uncle Walt exclaimed. Uncle Walt generally did not wait for people to respond to his proclamations so before Brewer could say anything, Uncle Walt announced, "I came up in the school of hard knocks. And look at me now!"

I am looking, Brewer thought. I can only wonder why.

"So what are you studying?" Uncle Walt said.

"I'm just doing my freshman requirements," Brewer said, searching for a way to step around Uncle Walt. There wasn't one.

"Like what?" Uncle Walt demanded.

"Well, I'm taking a physics course. . ."

"I remember that. Ol' Newton got hit by an apple. What's that got to do with the price of tea in China?"

". . .and an English course," Brewer said, trying to retain his composure, "and a course in early American history. . ."

"History?" Uncle Walt said in mock astonishment. "Big demand for historians, is there? Lotsa companies have history departments? Maybe I should hire a historian to tell me how Abe Lincoln went about selling houses. Ha!"

Uncle Walt laughed loudly, looking around to see if anyone else heard his brilliant observation.

When caught unawares by bad-mannered louts, Brewer always did the same thing. He froze. Later, he would think of all the pithy things he could have said, but at the moment of boorishness, he froze. It made him feel like a stock comic foil straight from Central Casting.

So it was now. Did Uncle Walt enjoy tormenting him? Or did he not know any better? Or did he simply not care? Most likely some of all three, Brewer thought. Uncle Walt was so used to blithering his brainless small-town conceit that it never occurred to him it might be insulting.

Brewer searched for a response, something that would catch Uncle Walt off-guard and leave him speechless. He considered Fuck you, you illiterate hick, but decided it probably would not play well at Christmas dinner. He remembered seeing a movie of Noel Coward's play, Blithe Spirit. In it, everyone smoked cigarettes in long holders and had incredibly witty responses to almost everything. What would they say at a time like this? Well, characters in Noel Coward stories did not live in the world of Uncle Walts, did they? And Mr. Coward sweated countless hours at a typewriter to make them sound so effortlessly suave. Razor wit was a myth.

So Brewer stood there like an ox waiting for the sledge hammer. Uncle Walt was perusing the room for acclamation at his wit. Apparently, none was forthcoming, so he wandered off.

Just then, Amanda and Joanie got in a fight - Joanie had dared to touch the gift wrapping from Amanda's present - and, as always, they expended most of their anger in the form of highly amplified sound waves. Aunt Edna's head popped out of the kitchen again, this time red with rage.

"Tom, what are you doing to those girls?!" Aunt Edna demanded.

"Nothing. They're in the other room," Brewer said.

Aunt Edna continued to glower at him. Clearly, he was lying. All boys lied. All men lied. The entire male gender was inherently brutish and cruel; drooling and lecherous and not to be trusted and Aunt Edna was duty bound to remind them of it ~ frequently. She glowered at Brewer a bit more to make it stick and then went back to pounding on the cookware in her scullery.

Brewer headed for the back door. Outside, he found Orrin smoking a cigarette.

"Thanks for the shirt," Orrin said.

"You're welcome."

"I'm going to start dressing better," Orrin said. "I want to square myself away."

Brewer was surprised, not just at the statement, but that Orrin actually said it. He never talked about himself.

"What brought this about?" Brewer said.

"The new job. Watching you."

"Watching me?" Brewer said.

"Yeah. If you can do it, I can do it. It's time," Orrin said.

"You mean go back to school?"

"Maybe," Orrin said. "Or maybe save my money and start my own business. I can repair cars. Or maybe I'll go in the Navy. They always need mechanics. I'm probably going to get drafted before long, anyway."

The brothers stood in silence for what seemed a long time. Then Orrin said, "Anyway, thanks for the shirt. It's a good shirt, the kind I need."

"DINNERRRR!!!"

It was Aunt Edna, shouting out the door. She was all of 18 inches away. Brewer and Orrin trooped in obediently.

Dinner was prime rib, cooked rare, which meant it was barely cooked at all, which suited Uncle Walt just fine. He liked to take a rib in both hands and chew on it like an ear of corn, with rivulets of semi-congealed gore dripping down the napkin he tucked under his chin. The more noise he could make gnawing, smacking his lips and licking his fingers, the better.

"I likes me the side meat," he grinned in his best Stepin Fetchit impression.

Joanie would not eat her peas and she and Aunt Edna got into a fight about it, with Joanie folding her arms across her chest and clamping her jaw shut. Aunt Edna glared at her – did Aunt Edna ever stop glaring? – and said things like, "You aren't leaving this table until you eat those peas, young lady." – which, of course, made Joanie all the more determined, which, eventually, made Aunt Edna say, "Walt, do something. She's being a monster again."

"Eat your peas." Uncle Walt mumbled thickly through a mouthful of greasy pulp. "There are kids starving in India."

Joanie was unimpressed.

Brewer's mother decided it was her moment to save the day. She took a huge forkful of peas and held it in front of her.

"Mmmmm, peas," she said, licking her lips. "I just lovvvve peas."

She shovelled the mushy mass into her mouth and chewed them with exaggerated jaw action.

"Mmmmm, yummy, yummy." She smacked her lips loudly for emphasis. "Joanie, you really should try some peas. Mmmmm."

Joanie continued to scowl defiantly.

I really can't blame her, Brewer thought. The peas were canned, overcooked and horrible. He suspected Edna had scavenged them from the back shelf of an Army surplus store.

Brewer's mother decided to change tactics.

"Don't you want to try just one little bite?" she said, moving a fork full of olive drab ball bearings toward Joanie's firmly pursed mouth. "Just a little? Oh, come on, just a little, for me? Just a little, hmmm? They're soooo good. Just a little, hmmm?"

Clearly, her tactics for selling Joanie on the efficacy of canned peas were falling short of their intended goal. She didn't care. She continued on in the same vein for another twenty minutes. Thus was dominated the family's holiday bon mot.

Eventually, everyone else finished eating and Aunt Edna started clearing the plates. With no more peas to force on Joanie, who never ate a single one, Brewer's mother had to concede defeat – but only to a point. She continued to simper and purse her lips at Joanie as Aunt Edna served up the cake and ice cream. Joanie ate that. The issue became moot.

Cake and ice cream can be God's own blessing. The Girls were too busy stuffing their maws to make any other noise, so the adults actually had an opportunity to converse. Uncle Walt and Brewer's father talked about the state of the nation, agreeing that the country was being driven to wrack and ruin by some vaguely undefined Them, and that good, honest, working folk were powerless to do anything about it. Oh well, you can't fight City Hall. Whatta ya gonna do. Such was their conclusion about everything from parking meters to the workings of the universe.

Aunt Edna told them to stop. Politics were not appropriate conversation for the dinner table. Neither was religion, sports, business, movies or any number of other vulgarisms. Which left Aunt Edna and Brewer's mother free to talk family gossip, much of it twenty years old or older, but still worthy of many a rolling of eye and clucking of tongue.

Brewer ate. There was nothing to drink. Aunt Edna did not serve coffee after noon and, of course, soda caused diabetes. Aunt Edna knew it for a fact. A glass of water was a glass that had to be washed by Aunt Edna, who already had spent Christmas working her fingers to the bone which, right on cue, she informed everyone as they ate their cake and ice cream.

Oh well. Once dessert was done, Brewer could take his book and retreat to the basement for the rest of the evening.

When everyone was nearly finished, Brewer's mother said she had an announcement.

"Well, I have good news and bad news," she said. "The bad news is, cousin Lee died last month." The Nicklemans looked around as if to say, "Who?" Even Edna, who was the self-appointed authority on all things familial, was uncertain.

"I know we'll all miss him," Brewer's mother continued with appropriate gravitas. Then she promptly changed her tone. Bubbling with perkiness, she exclaimed. "The good news is, Uncle Lee was a very generous man!" She winked at The Girls teasingly.

No, Brewer thought. Not that. Not here. Why, god, why is she doing this to me? Wasn't once enough? Don't these people ever give up?

"He left Tom here thirty thousand dollars!" his mother said. "And Tom wants to share it with The Girls!"

Brewer looked over at his father, who sat with his arms folded across his chest, nodding his head and smiling a small, smug grin. I gotcha, kid, that grin said. Let's see you try to get out of this one, fancy college boy.

A wave of humiliation enveloped Brewer, paralyzing him. He actually felt a little dizzy. He tried to make his mind work, but he could not. He was naked and alone, at the mercy of all.

"What a guy, what a guy!" Uncle Walt was bellowing as he slapped Brewer on the back and shook his hand. "I tell ya, Tom, you're a peach! A peach!"

"We are so proud of our Tom," his mother crooned.

Aunt Edna did not smile. She did not congratulate. Her jaw was set, her eyes were fierce. Her face drew together in determined, flint-like creases.

"How much money are you giving them?" she said with brutal bluntness.

Brewer tried to speak, but he could only choke.

"We're still working that out," his mother purred in a parody of June Cleaver good will. "We have to actually receive the money first. . ."

"When will you get it?" Aunt Edna demanded.

". . . and we have to work out lawyer's fees and taxes," Brewer's mother continued without missing a beat. "But I can tell you, there are going to be three very happy little girls!"

The Girls were looking around as if they had just been deposited on a raft is the Waddell Sea.

"What are you planning, a trust fund?" Aunt Edna snapped.

"As I said, we have to work that out. . ." Brewer's mother said uncertainly.

"They're my girls," Aunt Edna said. "I know what's best for them. Sign the money over to me." She was thinking fast, too fast for Brewer's mother to keep up.

"When will you get the money?" she demanded again. "Next month? February? March?"

Brewer's head finally cleared. He knew what she was doing: Be hard, be selfish, be demanding, make other people so uncomfortable they didn't know what else to do and they will comply. It had worked for Edna as long as Brewer had known her. Uncle Walt, his mother, everyone; they all gave into her simply because she was nastier than they were. And she was utterly relentless. Everyone eventually backed down to Aunt Edna.

Then something else became clear to Brewer, something in Edna's posture and tone of voice: She planned to keep the money for herself. The Girls? Oh, they were her little darlings, all right, and god help anyone who dared to question their perfection. But this was money, and Edna would get it.

"Who's the executor of Lee's estate?" Edna said.

"Uh, I don't recall his name. . ." Brewer's mother said, looking toward her husband for help. He shrugged helplessly.

"Tom?" his mother said plaintively.

Brewer did not answer.

"I want his name and I want a copy of that will," Edna said.

"Edna, I can assure you it's all on the up and up. . ." Brewer's father said.

"Tom, I want those papers," Edna said, her eyes boring in on him like a wolf.

Brewer wanted to cower. He wanted to hide. He had something they wanted and there were more of them. It was a simple as that. That it belonged to him, that they had no claim to it; none of it mattered. He was young and defenseless. That meant they could get it, that they would get it.

He could let them eat him alive or he could fight.

He would fight.

Brewer braced himself. There would be an explosion, of course; a crash of neuroses and vitriol, enmity and mendacity, history and resentments – and it was Christmas for chrisesake – and it would be distilled into one terrible, filthy crescendo. But he would fight.

"I won't give them to you," Brewer said. It took effort to say it calmly. "It is my private business. And I am not giving the girls any money. Please don't ask me again."

The room fell as silent as a vacuum deep in outer space, and as cold. No one spoke to Edna like that, certainly no one from the younger generation.

"What did you say?" she gasped in disbelief.

Brewer did not answer. Now he was the wolf. Edna's face was blank with astonishment. Brewer kept his eyes on her, unblinking. It was her turn to squirm.

"Why, I've never been so humiliated in my life!" Edna shouted, her chin dropping to her chest, her eyes popping. "How dare you?! The nerve! The nerve!"

She stood up as if to deliver a speech.

"Edna. . ." Brewer's mother began. Her bottom lip trembled and tears welled in her eyes.

"Who do you think you're talking to?" Edna spat at Brewer, her face contorted with hate. "What gives you the right to be so high and mighty? Just who do you think you are, anyway?"

Brewer started to speak.

"You don't talk to my wife that way!" Uncle Walt roared. Then, suddenly, he seemed gripped by confusion. Fifteen years acquiescing to everything Edna said collided with his habitual practice of bulldozing his way through things with booster club gibberish. The two would not mesh. He had no idea what to do.

"Edna, please," Brewer's mother whimpered.

"So this is what you bring to my house on Christmas," Edna snarled. "Mother always said you were weak, Clair. You've always been weak; weak and worthless." She pointed at Brewer in disgust. "No wonder you turn out kids like that."

The Girls suddenly got their bearings and erupted into a chorus of wailing. The room reverberated with their howls like a steel echo chamber. The air was mad and foul and diseased.

"Tom, I want to talk with you," Brewer's father snarled through clenched teeth.

Brewer headed for the door.

"Tom, I said I want to talk to you!" his father shouted. "Don't you turn your back on me!"

"That's right, you just leave!" Edna shrieked. "You degenerate. You communist!"

When Brewer closed the door behind him, it all promptly stopped. He found himself bathed with silent, clear night air. The full moon coated the land in a pale, luminous glow and it was clean and good. The psychosis in the Nickleman house seemed small and petty and far away.

He didn't have time to reflect on the moment for long. He walked fast, turning down a side street in case someone tried to follow him. He listened. No sound of a door closing, no sound of a car starting. Instinctively, Brewer searched the sky, found the Big Dipper and followed it to the North Star. Downtown Mount Vernon was due west, down the hill, maybe a mile away. There must be a Greyhound Bus station there, Brewer thought. He checked his wallet. Eight dollars, enough to get him to Seattle, probably. From the Seattle bus station to his home? Maybe not enough for that, even if there were any buses running at that hour.

He could walk, in any case. He knew the route, but he had no idea how long it would take. Did it really matter? What would happen when he reached home? Would they let him in? Would there be another fight?

But where else could he go? Dale's place? He envisioned himself knocking on Dale's door at 2 a.m. Dale was a friend, but not that good a friend. No, he couldn't do that.

He could sneak in his parents' house through the garage window, the one with the broken lock. He had done it before when he forgot his key. Then he could spend the night in the basement. No one would know. But what would he do the next morning? He could start walking and keep walking for the rest of the day. But eventually, he would have to stop. Then he would have to find someplace else to stay. But there was no someplace else.

Guess I'll have to worry about that when the time comes, Brewer thought. Maybe something will turn up. For now, I'm headed for the bus station. If it's not open, I'll hitchhike.

The bus station was open, but the bus to Seattle didn't come for another two hours.

The station consisted of a ticket window and a small, airless waiting room with battered oak benches and naked overhead light bulbs, one of them burned out. They turned the enameled walls the color of desiccated orange peel. Brewer was the only person there. He stretched out on one of the benches and tried to sleep. But he could not sleep. I could have gone along with them. It would have been easy to go along; give them what they wanted and they would have left me alone.

Sure, and it would have left you broke. And you still would be at their mercy. No. He had made his choice. Now he had to confront the consequences. What would those consequences be? Another huge family blow up? Maybe that's why families have blow ups, he thought; to bring things back on track – *their track, not yours* – by creating a situation so awful you will do anything to make it stop.

The situation already dark and incoherent with malignity. It could explode in any number of directions, none of them good.

Would his parents demand he apologize to Aunt Edna, and hector him about it mercilessly until he either gave in or went insane? That would be consistent with their general way of doing things, but it would take time and its results were not sure-fire. It would be more efficient to refuse to pay his tuition. Yes, that was a distinct possibility. It was, after all, the most solid leverage they had over him. He already had registered for winter quarter and his parents already had paid for it, but they could cancel that check, and they just might.

Or would they simply cut to the chase and throw him out?

With no home, no way to attend college and no visible means of support, that meant the draft. Again, somebody else had plans for him, plans that would benefit them, not him.

Did it ever let up?

Meanwhile, what about the thirty thousand dollars? If the lawyer's letter was accurate, it should arrive in the mail and that would be that. But legal matters have a way of becoming complicated, so who could say. And, it would have to arrive in the next day or two to be of any use in this predicament. No chance of that.

"Hi, sweety."

Brewer opened his eyes. A middle-aged woman with bright red lipstick and frizzy orange hair was standing over him, smiling with crooked teeth.

"Hello," Brewer said, rubbing his eyes. He sat up.

"So what brings a good-lookin' fella like you here tonight?" the woman said.

Brewer didn't want to talk to her. He didn't want to talk to anybody. But he was inherently polite. It could be a cross to bear.

"Nothing interesting," he said. "Just on my way home."

The woman sat down next to him. She slid over so their thighs touched.

"Have a good Christmas?" she asked.

If there was one thing in the world Brewer did not want to talk about, it was Christmas.

"I had to work," he said. "I'll see my folks tomorrow." Brewer was bad at lying. He hoped it didn't show.

"Ooooo, working on Christmas, that's too bad," the woman said. She was looking into Brewer's face with exaggerated concern.

Brewer had no idea what to say.

"Must feel pretty lonesome, here in the bus station all by yourself on Christmas," the woman said.

"Things happen that way sometimes," Brewer said with a shrug.

"Well, I know I'd feel pretty lonesome," the woman said. She took his hand and patted it.

"What brings you here?" Brewer said, and instantly regretted it. You want to get rid of her, remember?

"I was just walking by and I saw this handsome fella on the bench and I said to myself, now that looks sad. I bet he could use a friend." She lowered her chin and looked into his eyes with a soulful expression. "Could you use a friend?"

"Sure," Brewer said. What else could he say? What was with this woman, collaring strangers at the Mount Vernon bus station on Christmas? The second hand on the wall clock crept along the rim with exquisite lethargy.

"Here, I have something to show you, honey," the woman said. She reached into her purse, pulled out an ivory-colored business card and handed it to him. Brewer held it up. It read, "Hi. My name is Betty. You seem nice. I'd like to fuck you very much."

Brewer jerked back in surprise. He read the card again to make sure his eyes were not deceiving him. They weren't. The woman lifted her eyebrows quizzically and smiled. The edges of her teeth were stained with lipstick.

Brewer searched for something to say, but his mind tripped over itself. Fuck her? No one had ever come out and actually asked him before, certainly not in a bus station and certainly not with a business card.

Did she really mean it, or was this leading to some kind of a joke? If she really meant it, did he actually want to? Well, of course. He had a cock and it was hardening even as he thought about it. Funny how the introduction of opportunity can make you forget crooked teeth and a thirty year age difference.

He looked at her again. There was still some prettiness left in her face, albeit crinkled here, puffy there and too much makeup up everywhere. Well, you could do worse. Fuck when you can, you may not get another chance for quite a while, wasn't that the way it worked?

On the other hand, no question about it, the situation was distinctly strange, a disconnect from reality as he knew it. Was she a creep who would stab him and take his money? Unlikely. He didn't have enough money to make it worth the effort. Otherwise, why would he be in a place like this?

Was she a prostitute? In Mount Vernon? On Christmas? Also unlikely. And she didn't look like a prostitute, or at least like

Brewer's uninitiated vision of what a prostitute would look like. Her clothes were cheap, but conservative and reasonably tasteful, like a blue collar housewife applying for a secretary job.

There was something else about her, though, something in her posture, in the set of her face, something that reminded Brewer of friends of his mother; women who exuded a sad, quiet air of resignation and defeat, chronically tired women who reeked of stale cigarette smoke and complained about their feet. That thought unsettled him even more.

Still, what did he have to lose? Fucking was fucking. Would she want to do it in her car? Fucking was fucking. Or in some rat hole double wide down by the river? Fucking was fucking. Would she have sandbag tits and cottage cheese legs and bunions? Fucking was fucking. Would her crotch smell like a can of tuna left out in the sun too long? Fucking was fucking. Fucking was fucking was fucking was fucking. Do it when you can, you may not get another chance. . .

But, Brewer finally decided, he simply didn't want to. He couldn't understand it.

For God's sake, she has come right out and asked you! a voice in his head shouted. *What more do you want? Are you impotent? Are you queer?*

Neither, Brewer thought in response. And what do I want? A different life. The one I am experiencing right now is one I want to escape, even if it does have women asking me - in writing! - to fuck them. This day, this time; it reminds me of one of those hoppers full of ping pong balls at Bingo parlors. Around and around it goes, the balls tumbling and jumbling, bouncing off one another over and over for no purpose. I want it all to stop, Brewer thought. I want silence and solitude.

What?! Are you out of your mind?! Imagine her, under you, soft and smooth, her legs wrapped around you, enfolding you in her wet and warm – are you hard yet? – only her, only you, only that moment. The moment we have now is all we have. If you don't make the most of it, you aren't really living, you're just marking time, like a plant taking in air and water and releasing oxygen – carbon dioxide, in your case – doing nothing, feeling nothing, experiencing nothing. The world will little note nor long remember what you did here, and for good reason. For chrisesake, just say yes and see what happens.

Good point, Brewer thought. At least his cock thought so.

But he still didn't want to. Besides, he didn't know how to say yes "Yeah, sure, I'll fuck you." Or, "A most charming and attractive offer. I would be honored to accept." He couldn't picture himself saying either one, or anything else. The situation was too much for him.

He handed the card back to the woman.

"Thanks," Brewer said.

She smiled and raised her eyebrows again.

"So?" she said.

Brewer swallowed hard and did not answer.

"So?" the woman asked again, her voice a bit uncertain.

"Thanks," Brewer said. His hands were clinched together as in prayer. He stared hard at his shoelaces.

"So, are you interested or not?" she said.

Crippled with confusion, Brewer remained silent.

The woman waited a while. Finally, she patted him on the knee.

"So, that's that," she said. "Have a good evening, honey."

And she left.

Brewer continued to stare at his shoelaces for a full fifteen minutes. Fifteen minutes after that, the bus came.

Brewer found himself seated next to a Japanese girl; a student, apparently, for she was reading a textbook. The book was about genital chancres, lesions and ulcers and it featured large, color photographs of each kind.

Could this evening get any more strange?

Brewer couldn't help but look, if for no other reason than he had never seen such things before. The girl noticed and he looked away. Then, inexorably, his attention would be drawn back to the pustules and blisters and abscesses, some red, some yellow, some black (Brewer winced); oozing and festering, glistening in the flash of the camera; nauseating in other circumstances, oddly fascinating while enduring a Greyhound ride through Skagit County, Wash., on a dismal December night.

The Japanese girl apparently thought otherwise. After catching Brewer peering over her shoulder – for the third time – she gave him a dirty look and moved to another seat.

Finally, the lights outside the bus window became brighter and more frequent. Seattle. The downtown bus terminal was bigger than the one in Mount Vernon, but with the same look about it: Brown linoleum floors, urine-colored tile walls, battered oak benches and, permeating all, the sickly sheen of fluorescent lights.

Brewer rushed outside, past a twitchy heroin addict and a wino babbling about socialism, and hurried down Stewart Street toward the bus stop at Third and Pine. The city posted route schedules there.

Downtown Seattle on Christmas Night: Bright lights glimmering to no one, already old and stale, their joy evaporating into the emptiness. The streets, abandoned and stark, the buildings hollow; no one there, no one living, breathing, laughing, sweating. The only sound the hiss of bus brakes - ah, there were buses running on Christmas - and the arrhythmic bong-bong of halyards on flag poles, echoing into the loneliness. No flags on them tonight. No one to look at them. A couple walked by, speaking a language that sounded like Spanish but wasn't. Catalan, perhaps. The only other people on the street.

Brewer finally reached Third and Pine, the place of his holiday muse - was it only a week ago? - now even more empty than the rest of the city. The mannequins in the Bon Marche display windows looked like mannequins, nothing more. The plastic evergreen garlands looked like plastic. The strings of Christmas lights blinked on and off automatically, mechanically, devoid of souls.

Brewer went to the window at the corner. The toys were still there and still gay. They cheered him up. The Aerial Daredevil was still on his unicycle, going back and forth on the tightrope as earnestly as ever, a toy, a child's fantasy, magical, a wonder. Somehow, Brewer thought, wonder would find a way to endure; somehow, somehow.

Brewer checked the bus schedules. The holiday schedules were in small print at the bottom of the sign. The Number 15 to View Ridge last stopped here at 10:30 p.m. Brewer checked his watch. It was 11:15. The next bus was at 7 a.m. He looked over the schedules for other buses that might take him toward home. None.

Well, what did you expect, he thought to himself. It was Christmas, remember?

He considered his options, but not for long. He really had only one: Walk. Where? North. That's where his home was - if it still was his home. What he had done, he had done. The consequences, whatever they might be, were the consequences.

He started up Stewart Street. So this is what real loneliness feels like, he thought. He had no attachments, no obligations. He had only himself - but he did have that, and that sense of self, the feeling that whatever happened in the world outside his body, his mind, his being, it all was secondary to the fact he was here, in the now, solid in existence. Nothing could change that - at least nothing that had happened yet.

The only thing to do was keep moving and see what developed. If nothing else, it was an improvement over sleeping in a doorway, although he might very well end up doing that anyway. At least the North End featured a better quality of doorway.

After a block of so, Stewart Street branched off to Olive Way, the route of his bus ride home. Brewer followed Olive past Val De Pena's tiny, old-fashioned barbershop - two chairs, one barber, a kaleidoscopic wall of multi-colored bottled tonics and lotions - then past the storefront where the Gypsy women lolled outside the door, smiling cloyingly at passersby. What did they really offer inside, behind the curtain? Probably not what the men who smiled back at them hoped for. Now, both places were locked and dark. Everything was locked and dark.

Olive Way branched off to Howell Avenue - there were a lot of idiosyncratic spurs and one-block streets in this part of Seattle - which curved into the dark cavern beneath the Denny Way overpass and emerged onto Eastlake Way. From there, it was about four miles to the University District and then another three miles to Brewer's home - if it was still his home. Keep moving and see what develops, keep moving and see what develops . . .

The first leg of the walk was through a canyon: The freeway on one side - loud even at this hour - and decrepit brick apartment buildings on the other. It was like a set for a movie. Give me a dark, foreboding, back street, the producer told the art director. Brewer pictured himself in a film noir, the man with secrets prowling the night. He turned up his collar and hunched down into his coat to replicate the look. For the first time that day, he found himself laughing; a quick, two-syllable grunt, actually, but it was something.

At Roy Street, Eastlake turned downhill toward the south end of Lake Union. He stopped at the crest of the hill and took in the view, the expanse of North Seattle stretching out before him in an infinite lattice work of twinkling light. When cities have no people out and moving around, no real activity except an occasional car, they all must have this look about them, Brewer thought; an empty stage patiently waiting to be put to life.

Or maybe it was something else. Maybe the city was a living thing, apart from the people who inhabited it. Brewer could almost feel the city inhaling and exhaling. Occasionally a light would blink, or a far away car would make a sound; the tics and sighs of a sleeping giant.

Brewer walked down the hill, past the old, smoke stacked, City Light power plant and, on the other side of the street, the old Buffalo Shoe Company building slowly moldering into the weeds. Someday, the power plant would molder away too, Brewer thought. Eventually, everything he saw and understood would molder way, including this time, this 1964. It would become a myth, an illusion, a dream. For a very long moment, Brewer felt his own mortality. Someday he would be gone and no one would know or care. Who knew or cared now? Few. His family cared about him, in their way, but did they know him? No. Therefore, who exactly did they care for? An illusion of their own making? Did it matter? The world outside Brewer's mind evaporated into ephemera.

The street leveled out for a few blocks, then started up a long, slow hill to the old residential neighborhoods on the northwest slope of Capitol Hill. An old neighborhood, in Seattle, was a relative term. The city was barely a hundred years old and its neighborhoods had developed in fits and starts as dictated by a notoriously erratic boom and bust economy and a topography of high hills and steep ridges interrupted by deep ravines, broad bays, twisting creeks and marshy lakes.

Things rarely remained stable for long – buildings were leveled to make way for something bigger in as little as ten years – and the concept of historic preservation occurred to no one. So, a thirty-year-old neighborhood was considered old in Seattle. Forty years and up was considered a curiosity.

This part of town was one of those curiosities. The glow from its old neon signs roused Brewer from his introspection. He looked around and found himself in a place lost in time, a time of one-story, courtyard apartments, small cafes and mom and pop stores, modest brick buildings with terra cotta trim, idiosyncratic, an expression in scale, an intimate scale. There was an inherent warmth about it all. You could almost hear the old Jack Benny radio programs wafting through the night air.

Brewer's hands were beginning to hurt from the cold. The air had become dry and the small puddles in the gutters were frozen solid. No wind or snow, thank god – at least not yet.

The road turned downhill again, this time toward the curve at Hamlin Street where Tim Conway, twenty feet tall on a lighted billboard, had been trying to lift that barbell since September. Brewer was musing about its familiarity when the cop drove up.

The patrol car was a big Plymouth; black, brutal and menacing. It slowed to a creep to match Brewer's pace. Brewer started to look at it when the spotlight hit him in the face, blinding him.

"Stop right there!" a voice barked out of the glare. "Keep those hands where I can see 'em!"

Brewer stopped and held his hands out from his side. Oddly, the posture resembled nothing so much as Wyatt Earp waiting for the Clanton boys to make their move. There he stood for a full two minutes while the cop spoke into the radio and scribbled something in a notebook. Finally, he got out of the car.

He was a young man, still in his twenties, and he was short, five-foot six, tops. He was smiling. Brewer did not like the look of that smile.

"Well, well, well, so what brings you out at this late hour, sport?" the cop said in a smug, amused tone.

"I'm on my way home," Brewer said.

"Really? And where's home?"

"View Ridge."

"Oh?" the cop said, his voice taking on a hard edge. "You're quite a ways from View Ridge."

"We were visiting relatives. . ."

"I don't remember asking you a question!" the cop snapped. His voice took on an insinuating tone. "When I want you to talk,

I'll say so. You understand me?" He let the moment hang in the air. "Got any ID?"

Brewer reached for his wallet.

"I said keep those hands where I can see 'em!" the cop barked. "You tryin' to make trouble for me, HUH?! You tryin' to provoke me, HUH?!"

Brewer did not answer.

"I think you are. I think you're trying to provoke me," the cop said, his fingers drumming on the handle of his billy stick. "Out here at midnight, all by yourself. Been checkin' the locks on those doors?"

Brewer shook his head. He sensed that the less he said, the better. The cop was looking for an excuse.

"Oh, really? Now let's see some ID."

Brewer gestured, asking if it was all right to reach for his wallet. The cop nodded. Brewer opened his wallet to take out his driver's license. The cop shook his head.

"Nonono, hand me the whole thing," he said.

Brewer handed him the wallet. The cop thumbed through it. He counted the cash, all four dollars of it, took it and put it in his pocket.

"Well, well, well, so you do live in View Ridge," he said. "One of them fancy rich kids, huh?"

Brewer didn't answer.

"Oh, and lookee here, you're a college boy, too," the cop said with exaggerated geniality. "Now isn't that just special."

He handed the wallet back with a condescending smirk.

"So, what's your story again?" he said.

"We were visiting family for Christmas," Brewer said in the flattest monotone he could manage. "There was a big family fight, so I left. Now I'm walking home."

"Oh really?" the cop said. "Now, how do I know you just weren't out here pickin' locks, maybe thinking about busting a back window or two?"

"I wasn't doing that," Brewer said.

"Can you prove it?" the cop said. "I mean, all I have now is your word for it. What kind of proof can you show me?"

Brewer's mind flashed to the unit on logic in freshman English: It is impossible to prove that you did not do something because it is impossible to prove something did not happen. Random chance makes anything possible, however unlikely. Hence, the burden of proof is on the claimant: The cop, in this case.

Jesus, what a time for a treatise on the Socratic method.

The cop turned his flashlight on Brewer.

"Turn around," the cop said.

Brewer turned around.

"Keep turning."

Brewer turned some more. He was facing the cop once again. The cop ran the flashlight up and down him slowly.

"Oooeee, you're a tall one. Just how tall are you, big boy?"

"Six two."

"Six two, you say? Well, where I come from, a man that tall has to prove he's worthy of his height. You worthy of your height there, big boy?"

Brewer had no idea what the cop was talking about. There was a long pause.

"Oh, cat got your tongue? That pretty much tells us what you're made of, now doesn't it."

The cop turned the flashlight off and stepped forward so he was face to face with Brewer.

"Now listen good, big boy," the cop hissed. "I know what you look like and I don't want to see your face again." He punched his finger hard against Brewer's chest. "You got that, big, important college boy?"

"Yes."

The cop glowered at Brewer for a few seconds more. Then abruptly, he went back to his car, slammed the door and sped off, tires squealing. In less than ten seconds, Brewer was alone again in the silent night.

SHIT!

SHIT, SHIT, **SHIT!!**

Brewer kicked a metal light pole with the sole of his foot. Then he kicked it again, as hard as he could, so hard it sent him staggering backward.

SHITHEAD!

ASSHOLE!

Cocksucker bastard motherfucker son of a bitch prick boil-sucker snot-eater buttcunt buttfucker dickhead, ass-licker pus sac kotex-sucker turd-maggot jerkwad cuntface cockface faggot puke bucket fuckhead fuckbag jizz-eater piss-drinker. . .

SHIT!!

. . . go fuck yourself lick a dog's ass piss in your mother's milk eat hot cat shit shove it up your ass suck a dead donkey's dick jerk off to the Bible choke on your own farts. . . .

DIE, DIE, *DIE!!*

SHIT!!

Brewer kicked the light pole again. But it wasn't enough. He looked around for something else on which to vent his fury, but he didn't see anything, except the windows to the little shops, and no matter how mad he was, he couldn't bring himself to attack them. Exploding with rage and frustration, he jumped up and down, pounding on his thighs with his fists, slamming his feet on the pavement as hard as he could.

"Shit!" This time, he shouted it out loud. It drifted off weakly into the cold night air, heard by no one. Then there was silence, save the fevered panting of the tall young man, enveloped in his wrath, alone in his anguish.

FUCK YOU!!

Fuck all of you! Fuck you until you bleed! Fuck you until you fucking die!

But the words had taken on a weak and flaccid tone. Drained, Brewer could manage no other coherent thoughts. He could only stand, panting and shaking, waiting for the blast furnace in his head to burn itself out.

After a while, it dwindled; enough that he once again was a rational human being, back where he started, trying to find his way to a home where he may no longer live, to a family he may no longer have. But an ember continued to glow and smolder in the back of Brewer's mind, an ember of resentment that would never go out completely, no matter how lost and alone he might be, even when he wished it would.

Keep walking, keep walking, do not stop. The University Bridge, steel lace over polished onyx, lights, gems, shimmering, glistening, sparkling. Keep walking, keep walking. Roosevelt Way, a stygian tunnel through run-down buildings disintegrating into the gloom, claustrophobic, spectral. Keep walking, keep walking. Northeast 45th, into the heart of the University District, incense and peppermint, a blurred mosaic of time in ferment, ideas, perceptions, vibrations sparking off into space, intoxicating, breathtaking, young. Keep walking, keep walking. Stride long and determined, jaw set, eyes hard, focused straight ahead.

Down the long, precarious viaduct to Sand Point Way, steep, cold, dirty, a concrete catwalk, treacherous, scoured by sleet and grit, a place where no one stops. Keep walking, keep walking.

Along the rim of Sand Point Way, crumbling asphalt, no sidewalks, the blast of passing cars pounding on eardrums, cold, cold, cold, a lone figure, singular amid the erratic pops and flashes of a city at night. Keep walking, keep walking.

Keep walking, young man, for motion is life. To stand still is to admit subjugation, to accept suzerainty, to die. Keep walking, keep walking, keep walking.

It was 2:40 a.m. when Brewer finally reached his parents' house. Snug and comforting at other times, it stood morose and forsaken now, only the front porch light glowing dimly, a pale straw color evaporating into the gloom.

Brewer walked past it, around the corner and then down the alley in back. He approached the house on little cat's feet, stopping frequently to listen for any other movement, any other sound. There was none.

The lock on the garage window was still broken. The window swung open inward and upward, with a hook on the inside ceiling to hold it. Brewer opened it slowly, listening for a squeak. The hinges were silent. Awkwardly, stretching his arms painfully, he held it open with one hand and searched for the hook with the other. He finally located it, affixed it, and then started his crawl in, head first. The window was small. He had to wriggle. It was hard to do without making a sound. It took what seemed like a very long time.

Finally, his hands found the floor. Carefully, he pulled his legs through. He crept around the car to the basement door, opened it very carefully – it had a loud spring hinge – and found himself face to face with Orrin.

Orrin put his fingers to his lips. Brewer nodded.

"Sleep under my bed tonight," Orrin whispered. "I put a blanket down for you."

"How mad are they?" Brewer asked, pointing upstairs.

"Mad."

Orrin put his mouth next to Brewer's ear.

"I go into work late tomorrow, after they've both left. I'll give you a ride."

Brewer nodded.

The blanket under Orrin's bed was the only padding between Brewer and the basement's concrete floor. Brewer didn't care.

He awoke to the feel of Orrin's toe nudging his ribs.

"They're gone," Orrin said. "I leave in a half hour."

Brewer showered and shaved quickly, then went to his room, gathered his books and notebooks, some shirts, a sweater, a pair of trousers, some underwear and whatever other clothes he could find and stuffed it all into the athletic bag he kept under his bed.

He took a quick look around. It had been his room his entire life, his haven, his retreat, a place of boyhood, of football pennants on the wall, baseball cards in the drawer, model airplanes hanging from the ceiling. He felt his throat tighten. He knew he would leave home eventually, and he wanted to. But not like this, not like a fugitive. His life had not evolved to this moment. It had stopped the day a letter from J.P. Addelton, Attorney at Law arrived. Actually, it probably had stopped long before that, whenever it was he stopped being his parents' little boy and they stopped being his mommy and daddy. It's just that none of them saw it. In any case, it was over now, whether he wanted it to be or not. Given that his parents were what they were - which was what, exactly? - it probably couldn't have happened any other way. What a shame, what a shame.

As they drove away from the house, Orrin was, as usual, silent. After a while, he said. "You wanna go to the garage or to SPC?"

"SPC, I think," Brewer said.

Orrin handed him a card.

"Here's the garage's number. Call me if you need a ride."

"Thanks."

They continued in silence. Then, as they waited for the Stone Way traffic light, Orrin said, "You get the money yet?"

"No," Brewer said. Good god, now Orrin's joining in the gang bang.

The light changed. They drove on. As they turned on to the Fremont Bridge, Orrin said, "I don't want any of it."

"What?" Brewer said, surprised.

"I've seen what it does to people. I don't want to be like that."

More silence. Eventually, Brewer said, "What if I gave you some of it?"

Orrin shrugged.

"If you want to give me money, I'll take it. If you don't, I don't care. It's yours, not mine." His voice was flat, but declarative. He wasn't arguing, he wasn't trying to make an impression. He was stating a simple fact. It was not open to debate.

Brewer looked at his brother. As usual, Orrin was hunched forward, his hair untidy, his face an expressionless mask. Brewer had always assumed that Orrin was simply a mope and an oaf, and maybe he was. Or maybe there was more and people had been too busy making Orrin fit their preconceived notions to see it. In any case, his moody, silent, inscrutable brother was probably the only person left in the world Brewer could depend on. He was moved. He didn't know what to say. But the good thing about Orrin was, you didn't have to say anything. The old DeSoto pulled over next to Brougham Pavilion.

"Thanks for the ride," Brewer said.

Orrin lifted two fingers off the steering wheel in acknowledgement. His eyes never left the road. Then he was gone.

Few things are as melancholy as a small college between terms. Where once was the hum and hurry of constant motion, now was bleak emptiness and cold silence. A fog had settled on the campus. No pretty girls walked through it, parting the air with their brightness. No young men, either; stronger than they knew, bolder than they knew, the force of their being echoing around them. No smiles, no laughs, no frowns, no sobs. No life. All was gray, deserted, abandoned. Other students had homes and families and lives to go to. Brewer did not.

The SUB was open but empty, save for the acne-scarred girl at the switchboard. She was idly thumbing through a magazine, her chin propped on her fist, a caricature of boredom. She did not notice as Brewer walked by.

Downstairs, he opened his locker and stuffed his bag in it. He had to push his shoulder against the door to force it shut. Back upstairs, he checked his mailbox. Nothing.

Where to now? The SUB coffee shop was open, but the cafe counter was closed. The big meeting room next door was open. Brewer had, at the most, four hours sleep the night before. May as well make good use of time he had now. The couches were too short to stretch out and the steel and naugahide chairs were notoriously uncomfortable. But that's what there was. Brewer found a chair partially hidden from sight by the big, jutting fireplace, did his best to settle in and closed his eyes.

He dreamed, as he often did, of places; of parks with weeping willow trees on the shore of a lake, soft and gentle in a Seurat-like summer haze; of cityscapes of beams and braces and high buildings, a world of art deco steel; of Venice-like cities with one-story houseboats and barges where people navigated narrow passages in kayaks; none of it real, all of it fanciful, the way he wished places would be.

"Brewer?"

It was McLean.

"What are you doing here?" Brewer said.

"I could ask you the same," McLean said with an amused expression.

"Oh, fuck," Brewer said, sitting up.

"What?"

"The shit hit the fan," Brewer said.

"What? You flunk out or something?"

"Problems at home. My parents kicked me out."

"Oh," McLean said, his face turning serious.

"This seemed as good a place to go as any," Brewer said.

"Hmm. Well, I'd offer you a couch to sleep on, except we don't have one. . ."

"Nonono, I'm not trying to hit you up," Brewer said.

". . . but you can use the floor for a few days."

Brewer's attention promptly snapped into focus.

"I can't pay you," he said. "I'm broke."

"No need, not for a few days," McLean said. "You can work it off by doing the dishes and taking out the garbage, stuff like that."

Brewer didn't wait to think about it.

"Deal," he said, sticking out his hand for McLean to shake. A roof was a roof. What would be would be.

Chapter 18

McLean was a pig.

Brewer should have known. McLean walked around campus in wrinkled shirts, carelessly buttoned and usually untucked, scuffed shoes and faded Levis with frayed cuffs scraping along the pavement. He neglected shaving for three days at a time, and it showed. He was the first at SPC to adopt Beatles-style long hair, but he found it too much trouble to care for, so he let it grow until it fell over his eyes. Then he got the cheapest haircut he could. That showed, too.

Brewer liked to think of himself as tolerant, so he shrugged McLean's slovenliness it off as personal eccentricity. And he liked McLean; a bright, funny, interesting guy, and an individualist, a rarity at SPC. To each his own, live and let live and all that.

None of which prepared him for what he found at McLean's house on Dravus Street behind Adelaide Hall.

The house was typical of the small workmen's homes erected throughout the neighborhood at the turn of the century: Built fast and cheap because no one expected them to last twenty years, certainly not thirty. But there, in 1964, it still stood, albeit at a few degrees off vertical, its roof sagging, its siding shingles falling off one-by-one, its walkway cracked and uneven; the very picture of abandonment.

But abandoned it was not. Every year or so a new batch of SPC students would rent it, ignore the holes in the floor, the dark stains on the ceiling, the rusty pipes, the unidentifiable smells – in short, all the features that made for a captivating ambience – and live out their undergraduate years free from the school's compulsion to regulate students' private behavior. Or so they liked to think.

In reality, the house, and similar old houses around the campus's periphery, were a source of aggravation for both Chester Dalrymple and Layton Fleming. Not because anything troublesome ever happened at them – beyond occasional acts of sexual congress, nothing much happened at all – but because something might.

Dalrymple worried about the potential for adverse publicity; not the kind that made the news - Dalrymple knew the rest of the world barely cared that SPC existed, although he was careful never to say so out loud - but the kind that might get stuck in the constantly grinding gears of the evangelical subculture's omnipresent, omnipotent, omniscient, omnificent rumor mill. Once something did get stuck there, whether it was true or not, it became endlessly magnified, dissected, interpreted and confabulated, with the usual conclusion that SPC was on the road to godless decadence and why wasn't the administration doing something about it.

Such canards were not pleasing to President Donald A. Fotheringham, Ph.D. The vision of SPC he wanted to project was of a collegium of like-minded believers, a crucible of proper Christian behaviors synergistically molding its protégés into an impassioned cadre for the faith - or into lobotimized Republican Babbitts, whichever came first. Overseeing this wondrous process was, of course, President Donald A. Fotheringham, Ph.D., and the rest of the world should know it.

It was Chester Dalrymple's job to make sure it knew, and if anything put a crack in the plaster, he was responsible for it. One drunk and disorderly call at one of the old houses and Chester Dalrymple would have to rearrange reality to fit the college's predetermined version of it. The contortions of logic and the process of uncoupling language from its meaning necessary to accomplish that could be unusually tortuous and Chester Dalrymple had both to administer and endure the torture. In short, he had to lie.

It wasn't that he minded lying. It's what directors of public relations were paid to do and once one got used to it, it rested on the conscience with surprising ease. Chester had even come up with a comforting name for it: "Reinforcing positive outcomes."

What bothered him was that the lies he told on behalf of the college usually ended up being convoluted beyond comprehension and, all too often, unconvincing. It was hard. And no one ever thanked him for it.

Layton Fleming's aggravation was a matter of principle. The students in the houses did not meet his standards. A paragraph in the Student Housing Policy stated that seniors or students over 22-

years-old could live in their own apartments off-campus. Fleming hated that loophole, which he had inherited from previous administrations. Just who did these punks, these nobodies, think they were, assuming they knew how to run their own lives. If Fleming had his way, only varsity athletes would be allowed to live off campus, and only some of them, the ones who *looked* like varsity athletes. But, for the sake of compromise, student body officers, Youth For Christ leaders and the children of wealthy donors - the right *kind* of student body officers, Youth for Christ leaders and children of wealthy donors - also might be considered from time to time. Fleming thought that a reasonable concession.

The old houses also meant empty dorm rooms, which could be discomforting when federal funding officials did one of their periodic reviews. The federal loans that had paid for Hill Hall were granted on the condition that at least 90 percent of the college's dorm rooms were occupied.

So Fleming and Dalrymple kept their eyes on the old houses.

Brewer knew none of that. He needed a place to stay, McLean offered him one and that was that - until he discovered McLean was a pig.

He discovered it when he came through the front door. To say the place was littered would be to give litter a bad name. Inundated was a better word. Piles of clothes - some men's, some women's, all dirty - lay in islets amid a sea of mismatched shoes, crumpled papers, carelessly-tossed books and magazines - some Playboys, Brewer noticed - and the occasional moldering pizza box and empty wine bottle. Random paths twisted through it to the kitchen, which was a little neater, but not much. It was clear the dishes had not been washed in a few days and if the stove had ever been cleaned off, no one could recall when.

Brewer did not look in the bathroom - he didn't want to - and as he passed a bedroom, he saw a pallid, skinny young woman laying on the bed, her head propped up on the pillows, reading and smoking a cigarette. She was not wearing a shirt. Or a bra. She looked up at Brewer as he walked by, her face a blank map of disinterest, then went back to her book.

"Here, we have a spare mattress," McLean said as they entered a small room lined floor to ceiling with crates, books and various accumulations of unidentifiable junk. More boxes and bags covered the floor. The mattress, a stained, threadbare affair with the look of U.S. Army, circa 1942, was propped against the wall.

"It's all yours," McLean said. "Find a spot in the living room, I guess."

To take his mind off it all, Brewer started cleaning. He spent the rest of the day sweeping, vacuuming and picking up the litter in the living room.

"Dinner in about a half hour," McLean said. "You like Spaghettios?"

"Sure," Brewer said. In reality, he was worried about anything that came out of that kitchen.

Dinner was indeed Spaghettios, with canned corn and a large jug of red wine. Brewer, who had never drank wine, took one sip and concluded he probably never would. He got a glass of water. They talked through dinner. That is, McLean talked and Brewer listened. The girl, who was named Pam, no last name offered, alternately nibbled at tiny forkfuls of food and puffed on a cigarette, all the while staring straight ahead as if the wall, which was six feet away, was something far, far distant. She had donned a t-shirt for the occasion. Brewer was glad he didn't have to see her breasts, perverse as that seemed to him.

"Now the Rolling Stones, that's the group to watch," McLean said. "The Beatles are a flash in the pan. And this other group, the Byrds, they're sounding pretty good too. And have you heard Barry McGuire?"

Brewer had not.

"Oh, you gotta, you gotta. I have one of his records. He's definitely on the edge, a voice for our times."

From there, McLean shifted to movies. David and Lisa was sentimental pap, but Zorba the Greek, now there was a flick with soul. So was The Americanization of Emily - laughed my head off, the rest of the audience didn't seem to get it - and, believe it or not, Mary Poppins is pretty good, too. So is The Pawnbroker, but I'm not sure I'd recommend it. Bleak as hell, depressed me for a week.

And so McLean went on. Politics ("You know what you call those monks in Vietnam who keep setting themselves on fire? Crispy critters!") Religion ("Wanna hear my Billy Graham impression? 'We live-ah at the most critical-ah mo-ment in human his-tore-ee.' Says it every time he starts thumpin' the tub, guaranteed. I think he has one of those rings you pull on the back of his neck, like a Chatty Kathy doll.") And, of course, about SPC. ("When I lived in Moyer, we had these guys down at the end of the hall, the Odd Clods for God Squad. I don't think they'd know a can of Right Guard if you bounced it off their foreheads.")

McLean could go on indefinitely and never repeat himself. Sometimes Brewer tried to join the conversation, but he never got far. Pam blew smoke rings, stared at the wall and occasionally scratched her crotch.

****

Brewer called home Thursday morning. He remembered Orrin had Thursday off. His parents probably would not be home during the day. If they were and one of them answered the phone, he would silently hang up.

"'Lo?'"

It was Orrin.

"This is Tom. I'm calling to find out if there's anything I need to know."

"Not really. Mom whines about the girls sometimes and Dad gripes about what is he supposed to do with your room, but they haven't done anything. Same as always."

Brewer sighed with relief. The situation might be bad, but at least his parents weren't making it worse.

"Any mail for me?" he said.

There was a pause. Orrin was thinking. Finally, he said, "Uh, yeah, I think so. Wait a minute."

Orrin put the phone down. Brewer could hear rustling and clattering as Orrin rummaged around. Eventually he returned.

"There's a letter from Aunt Edna and Uncle Walt. Want me to open it?"

Brewer had a pretty good idea what it would say, but he was curious.

"Can you read it to me?"

There was a tearing sound.

"Let's see. . ." Orrin said. "'. . . hope you are proud of yourself. . . the girls are heartbroken. . .'"

"That's enough," Brewer said.

"Really?" Orrin said with a slight chuckle. "Can't imagine why." Brewer heard Orrin wad the letter up.

"There's something else," Orrin said. "Something from the college. Looks official."

"Okay," Brewer said. "Let's hear it."

Another tearing sound.

"You got your grades," Orrin said.

Brewer tensed. He had done pretty well in his classwork and his midterms had been good, but he wasn't sure about his finals. He had never taken a final before. And, of course, teachers could ding him on grades for no reason whatsoever. There was one teacher who was known to knock students down a full grade point if they didn't remember a textbook's footnotes. Teachers had that power.

Well, might as well get it over with.

"What are they?" Brewer said.

"Hmmm," Orrin said. "Hmmm, hmmm, hmmm."

"Come on, what are they?" Brewer said, bracing himself. Jesus, what if he was on probation? Then everything his family said about him would be true, at least in their eyes. And worse, his little campaign for freedom would be a joke. One more quarter in school, maybe two, then it was the draft, or some shit job on a loading dock toadying to any clown who had power over him. Brewer's stomach started to tighten. His throat went dry. His. . .

"All Bs," Orrin said.

"What?!" Brewer gasped.

"All Bs."

Brewer couldn't speak.

"Still there?" Orrin said.

"Are you sure?" Brewer said.

"Eng. 101. Habib. B. 3.0. Hist. 142. Schnieder. B. 3.0. Physics 114 Van Holder. B. 3.0. P.E. 122. Bdybldg. – what the hell is bdybldg? – Hoffman. B. 3.0. Cum. GPA 3.0."

Brewer struggled to catch his breath. Finally, he croaked, "I'll be damned."

There was silence on the other end of the line.

"I'll be damned," Brewer said again, a far away tone in his voice.

He had survived. No, more than survived. He had done well, better than he had any reason to expect. It all had been so hard, so uncertain, so lonely. He had never dared hope for anything beyond skin-of-the-teeth survival. And now this.

Brewer remembered that he did his best work, the work that got him out of the muddle of the first half of the quarter, by doing it his way. The ideas in his essays were his ideas, not the ones people expected him to dutifully regurgitate. The answers on the tests were his answers, as best he could express them based on his – not someone else's – understanding of the material. And – here was the craziest thing of all – he actually *did* understand the material, at least most of the time. For the first time in his academic life, he *did* find it interesting. And challenging. And stimulating.

Damn. Was this what it was like to become *educated?* The idea was disconcerting. Up to now, education had largely been a matter of obedience and rote; do what you're told, don't ask questions and give your teachers the answers they want to hear. Be a Good Citizen, which was code for shut up and conform. And so on. And now this.

Jesus, I might be beginning to like school.

Then he remembered the hours at Weter, the impenetrable text books, the interminable note-taking, the ever- present specter of failure hovering over his every move...

But, damnit, he could do it. All Bs, a 3.0. He could do it.

"You still there?" It was Orrin.

"Yeah, yeah. Sorry. I just wasn't expecting a 3.0."

"What do you want me to do with it?" Orrin said.

"Can you mail it to my campus box?"

"Yeah, I guess so."

Brewer recited the address.

"Got it," Orrin said.

"Thanks," Brewer said. "I owe you."

"I told you, I don't want your money."

"That's not what I meant."

"Okay," Orrin said, his voice its usual near-monotone. "You gotta place to live yet?"

"Not yet. Staying with a guy. Not sure where things are headed. What about you? How's the job."

"It's okay. Kinda boring, but I've learned a lot about tires. There's a lot of money in the tire business."

"Hmmm. Well." Brewer couldn't think of anything else to say. And he knew Orrin wouldn't initiate conversation.

"I'll be in touch," Brewer said.

"Yeah."

Then Orrin hung up. Someday he would understand his brother, Brewer thought, but not any time soon. Meanwhile, a 3.0. in the fall quarter of freshman year! Damn! Brewer shook his head at that imponderability of it all.

Brewer smiled. He kept smiling, on and off, for the rest of the day and on into the night. Pam looked at him like he was trying to make a pass at her. McLean looked at him like he was nuts. Brewer didn't care. He kept on smiling.

****

On Saturday morning, Brewer decided he had been stalling long enough; his parents deserved a call to let them know he was all right. As he dialed the phone, he wondered what would happen next. A blowup for sure, but so what? He had made his decision. And, while he was sorry if he hurt his parents' feelings, they were their responses, not his. They had control over them if they wanted to. No one had seemed particularly concerned about his feelings throughout this whole mess. That thought, particularly, settled in his mind. It didn't anger him. It didn't upset him. Would he ever understand human nature? It was a boundless universe of irrationality.

"Hi mom."

"Tommy? Tommy is that you?" His mother's voice was choked and anxious, sliding inexorably toward tears. "Where are you?"

"I'm staying with some friends. I'm fine."

"Friends? What do you mean, friends?" Her tone was a mixture of fear and accusation. Brewer had heard it many times before. What usually happened next was that he would offer a detailed explanation of things, and she would either refuse to believe any of it or not listen at all. She would simply become more angry and frightened and unreasoning. It was just a question of how much.

"I'm fine, mom," Brewer said again. "I'll let you know when I get a little more settled."

"What do you mean settled? Where are you? Who are these friends of yours?" she demanded again, her voice rising.

Brewer did not answer. He waited. Finally his mother said, "Oh, Tom, Tom, Tom. You can't believe how awful things have become. . ."

Here it comes, Brewer thought. As certain as an inside fastball on a two and three count. . .

"Oh, Tom. The Girls are just crushed. I've never seem them like this. The cried and cried and cried. The poor little things. . ."

Well, she's consistent, Brewer thought. He stopped listening. He could hear her tone of voice; histrionic, melodramatic, and he could hear the choruses of whimpers and sobs she trooped out when she went on one of her emotional rants: "Oh, no, no, no. . ." or, "I just don't know, I just don't know, I just don't know," anything to keep the conversation under her dominance while she let her emotions have full sway. He used to feel sorry for her at such times, or at least feel some empathy. But not now. She would go on until she wore out, not really saying anything, certainly not trying to solve anything, and, throughout it all, she would save her most intense expressions for the plight of The Girls.

Sure enough, just as Brewer thought about that, he heard her sobbing begin.

". . . oh, Tom, they were so frightened and confused, the poor little things. Couldn't you just give Edna a call. . ."

She'll never give up, Brewer thought. Never. Not until I give them my money; probably not even then.

He found himself wondering about his mother's sanity. Doting on her nieces was one thing, but this was beyond doting. Obsession? Worship? Fetish?

Then Brewer realized, suddenly and with startling clarity, that something was not quite right with the woman he called mother. Claire Brewer was, to one degree or another, cuckoo.

Think about it: Other than The Girls, what else had she ever shown interest in? Gardening? No. Cooking? No. Current events and politics? No? Art, music, theatre, books, movies? No on all counts. Weekly get togethers for coffee with her friends? Brewer didn't know for sure, but he doubted it. He ran some other things through his mind, the typical things that interest most people to one degree or another. No on all counts.

He should have known it all along. Why her fixation on The Girls? Was it because she hated boys? He had ever noticed, but it was possible. Many women did. Did it have something to do with her relationship with Edna? Probably, but what? Edna was a vicious neurotic. A healthy relationship with her was all but impossible. But then, relationships don't have to be healthy, do they, Brewer thought. The less healthy they are, the more they monopolize you.

Brewer stopped himself. He was out of his depth. Besides, what difference did the whys and wherefore make, particularly now, after all that had happened?

As that thought settled in Brewer's mind, he found himself no longer resenting his mother. She was what she was and she would never change. He loved her, but he had made his break from her and from her control over him, and that would never change, either.

There was a rattling sound on the line, as if someone had dropped the phone.

"Well, you've made your mother cry. I hope you're proud of yourself," the voice on the line snarled.

"Hi dad."

"I can't believe you've done what you've done," his father said. "What do you have to say for yourself?"

Hmmm, what indeed, Brewer thought.

"I love you, dad."

He could almost hear his father jerk back in surprise, his eyes widening. He waited for his father to say something. There was silence.

"I don't really have anything else to say," Brewer said. "School starts next Monday. I'm fine. Don't worry about me." He waited for a few seconds more. Still silence. Brewer gently hung up the phone.

Well, that was a bold stroke, he thought, except there was nothing bold about it. What else could he do? He would not give them the money, his money, and he would not yield to their unrelenting obsession to control him. But he was broke, alone, with no visible means of support. It made him vulnerable and that made the world want to attack him, like wolves going after a crippled fawn.

The irrationality of it all unnerved Brewer. Was this the way The Real World functioned, the world adults had been warning him about for as long as he could remember? If so, it was a boundless anarchy of madness. Brewer's future in that world depended on the money. But, in an insane world, a world where ownership, legality and similar supposed stabilities were the provenance of psychopathy, would he actually ever get it?

So far, all he had done was exchange letters with a lawyer he had never seen. Was there really such a person as J.P. Addelton, Attorney at Law, 202 State Street, Albany, N.Y. ? Maybe the whole thing was some sort of con game. And even if it wasn't, what about all the laws regarding inheritances and taxes? Brewer knew nothing about them. Maybe the federal government, or the state, or the county or the city, or almost anybody with more power than an eighteen-year-old college freshmen ~ and that was pretty much anyone at all ~ could take the money from him for perfectly legal reasons and there wasn't a damn thing he could do about it.

Brewer felt like he was standing on a plank sticking out over the Grand Canyon. The plank was old and rotten and falling apart piece by piece. He couldn't stay on it and he couldn't go back. All he could do but stand there and wait for the inevitable to happen.

Before now, his life had never been his to control, but at least it had been stable. Now all he had was a mattress on McLean's floor. Tomorrow? Maybe he would, maybe he wouldn't. He couldn't expect to McLean to keep him around like an old cat that refused to die.

Good god, what have I done?

His thoughts raced into overdrive, beyond his control; a crazy quilt of snarling parents and shrieking cousins; of intimidating textbooks and difficult classes and ideas, oh so many ideas, ideas with power, ideas that changed his perceptions, god, how he was eager for more; of a girl named Marilyn, the deep sheen of her hair, the glow of her skin - *how could I have been so fucking dumb?!*

Brewer was breathing heavily. He looked about with wide, feral eyes. He had to act. He had to do something before he went mad.

He spotted a broom.

He leapt at it, took it in his hands and gripped it with white-knuckled intensity, glaring like a Visigoth who just taken a gladiolus from a slain legionary.

Then he launched into what would become the legendary Brewer Cleaning Frenzy. The broom became his weapon as he attacked every corner, every nook of the house, destroying dust balls, annihilating cobwebs, eradicating mouse turds; back and forth, back and forth, hunting for dirt, prowling for crud. When he couldn't find any more, he filled a bucket with hot water, added a bottle of Lysol, found a rag and began scrubbing. He scrubbed the floors and baseboards, scouring them, abrading them in his ferocity. He assaulted the windows, washing and rinsing washing and rinsing until there were no streaks - *You Better Fucking Believe It!* - and then he went after the cabinets. He emptied them, cleaned inside and then filled them again, their contents orderly for the first time since, well, since forever. Then he scrubbed down shelves and counters and anything else that crossed his sights.

McLean stood aside, quietly drinking a cup of coffee and contemplating the demonic wraith crashing and swirling about his home like the Tasmanian Devil. Well, maybe he's nuts, but the place could use a good cleaning. . .

Brewer attacked the kitchen. He scoured the stove, including under the burners and the oven; no oven cleaner just a Brillo pad and a lot of primal grunting and cursing. He swept the mouse turds from under the sink and then scrubbed that.

He scrubbed down the bathroom sink and the toilet and the tub. He found a bottle of rubbing alcohol and polished all the fixtures. He thought about emptying the drawers and cleaning them, but when he opened one and saw all of Pam's tampons, douches, yeast infection ointments and the like, he decided against it. Even cleaning frenzies have their limits.

He wiped off every door knob, light switch, drawer pull and cabinet handle in the house. He took the throw rugs out into the back yard, hung them on the line and savagely flailed at them with a broken axe handle until they all but bled.

He spotted a rusty lawn mower leaning against the house. Mowing the lawn in December? Clearly not the act of a sound mind. Brewer didn't care. The collection of weeds that passed for a lawn never had a chance.

He stomped back inside and ransacked the house of every item of clothing and bedding he could find, gathering them into a large ball, stuffing it in a garbage bag and demanding McLean give him coins and soap for the laundromat down on Nickerson. Wordlessly, so as not to provoke the panting lunatic before him, McLean complied.

Brewer washed it all, dividing it up among three washers to save time, pacing back and forth maniacally, a man possessed as the machines chugged and groaned through their cycles, the only thing distracting him the sharp smell of hot water and soap. Brewer liked that.

Into the dryers the textiles went, tumbling and roaring before the glaring, intolerant eyes of the tall young man who tapped his foot furiously, demanding they hurry up.

Back up the hill he walked, a deranged Santa Clause with a bag full of other people's clothes, past the donut shop, closed, past the barber shop, closed, past the college, empty and dormant. He saw little, he heard little. He thought only of muscle and sweat, and breath cold in his chest, hard and fast, forcing the fear from his body, routing it from his mind. The air around him was clear and life-giving, the night was his cloak. The world was big, immense, endless; he would never see all its sights, never smell all its smells, never run his hands along the flanks of all its girls. It was huge, he was small, but he was in it, part of it, sweat and strain, sweat and strain, and his fear evaporated into its greatness and it was a wondrous thing.

Back at the house, he dropped the bag in front of McLean.
"Here!" he barked.
McLean was impressed.

Brewer looked around, searching the room with a predator's eyes. But there was no more. He was done.

He hadn't rested all day. He hadn't eaten all day. Call it purging, call it purification, call it madness, *call it any fucking thing you want, but goddamnit, that place was CLEAN!*

McLean offered him a glass of wine. Brewer said no thanks. McLean offered him a glass of Bourbon whiskey. Brewer, who up to now prided himself in being a non-drinker, thought, aw hell why not. He took a deep breath and knocked back the big drink in one gulp.

For a second, he stood paralyzed, like a freeze frame in a movie. Then his body jerked in a head-to-foot spasm, his eyes went out of focus and his legs took on a mind of their own.

He staggered into the wall, gasping and gagging. McLean exploded in laughter, caught his breath, took another look at Brewer, whose red face and bulging eyes resembled something out of a Looney Tunes cartoon, and went into a convulsion of laughter that sent him to the floor. Brewer started laughing too. But it made him inhale some of the fumes left in his mouth and that made him to stiffen and fall with a resounding crash, not unlike a felled fir tree.

Pam wandered out of the bedroom to see what was going on. When she looked around and saw that she was the only one in the room standing on her own two feet, she actually smiled - a very small twitch at the corners of her mouth, but a smile nonetheless. And that made McLean and Brewer laugh and gasp and gag and roll all the more. It was a merry climax to the day's activities.

Chapter 19

Seattle in winter is four shades of gray, none of them interesting. It is short days, often rainy and usually dark; wind, often, and snow, with its crystalline, alabaster drifts and sapphire skies, rarely.

The city is hilly; a series of long ridges, actually, many very steep and five of them more than four hundred feet above sea level – and the city begins at sea level. They make it difficult to navigate at any time, and in the dark and cold, they create a singular sense of gloom and foreboding. There is no release from the watery murk. It drives people indoors, where they stay and endure, waiting for better times.

At SPC, winter quarter 1964-65 was characterized by huddled figures with long coats and umbrellas, wading through the perpetual dusk to classes or meals; rote, their heads down, their expressions resigned. In class, they usually were equally stoic, taking notes and answering questions mechanically, their minds elsewhere – except there was no elsewhere. It was Seattle in winter.

Or so it seemed. But there was more. For, in the dorm lounges, in the student lounges, in the dining halls, over formica tables and overbrewed coffee, there was unrest. Forced together against the darkness, the young were like electrical wires in the rain, sparking ideas, insights, doubts.

"So, what Buber says is that we need to view the world around us in two ways; the I-It relationship and the I-Thou relationship."

"Huh?"

"Okay, let's say you look at a tree. It's a tree, that's that and you move on. No need for further consideration. That's an I-It relationship. But let's say you feel something for that tree. You feel a relationship with it."

"Wait a minute, a relationship with a tree?"

"Sure. Think about it. You've felt attachments to inanimate objects: Your teddy bear when you were a kid, your favorite jacket, whatever."

"Maybe that's just a projection of your own needs. You just can't express them."

"Maybe. But what Buber says is that when there is a relationship between you and another thing, you can eventually enter into another realm; one where there is no 'between.'"

"Wait a minute. . ."

"The Plains Indians believed that. They believed rocks, trees and other things had spirits. So they would go out alone, fast, meditate, chant and so forth until they were free of physical sensation. Then, they believed, they were part of the greater universe, there was nothing between them and it. They achieved I-Thou."

"Okay. I don't agree, but even if I did, what practical value is all of this?"

"No idea. But if Buber is right, most of us spend our lives walking through a world and never sensing its reality. We are inherently narrow-minded and unaware. I can't believe that does a person any good."

Sometimes, they ushered in new ways of thinking.

"The big bang theory makes a lot of sense. The universe is expanding. But what I keep wondering is, what caused the big bang to go off?"

"Maybe nothing caused it."

"Something must have caused it."

"Why?"

"Cause and effect. It's an essential law of physics."

"Does physics explain everything?"

"Yes."

"Does it explain the human soul? No equations for that that I'm aware of."

"Okay, okay. Your point being . . ."

"Maybe the big bang had no cause. It just happened. It's called moot logic. We've been studying it in Andress's class. A thing has no cause. Poof, it just happens. The concept can drive you nuts."

Sometimes, they provoked brutal pragmatism.

"Now, we know the sound of two hands clapping, right?"
"Right."
"So what is the sound of one hand clapping?"
"Actually, I know the answer to this one."
"You do?"
"Sure: Who cares?!"
"But in the Tantric, spiritual sense. . ."
"Oh, bullshit. The question is nonsense. Buncha beatniks hang around a coffee shop all day, listen to bongo drums and talk about half-assed hogwash. It makes them feel soooo deep."
"Maybe they are."
"Oh right, you bet. People invented the light bulb and the telephone and the polio vaccine by contemplating their navels. Shakespeare shouldn't have wasted his time writing plays. Bad poetry is where it's at, man. Tchaikovsky should've scrapped symphonies and taken up the bongo drums. Posing and jerking off; that's where the real action is."

Sometimes, they touched upon disquieting realities.
"But we are a free country."
"Are we?"
"Well, sure. Of course."
"Not if you have to work for a living. Then you spend a third of your life making money for somebody else. Then you are free to say, 'Right you are, J.B.!' and 'By golly, Mr. Gotrocks, I wish I'd thought of that!'"
"You can always quit."
"Sure, then get another job where the rules are just the same. Try exercising your right of free speech, or free press or free assembly - or free thought! - in your basic American workplace and you'll end up broke and on the street in a hurry. "
"You would prefer communism?"
"Show me where the Constitution says anything about capitalism. It didn't even exist until the Industrial Revolution. Capitalists have been making people kiss their asses ever since. The best way to succeed in our world is to take whatever resembles self respect and throw it in a drainage ditch. Then you can get on with being as sniveling little suck-up for someone else's benefit. That's the real American way."

Sometimes, there were quiet, reasoned moments of insight.

"So Machiavelli is saying we shouldn't waste our time by doing the right thing?"

"No, no, not at all. What he is saying is that no person can ever be completely good all the time. We are flawed humans. And, we live in a world where virtue by itself serves no practical purpose. But, by recognizing virtues, by categorizing them, you can pick and choose when to use them for maximum benefit."

"Sounds a bit hypocritical."

"Look, here's an example: generosity. Let's say you are a king. You want to make people's lives better, so you give liberally to good causes. That's good, right?"

"Right."

"Wrong. You'll have to tax the people to raise the money for all your good works. They will resent that. And you'll become known as a soft touch for every freeloader with a sob story. People hold that in contempt."

"Better you should be a miser?"

"Yup. Get a reputation for it. Spend rarely. Don't flaunt your wealth. Keep your private life private. Then every now and then, if the occasion arises, give to some worthy cause, one that will generate a lot of publicity. That way, people will admire your generosity – or the appearance of it, which is what really counts. The kingdom will have low taxes, you will have the authority to run it efficiently and everyone will be happy."

"But there will still be suffering and misery."

"Sure, but there always has been. No point in destroying a kingdom over something that will never go away. You can't do anybody any good if you are on your way to the guillotine."

Sometimes, it challenged the most sacred of sacred cows.

"A girl has to be careful about her reputation."

"Her reputation for what?"

"You know."

"Why is that anybody's business but hers?"

"I mean she has to have high standards, for herself."

"What standards? There's some one to ten rating systems for girls, all spelled out and ranked for what you do in your private life?"

"That's not what I meant. I mean we can't have free love, with everybody doing it with whoever they want all over the place."

"Why not? As long as there's contraception and mutual consent, what difference would it make? Just keep the door locked."

"There's no telling where it would lead. There would be chaos."

"You don't know that. There's no evidence at all to suggest that would happen. It's just another way to keep the whole business hushed up and mysterious; it's a big, dark secret so let's be terrrribly afraid of it. Just a bunch of superstition."

"You're just looking for a way to get girls to go to Golden Gardens with you."

"Well, now that you mention it . . ."

And occasionally, on very rare moments, there was transcendence.

"I was walking toward Peterson and my mind was playing music, the way it usually does, music with a rhythm and a beat, the theme from The Man From UNCLE, of all things, and this girl is walking toward me. I'd never seen her before. She was really tall and she was looking straight ahead like I wasn't there, like no one was there. Her steps matched the rhythm in my head, beat for beat. And her body seemed to pulse every time her foot hit the pavement, as if all her muscles were tensing and stretching to the beat, as if there was some kind of special life in her. And I don't know why, but that's when I realized that it's all happening right now, this moment, right here."

"I'm not quite clear. What is happening?"

"Life. Wonderment. Call it whatever you want. Music expresses it better than anything I know, but even that can't capture it, really. Now, this moment, *this moment,* that's reality. Incredible things are happening *right now.* But we miss them. We're too busy thinking about the past or worrying about the future."

"So?"

"The past and the future aren't real. Now is real."

"Wait a minute . . ."

"You can't experience the past or the future. They are abstracts. You can't do anything about them. This moment is all we have. You have a responsibility to understand it, to feel it. You have to make the best of it, and everything about it *now.*"

"What about the girl with the walk?"

"Don't know. Haven't seen her since."

****

Marilyn Pennell returned for the second quarter of her freshman year of college to find her room half empty.

Every trace of Janet Small was gone; not a good bye note, not a mark on the wall where she had put pictures, not even a dust ball. Marilyn was not surprised. If ever there was a dumb, naïve girl destined to flunk out, it was Janet Small. Still, Marilyn found it disconcerting that every trace of Janet had disappeared, that any evidence that she even existed was gone.

Janet and her parents must have come in during Christmas break. Marilyn tried to picture the scene: A Norman Rockwell tableau retouched by Edvard Munch; Her parents, so proud and hopeful four months earlier, now grim-faced and terse, trying hard not to show their heartache, their disappointment and only partially succeeding. Where goeth one's child, one's hope, one's dreams, now, when failure comes at such a young age? What a world. Marilyn felt pity for them

She did not feel pity for Janet. A twit is a twit, she thought. All the sympathy in the world won't change them. The best thing to do with them is keep them out of your life.

The thought made Marilyn feel guilty. She had been raised to show kindness toward the weak and helpless and she knew, intellectually, that was the proper attitude. But she didn't feel it. She had her own problems; a quarter more of college, maybe two if she was lucky, and then what? She had no idea. Janet was weak and foolish. Marilyn was strong and smart. But she also was unlucky. The thought irked her. People who blame their misfortune on bad luck are simply quitters . . .

My, my, she thought; how pat, how simple – and how arrogant.

She looked again at the bare half of the room. Poor, dumb Janet. Maybe she would enroll at a local JC. Marilyn pictured Janet, open-mouthed and lost, wandering amid the zombies, drop-outs, unwed mothers and general flotsam of a local JC, a kitten among jackals.

Or maybe Janet would move home with her parents and spend the rest of her young adulthood in her room. What else could she do? Perhaps a job as a church secretary or some such thing, something in a properly safe, secure fantasyland.

Maybe she would even get married.

Marilyn's brain zigzagged loudly, like a phonograph needle gone astray. Janet Small Doing It? Marilyn pictured the scene: Janet, wide-eyed and terrified, quivering under the covers, waiting to be violated by some leering, slavering fiend. Marilyn chuckled dryly, without humor. Well, she's gone now. I have the room all to myself. When the lights go out, I can play with myself in peace.

Oh, what have I become?

Well, it's the truth, isn't it? Welcome to reality, and if ever there was a time to face reality, without illusion, this was it.

Janet was not the only one gone. Of the Class of '68's 502 members, 87 did not return for winter quarter; whereabouts unknown. Others would be gone soon. Their bad grades put them on academic probation, which meant they had one quarter to bring them up to a 2.0 – which most would not.

The winnowing had begun; a cold, brutal process that would last the rest of the year and into the next. Like Marilyn, those who survived it did not expend compassion on those who did not. The difficulties were the same for all and the laws of self-preservation were plain. Adulthood, in the form of accepting cruel realities, was settling in.

God, I need some fun, Marilyn thought; some gaiety, a room full of witty, carefree people; Champagne and music and bright lights.

At SPC?

The place was a mausoleum of goody two-shoes. The pizza parties they threw in the dorms are all right, as far as they went, but they don't go very far, and there wouldn't be any for another week or two.

Maybe she could catch a bus downtown and find some action. But where? Too young to go in a bar and, really, where else was there? One of those beatnik coffee shops in the U District? No. Stale cigarette smoke and unwashed bodies did not suit her mood, if indeed they ever would.

She was stuck and she knew it. Welcome back to school.

****

Every morning, Brewer would cook breakfast, serve it, wash the dishes, clean the stove and kitchen counters and vacuum the living room. Then he would go check his mail.

To McLean and Pam, he seemed a rather comical figure; a fussy little man constantly cleaning and straightening the chaotic mess that characterized their habitat, his persnickety routines as foreign to them as their porcine proclivities were to him.

What they didn't know, although McLean had an inkling, was that Brewer's rituals constituted the slender thread of sanity that kept him from total despair. When in doubt, concentrate on practicalities, he told himself, and it worked - to a point. Sometimes, he still found himself waking up at 3 a.m., terrified, alone, thoughts of ruin overwhelming him in icy waves.

At 8 a.m. sharp, never a minute early or a minute late, Brewer left the little house on Dravus to walk to the SUB and check his mail box. On the way, he concentrated, as best he could, on practicalities. How would he retrieve his clothing and personal items from his parents' home? Orrin would probably do that. He would give him a call. How would he pay for his books for winter quarter? He had $82 in his savings account. It might be enough. If not, maybe some of the books would be in the library. Either way, he could no longer afford the bus, so he would have to hike to the bank, a six mile round trip in the rain. He could ask for a ride from McLean but, damnit, he would not. He had been obligated to other people too much and too long. Better to be wet than beholden.

Assuming he got the books, where would he study? Certainly not at McLean's. McLean may have thrived on disorder, but Brewer did not. That left the library, which was fine, except it closed at 10 p.m. Maybe the basement of one of the dorms. Yes, that would work. No one would notice. No one would care.

He needed his typewriter. Maybe Orrin could get it for him. Or maybe that was asking too much of Orrin. When he called him he would find out.

How long would McLean let him stay at the house? They hadn't discussed it. Brewer hoped his constant cleaning could delay discussion. Already, Pam was giving him dirty looks. But then, Pam gave everybody dirty looks. That and glazed stares constituted her range of expression.

As he walked past Moyer, Brewer shifted his thoughts to the $30,000. If he got it, his first expense would be an apartment. He heard that you could get a furnished, one bedroom at the apartments by the Ballard Bridge for about $120 a month. That came to about $1,400 a year. Twenty eight thousand, six hundred dollars left. A car? He saw new Mustangs advertised for about $3,000. Tempting, but no. A used car, say $1,000 to $1,500. Gas? Insurance? He had no idea. Food, clothing, miscellaneous? Again, no idea.

Tuition? About $1,800 a year at SPC. Half that at the UW. Girls?

That thought stopped him. Girls. Well, they didn't come free, that's for sure. A movie and pizza? Ten bucks or so; $520 a year if you want to calculate it that way. Dinner and a play or a concert? More, to be sure, but if you don't spend, you don't get.

Jesus, that's crass, Brewer thought. Did he want to take off their clothes? Of course. But he also liked them as people, whether fuckery was involved or not. Their company, the fact they actually wanted to spend time with *him*, of all people; yes, that could be very pleasant indeed.

Anyway, he would have expenses, lots of expenses. He would have to find some type of summer job to make the money last four years. He could probably get his old job bagging groceries at the University Village QFC. It didn't pay much, but when added to the thirty thousand, it should be enough.

It would take him about twenty minutes each way to drive there, much faster than when he used to take the bus from his parents' home, even though it was only two miles away.

Would his parents see him working there and precipitate a big, imbecilic scene? Probably not. They had bought their groceries at the same Albertson's on Northeast 55th and 40th Northeast for twenty years. Never anywhere else. As with most things, any deviation from what they were accustomed to was something to be feared.

In any case, Brewer decided the $30,000 just might get him through all four years of college, if he was careful ~ and if indeed it ever arrived.

It did not arrive on Monday. It did not arrive on Tuesday. It did not arrive on Wednesday or Thursday. Oh well, Brewer thought, time for Plan B: Finish one more quarter of college, then wait for the draft. Or go enlist. Yippee.

On Friday, it arrived.

Mr. Thomas J. Brewer

Mail Box 73
Student Union Building
Seattle Pacific College
Seattle, Wash. 98119

Dear Mr. Brewer;

In accordance with your instructions, I liquidated the portion of funds allotted to you in the estate of Mr. Lee W. McEwen. Because some of the stocks and bonds had accrued interest and earnings, the final amount was $31,814.67.

The broker's fee for this transaction was $206.14. My fee for the legal services necessary to oversee the transaction was $154.26. These fees were deducted from the inheritance. A check for $31,454.27 is enclosed.

Brewer carefully peered into the envelope. A blue piece of paper, one that definitely looked like a check, was neatly tucked among its folds.

He glanced around quickly. The hallway was empty, save for him. Good. He reached in the envelope with two fingers. Carefully, so as not to damage it, he slowly extracted the check.

There it was: $31,454.27 made out to Thomas J. Brewer.

Brewer waited for a few seconds. Wasn't something supposed to happen? Wasn't he supposed to have his breath taken way? Wasn't his head supposed to spin?

Something?

Nothing. It was a piece of paper, no more, no less. So this is what it feels like to have a lot of money, Brewer thought. It doesn't feel much different than being broke. He laughed. What a game, what a silly, brainless game.

Then he remembered: Practicalities. He looked at the letter again. It continued:

In your recent letter, you asked about taxes on the inheritance. The state of New York and federal government do not tax inherited amounts under $50,000. Your home state, Washington, does not tax inherited amounts under $70,000. Nor does your state have an income tax.

So, the full amount belongs to you, free and clear.

If I can be of further assistance, please to not hesitate to give me a call.

Respectfully,

J.P. Addelton
 Attorney at Law
202 State Street
Albany, N.Y. 12210.

    Well well well. Thirty one thousand, five hundred forty four dollars and twenty seven cents, and it's mine. No one can take it from me – unless the State of Washington really does have some half-assed law that doesn't allow anyone under twenty one to inherit this much money.
    But the State of Washington doesn't know anything about it and I'm sure as hell not going to tell them.
    The thought made Brewer feel shady and conspiratorial, a character from a cheap detective novel. He had gotten away with something illicit and he liked it. He found himself turning inward, happy within himself, happy that he was a private citizen with private affairs *that were nobody's else's goddamned business!* He wouldn't have to justify them to anyone.
    Was that freedom, ultimate freedom?
    Well, yes, it probably was.
    But back to practicalities. Get the check to the bank. Now.
    With calculated, delicate movements, he eased the check back in the envelope. With equal care, he slid the envelope into the breast pocket of his coat, where it wouldn't wrinkle. Then he set off walking. No rain today, blessedly, just gray sky, muffled and still. Morning traffic had cleared. A young man walking alone would be anonymous, hardly noticed by the rest of the world.
    Up Nickerson, across the Fremont bridge, along the shore of Lake Union to Stone Way, then up 45th and over the freeway to the bank at 12th N.E. It took Brewer a little over an hour.
    At the bank, he found his hand shaking slightly was he filled out the deposit slip for his savings account. The teller was a young woman, Brewer's age, give or take, and she had the waxen, resigned look of those who are stuck in dead end jobs for the rest of their lives and know it. She did not smile at Brewer when he

stepped up to the window. She did not say Good Morning. She barely looked at him at all.

Then she read the amount on the check.

Instantly, her face took on a glow.

"Oh! Well, this will take just a minute. And how's your day so far, Mr. Brewer?"

"Pretty good," Brewer said. He put his elbow in the counter, leaned toward her and smiled. "And please, call me Tom."

She smiled back shyly.

Flirt with a bank teller? Well, why not? He was rich now. Isn't that what rich guys did? He continued to smile at her as she tapped on an automated adding machine. Befuddled, she missed a key and started again. Finally, she handed him the receipt, her face still glowing.

"And have a really nice day," she said.

Brewer continued to smile at her for a moment longer, enjoying her befuddlement.

He found an assistant manager and opened a checking account for $15,000. As with the teller, the assistant manager was all smiles and good will. Brewer, who had been in the receiving end of officious contempt so long and so often he had come to expect it, chuckled inwardly. What a game...

A half hour later, he was back on the street, checkbook in hand, wondering what he was supposed to do next. He was, after all, in new territory. Then he remembered: Practicalities. It was about noon. Eat. On University Avenue, just south of N.E. 50th St., there was a Chinese restaurant, Kau Sing, which he had seen from the bus every night, wondering what it would be like. Moot point. He couldn't afford it. But he could now.

Chapter 20

The day after he deposited his $31,454.27 in the bank, Brewer set off walking up Nickerson Street, checking the manager's office of every apartment building until he found one with a vacancy. It was on the second floor, had one bedroom, a small balcony and was furnished. "Furnished" meant chairs and couches and tables that were cheap ten years ago and had not improved with age. They had no tears, stains or cigarette burns, however, and that was good enough for Brewer. The carpets looked reasonably clean, the bathroom fixtures had no rust. The refrigerator had no mildew.

There was a dishwasher.

It was as good a place as any, Brewer decided. He signed the lease, paid first and last month rent and that was that. The landlord, a weary-looking old woman, asked no questions about his age, his income, his status as a student or anything else. As one used to being scrutinized almost constantly by every authority figure in range, Brewer found it all oddly anticlimatic.

He looked the apartment over. There were no pots and pans in the kitchen, no silverware, glasses or cups. There were no towels in the closet, no sheets or blankets in the bedroom. No television or radio. Not even a clock. I suppose I should expect that, Brewer thought. People steal things.

That night he slept on the bare mattress, dreaming of nothing, nothing at all. It was a blessed relief.

The next morning, he had coffee and a donut at the little shop on Third West and caught the first bus downtown.

He had browsed the Bon Marche occasionally during his commutes and he knew it probably had everything he needed. But he didn't know much else. What constituted a reasonable number of towels, or plates and saucers or bed sheets? What were the good brands? What was the terminology for such things? Brewer felt like a rube going to town for his first store-bought suit.

In addition, the world of shopping was a woman's world, and the female approach to shopping – endless walking, endless talking and a seeming genetic incapacity for simple yes or no decisions, had aggravated him since childhood pull-alongs with his mother.

He slinked and sneaked through the aisles, furtively looking over his shoulder, worried that someone might be watching him. Finally, he found the kitchenware department. There was a great deal to choose from: Row upon row of boxes with bright pictures of plates and saucers and cups on them, along with enthusiastic descriptions of the latest space age materials they were made from. Some of the pots and pans were coated with something called Teflon. What the hell was Teflon? Brewer had no idea what any of it meant. But, he eventually concluded, he could count - "Service For Four" was clear enough - and he could read a price tag. He bought the cheapest and the least.

"Well, looks like you're setting up house!" the woman behind the counter chirped.

Yeah, and I'm eighteen, I don't know a thing about any of this, I don't want to be reminded of it and the sooner I can get the hell out of here the happier I'll be, Brewer thought. But he didn't say it out loud. He forced a smile, paid and, burdened with a jumble of awkwardly-proportioned boxes and bags, each with its own interpretation of the laws of gravity, did his best to make it to the door.

Back on the bus. He was coming to hate the bus. It was impossible to walk down the aisle with anything approaching normal coordination and the only seat he could find with enough room for all his cargo was at the very back. People stared at him, including a blue-jowled man with taped-together eyeglasses and a permanent, moronic grin. He continued to stare at Brewer, grinning, the whole three miles to Brewer's stop.

Brewer lurched and stumbled out of the bus, staggered across Nickerson blindly - the damned boxes kept blocking his view - and then managed, with a lot of crashing and cursing, to make it up the stairs and through the door of his apartment.

After he put away the kitchenware and hung up the towels, he went to the bedroom. Shouldn't you wash sheets before putting them on? He vaguely remembered something about preservatives they put on them at the factory. To hell with it. On they went.

He had forgotten to buy a pillow.

To hell with that, too. He ordered a burger at the SUB for dinner, bought a newspaper and spent the rest of the night reading it.

The room was very quiet.

Brewer thought he should feel lonely and isolated, but he did not. He felt satisfied. He was getting there. This place, this stuff; it was his and no one could take it from him. No one could even come through the door if he didn't want them to.

So, what would he do with his new-found independence? Nothing. He liked nothing. The state of being left alone was enough.

The next day, Brewer bought a car. He considered going to a used car lot, but the byzantine world of automotive registration, licensing, warrantees and the like was totally beyond his comprehension and he doubted a used car salesman would be conscientious about educating him. Again, he felt like a hayseed fresh off the turnip truck.

So he checked the want ads. Someone on Capitol Hill was selling a 1960 Pontiac Catalina four-door ("Low Mileage! Clean!") for $1,300. Brewer gulped at the price. He saw his thirty thousand dollars crumbling into dirty, gray particles, casually blowing away into the grimy winter dusk. Then he checked the other ads. The price was typical for four-year-old cars, and, for the sake of repair costs, he didn't want anything older than that. And he didn't want a Falcon or a Valiant or some other compact. It was pretty hard to get a girl interested when you are both too wedged in to move. He took a deep breath and forced the money from his mind.

Brewer knew the 1960 Pontiac, one of the rare cars of the period to have understated styling and a certain air of good taste about it. How was it mechanically? Brewer had no idea, nor any idea how to find out. He called the number in the ad. A tired-sounding woman answered. Yes, the car was still available. Come by at 2 p.m.

Again, a bus ride, this one with a transfer and two long walks in the rain, one up a steep hill. The house was for sale. The woman, once young and pretty, looked haggard and sad. Brewer knew the signs of a divorce when he saw them.

The car's finish was still reasonably shiny. No dents. The tires had tread. The upholstery was a bit worn, but not threadbare.

The woman let him start the engine. No smoke, no rattles, no pings.

Brewer didn't know what else to look for. He offered the woman $1,200 cash on the spot. She sighed resignedly and accepted. She gave Brewer a receipt, the deed and registration and the keys. The entire transaction had taken fifteen minutes.

No more bus rides, no more getting stranded far from home, no more cops rousting him because they had nothing better to do. Freedom. Brewer could not recall ever having felt better.

He knew he would need insurance. He knew nothing about insurance. While riding the bus - *The Goddamned Bus!* - he had seen a big insurance company on Eastlake next to the freeway. It would have to do.

The receptionist sent him to a young man far in the back of the building. The young man, not much older than Brewer, had uncombed hair and a tie pulled loose to the third button of his rumpled shirt. His desk was cluttered, his ashtray was full. Brewer decided to cut to the chase.

"I just bought a car," he said, pulling out the sheaf of papers. "I need insurance. I'll be straight with you; I have no idea what kind to get. Please don't screw me."

The young man sat up straight in surprise. Then he laughed.

"Okay, okay, I won't screw you," he said. "I've made my screwing quota for the day and I want to go home. Let's see the papers."

He looked them over quickly.

"Any accidents or tickets?" he asked Brewer.

"No."

"Okay. Here's the deal. Accident and collision coverage will pay for any damage to your car and anybody you hit. You don't need anything else, unless you want towing coverage, which you'll probably never use. If you get in a wreck, don't admit to anything. Make a sketch of what happened, write down the time and place, get the other guy's name, license number and insurance company and send it to us. If it was your fault, we'll pay. If it was his fault, we'll pay for your damage then get the money from his insurance company. Costs you eighteen bucks a month."

"That's it?"

"That's it."

"What about deed and registration and all that?"

The young man handed Brewer a form.

"Fill this out and sign it. We'll take care of the rest and send it to you."

Brewer laughed.

"You're not what I expected from an insurance salesman," he said.

The young man laughed too.

"I hear that a lot. As far as I'm concerned, you need insurance, we sell insurance and that's that. The rest is b.s. Insurance salesmen aren't supposed to believe in b.s. I'm not sure I'm cut out for this line of work."

He held out his hand. Brewer shook it.

"Well, you're covered," the young man said. "Try not to wreck the car."

****

The experience of having a home of his own home took getting used to. Brewer would read a great deal, luxuriating in the quiet. Or he would sit out on the small balcony front Nickerson and gaze out at the view. It was a plebian view of the hills of Fremont and Ballard, but it was his to take in any way he wanted. He took drives around town. The beaches at Golden Gardens and Carkeek Park were favorites. He went to the bookstores. He paid cash for his winter quarter textbooks. He liked it all.

The day before classes began, he found himself feeling itchy. He remembered riding the bus. One day a man got on. He was as unlikely a bus passenger as one would ever see: Silver-haired, ram rod straight and imperially slim in a perfectly-cut three-piece chalk stripe suit; tie precisely knotted, trousers razor-creased, shoes plain but expensive, polished to an onyx finish; the personification of understated patrician elegance.

He only rode a few blocks, but it was enough; enough for Brewer to notice, enough for Brewer to be struck with angst.

I'll never make it, Brewer thought. At least once a week, usually more, he would find himself staring at an impenetrable block of academic prose and understanding not a word. Three chapters to finish before morning and he couldn't get past the first page; one page out of thousands, one assignment out of hundreds, one day out of four years – if he survived four years.

Brewer felt as only those who must face themselves and their limitations without defense, without protection: Four years of college, sweating out every day, always on the fine edge of failure and ruin, his existence sliding slowly, inexorably down a formless slope toward the blank, desolate haze that is the future.

Would he ever, *ever*, have an expensive suit, little less cut an elegant figure in it? It was so far from the world of struggling through college every day; so remote, so hopelessly out of reach that it was painful.

Then he inherited $31,454.27.

He had been careful with the money so far; a used car, a modest apartment. He had kept track of it with meticulous attention, constantly calculating and recalculating his expenses, always wary of seeing it melt away and leaving him abandoned in a cold, hostile world. But, he decided, he could probably spend some of it on clothing; not too much, of course, but some, enough to see him through for a while.

His first stop was at Frederick and Nelson, Seattle's premier department store. During his commutes, Brewer had wandered through its men's clothing department a couple of times. He had always noticed the neckties, folded neatly, row on row in a mahogany-framed display case, their colors lustrous and rich, bespeaking a world of cherry-paneled rooms and expensive brandy in cut crystal glasses, of stimulating conversation and thick, dark cigars . . . a world Brewer had never seen and, he suspected, never would. But the muse still captivated him. So he bought some ties – a lot of ties: Regimental stripes, strakes of ruby and emerald and sapphire against a midnight sky, pure color, deep in the shimmering silk . . .

Nearby was a wall of shelves filled with sweaters. Brewer found his size and started to explore. As he did so, the touch of the wool, thick and soft, began to affect him. Tweed in the cool morning mist, heather and bracken, folds of the land, curvatures and undulations, pastures rolling off to the sky, you whistle to a dog . . .

He looked over the sports shirts. A bit staid and behind the times for his taste, so he started to leave. Then he spied the dress shirts. He had always worn the same kind, oxford cloth button-downs, and there were lots of those. But when Brewer picked one up to look it over, he noticed something unusual. The cloth had a very fine finish, a sheen, silky to the touch. Elegance; diamonds on ermine, a beautiful woman, black hair and red lipstick, hissing a thin haze of blue smoke across a darkened room . . .

The label called it "pinpoint oxford," and it cost twice as much as Brewer had ever paid for a shirt in his entire life. He had to have it; glacier white, ice blue, pale sage, yellow, stripes, tattersalls.

Brewer wrote out the checks, tried to ignore the amounts and headed off to the University District, the trunk of the car, his car, his freedom, stuffed with bags.

At Vaughn's on University way, he bought sports shirts. Solids, plaids with small, neat checks, madras; bright days; head back, laughing, pretty girls and lemonade, sailboats on the horizon . . .

A pattern was emerging. What did the combination of burgundy, navy, tan and oxford cloth blue mean? To be like the man on the bus? To never again have to wade through grit and slush and accept second best and take whatever disrespect others dished out because they have more position than you? Yes, all those things, but also something else, something about the depth, the self-assured understatement, thoughtful, the antithesis of the loud and overbearing and cheap and shallow; a cool, clean intelligence. Brewer couldn't express it, but he felt it. It was real.

He decided to buy his trousers at Bernie's a few blocks away, simply because he had never been able to afford anything there before. Chinos, simplicity, a zen of confidence; cords the texture of old schools and autumn days; wool slacks, a knife's edge, the perfection of a single vertical line, a snap to the walk, flawless grace . . .

The slacks had to be hemmed. "Straight or break?" the salesman asked. Brewer had no idea what that meant. He ordered break, trying very hard to act like he knew what he was doing.

Three pairs of shoes at Nordstrom. At Werner's, a blue blazer – *poise personified* – a sports coat, a trench coat – *Bogart!* – gray suede fleece-lined gloves and an umbrella. Brewer couldn't think of what else to buy. He added up the checks he had written. $514.62.

WHAT?!
FIVE HUNDRED BUCKS?!
ARE YOU OUT OF YOUR FRICKIN' MIND?!

 Brewer swallowed hard. Well, it was spent now; gone and not coming back. He felt strange. Unlike the apartment and the car, he didn't really need all this stuff. But he wanted it and now he had it; more of it than he was quite sure what to do with. You could only wear one suit of clothes at a time, after all. But all those fabrics and shapes and colors and patterns represented a statement, a declaration of who he was. Some guys prided themselves on rumpled shirts and Levi's with frayed cuffs. It proved they were authentic Kerouacesque free spirits, or some such thing. Not Brewer. For what was and would be the only time in his life, he had indulged himself, and it felt, well, it felt great, goddamnit! Maybe Indian swamis found spiritual enlightenment in wearing rags and sleeping with bugs, but Brewer did not. He had found what it was like to not feel want, and he liked it.

 A cautious voice in his head warned him that he was overdoing it and Brewer knew that voice was right. The thirty thousand would run out one day and that day could come very easily and a lot sooner than he wanted. But, if he found some summer jobs, he could stretch it for four years and maybe even have some left over. He wouldn't have to worry about spending any more of it on clothing, that was for sure.

Chapter 21

"Lookin' good today, my man," McLean said.

It was Brewer's first public display of his clothing binge: Merino wool sweater, starched pinpoint oxford shirt, worsted slacks and new loafers shining like polished mahogany. If it impressed McLean, what must the opposite sex think?

"Thank you. I've decided to turn over a new leaf,," Brewer said.

"You're off to a good start. You survived fall quarter?"

"I did. Only three years and eight months to go."

"And the ladies? That girl from Wenatchee?"

"Don't ask."

"Perhaps I can help," McLean said.

"Oh?"

"A party at my place Friday night. To kick off another quarter. Or whatever. Any excuse will do. Free food, free booze. And available members of the opposite sex. I'm not sure they're your type. Uh, what is your type, anyway?"

"I have no idea," Brewer said.

"Then you have nothing to lose! And I guarantee you'll be the best-dressed one there."

****

Brewer had never been to a college party, at least not the kind that McLean was rumored to throw, and he was curious. Booze, wanton women and irresistibly depraved acts; while he doubted he would find that level of debauch, he hoped he might at least experience something beyond his day-to-day slog.

Every light in McLean's house was ablaze, glazing the front yard and walkway with light. Even from the street, Brewer could hear the low hum of voices and music and laughter.

The door was unlocked. Once inside, Brewer took in the scene.

The atmosphere was a thick mixture of music, cigarette smoke and perfume; English Leather and Jade East for the men ~

"Brewer!" It was McLean, scruffy as ever, with a wide-eyed, almost feverish expression. He was smiling broadly.

"Have a drink!" McLean said, pressing a plastic cup into Brewer's hand. It was filled with a murky maroon fluid. Brewer glanced at the counter. Jugs of Gallo, Italian Swiss Colony, Thunderbird and other cheap wines were crowded together, precariously vying for space. McLean probably conned them from the blind grocer in Lake City. All you had to do was show him your driver's license. He couldn't read the printing.

McLean turned to the young man beside him. He was hunched and balding, with flabby jowls, a paunch hanging over his belt and a general air of effeminacy.

"This is Clayton," McLean said. "He's an editor at The Spiral."

Brewer held out his hand. Clayton did not shake it. His lip curled slightly as if in distaste.

"Brewer here studies a lot," McLean said. "They're going to put a plaque on his chair in the library."

Clayton raised an eyebrow indifferently.

"Left the monastery to find a little sin, ey?" McLean said, gesturing around the room.

"I was hoping for more than a little," Brewer said.

"This is a good place to start," McLean said with a laugh and wandered off toward the crowd.

"So, you're an editor at the Spiral," Brewer said, hoping to start up a conversation. Clayton looked Brewer up and down coldly, inspecting him. Then he looked away, as if there were far more interesting things to contemplate. Brewer decided to call him on it. He stepped closer to Clayton, almost touching him. Then He locked his eyes on him and kept them there.

After a bit, Clayton started to shift uncomfortably from foot to foot.

Finally, he sighed, "So you're a student at SPC."
"Yes."

Clayton looked Brewer up and down again.

"Are you a believer?" He sneered the word believer.

"Not really," Brewer said.

"Well, I heard that you can't go to SPC unless you're a believer," Clayton smirked. "Isn't that why you people enroll?"

too much of it ~ and hairspray and Emeraude for the women. In the kitchen, something involving onions was on the stove, a lot of onions, and there was yet another smell occasionally wafting through the smog, one Brewer had never experienced, something like smoldering burlap.

Groups had formed around the room: Young men with beards and scarves and young women in bulky, black sweaters, all very serious; pretty girls, mini-skirted with long straight hair parted in the middle, boys in button-down collar shirts and tweed jackets; fringies, both genders in loud-colored, loose-fitting clothes reminiscent of an Erroll Flynn movie; a sensitive soul strumming a guitar; a muscular Brando wannabe in a tight t-shirt leaning against the wall and scrutinizing the scene with practiced scorn; an occasional freshman sorority girl trying very hard to act like she was wasn't out of her depth; posers and snobs and bums and generic hangers-on, all of them acting out private tableaus of one kind or another. Very few were from SPC, which suited Brewer just fine. He didn't know any of the rest. That suited him too. On this night, he was looking for the new, the different, the unexplored.

He started edging his way toward the kitchen.

"Tom! Tomtomtom!" It was Pam, dressed all in black, silk or rayon or some such filmy thing, and sporting a cigarette holder. "I'm so glad you're here!" Pam gushed. She took Brewer's arm and started guiding him across the room. Brewer was taken aback. It was the most words he had ever heard Pam speak. Her usual contributions to an evening's proceedings were to scratch her crotch and grunt.

"Here, this is Jeff and this is Elaine and this is Gail," Pam said, gesturing at a group sitting on bean bag chairs in a semi-circle. "And this is Tom. The one I told you about, who cleaned our house."

"Hi," Brewer said with a nod. Before the three could respond, Pam was whisking him off toward the kitchen.

"Oh, you won't believe some of the people who are here tonight," Pam was saying. "There's Bud Lothian, who's doing publicity for the Sonny and Cher concert next month, and Bruce Toros, the columnist for The Spiral, and Suzanne Aft, the wife of Bobby Aft, that radical over at the UDub, and. . ."

"Not everybody there is like that," Brewer said. "A lot of us just ignore all that sort of thing."

"You mean you haven't been saved?" Clayton sneered the word saved, clearly amused with himself. "Don't you know you can't go to heaven if you haven't been saved?"

What was this guy's problem? Brewer wondered. Is it because he's fat and queer and I'm not? Or is it because he thinks I'm some hick freshman he can antagonize and get away with it? Clayton wasn't aggravating enough that Brewer wanted to punch him in his supercilious mouth, although the thought did briefly cross his mind. It was a pleasant thought.

Brewer looked around. McLean had disappeared. Then he spotted Pam, flitting from guest to guest, her cigarette holder at an elegant angle, her white teeth sparkling in the light. Brewer had never seen her teeth before because he had never seen her smile before. He caught her attention and cocked his head in invitation. She came over.

"So, you've met Clayton," she enthused. Brewer still found Pam's perfect hostess act disconcerting.

"Who did you say those folks on the bean bag chairs were again?" Brewer said.

"Oh. Gail and Elaine and Jeff. Want to meet them?"

"Sure," Brewer said, turning his back on Clayton as quickly as he could. He guided Pam across the room more than she guided him. Along the way, he spotted a bottle of MD 20/20 on a table and grabbed it.

"Wine, anyone?" he said to the bean bag three. It was an instant introduction. Brewer sat down.

" . . . and don't even get me started about Sandy Meeks," the girl called Elaine was saying. She was slender and dark, and attempting a Nefertiti look via a dense plastering of green eye shadow.

"She's dating that Dan Ruskin guy," Elaine said, "and you know what? He's gone and signed up for the Marines! The Marines! Going to be a second lieutenant or some such thing. I mean, how establishment can you get! Can't you just see Meeks on the arm of some fascist?"

The others nodded knowingly. Brewer sipped his wine. It tasted like something that had recently decomposed.

"Well, what do you expect?" Gail said. "Good old Sandy Super Straight. Headed for split level heaven in an Edsel."

Jeff leaned back and stared at the ceiling.

"Sure won't find me joining no Marines," he said. "The draft ain't getting me."

"Jeff is looking into the Peace Corps," Gail said to Brewer. "He wants to teach school in Cameroon."

Brewer nodded as if was impressed.

"What's with that music?" Elaine said, straining to hear the stereo.

"Peter and Gordon," Jeff said.

"Bubble gum." Elaine huffed, waving her hand dismissively. "So last year. Don't they have any Phil Ochs?"

"Who?" Brewer said.

The others seemed to stop in midbreath. They stared at him for a long moment.

"You don't know who Phil Ochs is?" Elaine said, smiling in mock amazement. "Hey, Brian," she shouted across the room at McLean, "This buddy of yours doesn't know who Phil Ochs is!"

Others in the crowd looked Brewer's way. He did his best to betray no emotion. Up to that moment, he had wanted to know more about Elaine. Among other things, the hemline of her skirt had hiked up, revealing a long flash of velvet upper thigh. Now he was contemplating the suggestion that she go fuck herself.

"Ochs isn't all that great," Jeff said. "Tom Paxton is a lot better. Besides, they're all just copying Pete Seeger and Lee Hayes."

"Oh sure," Gail snorted. "Pete Seeger and Lee Hayes: 'On Top of Old Smokey,' there's real derivation."

"So who do you think is hip. . . what did you say your name was?" Elaine said to Brewer.

"I don't think about it that much," Brewer said. "I listen to music because I like it. If it resonates with me, great. If not, so be it. Whether it's hip or not, I don't care."

It was as if he had farted loudly. Elaine's jaw dropped in stupefaction. She fought to regain her composure.

"But. . . but how do you expect to keep up on the latest trends?" Elaine said, trying to sound condescending.

Jesus, why me? Brewer wondered. *I was just hoping to have a little fun, maybe meet somebody I liked, maybe even get layed,* remote though that possibility might be. But not this. But something about Elaine, her pretentiousness, her smugness, had touched a nerve in him.

"What's a trend?" Brewer said. "What somebody says is a trend? And why is it important? For the sake of some kind of status? To show that I'm cooler than thou? Seems to me that keeping hip with the latest trends is just conformity with a different name. Half the world is trying to make me conform to one thing or another already. Why would I want more?"

Brewer's pronouncement left Elaine speechless. She had never heard anyone challenge the sanctity of hip. It simply was not done. She was the font of all things with-it and this Brewer, this nobody, had embarrassed her. She glowered impotently.

Gail, on the other hand, seemed mildly aroused. She lowered her chin and contemplated Brewer through her eye lashes. Brewer noticed. Gail was a little on the chunky side, with a broad face and big teeth. But still . . .

Jeff leaned back again and stared at the ceiling.

"More Mad Dog," he said. "A lot more Mad Dog, please."

Brewer filled Jeff's glass with the blackish syrup. Jeff took a long draw.

"Ah, that was a good week," he said, exhaling MD 20/20 fumes into the ambience. "You know, Tom, I think you have a point there. Fuck hip. Fuck everything. Let's drink."

"I'll get some more wine," Brewer said, rising. He had no intention of getting more wine, he just wanted to find better company, the potential in Gail's expression notwithstanding. Maybe he could connect with her later. Meanwhile . . .

Brewer weaved his way through drinkers and talkers and hustlers and hipsters, all the while wondering what he should do next. When he got to the kitchen he noticed the back door was open.

The party had spilled out into the back yard, with small copses of people talking and laughing. A few had drifted behind the shrubbery to exchange hand jobs and finger bangs. One guy was down in his knees, retching into the rose bushes.

"Nice night," someone said with the trace of a Texas accent. Brewer turned to see a thin, nondescript young man with thick horn-rimmed glasses.

"Yes it is," Brewer said. He paused for a minute.

"Actually, it hasn't been that great," Brewer said. "So, no offense, but if you're queer or something, just leave me alone, okay? I don't need any more bullshit."

"No, no, nothing like that," the young man said with a soft chuckle. "I noticed you were alone, that's all. Just making polite conversation." He was holding a rumpled cigarette. "Want some?" he said.

"What it is?" Brewer said.

"Pot."

Brewer inwardly recoiled. Pot was illegal, a felony, three years in jail and, he was told, it led to heroin.

"No thanks."

The young man held up to cigarette and inspected it.

"I probably shouldn't," he said. "It makes me hungry and I've got an ulcer. I'm Evan Morrison, incidentally."

"Tom Brewer."

"You're the one who cleaned Brian's house," Morrison said.

"That's me. How do you know McLean?"

"He used to attend the church where my father was minister."

"Let me guess, he was the resident little troublemaker," Brewer said.

"No, and neither was I," Morrison said. "It took SPC to bring all that out."

Brewer noticed that Morrison had a soft, almost detached way of speaking, as if he was in a continuous state of amused reflection.

"I don't think I've ever met a preacher's kid," Brewer said. "Is it true what they say about them?"

"What do they say?"

"That they go all wild."

"I suppose it's true sometimes," Morrison said. "We come from a strange upbringing. On one hand, you're in a position of status, which can make you conceited. On the other hand, you're supposed to set some kind of example, one that nobody can live up to. And we're indoctrinated with church subculture from the day we are born. That can turn you really weird, especially when you start to discover the world outside it."

"Sounds like you've talked about this before," Brewer said.

"It tends to come up."

"So, you go to SPC?"

"I do. Never a question about anyplace else. Mom and dad wanted to keep me close to the fold."

"What do you think of it?" Brewer said.

"Can't stand it."

"Why is that?"

"Hmmm, good question," Morrison said in his detached way. "The answer is kind of long. Sure you want to hear it? It might bore you."

"It's not like I have a lot of action tonight," Brewer said.

"Okay. Well, when I arrived as a freshman, I was very sure of who I was and what I would do. I was going to be a minister. It's what I had been groomed for all my life, after all. Then I started meeting other people like me – and I mean *just* like me. It's like we came off a printing press.

"At first, it was okay – people are attracted to what's familiar and all that. But then I realized how boring they were: Same opinions, same politics, same clichés; not an original idea in the lot of them. So I started looking around."

"What did you find?" Brewer said.

"Not much. Most philosophies are mostly concerned with justifying their status and being holier than thou; religious, atheist, capitalist, communist, whatever."

"Then you found nothing?"

"Then I got layed. Didn't plan it; a nice Christian girl at a dorm sing-along, a drive afterward and bingo, it happened. Never felt anything like it. For that moment, there was nothing else. All the neuroses, all the bigotry, all the bullshit of the world was gone. There was only that moment. It defined itself; the essence of existence. Do you like being alive?

"Yes."

"For that few minutes I felt what it was to be alive, not just putting in your time and hoping for something better. I sensed the nature of existence. You can experience it anywhere, I suppose. Emily Dickinson experienced it watching bumblebees. I experienced it in the front seat of a '57 Chev. I actually felt the essence of life."

Morrison looked down at the ground.

"Sorry," he said. "It must be the pot talking."

"No, go ahead," Brewer said.

Morrison said, "And yet, religion forbids us from experiencing that essence. We're supposed to be contemplating the state of our souls or some such thing. There has to be something wrong with an institution that wants to deny people the experience of their existence.

"Then I took an anthropology class. We ended up studying the cargo cult in the New Hebrides Islands. Ever hear of it?"

"No." Brewer was curious where this was going.

"The people on the islands had a stone age culture. Then the Second World War came along. We landed and converted the islands to airstrips and supply depots. For the islanders that meant that all kinds of miraculous stuff literally dropping from the sky; thirty centuries of progress in one day. Not unreasonably, they decided it must be supernatural. They ended up inventing a beneficent god, John Frum – probably the name of some GI who gave them stale Hershey bars and used girly magazines.

"In '45, the Americans left and the freebies stopped, but the people kept right on worshipping; building mock airplanes and tractors and stuff and praying for the day John Frum will return and bring them paradise on earth. They still do."

"The point being?" Brewer said.

"The point being, God didn't create people, people create God."

Morrison said it in a voice that was low and tired and resigned, with a cold finality in distinct contrast to his easy-going style. He wasn't fucking around.

Brewer let Morrison's statement settle in his mind. Finally, he said, "One isolated incident convinces you of that?"

"Look back at the origins of any religion and you'll find the same thing pretty much everywhere," Morrison said. "People are confronted with a phenomenon they can't explain and conclude it must be the work of a supernatural power. Then the belief gets entrenched. When somebody like Galileo or Darwin comes along with facts to challenge it, they get thrown in prison, or have their eyes put out, or get burned at the stake or whatever other creative exercise god-fearin', Bible believin' Christians can come up with. I once read that the president of Yale, an eminent Leader of the Faith, declared that vaccination against smallpox was a sin because it was contrary to God's grand plan. Who knows how many of the faithful dutifully kicked the bucket from that little pearl of divine inspiration."

"But in the Bible, there were witnesses to what happened," Brewer said.

"Were there?" Morrison said "The witnesses, if there were any, didn't write the books. The people who did wrote them a century or more after the events supposedly took place. So, it was hearsay. A lot more of it probably was folklore. For example, there are no Roman records of Jesus, and the Romans loved to keep records. Seems to me somebody would have made note of a guy tippy toeing across the whitecaps in a wool nightshirt. And answer me this: Why haven't we had any miracles like that since? It's been nearly two thousand years. You'd think something would pop up, a least turn a little water into wine when they run out at a party."

Brewer was stumped. He had his doubts about religion but he also wanted to believe it. It was comforting. It gave him hope. On the other hand, the various cranks, church nerds and religion majors around campus were indeed a strange lot. Their certainty, their bulging-eyed, sweaty-browed certainty, could be a bit creepy.

"Okay, but how can you be sure?" Brewer said "It is impossible to prove or disprove there is a God. Even I know that."

"True, true," Morrison said. His voice was relaxed and contemplative again. "Maybe the best conclusion is to be an agnostic."

"A what?"

"An agnostic simply says, 'I don't know.' There isn't enough evidence on either side to make a declarative decision. I've always admired that kind of honesty."

"Then why aren't you an agnostic?" Brewer said.

"Maybe I should be," Morrison said. "But it's an awfully cold and lonely belief. Atheism gives me something to resent. Resentment gets me up in the morning."

"Is that honest?" Brewer said.

"Probably not as honest as agnosticism, but organized religion provides me plenty to resent.

"See, religious people are obsessed with imposing their beliefs on others, probably because they don't have enough confidence in their own beliefs to tolerate another way of thinking. So, they excommunicate people or declare war on them or simply slaughter whoever happens to be hanging around because it seems like an interesting way to pass the time. The crusaders were particularly good at that last one. I suspect most of those evangelists on TV fantasize about doing the same sort of thing, but it would be bad for public relations."

"Come on," Brewer said. "That's overstating things."

"Maybe," Morrison said. "But they definitely do try to control you. It's like what I said about sex: It's an expression of the essence of what we are as human beings. Control that and you control the individual. They have lots of other bans too, depending on the religion: What you eat, what you drink, what you wear and, oh yes, what you say. Show me in the Bible where it says Thou Shalt Not Say 'Shit.' Or fuck or whatever."

"But we do it or say it anyway, at least every now and then," Brewer said. "That's human nature."

"Yes, but I would suggest that even the most liberal person feels a twinge of guilt when he does it. That brings up my favorite religious practice: Extortion."

Brewer looked at Morrison quizzically. He was truly curious now.

"It's simple: Believe what I tell you to believe, do what I tell you to do, think what I tell you to think or you'll be roasted over a bed of hot coals for eternity. Like you said, you can't prove it *won't* happen. None of us knows what happens after we die, so we carry around a built-in fear. The church makes the best of it."

"I have to ask: In view of all that, why are you still at SPC?" Brewer said.

"Why do people go to the zoo?" Morrison said. "After a while, it just becomes a good way to have some laughs. My favorite are those evangelists who say 'We are living at the most critical moment in human history!' First time I heard it, I was five. I've heard it about twice a year ever since. That's an awful lot of most critical moments. But the suckers keep lapping it up; the fear thing again. Now, let me ask you something."

"Okay."

"Do you care where other people go to church?"

"No."

"Well, according to the religion majors on campus, God does and if you go to the wrong one, you're in or a long run as the featured attraction at the celestial barbecue. Would you do that to people who disagree with your religion?"

"Good grief, of course not," Brewer said.

"Well, God would. Now is that what you would call a loving higher power? Is that a higher moral and spiritual plane than we mere mortals are capable of?"

Brewer could find no flaw in Morrison's ideas. But they still made him uncomfortable. Then he had a thought.

"Okay," he said, "but people do all kinds of terrible things for reasons that have nothing to do with religion."

"Yes they do," Morrison said.

"So you can't blame religion for everything that is bad in the world."

"No you can't. Your point being?"

Brewer thought fast. But he knew there was no point. People did evil things, that's all. Their reasons were many, most of them contradictory, none of them valid. They just did them.

He looked at Morrison. Morrison was smiling.

"So, did I destroy your faith?" he said.

"I'm not sure there was much to destroy," Brewer said. "I'm curious, what are you majoring in?"

"I started out as a religion major, then I switched to philosophy so I could learn something about logic," Morrison said. "Last year, I declared an economics minor, emphasis in investments. I want to go to law school. Corporate law is where the money is."

"Money is the answer?" Brewer said.

"It makes the questions a whole lot easier to take."

"Thanks," Brewer said.

"Thanks?"

"I needed some clarity," Brewer said. "Thanks. Hope you make a million bucks."

Morrison laughed.

"Oh, five hundred thousand would be enough," he said. "I have pretty simple tastes."

Brewer extended his hand. Shaking hands seemed like an out-of-place formality. But he honestly was thankful. Morrison shook it. Then he went back to gazing at the stars.

Back inside, Brewer tried to strike up a conversation with Gail, but she turned out to be sloppy drunk, with runny mascara and the intelligence quotient of chopped eggplant. Was it easier to make time with smart girls? Probably - unless they are hipper than thou.

Arrrrgh!

The whole business wasn't worth the trouble; futility incarnate.

With that in mind, Brewer left - to return to his apartment, alone, always alone, for ultimately, he would forever be alone. Such was the essence of his existence as he knew it.

****

Sarah Gray had just survived a particularly horrific Economics mid-term. Her brain was popping like static electricity and she desperately needed coffee. As she walked to the SUB, it began to rain. Sarah did not notice.

Sarah Gray was a freshman, the daughter of Herbert Gray, professor of Religion. She was a fourth generation Free Methodist and discontent.

She had grown up in the evangelical subculture, knew all its rules and strictures, all its ins and outs. But unlike many children raised in a church setting, she did not automatically adopt its sociology and psychology. She had spent her young lifetime observing its narrow-mindedness, its judgementalism, the foolish jealousies and bigotries of its practitioners, and had decided she would not let it become part of her.

For the sake of her parents - truly kind and decent people - she still attended church, dutifully sitting in the pews, singing the hymns from memory and forcing herself to laugh at the same stale jokes year after year. She didn't resent it, at least not in the standard sense. That would be as pointless as resenting the weather. To Sarah the culture of the church was part of a larger societal onus. That onus expected her to meet the requirements of a predetermined formula: Virginity plus marriage plus motherhood, then grand motherhood, equaled virtue, fulfillment and, when you died, some sort of sanctification -- although you would not be around to accept the honor. Somehow, that little factoid always got left out.

Along the line, you probably should become educated to one degree or another- preferably in nursing or teaching or home ec; something that involved nurturing others at the expense of your own identity.

Sarah had seen how the world rewarded those who nurtured others. There was, for example, the time a group of church ladies put together a care package for a missionary in Indonesia: Second hand clothes, shoes with holes in them and this prize bit of Christian charity, used teabags. ("Used only once!" one of the church ladies proudly proclaimed.)

Another aspect of nurturing others involved helping people with trying personal problems. Sarah concluded that amounted to little more than a lifetime spent responding to other people's whining. She had heard enough public recitations of private gloom, tribulation and general woe to conclude that people prone to such things usually wanted to be; a way to justify weakness, a cry for attention, a socially acceptable method for blaming your failures on the cruel, cruel world. . . Whatever. Such people needed to take a good, long look in the mirror, Sarah thought. They should solve their own problems, privately, silently and with dignity - assuming they wanted to. Which they clearly did not.

When Sarah tried to voice her discontent, she got nowhere. The world had all kinds of pat answers for the concerns of 18-year-old girls; pat answers that, when you analyzed them, as Sarah did, were clearly designed to serve the interests of someone other than 18-year-old girls.

Was there a wild woman inside her, screaming to get out, to tear off her clothes and shriek obscenities and run from it all - and keep running and running and running? No. Sarah could see no advantage in such things. Instead, she kept her emotions to herself and, through a process of transference, used them to sharpen her skills of observation and analysis.

Somewhere in high school, Sarah was introduced to the concept of pragmatism. Its insistence on recognizing reality for what it really was, without sentimentality, and then applying cold logic to produce equally unsentimental – but realistic – outcomes transfixed her. A world free of silly games; what a wondrous concept.

She got in the habit of quantifying things in pragmatic terms. She observed, she studied, she measured. People, things, events; they all were subjects for her dispassionate analysis. She came to believe that all things could be understood, all situations could be mastered, all problems solved with the application of unsparing logic. In that way, it became her way of resisting the society in which she was raised.

Sarah had enrolled at SPC because it was expected of her. She didn't resent it. She neither liked nor disliked the school. It simply was where she ended up. It had its good points, after all. It was easy to make friends on a small campus. The classes were good. She saw the value in them. She would put in her four years, get a degree in something involving logic – statistics, perhaps – and then move on to independence. It was the pragmatic thing to do.

But something was still missing in her existence, something Sarah couldn't quite define and she was discontent about it.

When Sarah walked into the SUB coffee shop, she saw Nancy Siegleman at a table with three boys. One of them was Brian McLean, SPC's resident radical. Everyone at school knew who he was, probably because he worked hard to make sure they knew. She didn't know the other two, although she had seen them around campus.

Nancy Siegleman was Sarah's floor proctor, and a good one. She didn't especially care what the other girls did just so long as they did it quietly. She would look the other way if someone had her roommate forge her signature on the sign-in book so she could sneak in a window after curfew. She knew that Holly Ford and Celia Gillis in Room 408 were lesbians, didn't care and, in fact, had the kindness to warn them that the word was out and they needed to be more discreet. Nancy was cheerful and honest; a good person, all-in-all. Sarah liked her. Nancy waved at Sarah and gestured she come over and have a seat.

Nancy was listening to something one of the boys was telling her; a tall boy, well-dressed, with deep-set eyes.

Sarah liked the look of him. Ah, hormones. Sarah appreciated the opposite sex and wasn't afraid to say so – to herself, that is. As with most things, she saw no profit in exposing her inner feelings to the world.

"This is Sarah," Nancy said with a gesture in her direction. "This is Dale Griffiths and Tom Brewer." Tom Brewer, Sarah thought. She liked the name; clean, simple and direct. It fit him.

"You know Brian, I believe," Nancy said. McLean looked at Sarah, tried to suppress a leer and failed. He had the innocent young daughter of a professor at his table, in his clutches, and the daughter of a professor of *Religion* at that.

"I hear your dad got mugged," he said, with a smirk. Sarah knew what he was trying to do: Embarrass the poor, naïve little churchgirl. She breathed a resigned sigh. She'd been down this road before.

She looked McLean straight in the eye and very slowly said, "Yes. He did." She continued to stare him straight in the eye, with icy calm. She did not blink. It was disconcerting.

It wasn't much of a mugging. Herbert Gray was taking his evening walk when two punks jumped out of the darkness, stuck a gun in his face and demanded he give them money. He gave it, they ran and that was that. He was more surprised than anything else.

It happened on a Sunday, a notorious black abyss for news and the night reporter for the Post-Intelligencer was nervous. His by-line count was down and his editor wanted to have a little "talk" with him.

So, as he perused the police blotter, the reporter was desperate to find something to stop his slide into journalistic oblivion; a one-legged transvestite having intimate relations with a whooping crane in the parking lot of the downtown YWCA would have been ideal. But he had to settle for a professor getting mugged. At least he was a professor of Religion. It was a thin news hook at best and Herbert Gray didn't have much to say about it other than he hoped the miscreants would see the error of their ways and repent.

But it was something and the story, as long as the reporter could make it, ran on Page 4 the next morning.

It was of middling interest to readers, even at SPC, but in McLean's eyes, it presented an opportunity. McLean could be a real prick when he felt like it.

"Did he come home all scared and shaking?" he said, leering at Sarah.

"No. He found the experience kind of strange, but that's about all," Sarah said, sounding almost as bored as she felt with McLean's attempts to embarrass her.

Nancy saw the need to change the subject.

"Tom here thinks we should use the surplus in the ASSPC budget to buy some pool tables for the basement," she said. Nancy was the senior class representative on the student council.

"Sounds like a good idea," Sarah said.

"I'm going to recommend it to the council," Nancy said. "Nobody else has had any suggestions, so we'll see."

Sarah nodded.

"You play pool?" Brewer asked.

"I've never tried it," Sarah said. "But it looks like fun."

"Don't you think the council would better serve the school's mission by donating the money to gospel teams or some other right-thinking good work?" McLean sneered, looking Sarah's way.

Brewer shot McLean an angry look. McLean backed off. Sarah noticed.

"Pool tables sound better to me," Sarah said. "If you put it to a vote of the student body, I bet they would agree."

McLean had nothing to say to that. The other two boys looked at Sarah with expressions of respect.

"Yeah, I think so, too," Nancy said. "I'll have to find out how much they cost and how much room we have for them. But that shouldn't be too tough."

They all talked it over for a while – except for McLean, who quietly sulked.

"Where did you get the idea?" Sarah asked Brewer. She wanted to know more about him.

"Some friends took me to the pool hall on Stone Way," he said. "I'd never played it before. I had a good time. Then Nancy mentioned the surplus. I thought pool tables might liven things up a little."

McLean decided to be a prick again.

"What's the matter, isn't sitting around the dorm on a Friday night drinking cocoa and singing Kumbaya enough? Maybe finish off with a hot round of devotions?" The others ignored him. He went back to his sulk.

"In church, they told us that pool halls were dens of sin," Sarah said, smiling at Brewer.

"Nah, mostly it's just people shooting the breeze and playing pool," Brewer said. "The loser has to pay for the next round, but that's about all. It's just a game."

The bell rang. Everyone got up to go their separate ways.

"I'm sorry your dad got mugged," Brewer said. Sarah could tell by his expression that he actually meant it.

"Do you have a class?" she said.

"No, I'm headed up to the library."

"I'm going to Hill," she said. "You can share my umbrella if you like."

As they crossed campus, the rain began to beat down harder. Sarah found sharing an umbrella with Brewer singular and tactile; two warm bodies encircled by the rain; a cool, clean intimacy.

"Do you have to study for a test?" Sarah said.

"Philosophy mid-term with Professor Ordway," Brewer said.

"Oh. I had that class last quarter," Sarah said. "He always gives the same mid-term. You'll need to know the name of Socrates's wife."

"You're kidding."

"Nope. It's Xanthippe. And you'll need to know Plato's nickname for Aristotle."

"Wait, I know this one," Brewer said. "Nous. It means wiseas. . . uh, wiseguy."

Sarah giggled.

"I suspect you were closer to the real meaning the first time," she said.

Brewer smiled. She liked his smile.

"So, you're friends with Brian McLean," Sarah said.

"Yeah," Brewer said. "Don't be too hard on him. He likes to be contrary for the sake of being contrary."

"I suppose it's better than being a conformist for the sake of conforming," Sarah said.

"He's actually a good guy, he just doesn't want people to think so," Brewer said. "He put me up when I needed a place to bunk. It was really decent of him."

"Why did you need a place to bunk?" Sarah said.

"Long story," Brewer said. "I have a room now."

"Which dorm?"

"Actually, I have an apartment," Brewer said, a hint of pride in his voice. "Six six three Nickerson Street, number 204. It's not much, but it's mine."

Sarah was curious how a freshman managed to get an off-campus apartment of his own, but she didn't want to pry. It started raining even harder.

"McLean asked me to be on this interview panel for The Falcon," Brewer said. "I don't really want to, but I owe him. Seems we'll be interviewing the dean of students."

Sarah knew Layton Fleming from her church. He impressed her as a loudmouth and a boor.

"About what?" she said.

"I don't know. Policies, I suppose." Brewer grinned a little. "I think my job is to sit there and look earnest. I'll have to practice in the mirror."

The rain was coming down very hard now. Brewer moved over so Sarah had most of the umbrella to herself. How considerate, she thought; a gentleman. They reached the steps to Weter.

"This is where I get off," Brewer said. "Thanks for the umbrella."

"Maybe it will rain again soon," Sarah said.

Brewer missed the hint. He waved and started down the steps, the rain pounding on him as he went.

Chapter 22

At noon, when there were no P.E. classes in the gym, students and an occasional faculty member spent the lunch hour shooting baskets. That was how Paul Trimble came to meet Layton Fleming in person.

Trimble was practicing his hook shot. It was an unusual hook shot, one he had learned while he was in the Air Force. Desmond Grace, better known as Daddy Grace and a genuine Motor City homeboy, taught it to him while they played together on evenings when they didn't have enough money to go to town.

It was delivered while running parallel to the sidelines. Trimble came down crouching on his right leg, and then sprang up in one fluid motion from ball of foot to fingertips. It took a lot of practice, particularly the part where he used his right leg as his push-off for the jump. Left leg was natural for him. Anyway, since it was delivered on the run, the shot was hard to block. When he was warmed up, Trimble could shoot the hook at full speed without breaking stride. Depending on where he was on the floor, he could hit it with about ninety percent accuracy.

Trimble played basketball for fun. While other players concentrated on being intense and competitive, Trimble simply enjoyed himself.

Daddy Grace also introduced him to a particularly effective turnaround jump shot that involved turning to the right, as opposed to the left, which was normal for right-handed shooters.

Trimble came to be pretty good, better than the average player in playground pickup games, but because he played for the fun of it, it never occurred to him to call any particular attention to his skills. That tended to make other players underestimate him.

Trimble had just finished ten hook shots in a row and was starting to lazily shoot some jumpers when Layton Fleming entered the gym. And an entrance it was. Fleming immediately started shouting at a group of students engaged in a three-on-three half-court game. It was clear he was giving orders. The students obeyed dutifully as Fleming assigned them to teams. When he found he was a man short, Fleming looked around. He spotted Trimble and gestured at him to join them. It was not an invitation. It was an order. Trimble shrugged. A game was a game.

"You, you're with them," Fleming said, ushering Trimble toward a group of three boys. "We've got the ball, first outs." And the game was underway.

Trimble found himself playing forward. A blond, curly-haired kid was the point guard and he knew what he was doing; his moves sure, his eyes calm and alert.

Fleming played point guard on the other team and it became obvious early on that he was a gunner and ball hog. He also was what Trimble called a Hollywood basketball player. Any kind of bump or collision and down he went, often throwing his arms out dramatically and shouting as if he was in pain. Then he would rise slowly, coming up to one knee, his head bowed as if he were clearing away the cobwebs.

Where Trimble came from, such individuals were ridiculed as pussies and laughed off the court. But this was SPC and Fleming as an administrator. No one dared to call such exalted personages pussies, little less laugh them off the court.

On the other hand, there was no stricture against putting them in their place nonverbally.

Trimble got the ball and broke for the basket. Fleming was guarding him, his face a mask of intense ferocity. Trimble came down on his right foot, sprang upward and released his hook. Two points. Fleming looked confused.

"Hey, what was that?!" he roared. "You travelled! You travelled!"

" Come on, man, I didn't travel, " Trimble said with a modest chuckle.

"You calling me a liar?! You calling me a liar?!" The veins on Fleming's temples bulged and throbbed and his eyes popped with indignation.

Trimble held up his hand in a calming gesture.

"Your ball," he said.

Fleming took the inbounds pass and dribbled around, looking for an opening. There wasn't one, so he passed inside. That is, he tried to pass inside. Trimble saw it coming, jumped like a shortstop stretching for a tough one and slapped the ball out of bounds.

"Hey! Hey! What are you trying to do?! What are you trying to do!?" Fleming shouted. He was not used to people daring to block his passes. He was Layton Fleming. Trimble smiled, as if to be friendly. It seemed to make Fleming all the more furious.

And so it went for the rest of the game. Fleming was helpless against Trimble's running hook and when he got the ball himself, he found Trimble bent on taking it away from him. Trimble even had the audacity to outmuscle him on rebounds, one time throwing an elbow that caught Fleming on the chest and sent him sprawling. As Fleming got up - head bowed, one knee at a time (he had performed the act so many times it was automatic) - his face was a dark mask of rage. And that was not an act. No one did such things to Layton Fleming.

By this time, Trimble was over his little grudge against the loud, conceited man and was playing basketball for fun. And he was having a lot of fun. He especially enjoyed playing with the curly-headed kid. The kid knew his basketball, hitting his teammates with dead accurate passes and playing tight defense. He shot rarely, but when he did, he never missed. It was basketball the way it should be played. Paul Trimble as a happy man.

Layton Fleming was not. The more angry he got, the worse his game became. He started dropping the ball and throwing it away. His shots missed the rim completely. The rest of the players ignored his Hollywood theatrics.

Then it was 12:50 p.m.

"Gotta get back to work," Trimble said, flipping the ball to the curly-headed kid.

He headed for the stairs to the shower room. He felt a hand grab his shoulder.

"I suppose you think you were really hot stuff out there!" Fleming shouted. His face was glaring and contorted.

"Glad you liked it," Trimble said amiably. It was a pickup basketball game. Leave your feelings at the door, there were far more important things in the world . . .

"I did not like it!" Fleming said. "I think it was stinko! Just who do you think you are, anyway?"

Trimble was momentarily confused. What was with this guy? He gently nudged his way past Fleming. Fleming jumped in front of him.

"Don't you walk away from me!" Fleming's voice was shrill, almost hysterical. He grabbed Trimble's shoulder again. This time, his hand stayed, clutching hard.

Instinctively, Trimble reached up, took Fleming's wrist and pulled the hand away and gave it a hard twist. Fleming gasped and his eyes popped in rage. Before he could move, Trimble was already past him and on his way to the showers.

As he walked down the stairs, Trimble thought, that guy needs to do something about his temper. Then he shrugged the incident off. He had a lot of work to do and he wanted to get home before seven o'clock if he could.

It was a minor event, meaningless, really; the sort of thing that happened scores of times every day across the country. Within an hour, Trimble had all but forgotten about it. But Layton Fleming had not. No one bested him, particularly some flunky from the public relations department. Just what was his name anyway? Truman? Triplett? Something like that. He wasn't important enough that Fleming needed to know his name. But he knew who he was.

Chapter 23

Suzzallo Library at the University of Washington is golden bricks and soaring arches and carved sandstone and stained glass and dreams.

It is big: More than a hundred feet tall, more than two hundred fifty feet wide, more than three hundred feet deep, holding some two million books and more periodicals, microfilm reels, movies, photographs, research papers and historical documents than anyone has ever cared to count; an exercise in magnitude that awes those who see it for the first time – or, often, the second or third. Even the hundreds of students who trudge by it every day in the rain and the murk occasionally find themselves taken in by its grandeur and they nod and sometimes, for a moment, despite the daily tedium of lecture and study and tests and parking permits and all the petty aggravations of college life, a few of them sense that they are they are part of something wondrous, the wonder of human learning, the wonder of a generation on a journey to destiny.

The designers planned it that way. Suzzallo's gothic arches and patinaed oak and the eighteen terra cotta statues that adorn its entrance are carefully composed to look the way one thinks halls of great learning should look: Echoing with history and tradition and character. Here thought abides.

It is all contrived. For all its awe-inspiration, the main library building embodies no original architectural ideas. It simply copies gothic styles from England and France. But, in the way of America, it does so with such flair and Disney-like attention to detail that, in many ways, it outshines what it copies. Authenticity is, after all, a devised construct.

Brewer knew none of this when he climbed Suzzallo's front steps on that cold, clammy February morning. He was at Suzzallo because SPC's library was too small to contain all the material he needed. He had been assigned a research paper exploring the question of to what degree Joan of Arc expressed ideas that would later become tenets of Protestantism. And, therefore, was Joan a Protestant herself?

It wasn't a subject he chose. He had little interest in theology – none, actually – and little more in Joan of Arc, despite the fact he had been studying her for more than a month. But such was English 102, Research Techniques. You studied what you were assigned to study and researched what you were assigned to research. Then you wrote up your findings in properly footnoted form, with all its arcane ibids. and op. sits. and abbreviations and the rest that had to be done exactly according to style rules or you risked getting bumped down a grade.

Besides, Brewer had come to understand the purpose of it all, and he respected it: Conclusions based on verifiable evidence rather than intellectual conceits and hipshots.

But it certainly wasn't easy.

His efforts to find books addressing Joan's Protestantism didn't take long. There weren't any. Nor were there other books about her that alluded to it. That left the periodical stacks.

They were down a long, curving grand staircase that made Brewer feel like he had been transmogrified into the world of Prince Valiant and Robin Hood. Worn stone floors and textured glass windows that let in light but no distracting views of the outside world heightened the effect.

The periodical stacks themselves were in a cave. At least that's how it seemed to Brewer. The room was low and windowless, with row upon row of shelves holding folder upon folder of old magazines, along with bound volumes of the really old ones, often going back to the mid-Nineteenth Century. Brewer had drawn up a list of articles from the Reader's Guide to Periodic Literature going back nearly that far, at least to the early 1900s.

He put his books in a cubicle, hung his coat on the chair and started to search. He would gather four or five old magazines, take them back to the cubicle and pull out his stack of 3x5 note cards. On them he would write things like this:

Criticism
The Commonweal
Dec. 23, 1955
Vol LXIII
P. 304

Or:
"A Joan with Gumption"
Newsweek
Nov. 28, 1955
Vol XLVI
P. 110

The style – underlines, capitalization, abbreviations and the like – were the same on every card. That would be graded too.

Then, on other cards, he would write down a synopsis of what the article said, along with any good quotes.

And so it went, card after card, magazine after magazine, hour after hour.

It should have been tedious, but after a while it wasn't.

The room itself affected Brewer, the musty parchment smell of it, the endless rows of magazines, once bright and new, now out of their time; their illustrations and ads current and relevant to those who first saw them, now merely curious and quaint, a reflection of a world long since gone. Strange.

There were so many ideas, so much thought, so much reason all in one place. A lot of silly ego and shallowness as well, but in its way, that said something too. Many of those who thought both the worthwhile and the trivial, then said it and wrote and printed it, were dead. But their thoughts lived on; still there, immortality in old ink on old paper.

Elements of Brewer's assignment emerged. Was Joan a Protestant? She believed in a personal relationship with God, not one filtered through the church, a basic Protestant tenet. But she considered herself a Catholic and repeatedly said so.

She often spoke directly with God, which some Catholic saints did. But that assumes she was a saint, something the church itself didn't recognize until 489 years later. When she was alive, a tribunal of the church's most learned and influential declared her a heretic and burned her at the stake.

Brewer's stack of cards grew, first one inch, then two inches and still growing.

Was Joan a Catholic? She never said a word against those who judged her. And she never questioned the church's spiritual authority. She requested that the transcripts of her trial be sent to the Pope for a final decision.

Later, other scholars quoted that most catholic of Catholics Thomas Aquinas who wrote, "It is better to die excommunicated. . . than to submit to something which is contrary to God's law." In addition, Medieval doctrine held that one needed to obey the accepted body of Divine law, not every single ruling or opinion handed down by individual tribunals or clergymen. Finally, excommunication was not a final judgment. Only God was the final judge in such matters.

The stack of cards grew to three inches, then four.

The pro-Protestant camp pointed out that the final straw which got Joan burned was the fact she wore men's clothing while on military campaign; a matter of common sense practicality and hardly a major sin, even in those days. They also pointed out that the church later reversed the verdict against her. So clearly her trial involved something other than religious questions and, therefore, clearly it was a sham.

They also noted that, in following the voices that spoke to her, Joan answered directly to a power higher than any church, a very Protestant concept. Some argued that the voices were not voices at all, but simply a particularly accomplished form of visualization, a mental skill many people have, especially musicians and athletes. Therefore, Joan was merely exercising her intellect.

What was missing in much of the learned discussion was Joan herself. She was no theologian. She was, in fact, semi-literate at best. Her faith was the simple faith of a devout country girl and she never claimed otherwise. So, much of the discussion about her Protestantism/Catholicism was, Brewer decided, irrelevant. The arguments were mainly from Catholics, who took bits and pieces of the facts and selectively assembled them to prove their foregone conclusions, and Protestants, who took bits and pieces of facts and selectively assembled to prove their foregone conclusions. Joan herself? No one seemed to particularly care.

But Brewer did care. Who was this girl? What did she look like? There were portraits but they were contradictory. What was she like to talk to? There was no record. The men who fought with her were devoted to her to the death, partly because of her unwavering sense of mission, partly because of her utter indifference to danger. When in doubt, Joan drew her sword and charged. She never looked back to see if anyone was following her. But they did. They always did.

But there was more to her than that. Brewer's card stack grew to five inches, then seven, then more. Still Joan the person continued to elude him. Finally, it was eleven o:clock, closing time. Brewer looked at his stack of cards, now so high it was unwieldy. He would never understand Jeanne d'Arc d'Domrémy. For, he found, the people who knew her did not understand her either. But they recognized transcendence when they saw it. And they knew they would never see it again.

As Brewer walked down the front steps of Suzzallo, he thought more about Joan, but he also thought about the work he had just done, the work itself, regardless of the subject. The process of understanding had gripped him in ways he never expected. He no longer was confined by his own ignorance, prejudices and whims.

His throat pinched and his insides felt loose and empty. He drew deep breaths. But the feeling did not go away. Freedom of thought; what on odd, powerful thing. He never expected to find it working on an assignment he didn't volunteer for in the basement of a library he knew nothing about until he went there.

There are dreams that come from watching clouds drift across the infinity of a summer sky and there are dreams that are focused by concentration and work; and those dreams a person can give substance. So this was the reality of learning: Imagination and discipline becoming one. It moved Brewer as much as anything he had ever felt.

As he walked across the broad plaza in front of Suzzallo, a cool wind washed over him. The night was clear and the sky a deep, deep blue. The world felt very big.

Chapter 24

After his noon basketball game, Layton Fleming showered quickly and headed to his office. He was still simmering with anger when he arrived. His secretary informed him that the editor of The Falcon, the student newspaper, had called for the fourth time, asking for an interview about a Student Bill of Rights. Fleming had hoped the two-bit little pipsqueak would simply give up, but apparently he was determined. Fleming sighed. Well, if I must...

The Student Bill of rights had originated at Berkeley or some such place, where the administration summarily buried it, as administrations traditionally did with anything emanating from undergraduates. But it got mentioned in the local papers, the wire services picked it up and it had been showing up here and there on college campuses ever since.

It called for prohibiting professors from flunking students for their political activities; for stopping the practice of requiring student organizations to register membership lists with the administration; for the freedom of students to publically discuss on campus whatever issues they wished; for an uncensored student press – and on and on.

When Layton Fleming saw it, he laughed. Pathetic. Not a single college or university in the country had adopted the bill of rights and none ever would.

SPC? The students there, at least the ones Fleming associated with, would find it all rather frightening. Proper little raised-in-the-church boys and girls did not choose SPC because they were in the habit of challenging authority. Others, more than the school cared to recognize, were there because their parents gave them a simple choice: Go to SPC or don't go to college at all unless you can find a way to pay for it yourself – which, at age eighteen, they most assuredly could not. The result was resignation and apathy.

Finally, and Fleming liked this best of all, the school let it be known, indirectly but clearly enough, that survival for a student could be a very thin thread indeed. Grad school recommendations could be rescinded with the flick of a pen, draft boards could be notified with a phone call.

But the Bill of Rights might prove a problem for SPC's Board of Regents. The board consisted of carefully-selected representatives of two distinct groups. First, there was a covey of church administrators; sixty-plus-year-old evangelical preachers who had never attracted a national following and couldn't understand why. Now they were stuck in desk jobs; a world of budgets, church politics and attending endless meetings at places like SPC. It made them narrow and embittered.

Then there was a boisterous cadre of Business Leaders; affluent members of the Babbitt set who felt required, compelled, duty-bound and all but destined to apprise the rest of the world that all schools, all government bodies, all institutions – nay, the entire universe – would function with clock-like precision if they were merely Run Like A Business.

Such a body would become deeply anxious at any suggestion the school was not living up to its responsibility to provide then with a steady stream of corporate toadies and devoted tithe-givers. They would be sent into paroxysms at the suggestion of something as bolshevistic as a student bill of rights. They might very well end up demanding to know how the college president had allowed such a threat to the American Way to foment.

Not to worry, Fleming thought. The students promoting the bill of rights were a small handful of cranks and malcontents. Nobodies. Layton Fleming, winner, would brush them aside without breaking a bead of sweat.

He told his secretary to set up an appointment with the Falcon editor. An hour later, she had it confirmed: 2 p.m. Tuesday at The Falcon office. Fleming frowned. He, the dean of students, would come to *them*? One dared not risk such a breach of status. He thought some more. Actually, he could use it to his advantage. He could come off as the young, hands-on dean who knew how to talk to the kids in their language; who rolled up his sleeves and took on the big challenges, the can-do guy you can count on.

That sounded good. An opportunity.

****

When Layton Fleming strode into The Falcon office, he expected to be met by an awkward undergrad with scuffed shoes, chewed pencil and a list of clumsy questions. Instead, he found himself facing three neatly-dressed young men and one beatnik wannabe seated behind a large table. They did not look the least bit awkward.

He knew the editor, Parris, but he had never paid any attention to him because Falcon editors didn't rate attention. He knew about McLean, the beatnik seated in the middle. He was the campus's self-appointed radical and resident wiseass. Weldon, the third one, was a buddy of McLean's, another wiseass. The fourth one, a tall kid with deep-set eyes and thin, unsmiling lips; him he didn't know at all. Fleming didn't like the look of him. He didn't like the look of any of them, but particularly the kid with the deep-set eyes. He wasn't sure why.

Then he noticed that Parris had a tape recorder in front of him. For a moment, Fleming felt a twinge of trepidation, but only a twinge. So, they wanted to play like grown-ups, eh? These twerps? Who did they think they were dealing with?

"Well, looks like we have quite the little inquisition here," Fleming said with a pat Rotary Club smile. It usually had the effect of throwing people a little off-balance.

Parris smiled, as if responding to a joke. It was a way of camouflaging discomfort and Fleming knew it. Weldon smiled too, but it was more like a smirk. McLean had his head down, thumbing through a paperback book and jotting down notes. The kid with the deep-set eyes looked on coldly, almost accusingly, as if Fleming hadn't said a thing.

There was a chair in front of the table. Fleming sat down.

"Thanks for coming," Parris said, his voice pleasant, even a little deferential. He nodded at the other two. "This is Brian McLean, Mike Weldon and Tom Brewer. We have some questions we'd like to ask you about some of SPC's student affairs policies and how they relate to the Student Bill of Rights."

"Well, I don't have a lot of time," Fleming said, checking his watch in an exaggerated motion. "We'll have to keep it brief." It was another planned gesture, one he had learned long ago. It let the other guy know you have more important matters than this little tete-a-tete, which you are merely granting out of the goodness of your heart. But that was only the obvious message. More importantly, it set the parameters of the discussion. Fleming intended to take control from the start.

He was on his way. Parris looked disconcerted. McLean, however, didn't seem to notice and kept jotting down notes. Brewer continued to stare at him with those damnably cold eyes. What the hell was this kid's problem, anyway?

"Are you familiar with the Student Bill of Rights?" Parris said.

"If you mean that business that came out of Berkeley a while back, I've heard of it," Fleming said with practiced nonchalance. "It had some interesting concepts."

"How do you think it applies to SPC?" Parris said.

"Well, I haven't exactly heard anybody clamoring for it," Fleming said with a good-natured smile. "But as I said, it has some worthwhile ideas, so I suppose it falls into the same category as any number of elements to be considered in ongoing policy development."

Now they were on his turf. It would be easy to direct the conversation from here.

"On what do you base your policy development when it comes to student rights?" Parris said.

Sometimes, they make it too easy, Fleming thought.

"We view each person as a sacred whole, to be nurtured as a whole," he said in a tone that verged on lecturing, a tone he often used once he got things going his way. "Our commitment is to assist students in achieving that whole by encouraging the right balance of the intellectual, spiritual and social elements of each individual."

"How do you determine what constitutes the right balance?" McLean said without looking up.

"One of the problems you run into is trying to define the whole business through a lot of overly specific codification," Fleming said. There, that got rid of the Student Bill of Rights with one quick swipe. "Rather, it's more like coaching the person in a sport; lacrosse, for example. You teach the fundamentals. When a person masters those fundamentals, he's well on his way to becoming a winner. A bill of rights may be helpful in clarifying some of the fundamentals, but instilling values takes a more unified approach."

Parris and McLean looked at each other. Neither were sure what Fleming had just said. All the better, Fleming thought.

"So, are you saying that a student's personal goals should be defined by the college?" Weldon said. He was still smirking.

"Of course not," Fleming said with a pained expression. "As I just said, we want to assist students in achieving wholeness. . ."

"Who defines what constitutes wholeness?" Weldon said.

Layton Fleming was not accustomed to being interrupted, particularly by some nineteen-year-old punk. Anger boiled up in him. He took a quick, nearly imperceptible breath and got control of himself. As near as he could tell, the students hadn't noticed him doing it. In a voice oozing with calm and reason, he said, "We are here to facilitate students' growth. . ."

"But what if a student doesn't want the institution to facilitate his growth?" McLean said. He was looking up from the pages of a small paperback book. Fleming tried to make out the title. All he could see was "The Student As Ni . . ."

"What if he wants to define his own growth?" McLean said. "What if he doesn't want to define it at all? Shouldn't he be free to do that on his terms, rather than have the parameters defined for him?"

"Of course, of course," Fleming said. "But we know from national studies that people between eighteen and twenty three are still in a maturation process, psychologically. So, their decision-making processes vary, depending on the situation and where they are in their maturity, from one year to the next, from one month to the next. To manage all that, one needs a baseline. So, one of the objectives of a liberal education is to clarify self-discipline. That takes experience and, by definition, young people lack experience. There are no shortcuts."

"If that's the case, if they are somehow biologically incapable of controlling themselves with any consistency, why should they be held responsible for their behavior?" McLean said. He was looking at the small book again. What the hell was it? Fleming wondered. It was time for an end run.

"We are a community," Fleming said. "A certain amount of order is necessary for the well-being of any community. So we have guidelines for personal social management. It's one of the few privileges that private schools still have. As a Christian community, our emphasis in implementing those guidelines is founded on compassion. Through compassion, we try to help students actualize their potential in a Christian context."

Fleming liked that statement, particularly the As a Christian community and Actualize Their Potential parts. He had used it in a speech to the Ballard Kiwanis last year and the assembled were favorably impressed. When President Fotheringham heard about it, he sent Fleming a note congratulating him.

"But SPC's policies about smoking, drinking, dancing, card-playing and premarital sex are rules and they are written down," McLean said. "And we all have to sign a form saying we will obey them. And, correct me if I'm wrong, but if you break those rules you could be kicked out of school, could you not?"

I suppose he thinks that's a tough question, Fleming thought with an internal smirk.

"Technically, but only as a last resort," Fleming said. "We believe in the counseling approach: Talk to the person, find out the facts, put the incident in the proper context, offer some advice. There's a difference between a misstep or misunderstanding and a definable violation of the rules."

Actually, Fleming had never counseled anyone. Maybe his assistant deans did; they were fresh out of college, didn't really know what they were doing and were, therefore, irrelevant. If by some chance a student was brought before him, he usually gave the little shit a choice: Leave school or get kicked out. It was the perfect solution: No student, no problem. There were exceptions, of course, for varsity athletes, the children of rich alumni and the children of church leaders.

"But, of course, in some rare cases, we have to convene the Student Judicial Board," Fleming said.

The Student Judicial Board was Fleming's baby. It had well-defined rules of evidence, judicial procedures and such, all of which sounded very fair and reasonable. It also was made up of two representatives each of the administration, the faculty and the student body – all of whom were hand-picked by the dean of students himself, based on their reliability and predictability for doing just what he wanted them to do: Nod wisely, act interested, perhaps even ask a few questions – and then forward the final decision to, surprise, surprise, the Dean of Students. He then expelled the trouble-making little shit. A letter informing his parents cemented the process.

"Can a student be prosecuted for breaking SPC's rules while he's off-campus?" McLean said.

At least he could have let the moment gel a little, Fleming thought. Oh well.

"I suppose so," Fleming said. "The rules are the rules, but. . ."

"How do you propose to enforce those when it involves off-campus behavior?" McLean said. "Through spies?"

Fleming started inwardly at the bluntness of the question. It verged on disrespect. No one disrespected M. Layton Fleming. There was silence in the room. That kids with the eyes, Brewer, had fixed his stare on Fleming and for some reason, Fleming found it unnerving. Fleming stared back at him hard for a moment. His dislike for Brewer – *and those damned cold eyes* – was growing.

"Well, hopefully, we aren't the sort of place where people go around spying on one another," Fleming said with a light laugh. He noticed that Parris cracked a grin. The others did not.

"But if members of the SPC community observe something and bring it to our attention, then we are required to act upon it," Fleming said.

"How is that different than spying?" Brewer said. His voice was a cold as his eyes.

For a moment, for a very long moment, Layton Fleming did not know what to say. It had never happened to him before. It enraged him. Winners did not get tongue-tied. But the cold-eyed punk had caught him with a question for which there was no glib answer.

"Well, there are various levels of understanding involved. . . " Fleming began.

"What would your rules of evidence be?" Weldon said, his smirk firmly in place. "Is the word of one person enough to get a student disciplined?"

"As I said, there are various levels of understanding involved," Fleming said in a bored tone, as if he had answered the question dozens of times. He needed to play for time. He would try some standard institutional platitudes to throw them off. That worked wonders when he spoke to the local boosters clubs.

"This is a private school. By the nature of our Christian commitment and our institutional goals, our forms of due process are not necessarily the same as the civil justice system's. There, it's a question of who has the most evidence. We hope to look for a higher truth."

That should hook one of them into asking what that higher truth is, he thought. Then he could launch off on a collection of glittering generalities that would make Norman Vincent Peale and Richard Nixon proud.

"If a student breaks some rule while off-campus, in the privacy of his own home, how does that affect the rest of the community and this quest for wholeness you talk about?" McLean said. "They wouldn't even know about it, and the students I know wouldn't even care. They would be too busy trying to make it through midterms to give a hoot about some guy having a beer in his back yard."

"Well, if it is brought to our attention. . ." Fleming began.

"By who?!" McLean said, his voice rising in anger. "If they aren't spies, what are they? Snitches? Stool pigeons? Rats? What gives anyone the right to go around monitoring other people's behavior and then running to tattle to the teacher? What does that make them? How does it help them become these 'whole' individuals you keep talking about? What does it say about a place that encourages that kind of behavior?"

McLean's eyes were sharp. His jaw was set. Parris put his hand on McLean's arm to calm him. Fleming felt Brewer staring at him – *Oh, how I'd like to punch that little shit out.* – and he knew he was trapped. But Layton Fleming was never trapped. He looked at his watch.

"Sorry, but we're going to have to wrap this up pretty soon, fellas," he said with almost excessive calm. It threw them off just enough. "Time for just a couple more questions."

Parris – the dumb one, Fleming had decided – didn't see the dodge. He spoke just as McLean started to open his mouth.

"I wonder if you could talk a little about SPC's identity as a Residence College," Parris said. "To put it another way: The reasoning behind requiring students to live in dorms."

"First, they aren't required to live in the dorms," Fleming said. "They can live at home with a parent or at a place of employment that requires them to live there. You'd be surprised at how many SPC students have worked as night dispatchers at funeral homes."

He thought that would get a laugh. It did not.

"But seriously, residential living is yet another part of the concept of developing the whole individual," Fleming said. "We call it the learning through living process; where substantive relationships develop within a structure that creates a sense of wholeness and independence."

"You develop independence by forcing people to live in a dorm for four years?" Weldon said.

"First, as you know, the dorms are actually managed by resident advisors . . ."

"Who selects them?" Weldon interrupted.

"The Dean of Students Office, based on criteria . . ."

"So, you're the one who sets the rules." McLean said.

Layton Fleming actually felt himself start to sweat.

"The Inter-Resident Hall Council reviews all rules and changes of rules . ." he began.

"I looked that up in the Policy Manual. It's in the Library," McLean said. "It states that the council's recommendations are passed along to the dean's office for final determination, which means all they do is advise, which means all they do is nothing."

"Now, that's an overstatement," Fleming said. He was becoming angry and for a moment, a hot sweet moment, he did not try to rein it in.

"Gentlemen, gentlemen, maybe we all should take a breath," Parris said, again laying his hand on McLean's arm. "Mr. Fleming, perhaps you could tell us a little about the dorms and their funding by the federal government."

Fleming was surprised at the question. The federal government had paid for about three quarters of Hill's construction and it was paying roughly the same percentage for the new dorm going up on Dravus Street. The administration kept that information under wraps. It might aggravate donors, most of whom had politics slightly to the right of Attila the Hun, particularly where the federal government was involved. If ever Satan had strode the earth, it had been in the person of Franklin Delano Roosevelt and they weren't about to forget it.

In addition, federal funding ran askew to the college's lovingly crafted facade as a pious academie; a stalwart for the faith, above the ruttings and grubbings of godless politicians, some of whom were Catholics, even Jews.

How had these kids found out? There must by a spy in the administration, Fleming thought. Who? No time to worry about that now. There was a question to be dodged.

"There's not that much to tell," Fleming said. "The federal government contributed grants and issued low-interest loans to help with the construction of Hill and the new dorm. I'd tell you how much and what percentage of the costs they represent, but I don't know."

"That's not what concerns us," Parris said. "Isn't it true that the conditions of the loans require the college to keep its dorms full?"

"Yes, I believe so," Fleming said in an innocent tone, as if he wasn't well-informed on the matter. Actually, he knew all about it all too well. Yes, the feds required the dorms to be filled and yes, it was his job to see that they were. But with enrollment growing by about six percent a year, it was not a major problem.

McLean chimed in, "So, you want students to live on campus, even if it is cheaper for them to live off-campus, so they can pay off your debts, debts that were incurred in agreements in which the students had no say. Is that true?"

"Brian, Brian, Brian," Fleming purred condescendingly, "Now, you know as well as I do that we all must live up to our contractual obligations. . ."

"Are you familiar with the phrase 'No taxation without representation?'" Weldon said.

Very good, Fleming thought, very good indeed. You set up a trap and then you sprung it. For a moment, he felt a trace of respect for the young men behind the table. That moment, of course, did not last.

"Excellent question," Fleming he said with an approving grin. Then he looked at his watch.

"Well, I'd like to go into this further," he said, sighing indulgently, "but I have a meeting to attend. Hope you don't mind.

Maybe at some other time. Thanks for a stimulating discussion, fellas. Hope I was helpful."

And with that, he left. When he reached the door, he winked at McLean. McLean rose from his chair angrily. Fleming smiled. It camouflaged his fear.

****

Once Fleming was out of earshot, McLean exhaled hard and said, "What a phony."

"Well, I think we got some good stuff," Parris said. "Can Sally have it typed up by Wednesday?"

"Probably," McLean said. "Can't believe how fast that girl's fingers can move." He smiled a little at the double entendre.

"My guess would be we'll need a full page," Parris said. "Do we have enough photos of Fleming to fill, if need be?"

"Plenty," McLean said. "We should get some pics of the new dorm, too."

They were silent for a while, thinking.

"We really nailed the bastard," McLean finally said.

"We weren't supposed to nail the bastard," Parris said. "We were supposed to get some straight answers to questions that concern the average student. Truth is, he dodged most of the questions."

"Well, the fact he dodged them should tell people a lot in itself," McLean said.

"Then you and he got into a shouting match," Parris said.

"I did not shout," McLean said with an air of wounded dignity. Then he leered a sly, self-satisfied grin. "But I did deploy a certain, shall we say, *ton de la voix*."

Parris, Dale and McLean chuckled. Brewer did not. They noticed.

"So what do you think?" McLean said to Brewer.

"I'm not sure this was a good idea," Brewer said.

"Why not?" McLean said.

"I think he might try to get back at us," Brewer said.

"For asking some tough questions?" McLean said. "It's a college. We're supposed to have lively exchanges of opinons."

Brewer thought for a long moment. Then he said, "No, we aren't."

The room went silent as a crypt.

"What do you mean?" Parris said.

"In a class discussion, you can ask pretty much any question you want, express pretty much any opinion you want, just so it has something to do with the subject," Brewer said. "Even then the prof may cut you off. I've seen it; guys going off on a pointless tangent or some such thing. But unless you start acting like a lunatic or a complete jerk, it probably won't affect your grade. This was different."

"We have the right to ask questions, you know," McLean said, a sarcastic edge in his voice. "It's in the constitution."

"I don't think Fleming sees it that way," Brewer said.

"Oh yeah? And just what is he going to do about it?" McLean said in the pugnacious tone he adopted when he felt argumentative. He uses that tone too much, Brewer thought. He's always looking for a fight, whether there's one there or not.

"He has power and we don't," Brewer said. "He's more than a phony. He's mean and he's dangerous."

"We have the power of the press," Parris said. His voice was uncertain.

"He can shut you down," Brewer said.

"He wouldn't dare. Students wouldn't stand for it." McLean was angry again. No, not angry, Brewer thought. Self-righteous.

Brewer exhaled in frustration and looked up at the ceiling.

"Oh come on," he groaned. "They don't care. Most people just want to go to class, get their degrees and move on. The only ones who do care are the church nerds who'll go along with anything The Man says."

"We're just printing what he said verbatim," Parris said.

Brewer shrugged.

"Sounds to me like you're just chicken," McLean said.

Brewer considered the statement for a moment. He had seen McLean play intramural football – or try to play intramural football – so if it came to blows, he knew he could pound the snot out of him. But no, he thought, it was time to think with your brain, not your hormones.

"This sounded like a good idea when you suggested it," Brewer said. "Now I'm not so sure. I don't want to reform anything. I want to get a college degree. I want to get good grades. I want to learn something worthwhile. Mostly, I want to be left alone. Griping about SPC bullshit over coffee at the SUB is one thing. This is different. Call it chicken, call it whatever you want. I think we've stepped in too deep."

"You seemed pretty into it at the time," Parris said. "Your question really threw him off. You're good at this."

"I asked that question because it felt good to ask it," Brewer said. "It felt good to trip up somebody important. Is that why you are doing all this, because it feels good?"

Brewer definitely has a talent for getting on people's wrong side, Parris thought.

"Maybe we can change things a little," Parris said.

"I doubt it," Brewer said. "You can print this and it will create a stink for a few days, but that's all it will do. This place isn't going to change because of you."

"Well, I like to create a stink," McLean saod. "I do it all the time, right after I eat Mexican food."

Parris and Dale laughed. McLean basked in the glow of having made a good joke. Brewer looked pained.

"Cute," Brewer said. Then he walked out of the office.

Chapter 25

The call came on March 12, 1965.

"Oh, honey. . . " There was a long silence.

"I'm right here, mom," Marilyn said.

"Oh, honey, I'm so sorry."

"I know, mom. It's okay."

"We tried to save what we could, but the creditors took so much. And the lawyers. We even sold the house. But there's still not enough."

"It's okay, mom. It's okay."

Marilyn's mother sobbed. She was holding the phone away from her, but it was still audible.

"How long do I have?" Marilyn said.

"I'm. . . I'm, so sorry," her mother said, choking. "Spring quarter will be your last quarter." She started crying again. Marilyn waited until it died down.

"No sophomore year?" she said.

"No. Oh, god, I'm so sorry. If only I could make it up to you."

Marilyn let it sink in for a moment. Thus ended her college career. Now what?

"You'll come home, of course," her mother said.

Home to what? Marilyn doubted her parents would stay in Wenatchee. The public humiliation would be too much.

"I'll get a job here, mom."

"No, no, we need you here. We need you with us."

Maybe, Marilyn thought. But I have problems of my own. I can't be part of yours. Too much has happened. God, that sounds cold. But it's the truth.

"Oh, please, dear, please, please, please," her mother wailed. "We need you. You can find a job here."

Do they need me so I can contribute to the family income? Marilyn wondered. It's possible - unlikely, but possible. If so, it means I'll be tied to them indefinitely. All the more reason to make a break, whatever the risks.

The idea frightened her. She had no idea of what she would do or how she would do it. She thought fast.

"I'll call grandma," Marilyn said. "She'll probably let me stay there while I straighten things out." Marilyn's grandmother had a small house on Capitol Hill. She was a kind woman and generous. It could work.

The suggestion seemed to calm Marilyn's mother.

"Yes. Well, that is a thought," her mother said. "Hmmm, let me know what she says."

"How's daddy?" Marilyn said. It was probably the wrong time to ask. But there was no right time.

"He's. . . he's. . . well, you know your father."

Actually, I don't, Marilyn thought. Not anymore.

"Tell him I love him," Marilyn said. "Whatever happens, I love both of you more than I can say."

"Yes, yes, dear, I know." Her mother was now more her old, always poised self, even if her voice cracked.

They talked for a while more; nothing of substance, just soothing sounds, polite and innocuous, the sort of things people say to fill space until they can exit gracefully. Then they hung up.

Marilyn's home was gone, that place of doll collections and games of catch in the backyard and the smiles of adoring parents when she brought home yet another report card filled with As. She would never go back. There was nothing to go back to.

Her future was. . . well, was it gone, too? She thought about the girls who came to college to get an MRS. Degree: Go to class, of course, but mostly keep your eyes peeled for a Good Catch. Then marry, settle down and have the rest of your life taken care of for you. Marilyn shuttered. A Good Catch? Like who? Pipe-smoking offspring of the rich who majored in banking and finance, drones whose main appeal was ~ let's be honest here ~ money? No, Tom Brewer had erased any such silly pretensions. One look at him and she knew. . . she knew. . . she knew what? Some things you feel and they are the truth, even if you aren't sure what they are. And now Tom Brewer was gone from her life, too.

Good god, what a fool I was. All he wanted to do was neck, maybe more. So did I, maybe more ~ especially more, oh, god, more.

Maybe her whole life up to now was a sham, and the last six months of it, her college years - she chuckled bitterly at the word 'years' - were an exercise in pretentious self-delusion.

Her education, such as it was, certainly had not gone as she so arrogantly assumed it would. She had not been the star, the belle of the ball. It had been a dull slog, hard and grueling.

Did she actually learn anything, or did she merely survive? That thought brought her to a stop, and for some reason her mood changed from fear and desperation to a type of cold calculation. Well, let's take look at all that, she decided. Her statistics and psychology classes had taught her a lot about the nature of reality and human nature. English 101 and 102 had taught her about using language with clarity and the value of evidence-based conclusions. Other classes had done much to open her mind and, in that way, had given her forms of confidence she hadn't had before.

How useful would any of it be? "Oh, yeah? That and a dime'll buy ya a cuppa of coffee," the great minds gathered around the proverbial cracker barrel would say. But they would say that about almost anything: "So, ya found a cure for cancer, huh? That and a dime'll buy ya a cuppa coffee." "Nobel Prize in economics, ya say? That and a dime'll buy ya a cuppa coffee." It was the surefire mantra of the chronic mediocrity.

She had come out of school better than she went in. It was hers. No one could take it from her, even those too dumb to understand it.

The experience of surviving the grind had taught her some things, too. Her view of herself had proven seriously askew. The ethos of the country club princess doesn't mean much when the club won't let you in the front door.

Well, it all was in the past now. Marilyn set her jaw in determination. But it did not stay set. Instead, a tear started down her cheek. Then another, then another. She did not slump forward or put her head in her hands or break down and cry out loud. She sat erect and looked straight ahead. But the tears continued to stream down her cheeks and onto her collar. A few fell on the desk in front of her. She moved her papers so they wouldn't get stained. Whatever happened, she would finish her work. She would finish the first ~ and the last ~ year of her college education. Then it would be over. She had to find a job.

How? The college had no job center, not even a bulletin board announcing job openings. None of her classmates had jobs; not that she knew of, at least. They would start looking for summer jobs in a few weeks. She couldn't wait that long.

That left the newspaper want ads.

Most called for specific skills she simply did not have. Hydraulics mechanic? Investments returns accountant? Shipping traffic analyst? What did those even mean?

That left two other categories: Jobs with rather vague descriptions and waitressing.

Her first stop was one of the vague descriptions. The address turned out to be a bleak, four-story poured concrete building on Dexter Avenue just south of Mercer Street. The office was on the third floor. No elevator, just a covered outside stairway that smelled of mold and urine. A typing paper sign thumb-tacked to the door read, "Wonderware Inc." Marilyn knocked. No one answered. She knocked again. Still no answer. Gingerly, she opened the door a crack, waited for a response, then opened it a bit more. Finally, she opened it all the way. There was a small reception area with an unmanned desk. The desk had no desk lamp or telephone. A couple of cardboard crates were resting on its dusty top.

Beyond it was a door to another office. It was opened slightly and Marilyn could hear the noise of paper shuffling and drawers closing. She tapped on the door lightly.

"Yeah?" came an exasperated-sounding voice.

Marilyn opened the door and leaned into the room.

"I'm here about the job," she said, the slight lilt of a question in her voice. Was she in the right place?

"Huh? Oh yeah, come on in," said the man at the desk. He was a shabby man in a shabby suit in a shabby office. Everything about the place bespoke it; from the patchy, never-waxed linoleum floor to the fiberboard desk with the vinyl veneer peeling off its corners, to the dented institutional gray filing cabinets. Papers were stacked here and there. Half-opened crates were jumbled in corners. All the crates, Marilyn noticed, were emblazoned with red "Wonderware!" logos.

"You are. . . ?" the shabby man said.

"Marilyn Pennell."

"Hm. So you're looking for a job. What do you do now?"

"I'm a student at Seattle Pacific College."

"Oh, SPC, huh? You know Wayne Roebling?"

Marilyn nodded.

Wayne Roebling was an insipid young man with the perpetually vacant smile of the lobotomized; a somewhat exaggerated version of the affected, dewy-eyed piety you saw at SPC from time to time. She avoided him.

"One of our top people last summer!" the shabby man said. "Yes sir, if you want to know what Wonderware's all about, just ask Wayne!"

Marilyn looked over the half-opened crates. They appeared to be full of plastic bowls, spoons, spatulas, sauce pans and the like.

"So what have you heard about Wonderware?" the shabby man said.

"That you sell kitchen products," Marilyn said.

"Corr-ect!" the shabby man said. "But we like to think of them not just as products, but as part of an entire meal preparation and food storage system, a system that will last a lifetime."

Okay, Marilyn thought, but what's the job?

"Now we don't think of our people as salesmen," the shabby man said. "We prefer the term 'distributors.' It's their job to distribute the Wonderware lifestyle and it can be one heckuva rewarding job."

"How does it work?" Marilyn said.

"Well, our distributors invest a little of their assets and their district managers, that's what I do, help them stock up with the products they need. The products sell themselves! Then the distributors split the profits with the company."

"Wait. You said the distributors have to buy the products themselves first?" Marilyn said.

"It's an investment, a guaranteed investment. You'll make it back in a month," the shabby man said.

"And how do you go about selling them?" Marylyn said.

"Hey, hold parties with your friends. Or talk to your relatives. They can guide you to other potential customers. Some of our folks go door-to-door. You'd be surprised at how well you can do that way!"

Or you could end up walking through piss puddles every morning to an office with a leaky ceiling and piles of useless junk you can't get rid of, Marilyn thought. I may be from a small town, but I'm not that dumb.

"Any other jobs in the company?" she said. "I can type."

"Type?" The shabby man looked genuinely confused for a moment. Then he laughed out loud, an ear-pounding bray that echoed off the stained walls.

"Nonono, honey. Here we sell. Type; oh, that's rich."

I need a job, Marilyn thought. But this doesn't fit any definition of a job I've ever heard.

"Well, thanks," Marilyn said. "But I really don't think this is for me."

The shabby man's expression turned incongruously serious.

"Now wait," he said solemnly. "I'm presenting you with an opportunity here. You could do very well. You do want to do well, don't you?"

"Yes, of course, but. . ."

"And what about Wayne and that other SPC student. . . Jeff, Jeff Hadlock. Do you know Jeff?"

Marilyn remembered Jeff Hadlock as an adenoidal dipstick who sat in the back of English 101 with a pack of like-minded baboons, gibbering and snorting their way through class like seventh graders telling their first fart jokes.

She nodded and then regretted it.

"Well, they earned enough to pay for school for a whole year, and to buy a car too! Now how about that?! Do you really want to pass up an opportunity like that?"

If it's such a great opportunity, why are you trying so hard to sell me on it? Marilyn thought. And your elegant little setup here does not exactly engender confidence.

But then a voice inside her said, How do you know? You are not back home at the Wenatchee Country Club. Maybe this is the way the real world works. You had better get used to it. He might be right. You might not get another opportunity like this.

But it all made her skin crawl. If this was all there was. . . well, it wasn't all there was. That much she knew. There must be something better out there. There must be.

Marilyn rose to leave.

Her next stop was at a restaurant near Woodland Park. It was called The Dutch Kitchen and it did its best to look the part; a white storefront with blue doors and shutters surrounded by borders of intertwined tulip designs.

Inside, it looked the part too – more or less. Ersatz Delftware plates adorned the walls, along with posters of windmills and the like. It was all quite cheery, suggesting, to Marilyn, fresh-baked bread, hearty cheese and rich, foaming beer.

No one was to be seen. Marilyn spotted a pair of swinging doors at the rear of the dining room. She went through them and into a hallway. The first door on the right was ajar. She tapped on it and poked her head through.

A pallid, baggy woman with unwashed hair was sitting at a scratched and dented table, counting receipts. A cigarette with a long ash drooped from her lower lip. She looked up at Marilyn with nicotine-glazed lizard's eyes. She reminded Marilyn of a termite larva.

Marilyn waited for her to speak. She did not.

Finally, Marilyn said, "I'm here about the job?"

The woman continued to stare rheumily. Marilyn noticed that the lids below her eyes had lost their elasticity, exposing red, inflamed tear ducts. Her expression remained frozen in torpid rictus.

"The job in the P-I want ads?" Marilyn said, hoping to prime the conversation.

The woman inspected Marilyn coldly for a moment or two more, then grunted, "Mmmph. The job. Mmmph. Come on."

She rose from her chair, puffing and wheezing as if in pain and then waddled past Marilyn and through the door. Marilyn followed.

"You work for tips, we keep half," the woman said without looking back. "You get fifteen minutes for lunch or dinner, depending on your shift; one plate of whatever's left over in the kitchen and a glass of water. Coffee or tea and you pay for it."

"A hot meal sounds nice," Marilyn said, trying to engage the woman, an effort she suspected was hopeless.

"Who said anything about hot? It's hot if it's still on the stove. We won't heat it for you. We got a business to run. Electricity costs money."

They reached the kitchen. It was a small, windowless room, like a corridor. The walls were coated with an umber patina of rancid grease and dirty smoke. The perforated rubber mat on the floor was imbedded with granules and globules of food scraps. When Marilyn stepped on it, a greasy liquid oozed out, like something from crushed caterpillars. The garbage can had no lid. It had not been emptied for a few days. A cockroach skittered through a trail of mouse turds at the base of a cabinet.

A young man was busily washing dishes at the sink. He turned to look at Marilyn. His face was stamped with flat features and vacant eyes of a Mongoloid. He was drooling slightly.

"Damnit, who forgot to put that mayo in the reefer?!" the woman suddenly roared. "Carl! Carl! Godamnit, where's Carl?!"

The dishwasher stared at her uncomprehendingly.

"Goddamnit, get back to work, ya idiot!" she snarled. "Carl!"

Marilyn heard a toilet flush. A minute or so later, a tall, stooped man came through the doorway. Carl was a male version of the larva woman, the only noticeable difference being in his expression, a distinctive cruel, slack-jawed resignation. He was wearing a sleeveless undershirt and over that, a stained, greasy apron. His white trousers were similarly bespattered. Mats of curly hair covered his shoulders in sweaty blotches.

Carl squeezed past Marilyn and the woman. His body odor, a concentrated stench of vinegar, wet burlap and dead snakes, stung Marilyn's nostrils.

Carl shambled over to a counter by the sink, lit a cigarette, and started rummaging through the jars and tubs.

"Didn't I tell you about the mayo?" the woman barked at him.

"Yeah, yeah," Carl mumbled without looking up. Although it was not particularly warm in the room, Carl was sweating heavily. He wiped down his face and neck with a rag and then squeezed the sweat into a small drinking glass with two inches of grayish liquid in it. The rag went back on a board which, if knife cuts and assorted detritus were any indication, was where food was prepared.

"So, so . . . what did you say your name was, honey?" larva woman said.

"Marilyn"

"So Mary Ann here thinks she wants to be a waitress," the woman said sarcastically.

"Oooo, a waitress, huh?" Carl said looking up with a sly leer. "Well, ain't that just special."

He cackled at his own wit. Larva woman started to laugh, got tangled in her own phlegm, choked, coughed and eventually wheezed out a thin giggle.

Carl sneezed into his hands and wiped them on his apron.

"Well, ya got the legs for it, sweetcakes," he said and then guffawed again in his best red clay tenor.

Larva woman pulled Marilyn by the sleeve and guided her out of the kitchen.

"And put that seafood seasoning in the reefer, too," the woman said. Carl dutifully picked up the glass of wrung-out sweat and placed it in the refrigerator next to some open cubes of butter. As they left the room, Marilyn heard Carl murmur, "Mmmm-mm, those legs. Ooo-ey."

"Show up late and you're fired," larva woman said as she and Marilyn walked across the dining room. "Drop a plate and you're fired. We get a customer complaint and you're fired. And don't give me any of that hooey about customers trying to grab your ass. It's your ass, not mine."

She started to laugh again, choked and then gurgled for a while. They reached the front door.

"Be here at six," larva woman said. Then, without another word or any other form of acknowledgement, closed the door in Marilyn's face. Marilyn walked away. She wanted to run; to run off the tingling sensation creeping up and down her arms and legs like centipedes. But she kept walking, steadily and purposefully. She did not look back.

Her next stop was in the heart of Seattle's retail and office building district. The ad said the job was in the mail room of the Hart-Schaefer Building, a particularly sepulchral exemplar of the modern architecture muse on Fourth Avenue. Marilyn had heard that captains of capitalism often got their starts in the mail room, so maybe there was opportunity to be found. And, the work probably involved a lot of physical exercise, which certainly would do her no harm. She had gained five pounds since school began.

The basement room had no windows. Its concrete floor was chipped, uneven and stained. The long metal sorting tables were dented and dilapidated. The mail bags may have been white at one time, but years of being dragged across the floor had burnished them to the color of generic grime. They were piled in a mound like slag from a coal mine.

Loudly buzzing fluorescent tubes, dim amid the cobwebbed rafters high above, bathed the scene in gangrenous light, mutating people's skin to jaundiced citrine and metamorphosing their eye sockets to burned-out shell craters.

Actually, none of that particularly bothered Marilyn. What would you expect, after all? But, oddly, the metal frames on the elevator doors and mail chutes did. They were painted at one time – institutional beige, actually – but now were so scraped and scabrous that bare metal showed through; more metal than paint. That metal itself was abraded and gouged, particularly at ankle level where day after day, year after year, generation after generation of carts mauled and gnawed it. Once brand new, fresh from the factory, bright and shiny; now shoddy and scarred. No one noticed, no one cared.

The mail room supervisor was a trim young man with an open, honest face and a no-nonsense manner. He greeted Marilyn with a handshake, asked her to sit down and invited her to tell him about herself. Two quarters of college and a part-time job as a receptionist back home, she said. She knew how green it must make her sound. She was embarrassed.

The young man didn't seem to notice, nodding curtly as she spoke. When she was done, he said, "The job is delivery. You pick up the mail here, put it on a cart and then deliver it around the building. We have a crew of two. Usually, one starts at the top floor and works down, the other starts at the bottom floor and works up. Beginners generally make two rounds a day. After a couple of weeks, you'll probably up that to three. There's always lots to do. That's about it. Interested?"

She was.

"Good," the young man said. "The girl we're replacing is leaving in two weeks and we may need a day or two after that to make up our minds. We'll give you a call."

He stood up, shook Marilyn's hand, thanked her for coming and then went back to his work.

On the elevator back to the lobby, Marilyn found herself next to a young woman pushing a mail delivery cart. The young woman's youthful prettiness was fading faster than it should.

"You're on the delivery crew?" Marilyn asked.

"Yes."

"I just interviewed for a job there."

"Oh?" The young woman tried to sound interested, but apathy annulled the effect.

"It sounds like a good-enough job," Marilyn said.

"Hmm," the young woman grunted wearily.

"Tell me about it," Marilyn said. "I like to know the temperature of the water before I dive in."

The young woman looked Marilyn up and down, apparently to discern if she was worth talking to. She paused, then let out a resigned sigh.

"Okay, since you asked," she said. "First of all, you have the same route every day, sometimes from the bottom up, sometimes from the top down, but still the same route. After a week, you'll be able to do it in your sleep. After two weeks, you'll be bored out of your mind.

"The same people get the same mail on the same schedule day after day after day. The art director in the ad agency on fourteen, for example, gets the same big brown envelope of photographs every Thursday afternoon."

"Okay, so it's tedious," Marilyn said. Her tone indicated she expected that.

The young woman smiled ruefully.

"I'm just getting started," she said. "There are the people. You will see the same receptionists twice a day every day; the lesbian in 1241 who resents she wasn't born a man, the zombie in 902 who had her personality surgically removed, the moron in 518. She has to be told everything at least three times and then she still looks at you like you're speaking Chinese.

"Most of them just ignore you, but some like to play games; hassle you about being late, crap like that. And they do it every time, always looking for some crack they can pry open so they can get at you.

"It's all they have. They're trapped. This building has more than a thousand people in it and most of them hate - and I mean *hate* - their jobs. And their bosses and their lives and themselves. But they keep coming back anyway. Something is dead in them. You can see it in their eyes.

"Anyway, watch out for the hotshots in the marketing department on the eleventh floor. The nice ones just check out your legs - twice a day, every day. The not-so-nice ones try to hit on you, tell you about what hot shit they are."

"What's wrong with that?" Marilyn said. "I'm not adverse to the opposite sex."

"This is different. They don't want to date you. They certainly don't want to marry you. They just want to fuck you. You're a lower caste."

Marilyn sensed it was time to change the subject.

"The supervisor seems like a nice guy," she said.

"Darrel? He is a nice guy," the young woman said, brightening slightly - very slightly. "Good at his job, too. I have to admit it; thanks to him, our department definitely is efficient."

"Why doesn't he do something about all the harassment?" Marilyn said.

"He works for the building owners. All they care about is lunch at the Cascade Club. The businesses in the building are tenants. Darrel has no authority with them. One time, when it really got bad with an outfit on seven, he went and talked to them. Then they talked to the building owners and the building owners talked to Darrel. We mustn't alienate our beloved tenants, you know. To put it another way: We don't give a shit, now leave us alone."

The elevator reached the lobby. Marilyn couldn't contain her curiosity.

"You're still here," she said.

The young woman smiled. It was not a happy smile.

"I let one of the eleventh floor hotshots fuck me. Now I have a two-year-old to raise on my own. Don't know what I'll do when my feet give out."

Marilyn fought to suppress a shiver.

"Well, thanks for the information," she said.

"Yeah. Good luck."

The elevator door hissed shut and the young woman disappeared.

And so it went. One job had a hundred people lined up to apply. At another, the man at the desk said he never hired anyone unless they already were employed. At still another, bagging groceries, the store manager explained that women employees were paid less than men – twenty percent less – because they weren't worth as much. When Marilyn asked, as politely as she could, why they weren't worth as much, the manager nearly bit his cigar in half. Marilyn Pennell would never work at Evergreen Grocers Inc.

Marilyn tried an employment agency. She stood unnoticed in front of the reception desk for ten minutes while the receptionist whispered and snickered with a nearby secretary about some other girl's love life. Finally, the receptionist deigned to give Marilyn an application. Marilyn filled it out. The receptionist looked at it briefly, then handed it to the secretary. They shared a giggle.

Eventually, a short man came mincing out of a glassed-in office. He wore a bow tie, wire-rimmed glasses and prissy expression. He scanned the application.

"My, almost a whole year of college. How impressive," he said, stifling a smirk. "So, what kind of things did you study, dear?"

Marilyn told him.

"Oh really?" he said with exaggerated earnestness. "Just a regular little renaissance women, aren't we? I'm sure your mother is very proud."

Marilyn had no idea what she was supposed to say. The receptionist and secretary simpered and tee-heed as if sharing a private joke.

The prissy little man raised an eyebrow, like a cat confronting a baby bird with a broken leg.

"Well, dear, our clientele usually possesses specific skills the business world requires," he said. "Perhaps you can tell me how classes in philosophy and psychology translate to marketability?"

"They've taught me how to think critically and how to analyze human nature," Marilyn said in a monotone which she hoped sounded fearless.

I've analyzed your nature pretty fast, you rancid little pygmy.

"Hmmm. How nice," the rancid little pygmy purred through a vaseline smile. Without looking, he flipped the application toward the secretary's desk. It fluttered erratically and landed on her coffee cup. Coffee started wicking up the corner of the application.

"Well, we'll certainly contact you right away when we find something suited to your, ahem, unique qualifications, dear," the rancid little pygmy said. He stood with his lips pursed and the corners of his mouth turned up, like a character out of Dr. Seuss.

Marilyn went job searching every Friday after her last class ended at 2 p.m., then again on Saturday, although many businesses were closed then. Mostly, she turned in applications then moved on to the next listing.

Occasionally, she was harassed and insulted. Often, she was humiliated, whether the humiliators meant to or not. Exposing yourself to other people's inspection, revealing over and over again your youth, your inexperience, your vulnerability; she found her humanity being chipped away, day after day, layer after layer.

In a way, she got used to it. When she would finish Friday classes and get on the bus to another round of degradation and futility, she would reflect on what was coming and how loathsome it would be. And she would find herself thinking, yes it will be awful, but now, at this moment, it is not. I am alone, free within my thoughts. Bad things will happen, guaranteed, and I will experience them and feel their kicks and stabs, and the pain will be real, oh so real. But I manage to bear it. I don't know how, but I do. Tomorrow, I will still be here.

At the end of her day's job-searching, Marilyn would return to the dorm. The unoccupied bed on the other side of her room haunted her; the ghost of poor, dumb Janet Small, a failure before her nineteenth birthday. Now I am in the same sphere, she thought. Will it destroy me, the same way it destroyed Janet?

She thought not, but sometimes, when she lay staring at the ceiling, she would find herself wondering, "Why? Why, God, is this happening to me?" No answer came, of course, and then she would cry a little and fall asleep, still wondering.

During the week, she drove her desolation from her mind with schoolwork. She would find an obscure corner in Weter, pull out her books and notes and set to studying. She looked neither left nor right. She did not notice those walking by. Her attention was fixed, riveted, immersed in reading, analyzing, synthesizing and memorizing; lost in the cool, pure workings of the mind.

Time would pass, then disappear and the next thing she knew she had gone through seventy pages of text, or written fifteen pages of notes, and there was a librarian tapping on her shoulder, politely informing her it was closing time. Then she would go back to her room and wrap herself in a bulletproof cocoon of intellect until her legs went numb and her eyes could no longer focus.

It worked. Her grades soared, her professors noticed. Her classmates noticed too and started shying away from her. Marilyn Pennell was becoming distinctly odd, they clucked. Marilyn didn't care. At dinner, she overheard their prattling about clothes and boys and, above all, gossip involving other girls, and she would find it childish and banal. Was she merely becoming sour and cynical? No, she concluded; much of what they concerned themselves with truly was childish and banal; a waste of mental energy, a waste of life. Reality had forced her into a different dimension. She couldn't afford to be frivolous and harebrained.

Was that good or bad? If she had lost her youth, she had lost it very quickly, so quickly she had barely noticed its passage. That saddened her. She had been led to believe that maturation was a gradual mellowing process, not a brutal ripping of a raw wound.

She thought about it some more, but not for long. She had studies to complete while she still had them to study and she had to find a job before June. Practicalities, practicalities; they dictated her life now.

Chapter 26

Layton Fleming walked down the hall casually, as if he was carefree, even bored. He hummed a little to enhance the effect.

When he got to his office, he told his secretary to hold his calls. Then he closed the door and took a seat in his top grain cowhide, aniline finish easy chair ($300, special-order from Neiman Marcus). He hunched over, his hands folded, his head down. He was sweating. His heart was racing.

The two-bit little shits. Think they can talk to me like that? Well, I put them in their place.

That was the first thought that went through his mind. It was autonomic, the sort of thing that always went through his mind when he thought about himself: Layton Fleming, quintessential winner, had once again prevailed.

But now it brought him no comfort. He gazed at the trophies and diplomas and autographed photos on his wall. There was his All-American lacrosse trophy. Next to it was his All-American certificate and next to it a photo of him receiving the his All-American award. Nearby was a clipping from the Hartford Courant announcing his All-Americanism – not the whole page, because the story was short and on Page 4, at the bottom to the left. Some of the trophies went all the way back to high school, some were for things like the Spring Arbor, Michigan, Rotary Club Young Man of the Year.

There was his degree from Wesleyan, striking in red and black. And there were photos of him with famous people. Billy Graham, of course, was displayed the most prominently. He even had a photo of himself shaking hands with Vince Lombardi. He had been at a banquet where Lombardi spoke, carefully positioned himself along Lombardi's exit route, then stepped out quickly and grasped the coach's hand. A newspaper photographer was covering the banquet and Fleming paid him twenty dollars to get the shot. Lombardi's surprised expression passed for joviality. Fleming forged the autograph.

He had spent most of his life accumulating such things. They constituted a solid wall of gleaming brass and polished walnut and framed vellum that proclaimed, with jut- jawed, steely-eyed belligerence, "Here's what I've done. You got better?" They were his shield.

But for now, at this moment, they seemed like a shield that has rusted to a crumbling scab. Fleming was beginning to fathom just how serious a mistake the interview had been. As he turned it over in his mind, he saw his trophies falling from the wall and landing in a dirty pile of corroded pot metal, yellowed paper and broken glass, pointless symbols of a life no one else cared about, a life of surface brightness camouflaging an infinity of banality.

He shook his head.

What had he been thinking? Meeting with undergraduates on something akin to even ground was contrary to all that SPC stood for. No, more than contrary. Threatening. Subversive. Authority must be maintained. Any tear in its fabric, no matter how microscopic, called into question the essentia of the institution and all it represented. At least that's how the people who ran SPC saw it, particularly Dr. Donald A. Fotheringham, Ph.D., President.

The president had brought Fleming with him from Greenville College, Illinois, where Fotheringham had been the youngest college president in the country, aged 32, a fact that was included on the dust jacket of every book he wrote, including his latest, "Without a Raincoat: Christian Leadership in Stormy Times."

Perhaps because Fotheringham was a young man alone in an old man's environment, he had a particular penchant for personal loyalty. If you were his confidant, you flourished. Competence helped you stay in his good graces, but it wasn't really necessary just so long as you let it be known, frequently, through word and deed, that you were a protégée of Dr. Donald A. Fotheringham, Ph.D., and a testament to his greatness.

It suited Layton Fleming just fine. Create convincing appearances and shamelessly kiss ass; a simple formula and it had served him well - although, of course, he certainly would never acknowledge it as such. No, no; his success was the result of vision and hard work - and he had a wall full of trophies and citations and autographed photographs to prove it.

And now it all seemed meaningless. Why, oh why had he agreed to that damned interview? Had he become the instrument of his own destruction? The idea struck Fleming hard. Fear washed over him. His began conjuring streams of horrible imaginables. Students would laugh at him behind his back. He would be asked to account for himself at the next cabinet meeting. He would be grilled and he would have no good answers because there were no good answers when you caused a rent in the fabric of the flawless, Fotheringhamian universe.

His career could dissolve, never to be rebuilt. Layton Fleming had never worked in private business. He had never run a loading dock. He had never made a sale. He could not operate a lathe or repair an automobile. He had succeeded only at being successful, at the *appearance* of success, and if he lost that, he lost everything. And now it had become all too clear to him.

The clarity did not last long. Parris and McLean and Weldon and that beady-eyed little shit Brewer: Goddamn them. He would make them pay. How? He could expel them, but on what grounds? They had broken none of SPC's rules, at least none of the written ones. The unwritten ones? There always was opportunity there. He could claim the discussion had turned threatening, that he actually feared for his safety. No, no one would believe that. Perhaps he could claim that they openly insulted him. That might work. There were no witnesses, but he could probably make it stick anyway. But a group of students insulting a dean? He thought of Fotheringham and he realized that such things could never happen at any college over which The Great Man presided.

What then? He would find something, no matter how long it took. Even if he couldn't get them all, he would get some of them.

For now, though, he had to figure a way to save his own skin. Nothing came to mind. Nothing came to mind for the rest of the day. Nor that night. Nor the next morning. Then, finally, he knew what he would do.

****

Sally Huddleston was not a typical college journalist. She did not drink, smoke or curse. She displayed no particular interest in challenging authority. She was not a wiseass. She was an English major who wanted to write; no more, no less. Her stories for The Falcon were good: Accurate, succinct and fair. Her choice of subjects tended to be leaden – Student Council meetings, administration policy, guest speakers on campus and so forth – but they needed to be covered and Parris and McLean were happy to let Sally cover them.

She was a bit of an enigma to the young men in the office. She showed no interest in them and if she dated at all, they wondered who. Sally was a pretty girl; tiny and delicate with freckles and a lovely smile. And she was pleasant, albeit reserved. She was courteous to the other staff members, rather than friendly. The young men could not understand it. The status of her virginity and, they occasionally ventured, her heterosexuality, were topics of much speculation among them.

It never occurred to them that their lack of understanding was a reflection of their own prejudices and stereotypes, that Sally was simply what she appeared to be; a quiet, intelligent young woman who wanted to master a skill and went about it with cool-headed diligence.

Anyway, she could type. People who saw it were often taken aback. Her fingers moved so fast that the typewriter did not click and clack, it buzzed, rather like the sound of someone thumbing a deck of cards. She never made typing errors and rarely misspelled a word or misplaced a comma. To a newsroom of people resigned to hunt and peck floundering, she seemed a wonderment.

Sally agreed to type up the Fleming interview. The others worried she might find it too controversial. Actually, Sally didn't care if it was controversial or not. She was interested in it because she had never typed from dictation and it seemed like as good a way as any to learn how.

It took her about an hour to get used to listening to the tape and typing at the same time and another hour to finish the job. She put the copy on Parris's desk, saved a carbon for herself, packed up her books neatly and then, the epitome of self-containment, she walked up to Gwinn for dinner.

Sally left the tape recorder where she found it, amid a typical pile of newsroom clutter on a large work table just to the right of the front counter.

About an hour later, Parris came to the office. He looked over Sally's work, found it flawless, penciled in some typesetting directions and then left to drive it to the printer on the other side of Queen Anne Hill.

He did not notice the tape recorder.

Shortly afterward, McLean came in, spent about a half hour finishing a story on one of the newsroom typewriters and left. That was at 8:30 p.m.

He did not notice the tape recorder.

At 9 p.m., Layton Fleming dropped by his office at the other end of the hall, ostensibly to catch up on his in-basket. He did enough actual work to make it look convincing, turned out the lights, locked up and then headed for the Falcon office.

The office's door was open and its lights were on. The tape recorder was visible from the hallway, exactly where Fleming had seen it when he had walked by at noon.

Fleming moved fast. He rewound the tape and listened. Yes, it was the interview. He rewound it the rest of the way. Then he put the tape in his pocket. He took a blank tape from his other pocket, put it on the recorder, threaded it through the mechanism and then fast forwarded it so it looked like it had been played a while.

He pulled out a handkerchief and wiped down the machine and everything else he had touched – an unnecessary gesture, he knew, but adrenalin was pounding through his veins. It makes you do things like that.

Fleming left the office as he found it. Next to the office was the building's west exit door, the one hardly anyone used. Fleming cracked it open and looked out. Next door, Tiffany Hall was dark. Across the quad, the big cube of Moyer was lighted, but no one was in it. You couldn't see the SUB's west door from any other buildings on campus.

Fleming knew the SUB was unoccupied, save the night switchboard operator. She had not seen him come in and since she was in a windowless room on the first floor at the other end of the building, she would not see him leave.

He started down the stairs, tiptoeing carefully.

Halfway down, he spotted something moving on the quad. It was a figure, probably a student, walking from Moyer toward the SUB.

Fleming was silhouetted against the SUB's white wall. If the student happened to look that way, he would see him. Slowly, very carefully, Fleming lowered himself into a squat. That way, he hoped, he hoped so desperately, his shape could be mistaken for a shadow.

There he stayed, for what seemed like a very long time, watching the student's every step, every movement as he drew closer. The student continued to look straight ahead, with an occasional glance at the pavement in front of him. He never looked in Fleming's direction. Then he disappeared under the eaves of the SUB entrance.

Fleming felt a rush of relief, like a deep breath of pure oxygen. Then he brought his senses back into focus. He had to hurry.

He was all but invisible as he carefully walked through the black canyon between the SUB and Tiffany. He made sure no cars or people were on Bertona Street, crossed quickly, slipped between the ramshackle buildings on the other side and found his car in back of a boarded-up gas station. In less than a minute, he, and the tape, were gone.

Fleming was nervous and sweating as he turned on to the Fremont Bridge, and then on to North 34th Street. Would he be seen? What if it all went wrong? He found himself breathing hard at the thought.

Something else was nagging at him, too, something in the far corners of his mind, something that would not be silenced.

So this is what you have become, a common sneak thief. Proud of yourself?

It's a tough world, Fleming thought in response. Sometimes you have to do distasteful things in order to get by. That's just reality.

Sure, you just tell yourself that. Tell yourself over and over again. Tell yourself for as long as it takes. Eventually, you might even believe it.

Fleming tried to push the thought from his mind. He was human, that's all. Sure, sometimes, he shaded the truth a little. Sure, sometimes, he engaged in ethical marginalities . . .

You mean you lie and you cheat. Now you have stolen. Have you turned the corner once and for all?

Go away, Fleming thought. Just go away. I don't have time for you now. But the thought did not go away. It continued to pick at his consciousness, setting his nerves on edge like stinging nettles.

On into the night he drove, a night full of car headlights and neon signs and constantly changing comings and goings; not at all the haven of darkness and secrecy he had envisioned.

When he reached University Way, he cruised up and down the street looking for a trash can. He reasoned that ditching the tape here would be a good bet because it was a busy part of town, with people throwing away all kinds of things all the time. No one would notice a tape reel amid the trash.

He spotted a can a few feet from a bus stop in front of a European pastry cafe. Perfect. Fleming parked his car in a dark corner of a lot across the street. He took the reel from his pocket and carefully broke off as much of the plastic rim and spokes as he could. He put the fragments in a paper bag and wadded it up. Then he put the rest of the reel, with its tape now loose and tangled, in another paper bag. He wadded it up.

Fleming crept through a back alley for two blocks and then cut over to University Way. He walked down the avenue as casually and inconspicuously as he could, losing himself amid the flotsam of pallid grad students, stringy-haired white girls and pseudo intellectual posers with beards. As he went by the trash can, he slipped the two wads of paper in it without breaking stride.

He walked two more blocks, crossed the street, found the alley and followed it back to his car. He had, he concluded, done about as thorough job of being invisible as one could. It was a satisfying thought. But he was still sweating. And his heart was still racing.

****

The SPC basketball team was playing Pacific Lutheran University in Tacoma, an away game within reasonable driving distance.

A group of girls from Marilyn's floor were car-pooling to the game. Marilyn agreed to go, although she didn't particularly want to. True, it was a chance to get away from the stifling environs of the SPC campus, and any such chance was welcome. And the experience of rooting for the visiting team in a hostile venue might prove fun. But riding forty miles down and forty miles back with a group of dorm girls? They would giggle and talk and talk and giggle, generally about nothing at all; an enjoyable experience if you were in the right frame of mind, the frame of mind of 18-year-olds feeling carefree, flirty and gay. But Marilyn was not and, she concluded, probably never would be again. The realities of her life, her future, had come down on such things like the blade of a guillotine. What gaiety there was in the world did not apply to her. There was no dodging that reality.

So she sat in the back seat, next to the window and watched the city pass by in the night as the others chattered and tittered, their words flowing by her like a light wind. They talked about boys and classes and gossip about other girls and shoes.

Marilyn listened but she didn't hear. Bits and pieces of conversation occasionally penetrated her consciousness, but they rarely made an impression. Was it because they were trivial and inconsequential or simply because she didn't want to hear them? It didn't matter, really. Nothing they had to say would alter the course of her life.

On the other hand, the concentrated atmosphere of lightheartedness did have some effect on her, similar to the way music affects one, by going to your core, past where words can no longer go, down to where you sense what you cannot express.

By the time they reached Tacoma, the gloom that saturated Marilyn's being was gone. The world seemed pleasant.

The girls bustled through the crowd and found seats four rows up from the court. The game started in fifteen minutes. The rival bands played back and forth as loudly as they could, the rival cheerleaders danced as prettily as they could and PLU's cavernous, old gym became a concentrated ecosphere of youth and enthusiasm and expectation. Expectation of what? No one knew. It wouldn't be until many years later that they would find that expectation itself is enough, and usually far more enjoyable than the event expected.

Marilyn soaked it in as best she could. It was, she decided, a form of theater and she tried to enjoy it was such.

The pavilion filled quickly. Soon every seat was taken and students started finding places on the floor along the sidelines and under the baskets.

That's when Marilyn spotted Tom Brewer. He was with a group of friends whose names Marilyn did not know. As always, he had an unmistakable presence, an unconscious command of the space around him as he and his friends moved toward the end of the court, looking for places to sit. He was dressed in a navy sweater, cords and desert boots. It all looked crisp and new.

No. No, not now. I can't let that become part of my life. Not now. Things are too complicated and confusing as it is.

She tried to force herself to take her eyes off him but she could not. Brewer and his friends found a place at the far end, to the right of the backboard. Brewer ended up sitting in a makeshift front row, about three feet outside the out-of-bounds zone. While the students around him were chatty and animated, Brewer seemed to be in a state of calm; not cold or bad-tempered, but calm; calm in the moment, attentive, in control of himself, on a plane of his own.

Just then, the teams came out on the floor, the bands played, the crowds cheered and, in all the commotion, Marilyn lost track of Tom Brewer.

It was a very good game. That year, SPC had one of the great teams in Northwest basketball history, led by a silky smooth forward named Howard Heppner and a cocky, swaggering point guard named Dave Rumpee. PLU, meanwhile, had its own All-American candidate, the cold, merciless power forward Curt Gammell.

Both teams played to their potential, the score going back and forth with rarely four points between them. Marilyn found herself caught up in it all; the speed, the grace, the tension, the split-second timing that made it all seem to be balancing on the precipice of disaster. For a while, she forgot herself.

Time out was called. SPC's yell leaders, young men Marilyn found rather obnoxious, took to the floor and led their favorite yell:

Rip 'em in the lip
Tear 'em in the jaw
Come on Falcons
Claw, claw, claw!

This was accompanied by a pantomime of teeth being bared, jaws being clawed and various expressions of savagery. Marilyn's eyes drifted.

Tom Brewer was still seated under the basket. As Marilyn watched, he drew his legs up a little and then clasped his hands around his kneecaps, all with an economy of motion, a grace, that was unconscious and somehow perfect.

The game started again. Rumpee shot a blind pass to Heppner, who threw an almost imperceptible fake and then rose effortlessly into the air, where he floated like a feather in a light breeze before releasing a jump shot that glided soundlessly through the hoop, barely rustling the net. You didn't have to be a student of basketball to appreciate the beauty of it all. Marilyn found herself dazzled. Her mind drifted away from Tom Brewer.

Then the game got rough, with players throwing elbows under the boards and fighting for rebounds like stray dogs over a scrap of food. Occasionally, a body went crashing to the floor. The coaches shouted in protest and the referees called fouls, but it made little difference.

The crowd, of course, loved it. Marilyn found herself liking it. It was honest, a glimpse of human nature in its reality. More and more, she found herself living in the moment, in the immediate. And, right now, a delightful immediate it was.

By the third quarter, skill started to win out. Heppner had scored twenty four points and seemed all but unstoppable. Slowly, surely, the Falcons pulled ahead.

Just near the end of the third quarter, the ball flew out of bounds. An arm went up and caught it on the fingertips, an arm in a navy sweater. Tom Brewer balanced the ball smoothly on his fingers and then flicked it to the referee in a seamless, elegant motion. Then he returned to his quiet, controlled posture.

A cold feeling formed in Marilyn's chest. It flowed down her arms and out to the ends of her fingers and there it stopped and stayed and overtook her senses. For a moment, she had trouble catching her breath.

No, not now...

It wasn't supposed to be like this. He was supposed to be a proper small town aristocrat, a scion of country clubs and luncheons, a boy from the world of outdoor weddings and women with hats and lemonade... He was supposed to be... he was supposed to be...

Yes, Oh, yes. Oh yes.

Out on the floor, SPC's Dick Smith caught a pass, stumbled and fell to his knees. He kept right on dribbling the ball, off the floor, off himself, left-hand, right-handed, whatever it took. But he never lost the ball and managed to flick it to Rumpee, who fed it to Gary Carnevali for an easy layup.

Again, it was a magical piece of basketball. But Marilyn did not notice.

The rest of the world had disappeared and she saw only Tom Brewer and she felt only the emptiness within her. She didn't understand it, she couldn't understand it and it left her feeling lost and bewildered. But it was him and him and him and him. Yes.

The game continued and then ended – the Falcons won – and everyone headed for the door. As she moved with the crowd, Marilyn tried to spot Brewer, perhaps bump into him, even a word with him would be enough. But she could not. She was pulled along, out to the parking lot, still searching. Ahead was a tall young man in a navy sweater. Marilyn pushed and squeezed her way to him and tapped him on the shoulder. He turned. It was not Tom Brewer. Marilyn stuttered an apology.

She kept searching, but she couldn't find him.

Then it was back in the car for the long ride back to the SPC campus. Girls had to be in by 12:30, so there would be no stopping along the way. The others talked. The others chatted. The others giggled. Marilyn heard none of it.

It was him. Yes, it was him. What would she do about it?

Chapter 27

"It isn't true! None of it's true!"

Layton Fleming slapped down the copy of The Falcon on the big mahogany table in front of him. His chin jutted, his eyes blazed, his breath shot out in enraged salvos.

The others at the table looked on; some curious, a few shocked, all attentive. Angry scenes were rare to the point of non-existent at the president's weekly cabinet meeting. Dr. Donald L. Fotheringham, Ph.D., believed in a smooth-sailing ship, with him the stately commander of an obedient, professional crew. But on this occasion, Fotheringham gestured at his dean of students to continue.

"They asked me to talk to them a little bit about student policies and this is what I get!" Fleming bawled, pointing to the newspaper on the table. There he was, in two, three-column photographs, resembling a gerbil who had just had a firecracker go off in his face. And there it was, the entire conversation, in single-spaced, 10-point type, taking up two full pages and including every one of his dodges, asides, bungles and attempts at humor. The overall effect made Layton Fleming, All-American, Young Man on the Way Up, look like a boob.

"Is this what passes for journalism these days?!" Fleming roared indignantly.

The best defense is a good offense. He had been telling himself that over and over since the paper hit the stands that morning. He hadn't expected them to print the interview verbatim and, as he read it, he found they hadn't missed a word. He thought the story might prove a problem, but nothing like this. This was SPC, after all, where students, including student journalists, were expected to show proper deference to their betters. "A tough, no-nonsense airing," he expected. He could have manipulated that to his advantage fairly easily ("Straight-forward questions, straight forward answers: The Dean speaks.")

But this? They had ambushed him. All right, all right, they were his own words. That didn't matter. The paper didn't matter. The policies didn't matter. The students certainly didn't matter. His image as the president's right hand man, the most capable man on campus, the consummate winner, that mattered.

So Fleming was fighting back where it mattered, at the cabinet. The cabinet was, in itself, weak. It advised the president, but that's all it did, advise. No vote it took was binding. But its members did have influence. And - and this was the important part - they considered themselves the stewards of SPC's academic prestige, its traditions and, most importantly for Fleming, its image.

"It says in the story that they recorded the entire conversation."

That was Richard Atkinson, dean of instruction. He was an earnest, conscientious man and easy to ignore. Atkinson didn't know it, but he was on the skids. He was dean before Dr. Donald L. Fotheringham, Ph.D., arrived at SPC. At that particular time, Dr. Donald L. Fotheringham, Ph.D., needed to keep him around to create the appearance of continuity. But that was three years ago. Richard Atkinson had not gone to Wheaton. He received both his undergraduate and graduate degrees from state universities, and universities west of the Mississippi River at that. The president tactfully ignored him and already had lined up his replacement, a proper Midwesterner with proper evangelical credentials.

Atkinson's little attempt at relevance gave Fleming the opening he needed.

"If there was a tape recorder, I never saw it and if there were tapes, I'd like to hear them," Fleming barked indignantly. Steady, steady. Maintain the tone, maintain the tone . . .

All the men in the room nodded, including Atkinson. Three students had conducted the interview, a fourth had photographed it and one more had transcribed it from the tapes. Fleming had no idea if others had heard it. One or two, probably. So, make it the words of six against the word of one. Ha! Make it anything you want, Fleming thought. He was a member of the administration, a cabinet member, no less. He would be believed. The students, those pimply little snots, would not even be considered. No, better than that, Fleming thought: They would be suspected of dark motives - if, that is, he played it right.

Fleming scanned the assembled. Atkinson was looking on seriously, genuinely concerned about doing the right thing. Byron Sawyer, director of finance, was leaning back in his chair, his hands folded across his belly, his mouth spread in the smug, oleaginous smirk he wore most of the time. He would voice no opinions save those he thought the president wanted to hear.

Peter Louden, vice president, was hunched forward and scowling, his jaw grinding on ill-fitting dentures, his dark eyes burning. Peter Louden was a man given to disapproval.

Chester Dalrymple was absent-mindedly punching holes in a styrofoam coffee cup with a bent paper clip. Typical, Fleming thought. Chet rarely seemed connected to realities other than his own. Or maybe he was enjoying Fleming's discomfort. He had held a grudge ever since that nonsense over Freshman registration back in September.

Others were there, too: the director of admissions, the registrar, the director of the Graduate School, but they were not part of the president's inner circle and therefore not worth worrying about.

But back to his performance. The best defense is a good offense, the best defense is a good offense...

"I'm worried," Fleming said, taking a deep breath in an apparent effort to collect himself. "We're seeing it more and more on campuses around the country; students disrespecting authority, flaunting bad manners and calling it independence. I wouldn't want to see it happen here."

Peter Louden's scowl deepened. Fleming knew he had him in his pocket, but he was the easy one. There was a long pause as the others considered.

"Perhaps we need to reassess our publications policy," Dr. Donald L. Fotheringham, Ph.D., said.

"Well, we certainly don't want to see something like this again," Louden grumbled.

"What does our policy say about quoting a member of the administration?" Atkinson asked. Good old Dick; he could always be depended upon to give me a good segue, Fleming thought.

"There is no policy," Fleming said. "They can pretty much print whatever they want."

A low, uneasy murmur went around the room.

"Up to now, we've trusted them to do the right thing," Fleming said. "But times are changing. They've even been talking about something called a student bill of rights."

Another uneasy murmur. Then silence.

Finally, Dr. Donald L. Fotheringham, Ph.D., spoke.

"How do you see the student newspaper fitting into SPC's institutional mission?" he said. The question was directed at Fleming. The paper was funded from the student body budget and its office was in the SUB.

Fleming was momentarily taken aback. He hadn't thought about the paper's mission because he didn't care about the paper's mission, just so long as it printed stories about basketball games, homecoming princesses and the wonderfulness of the school's Christian outreach programs. Then Parris had come along. It was Fleming's responsibility to appoint The Falcon's editor and Parris seemed like a good bet: Innocuous, malleable and not terribly bright. Then Parris took on McLean and Weldon as his assistants. Troublemakers, those two. The paper had been plaguing him ever since. And who was that other kid, the one with the icy stare? Oh yeah, Brewer. Mustn't forget that little shit.

"Our mission is excellence in Christian education and the efficient processing of educational services," Fleming said. It was one of the president's favorite platitudes. He used it in speeches to the Chamber of Commerce, the Rotary, the Lions and similar gatherings of great minds, and it always generated many posturings of gravitas and much nodding of heads. It was all but a mantra for the men seated at the big mahogany table. They could be depended upon to give it unquestioned deference.

"I would like to think the paper supports it through fair and accurate journalism," Fleming said. He gestured contemptuously at the page with his interview. "Not this."

What Fleming wanted was to see the paper shut down and its staff kicked out of school. But that was too obvious. Excellence in Christian education, in any education, required a free exchange of ideas – or so the academics at SPC liked to say. Fleming sneered. The *appearance* of a free of exchange of ideas, that's what mattered. Most people didn't notice the difference between appearance and reality because they didn't care. Then came those damned troublemakers from the Falcon.

Ideas were exchanged at SPC, of course. Classroom discussions could get lively and contentious, depending on the professor. In the coffee shops and dorm lounges, there was far more free exchange than the administration liked. Students could and did discuss original ideas, including ideas that challenged the institutional status quo and there wasn't much the school could do to prevent it, at least nothing Fleming could think of.

Blessedly, the conversations were fragmented and usually went no further than the rooms in which they were conducted. Their effect on the college as a whole was negligible. But a newspaper put ideas in writing, ideas that focused people's thoughts on a single concept or combination of concepts: Unity. In unity, there was power. No, Fleming thought, the college could not tolerate that.

Fleming sized up his situation. Not all the men in the room were fools and some, like Atkinson, were open-minded and well-meaning. But they all were products of their environment, and that environment was founded on hierarchy. Hierarchies could not abide challenges to their authority; certainly not challenges with any teeth to them, even the tiny baby teeth of an undergraduate newspaper.

So Fleming was on solid ground.

"We need to act before this thing starts to spread," Fleming said.

"I have problems with that," Atkinson said. "We need to think this out. It raises questions about freedom of expression."

"Does that mean they have the freedom to shout 'Fire!' in an overcrowded theater?" Louden grumbled.

"That's not the same thing," Atkinson said.

"As far as I'm concerned it is," Louden said darkly.

"There's more involved than just some students getting their facts mixed up," Atkinson said. Fleming perked up. Atkinson had acknowledged that the students were in the wrong. Good, good.

"I'm saying the people take freedom of the press pretty seriously," Atkinson said. "We need to consider what the general public will think about this."

"Well, they aren't us," said Dr. Donald L. Fotheringham, Ph.D. with weighty finality. And with that, he summed up much of his world view. The college and those who ran it were above the clamor about liberty, rights, democracy and similar gibberish emanating from the riffraff beyond its cultural borders. The elite were the elite for a reason; the academically elite because they were smarter than other people. They were smarter than other people because God had bestowed special blessings of intelligence on them – along with special blessings of leadership, vision and the like. It said so in the Bible, somewhere, if you looked hard enough. . .

"Peter, I want you to look into this," Fotheringham said. Louden nodded gravely. "Come up with a proposal for a committee to study the question."

"Chet, I want you in on this too," Fotheringham said.

Dalrymple's head jerked up in surprise. He looked quizzically at the president.

"I want some kind of public statement to the effect that we are reassessing our policies in regards to The Falcon," Fotheringham said. "Meanwhile, I want to make that assistant of yours – what's his name? Oh yes, Trimble – I want to make him the paper's advisor. Make sure he understands I don't want to see anything like this happen again."

"You mean make him a censor?" Atkinson said.

There was an awkward silence. The word censor had a nasty connotation, even in that room. Fotheringham's expression hardened.

"I wouldn't call it that," he said stiffly.

"That could be the effect," Atkinson said.

Fleming smiled inwardly. Keep it up, Dick, keep it up. Your slide is getting steeper every minute.

"Students have ample opportunities to make their opinions known through any number of avenues," Fotheringham said, "their class officers, their student body representatives." He nodded at Fleming, "The Student Affairs Office." He gestured at the copy of the paper on the table. "I fail to see the need for them to disrupt the educational process."

He looked around the room to see if anyone would challenge him. Atkinson shrugged and began doodling on his notepad. The rest nodded solemnly and in unison.

****

The moment Paul Trimble entered Chester Dalrymple's office, he knew he was in trouble. Byron Sawyer, SPC's finance director and the president's most trusted advisor was there, leaning languorously in his chair, the tip of a front tooth pinning his lower lip in a smirk, his unkempt hair hanging here and there like dirty straw. He reminded Trimble of a Missouri sharecropper settling down on the front porch for another day of whittle and spit.

He was contrasted by Peter Louden, vice president of the college, a sallow-skinned man with permanent mauve rings around black eyes buried in a head resembling a block of paraffin. His imposing jaw was set in the earnest, resolute attitude popular in the evangelical subculture. (It photographed well, particularly from low angle and particularly with a crucifix or stained-glass window in the background.) To Trimble he resembled Frankenstein's monster with a bad case of hemorrhoids.

Chester Dalrymple completed the firing squad. He gave Trimble the most pause of all. Dalrymple was hunched over his desk, his eyes darting right and left, a faint sheen of sweat glistening on his blue-jowled face. Trimble knew the look. Whenever Chet Dalrymple was feeling insecure, bad things were certain to follow for his staff.

"Have a seat, Paul" Dalrymple said. "Oh, and close the door."

Ah, the ritual of the closed door. Next would come solemn pronouncements of one kind or another leading to a conclusion that Paul Trimble was sure to dislike. For all his attempts at snark, Trimble felt the first twinges of fear. Inquisition time.

But for what? Trimble's work had been especially innocuous and insipid as of late, just what the college wanted. He almost felt more curious than nervous.

"Paul, are you familiar with what the Falcon is up to lately?" Dalrymple said.

The Falcon, like many things at SPC, was an exercise in respecting authority and reciting appropriate platitudes. It had been getting a little better lately, Trimble had noticed, with honest-to-goodness journalism occasionally gracing its pages.

"I scan it every now and then," Trimble said.

"Mmmm," Louden growled under his breath. Obviously that was not the answer he wanted to hear.

"Well, Paul, in nutshell, we're concerned about the direction it's been taking," Dalrymple intoned weightily.

"Which you would know if you ever took the trouble to read it," Louden grumbled.

Trimble did his best to maintain a poker face while he scribbled in his notebook as if he actually cared what Louden said.

"The Falcon's been pushing boundaries," Dalrymple said, licking his lips nervously. "And, well, lately, it's gone beyond the pale."

So what and according to who? Trimble wondered. It's only a student newspaper, after all. But he knew enough to stay quiet. More was coming.

"The final straw was that supposed interview with Layton Fleming," Dalrymple continued. "Have you seen it?"

Trimble had. It was one of the pieces that gave the paper some journalistic integrity. The students asked questions, Fleming answered them; a pretty straight forward exchange. Clearly the powers that be thought otherwise.

"I never thought I would see tripe like that at SPC," Louden said. "First they interrogate the dean of students about a bunch of trumped-up nonsense, then they deliberately misrepresent his answers. In my day, they would have been expelled."

Sawyer chuckled. "Well, we're not quite at that juncture," he said in a tone he tried to make jovial. He was a few inches off.

"Now, we don't want to throw the baby out with the bathwater," Dalrymple said. "We want to give them an opportunity to straighten up and fly right. So, we've decided to appoint an advisor to oversee them. Paul, we think you're the best man to run with the ball on this one."

Trimble's head jerked up. Suddenly he was focused.

"The action plan is the have a point man to interface verbally with the staff and move them on board to synergize with the institutional mission statement," Sawyer said. He said it very smoothly. He had a lot of practice in the dialect.

"Exactly, specifically, how am I supposed to do that?" Trimble said.

The triumvirate seemed upset at the question. Even Sawyer frowned slightly. Didn't he just conference Trimble on formulative actualization management of resolution exemplification?

"We would hope you will be proactive in establishing a functionality of responsible processing of information," Sawyer said. "Consider it a growth opportunity to demonstrate your facility at self initiation."

Usually, Trimble didn't mind wading through linguistic donkey shit. It's what you had to do in some places. But Dalrymple's canticle of clichés and Sawyer with his organization chic gibberish was too much. The thing was, these guys talked like that because they thought like that. Really. Were they from Mars?

When Paul Trimble was particularly frightened or nervous, his stomach would hurt. It hurt now, more than it had ever hurt before. It made him angry. Not enough that they fuck with my career – my life, really – now they're fucking with my body.

"Wait a minute, just wait a minute," he said. "I have a full-time job now. Where will I find time to do both?"

"You are a management person," Louden growled. "Are you unfamiliar with the concept of time management?"

What to do, what to do. . . Clearly, saying anything that revealed a hint of vulnerability was like blood to a shark in this room. And, in the rarified environs of SPC administration, expressing doubt, particularly doubt about decisions from on high, was tantamount to wiping one's nose on the Bible.

So Trimble remained silent. The moment hung in the air. Finally, Sawyer spoke.

"The question is the role of the student press in our institutional exemplar," he said. "Recent events suggest the Falcon is not integrated vis-à-vis the organizational cache. We would hope the input of an advisor would reeffectuate that calculus.

"Of course, we are firm believers in an active student press," he continued. "But, as I'm sure you know, with that privilege comes responsibility."

"Privilege?" Trimble thought. The freedom of the press is now a "privilege?" Those idiots who wrote the Constitution of the United States, what the hell did they know, with all that claptrap about inalienable rights? Clearly not SPC material.

Trimble thought about simply letting it go. (*You need this job, you need this job. . .*) You don't want to piss these fools off. (*You need this job, you need this job. . .*) They've made up their minds anyway. *(You need this job, you need this job. . .)* There must be a way to finesse this. . .

Fuck it.

The words hit Trimble's mind with a hard finality. They refused to go away.

Fuck it. Time to piss on the apple pie.

"So, you want me to be a censor," Trimble said.

Dalrymple and Louden jerked in their chairs as if they had just received an electric shock. How dare an underling speak in such terms.

Sawyer did not flinch.

"Yes," he said, his self-satisfied smirk never cracking, his smug expression never wavering.

Fuck it.

"How do you expect to know what students are thinking if they don't have a newspaper where they can express their views?" Trimble said.

"Now, Paul, let's not. . . " Dalrymple began. Sawyer held up his hand to stop him.

Sawyer kept smirking his smirk, the very picture of smug assurance. I'm not going to answer your piss-ant question, you small-time nobody, that smirk said. I'm not going to listen to your ideas. I'm not going to acknowledge your humanity. You don't matter and there's not a thing you can do about it.

It was all so obvious, Trimble thought. The administration didn't care what students thought. Why should it? Students were not rich Republicans. So, the only real issue was finding a way to make it appear like it actually did care. That's why they were appointing him advisor; a token gesture for the sake of appearances.

Their plan probably would work. If it didn't, they could simply blame it all on him; an elegant solution, when you think about it. He was cheap and disposable. Hardly anyone would notice.

Fuck it. Fuck i. . .

And then an odd thing happened. For a moment, a brief moment, all pretense and delusion and illusion left Paul Trimble. It felt cool and crystalline and unobstructed and not the least bit strange. He couldn't deny it. Maybe this is what yogis and Zen Buddhists experienced after years of meditation. And here it was happening to him; no particular reason, it just was. And what did it say?

This:

Fuck it? Oh, really? Fuck what? Okay, for a minute or two, you stood up like a manly man, valiant for that which is right and good. How very noble. But it didn't accomplish anything and you knew it wouldn't, so who is trying to create convincing appearances now? You, who spends your days typing up verbal vomit. You prays to god none of your classmates from journalism school will ever see it? You, who drinks yourself blind yourself every night because you don't know what else to do? Oh, you sure are a paragon of nobility, all right.

And besides, in the width and breadth of God's green earth, who gives a shit? Did anything, does anything, will anything - *anything* - change one sixteenth of an inch because of your gallant nobility?

No.

No, no, no. No to infinity.

In his moment of clarity, a voice in Trimble's mind spoke with the most clarity of all: Keep your mouth shut, do what you're told and collect your pay ~ and drink heavily; for truly, alcohol is the only comfort you will ever find in this world. Survive; survive any way you can, whatever works, however disgusting it may be. Don't live, just exist. That is the true, immutable law of the universe. Oh, yes. Oh, yes, it most assuredly is.

And with that, Trimble caved. He quietly took a deep breath. It calmed him.

"When do I start?" he said.

Sawyer's smirk twitched briefly. Another scalp on his belt.

"We told them you would be by this afternoon," he said jauntily. "Best of luck!"

****

Trimble was nervous about going to the Falcon office, and for good reason.

He was met by a phalanx of stone faces straight off a travel poster for Easter Island. He didn't blame them. But what they didn't know, what they couldn't know, and it was sad, was that it didn't make any difference. They were patsies in a setup. The deal was done. But who knows. He would talk. He would listen. He would reason. Maybe something could be worked out. Miracles did happen from time to time ~ or so he had been told.

Trimble sat on a small, battered couch against the wall. Notepads, pica poles, reducing wheels and galley proofs littered the desks; stacks of old newspapers teetered precariously here and there. The floor was unswept, the windows unwashed; the stuff of a newsroom, the look of it, the dusty, papery smell of it, the quality of light. God, how I miss it, Trimble thought. God, how I loved it so.

Four young men confronted him. They sat at scratched army surplus desks or on the cheap folding chairs. A petite girl with freckles was seated with perfect posture at a small typing table near the window. How to tell them...

"My name is Paul Trimble," he said. "I'm the college's publications director, which means I'm in charge of all the catalogs and brochures, the Alumni magazine, all that sort of stuff. I'm also temporarily in charge of the news bureau, which means I write news releases telling the rest of the world how wonderful everything is at SPC."

Trimble hoped that last part would lighten things up a little. It did not. The air felt like the interior of a storage locker that had been chained shut and forgotten.

"Okay. I have a B.A. in journalism from the University of Oregon. I worked on the student paper there for three years. In my senior year, I also worked as a sports stringer for Associated Press.

"I was going to get drafted, so I joined the Air Force. I ended up writing for a base newspaper in Korea, which means I spent two years grinding out stories about clean-cut young airmen who loved their officers."

He paused for a moment. Memories of writing things he knew weren't true – sins of omission rather than sins of commission, but untrue just the same ~ clutched at his throat. The moment lasted a second. Then he remembered the students expected him to say more.

"Now, if you can do that day after day and still maintain your sanity, then gang, you can do just about anything."

The students looked back and forth at one another. Just what was this guy getting at, anyway?

"So now I'm your advisor. I haven't made up my mind how I'm going to go about the job, not until I hear from you first. What do I need to know?"

A young man with a Beatles haircut and an earnest expression spoke. That would be Parris, the editor, Trimble decided.

"I assume this is all because of the interviews with Fleming," Parris said.

"So they tell me," Trimble said. "But I expect there's more involved. Anyway, let's hear about the Fleming interview."

"Did you read it?" Parris said.

"Yes."

"What did you think?"

"It was okay. Probably too long. I doubt anybody read it all the way through, but otherwise it seemed okay. You asked, he answered."

"What did you think of the questions?" said an athletically-built kid slumped over a desk, his head propped in his hand, his face the barren veil of who has achieved cynicism far too young. That was Weldon.

"They were pretty good," Trimble said. "You kept probing. Sometimes you got a little redundant. I would have edited some of that out."

"The idea was to run it verbatim, whatever transpired," Parris said. "If it was redundant and a little dull, so be it. It was accurate. What you saw is what you got."

"What did you think of his answers?" Weldon said.

"About what you would expect," Trimble said. "He tried dodging, but he was smooth enough that it barely showed. Problem is, he claims he didn't say any of it, that you made it all up, that it was a hatchet job."

"Well, we taped the whole thing," Parris said. His voice had an uneasy edge to it.

"Where are the tapes?" Trimble asked.

"Uh, that's a problem," Parris said. "They're gone."

Six-inch reels of tape don't just disappear. Were these kids that careless?

"You've searched?" Trimble said.

"Everywhere we could think of," Parris said. "They're gone."

"That's not good," Trimble said.

"No kidding," Weldon said.

"Okay, you conducted the interview, then transcribed it from the tapes. Who did that?" Trimble said.

"I did," said the prim little girl at the typing table. "My name is Sally Huddleston, by the way."

"Where did you type it up?" Trimble said.

"At this table. It took me about three hours. I put a copy on Jeff's desk, kept a copy for myself and then went to dinner. That was at about six thirty."

"Where did you put the tapes?" Trimble said.

"On that desk by the front counter."

"Did anyone else see them?"

The students all shook their heads.

"They may have been there, they may not. No one noticed either way," Parris said.

Hoo boy, Trimble thought. Your most important piece of evidence is missing and you can't explain it. It's the worst possible journalistic scenario.

"I'd like to say something here," Sally said." Her tone was even, measured and calm. Sally Huddleston was not a person who rattled easily, Trimble concluded.

"I read the transcripts I typed and I read what was printed in the paper," Sally continued. "Both are accurate. With the exceptions of the ums and ers - I left those out - they are exactly what was on those tapes."

"Are you sure?" Trimble said.

Sally nodded curtly.

"Look, she never makes typing mistakes, she never misspells a word or even misplaces a comma," Parris said. "She's the best we have. That's why we asked her to do it. If she says it's accurate, it's accurate."

"And we were there," Weldon said, gesturing at the others. "We were the ones who asked the questions and took notes. We all say the story was accurate. The only one who doesn't is Fleming. Explain to me why the administration chooses to believe him and not us?"

Trimble knew the answer, of course, but he didn't want to say it out loud. He had enough problems already. If it came out that he sided with the students, that he wasn't a good team player, that . . .

Fuck it

He remembered the last time he said that, a scant three hours ago, and how he had betrayed the righteousness of it. For a moment, he felt panicky. He fought to control himself, to keep his fear from dictating his thinking. Not this time, not this time. . .

Fuck it.

"Okay, here it is, no b.s.," he said. "You are in deep shit."

A couple of the students straightened in surprise. A member of the administration using the word shit, and using it like it was a perfectly natural thing to say? They couldn't quite believe it.

"They want to shut you down," Trimble said. "They sent me here as a last resort - or so they said. I'm supposed to turn you into nice little boys and girls who write what the administration wants you to write. More likely, they're using me as a plausible excuse. When you screw up again, the administration can say, 'See, we gave them a chance and they refused to take it.' Then they'll shut you down."

Trimble had caught the students completely off-guard. Now they were paying attention.

"You said earlier that you thought there was more involved than just the Fleming interview," Weldon said. "Like what?"

"No idea. You probably know better than me. But I think it's safe to say you've rocked the boat. That's one thing they won't tolerate around here." He shook his head in frustration. "Look, didn't you know that? I had it figured it out by the end of my first day on the job. What were you thinking?"

The students seemed confused. Not only was this guy using words like shit and fuck, he was being honest with them. He was treating them with respect. Nothing had prepared them for such an eventuality. Only Weldon seemed unfazed.

"We were trying to do our job," Weldon said. "A student newspaper is supposed to write about issues that concern students, so we did. Okay, so we were wise-asses sometimes. It was good for some laughs. People around here could use a few laughs."

"So you were irreverent," Trimble said.

"Yeah. What's wrong with that?" Weldon said

"Any place else, nothing. Here, a lot," Trimble said.

"People laughed," Weldon said.

"The people who can shut you down did not. When it comes to their own gravitas, they have no sense of humor. I'll say it again: Didn't you know that?"

The students fidgeted some more. Finally, Parris spoke.

"Not as well as we should have, I guess," he said. "We were having a good time. Is our stuff that bad?"

Trimble had just spent two hours at the library going through back issues of the Falcon; not the most thorough preparation for an advisor, but all he had time for.

"Actually, no," he said. "A little sophomoric here, a little clumsy there, but your instincts are good and sometimes you are pretty funny. I like that stuff Weldon wrote about the javelin throwers on the track team tossing around their pointy little sticks while everybody else ran for cover. And you did some solid grunt reporting." He nodded at Sally. "And your editorials were succinct and fair.

"So, if I was to advise you in the standard sense of the word, I would show you how to tighten up your writing and teach you a little bit about the difference between parody and self-indulgence. I also could help you understand the legal technicalities of libel, because you come close every now and then.

"That is, if I was an advisor in the standard sense of the word. But I'm not. I'm supposed to be a censor. I will not be a censor. So as I see it, what I can do, realistically, is help you finish out the school year without getting shut down. With a little luck, we might be able to do it in such a way that everyone keeps their integrity intact. Maybe I can help you improve your journalism, too, if you want me to."

"Oh?" said a scruffy-looking kid with a permanent sardonic sneer. That would be McLean, according to the descriptions Trimble had heard.

"Well, I have a question," McLean continued with the slightly sarcastic lilt of one who thinks he is your intellectual superior. "What if you can't find a way to do it and keep our integrity intact?"

"Then I guess you swallow your pride, do what you have to do to keep your jobs and carry on until it's over and you can move on to something else," Trimble said. "Look, this is only one incident in your lives. You have a lot of years ahead of you."

It was true but it wasn't true and Trimble knew it all too well. Sell out your integrity once, cross the line into self-deception once and you won't come back, at least not all of you. When you abandon honesty and integrity, you can't retrieve them. In this case, they wouldn't be abandoning much - One percent? Two percent? - but it didn't matter. When you do it, you feel something inside you change and you hate yourself for it and you convince yourself it's no big deal and then you hate yourself even more. There goes part of you, like an arm or a leg or an eye. And for what? So little, so little. . .

Trimble stopped and forced himself to concentrate on the moment.

"But I'm hoping it won't come to that," he said. "You be straight with me and I'll be straight with you. I think we can pull it off."

"I have one other question," McLean said with the sly leer of a playground weasel who just found a way to embarrass you in front of a girl you were trying to impress. "Why should we trust you? How can you do what you do all day, how can you shill for Fotheringham and his buddies and still have a clear conscience?"

Jesus, Trimble thought. I'm doing the best I can and all you can do it use it as an excuse to be an arrogant little prick, you two-bit. . .

He caught himself.

"I do it for money," Trimble said, meeting McLean's smarmy "Maybe you have an independent source of funds, but I do not. I have to work for a living."

McLean's eyes darted about nervously, then focused on the floor. They stayed there.

"Look, I'm what you have," Trimble said. "I don't want to screw you over, I don't want to impress Fotheringham, I don't want to make friends with Fleming. I just want to get you - and me - through this as painlessly as possible. That's it. Take it or leave it. But know this: If you leave it, you'll be shut down by tomorrow morning. They aren't bluffing."

The room was silent. The students sat frozen in the reality. This was no academic exercise. They understood they were indeed in deep shit. Finally, Weldon spoke.

"What would happen to you?" he said.

Trimble shrugged.

"Don't know. Maybe nothing. Maybe they'll fire me. Maybe they put my name on the shit list, then fire me a few months later, after things have died down and no one will notice. Depends on what suits their purpose."

"So, what do you have in mind?" Parris said.

"The next issue is due out Friday," Trimble said. "What's your copy deadline?"

"Five p.m. Wednesday," Parris said.

"Okay, here's what I propose: I'll go over the copy on Wednesday as it comes in. If something looks like trouble, I'll tell you. If you want me to, I will help you tighten up your writing and so forth, too. I'll help you lay out the pages . . . when?"

"Thursday afternoon at Grange Press down on Western Avenue," Parris said.

Well, I guess that means he's agreeing, Trimble thought. He nodded and looked around the room. No one showed any sign of disagreeing.

"Who will have the final say on what goes in the paper?" Weldon said.

"You will," Trimble said. "But, for god's sake, pay attention to my advice. I'm trying to save your ass."

Weldon nodded. Parris nodded. McLean did not, but at least his self-satisfied smirk was gone. Sally maintained her proper, hands-crossed-on-lap bearing. Whatever her opinions, she was keeping them to herself. That left the tall kid with the deep-set eyes, the kid with the expensive sweater – Was that cashmere? At SPC? – the one who hadn't said a word. His hands were folded like a steeple, the tips of his index fingers at his lips. He was thinking. You could almost hear the wheels turning in his mind. His expression was detached, as if he wasn't quite part of the events that had just transpired. Who the hell was he?

****

The Falcon came out on Friday. It was appropriately respectful and appropriately prudent and appropriately bereft of a soul. Trimble had seen to that and he hated himself for it. It's only evidence of sentience was Weldon's story on the track meet with Western Washington in which in he wrote about SPC shot-putters launching errant cannonballs at the hurdlers. This disconcerted them so much that they kept hurdling right out of the stadium – one, two three, jump, one, two, three, jump – then down the street – one, two three, jump, one two three, jump – until they hit a dead end, crashed into a hedge and were set upon by a family of irate chipmunks. Trimble chuckled thinking about it.

Meanwhile, his own journalistic effort, the Alumni Bulletin, which also came out Friday, had no such attempts at wit. Or originality. Or initiative. In the featureless wasteland of mediocrity that is public relations, it stood out the least.

There was only one thing to do. In a town noted for some of the great low dives in the western world, the Blew Eagle reigned infamous. It wasn't that the place was particularly dangerous, although in the right circumstances it could be; it had more to do with its unabashed sense of failure, its revelry in being the last stop for losers, malcontents and the mildly deranged. The Blew Eagle had opened some time in the dim yesteryear to cater to sailors from the tramp steamers anchored in that part of Elliott Bay. It had been in a gleeful downhill slide ever since. The walls were white when it opened, but decades of nicotine mist, beer splatters and sneeze had given them a yellowish patina that had never been washed off because everyone was afraid to.

It ideally suited Paul Trimble. No pretense at the Blew Eagle. He could hide in a corner and drink himself blind in peace.

It was payday, so he began by treating himself to a double of Black and White. When he was done with it, he would move onto to pre-mixed martinis that the Blew Eagle served in glasses the size of small soup bowls at a dollar fifty each; an eminently economical way to despoil one's brain cells, all things considered.

But first the Black and White. It caressed his tongue with morning mist and driftwood smoke and sweet amber. Ahhh, the finer things of life. He could pay for them now, at least every now and then, and maybe that made the excrement-shoveling he did day after day worth it. Or maybe not. Definitely not. Irrevocably not. *Jesus, who am I kidding?*

Another sip, another gust of thought. The juke box was playing a song called "Cast Your Fate to the Wind." *There never was, there couldn't be/ A place in time for men like me/ Who'd drink the dark and laugh at day/And let their wildest dreams blow away.*

Was there such a thing as romance? Trimble wondered. Was there a wind that carried us along, a current that bore our lives to some destiny? Or was the world merely a medium for the day-to-day ennui of a banal reality no one wanted to admit to? Or was all this Deep Thinking merely the seductive wiles of expensive Scotch whisky on a fatigued body; probably the most likely possibility. Keep drinking, keep drinking. Soon enough thought will go away. Good thoughts, bad thoughts, it didn't matter. Oblivion, blessed oblivion.

That's when he saw Weldon. Weldon was at the opposite corner of the room, nursing a beer. He was watching Trimble.

Oh shit.

Trimble stared back. Well, the wing has blown off the plane, he thought. May as well enjoy the trip down. He gestured for Weldon to join him.

"Gonna turn me in?" Weldon said.

"Well, since I'm here too and drinking like a flounder, that seems a bit unlikely," Trimble said. "Don't screw me and I won't screw you. Have a seat."

Weldon sat down.

"So what did you think of today's paper?" Weldon said.

"It got done on time and everything was spelled correctly," Trimble said.

"Yeah, there was that," Weldon said. "But you didn't really answer my question."

"I know," Trimble said. "I was hoping you would fall for the dodge."

Weldon gave a quick, sardonic smile.

"It did no harm, I guess." Trimble said. He took a long sip of his Black and White. "Like I said, with a little luck, we'll make it to the end of spring quarter intact."

Weldon nodded.

"Then what?" he said.

"No idea. People will graduate, a new year will begin in fall. A new world, really."

"I'll be back," Weldon said. "So will Parris, so will McLean. What will we do?"

"I wish I could tell you," Trimble said. "I'm going to spend the summer extricating myself from the job of advisor. With a little luck, it will be somebody else's turn in the barrel come September."

"Why did you take the job anyway?" Weldon said.

"I already told you. I needed the money."

"No, the advisor's job."

"I told you, I was assigned."

"Did you try to get out of it?"

"I tried reasoning with them, but it didn't do any good. They had their minds made up long before I came in the room."

"You could have quit," Weldon said.

Trimble sighed and took one last, long sip of his Black and White.

"Look, that's an easy thing to say when you're not the one facing the decision," he said. "Standing up for what is right when it means your personal ruin, sounds very noble, but I've never seen anyone actually do it, and I've watched. I suspect it's a cultural myth. Truth is, when someone else has power and you don't, there's not much you can do except take it."

"You could have quit," Weldon said again.

Trimble leveled his eyes at Weldon.

"So could you," he said.

He watched as Weldon turned the idea over in his mind. At first he was irritated that Trimble had outfenced him. Then realities began appearing, as if on a list: Leave behind three years of school. Say good bye to all your friends. Explain it to your parents. Argue with them. Apply to another school. Was there still time to make it for fall quarter? If not, you might get drafted. . .

The list went on. Weldon nodded.

"Yeah, sorry," Weldon said. "I was just being an asshole." He gestured around the murky cavern that was the Blew Eagle. "You come here a lot?"

"Depends on who I'm with," Trimble said.

Weldon laughed.

"How about you?" Trimble said.

"They don't check IDs and no SPC types come here - until you."

"I'm not an SPC type," Trimble said.

"I noticed. What exactly are you trying to do with that job of yours?" Weldon asked.

Trimble shrugged.

"I dunno. Build up a portfolio so I can move on to something better, I guess."

"You mean you don't want to save the wor-uld?" Weldon said, imitating the sort of bulging-eyed evangelicals who pounded the pulpit at chapel from time to time. It was a pretty good imitation.

"I don't hear the world asking to be saved," Trimble said, smiling despite himself.

"But friennnds, it is up to you, the young generation, to church the churchless, to salvation the salvationless, to lawfulize the lawless, to slather goodness and niceness on the ungood and unnice! And then, only then, can they bask in the assurance of an eternity curled up on the living room floor, a cozy fire in the fireplace, playing Parcheesi in their bathrobes while sipping cocoa with an everlasting supply of marshmallows!"

"But there are those who are beyond hope," Trimble said. "Those who reject the sanctity of marshmallows in their cocoa."

"Then we shall bring the blessing of pellets of puffed sugar to the marshmallowless whether they like it or not! And then, verily, they will be anointed in the glory of graham crackers and melted Hershey bars. There is smore! There is smore!'

"Personally, I'd prefer to drink," Trimble said. "Would you care for a martini?"

"Yea, I shall receive your offering of the vermouth of the lamb. Why are you always so fucking gloomy, anyway?"

"I think my face froze that way a while back," Trimble said. "Maybe I should order a marshmallow in my martini."

"Truly, that would be an abomination before the lord!" Weldon said.

The martinis arrived.

"So, how did you ever end up at SPC?" Trimble said.

"I got a track scholarship, not a full ride or anything, but enough to get me out of my hometown."

"Which was where?"

"Porterville, California, armpit of the Central Valley, home of the state's largest booby hatch for the criminally insane. If the DDT and the airborne fungus don't kill you, the escaped loonies will. Ninety eight degrees in the shade, all year around – except there is no shade. A true garden spot."

"Do you run now?" Trimble asked.

"Blew out my Achilles tendon my sophomore year and that was that," Weldon said. "So I started writing for the paper."

"Do you want to change the wor-uld?"

"Hell no. I just like writing stuff. It's kind of fun to grock people every now and then, too."

"Grock people?" Trimble said.

"Yeah, like once I turned in a paper for philosophy class with the hypothesis that God masturbates. After all, He created us in His image, which means He has hands. And sitting around for eternity like He does, He must get kind of bored. His mind starts to wander and. . ."

"You actually did that?"

"Only got a C-plus on it. So unfair. My logical structure was flawless. I put a lot of study into it."

"I take it the professor did not read it aloud to the class."

"Sadly, no. It would have stimulated some lively deliberation, don't you think?"

"I get the impression that half the people at that school don't know what masturbation is," Trimble said.

"You'd be surprised. During spring quarter when dorm rats forget to close their windows, you can hear mattress springs squeaking all over campus. First time I heard it I thought it was baby robins."

They drank on. Weldon, as it turned out, was an English major, with a particular interest in American poetry – "I'm looking forward to a lucrative career as a corporate poet." – and now that he couldn't run track anymore, he found himself frequently bored. Hence evenings at places like the Blew Eagle.

"I'd prefer to spend my time with wanton women, but they're scarce at SPC, particularly after you've gone through the first two. There is no three or four. Female virtue is God's curse on the rest of us."

Weldon liked to talk, which was fine with Trimble, who found discussion of his own existence depressing. Growing up in Central California had been a singular experience, Weldon said. The cultural muse was faded Levi's, a curled-up cowboy hat, squint and spit ("I thought gun racks were standard factory items for cars until I came here.") "Yup" was the epitome of eloquence and a scholarship to beautician school was an intellectual achievement worthy of a six-inch write-up, with photo, in the local paper.

Weldon's father owned a celery farm, the biggest one in the valley. Never a loquacious man, his most sage piece of advice came on Weldon's eighteenth birthday when he put his hand on his son's shoulder, looked him solemnly in the eye and in a voice weighty with import, intoned, "Son, one thing I learned is to never hire a man with leather bootlaces. I pay 'em to work, not spend all day tyin' their shoes."

Porterville's vin ordinaire was chelada, a mixture of tomato juice, clam nectar and beer – "beastly, truly beastly," Weldon said – and local sports, well, local sports were actually pretty good. Olympic decathlon champion Bob Mathias grew up in nearby Tulare and in spite of levels of air pollution that corroded house paint, the valley turned out a surprising number of world-class runners and jumpers.

"Probably because we spend so much time getting chased by Mexicans with big knives," Weldon said.

Weldon did not miss his hometown, although he did find Seattle rather aloof and full of itself.

"This place needs a chelada enema."

Weldon abruptly switched subjects to poetry, specifically the poetry of Emily Dickenson, whose rhythm and rhyming structures seemed odd until you got used to them, at which point her ideas started to reveal themselves. Note the word reveal, Weldon said. Dickenson didn't waste time with explanations. She was too busy exploring the nature of dimensional physics, which actual physicists wouldn't glimpse until forty years after her death.

"No bullshit with Dickenson," Weldon said. "If you don't get it, it's your loss, dipshit."

Not so Robert Frost, who Weldon considered a shining achievement in marketing department hooey.

"His weather-beaten Yankee act is a load. The New York literary establishment love it because they think it's authentic. They wouldn't know a snow job if you dumped it on them with a steam shovel."

More drinking. One martini, then two. They talked politics. Trimble thought Franklin Delano Roosevelt was the country's greatest president, at which Weldon offered, "Don't say that where I come from. Down there, they think Lincoln went too far." Football was a better topic. Weldon thought the 49s' million dollar backfield, Y.A. Tittle ("The Bald Eagle"); Joe The Jet Perry, Hugh The King McElhenny and John Henry Johnson ("The Battering Ram") was the greatest backfield combination in the history of the game. Trimble argued for a while -- "What about Jim Brown and Bobby Mitchell?" - but eventually conceded that Weldon was probably right.

Trimble was thinking about ordering a third round when he looked in his wallet. He couldn't focus his eyes to count the bills.

"I think I'm too drunk to drive," he said.

"No matter," Weldon said. "Lyle's here."

"Lyle?"

"Lyle, my car. He replaced Edward, who went to the great scrap yard in the sky last year."

Trimble was curious to meet a vehicle named Lyle. He was confronted by a once-blue Plymouth two-door, circa 1952 or so, with a look of a car that had spent a number of years trying to navigate around potholes and failing.

"That thing actually runs?" Trimble said.

"Ey, mano, don't go dissin' Lyle. He got heart."

Trimble eased into the front seat. He found himself perched atop a spring emerging from the upholstery. It was a large spring.

"Ouch," he said dispiritedly.

"Be a man about it," Weldon said. "Let's fire old Lyle up."

He turned the key. Nothing happened.

"What the fu. . ."

He turned it again. Still nothing. Not even the clickclickclick of a solenoid.

"My god, Lyle's dead! Lyle's dead! Lyle, how could you!?"

"Just sounds like a dead battery to me," Trimble said.

"Yes, yes, of course, just a dead battery," Weldon said. "You got jumper cables?"

"Nope."

"Maybe somebody back at the bar does," Weldon said.

"You really want to ask?"

Weldon thought for a moment. To interrupt the methodical dissipation of the Blew Eagle was to invite being pummeled severely about the head and shoulders for an extended period of time.

"We're screwed," Weldon said.

"Look, I'll drive," Trimble said. "We can come back and get Lyle tomorrow."

"What if somebody steals him?"

"Who'd want to?"

Weldon tried to look offended but couldn't manage it.

"But aren't you too drunk to drive?" he said.

"It's wearing off a little," Trimble said. "I know the way back to the college. Besides it's a VW. I can barely get it over forty, even when I'm sober."

They got into Trimble's VW. Weldon looked it over.

"And you make fun of Lyle?" he said.

"The rust spots aren't getting any bigger," Trimble said with an air of offended dignity.

He started up the VW. The distinctive, high-pitched whir of the air-cooled engine was comforting.

"Is it true these things run forever?" Weldon said.

"Seems like it," Trimble said. "And awaaaay we go!"

He popped the clutch, the car stalled and lurched to a bone-rattling stop.

"Still learning to drive?" Weldon said.

"I'm working on it! I'm working on it!" Trimble said. He took a deep breath to clear his head. It did not clear. Well, we have to get home some way or another, he thought. Concentrate, concentrate.

The car started. Trimble guided it smoothly away from the curb, did a u-turn under the Spokane Street viaduct, picked up the on-ramp to the eastbound thoroughfare and headed for Highway 99. Once there, he could steer into the middle lane and putt-putt along inconspicuously to the turnoff by Canlis's restaurant at the south end of the Aurora Bridge. After that, things might get a little tricky - a lot of short roads, very few of them running in straight lines - but police patrols in that neighborhood were rare. He would get Weldon home efficiently. And then? Well, he knew an isolated spot under the Ballard Bridge where he could sleep it off for a couple of hours before heading back to his apartment in Greenwood.

He turned on to Highway 99 northbound.

"This looks familiar," Weldon said.

"How so?"

"A big, straight road, perfect for neck cruisin'."

"Neck cruisin'?" Trimble said.

"Here, I'll show you." Weldon said. "You slide down in the seat like this, so your ass is on the edge and only your neck and head are touching the back. That way, your eyes are just over the dashboard. It's considered very cool in Porterville. 'Course, it helps if you have a cowboy hat. You pull that down over your forehead so just your eyes are showing. Keep your head still and move your eyes back and forth, real slow, like a gun fighter. Neck cruisin'."

"I'm not sure I can do it and still control the car," Trimble said.

"I'm not sure you can control the car anyway," Weldon said.

Trimble shifted around, trying to slouch in the seat for a proper neck cruisin' posture. He couldn't do it.

"Car's too small," he said.

"No matter," Weldon said. "This ain't exactly a pussy wagon anyway. Why don't you get some real wheels?"

"I probably should," Trimble said. "But I'm saving my money. I'm not sure how long this gig at SPC is going to last."

They passed over the Alaskan Way Viaduct, a long, raised section of highway offering a spectacular view of the Seattle waterfront, Elliot Bay and points beyond. It always left Trimble in awe, no matter how many times he drove it. Weldon seemed properly impressed too. Or maybe he was just perfecting his neck cruisin'. Trimble looked over at him. Weldon was passed out, his mouth agape, his chin resting on his chest.

They came to the Battery Street tunnel, a mile-long tube under the north end of Seattle's business district. They hit a bump. Weldon woke up.

"Good god, what's happening?!" he shouted. "The lights, the lights! We're being sucked down to a hellish fate worse than death!"

"Could be, could be," Trimble said, stifling a laugh. "A dark future can hold unseen perils."

"Do not trifle with me!" Weldon roared. "The Bosch is no man's fool!"

Trimble started to giggle, tried to stop, and couldn't. Drunk, giggling and struggling to keep a rusty VW under control through the Battery Street tunnel, he decided that life might very well be just one extended comedy routine.

"Wait, I think. . . I think I see an escape!" Weldon shouted,

"But who can say what lies beyond," Trimble said. "Fate is a capricious mistress in torrid tropic climes."

Where did I come up with that? he wondered. Need to mix Black and White and cheap martinis more often.

He dropped off Weldon a block from Hill so they wouldn't be seen. Weldon had a ground floor room and he left the window open. No one ever caught on, although one proctor kept eying him suspiciously until Weldon pointed out that legally his room was his private legal domain and, therefore, entering it without his permission constituted trespassing. He had no idea if it was true, but it sounded convincing.

****

Marilyn finally found a job. It was dumb luck, really. She stopped at the downtown Nordstrom's shoe store to fill out an application; one of a dozen places she visited that day, one of scores of applications she had filled out since she began her search. She expected nothing to come of it. Nothing ever did.

The receptionist at the personnel office looked at the application, paused, then told her to take a seat. The receptionist got on the phone. When she hung up, she said, "Can you wait here for a few minutes? Mr. Neville would like to see you."

Presently, a slender, balding man in a razor-creased light gray suit entered the room. He had a somber, almost cold air about him; moving as if on tiptoes, his eyes downcast, his entire aspect solemn and austere.

He exchanged a few whispered words with the receptionist, then looked over Marilyn's application. He looked it over very carefully, stopping at one point to raise an eyebrow slightly. Finally, he said, "Miss Pennell?"

Marilyn stood up. She was careful to adopt the erect posture, lifted chin and folded hands she had been taught in etiquette classes. It was, she had found, a posture that was neither fawning nor arrogant. It was impeccable manners and, Marilyn had concluded, impeccable manners were a very good way to keep the world at arm's length without looking like it.

"I'm Bill Neville," the well-dressed man said, his voice so hushed Marilyn could barely hear it. "May we talk?"

"Of course."

He motioned her to follow him. They wound their way through a maze of narrow corridors lined with shoeboxes; hundreds of boxes, thousands of boxes, on shelves reaching to the ceiling like the bricks of some secret passageway in an ancient castle. Every now and then, harried-looking young men in cheap suits rushed by, some carrying stacks of boxes, others clearly searching for shoes. None seemed to notice Marilyn.

Eventually, Marilyn and Neville came to a small alcove deep in the core of the cardboard citadel. It contained a battered desk with an old goose-neck lamp on it. Nothing more. Neville sat down behind the desk. There was no other chair in the room. Marilyn stood, again with perfect posture.

"I see you have nearly completed a year of college," Neville said. "Your grades?"

"Two point four GPA," Marilyn said.

Neville paused. Marilyn wondered why. Then Neville said, "Why are you leaving school, if I may ask."

Marilyn inhaled deeply, but carefully so as not to show it.

"Poverty," she said, looking Neville square in the eye and betraying as little emotion as possible. "I'm out of money."

"Umm," Neville said indifferently and looked back down at the application. He thumbed it over some more. He wasn't reading it. He was merely going through the motions for something to do.

After a while, Neville said, "What do you know about the shoe business?"

"I buy shoes," Marilyn said. "And I try to keep up on the latest styles."

"Oh. Really." Neville tried to sound interested. He failed. There was another long pause.

Finally, he said, "We just got an opening for a floor girl in Northgate. For now, the job will be Monday 2 p.m. to nine thirty and Saturday nine to six thirty. After June, it will be five days a week. Your day off would vary according to the flow of business. Tuesdays and Thursdays are usually the slowest days. Does that sound like something you would want?"

Marilyn quickly ran through her options. The only other lead she had was at the mail room in the Shafter building. That had been last week, and she hadn't heard from them since. And, whatever else its advantages, delivering the daily mail didn't seem to have much of a future. Would this job be any better? Well, at least it was out in the public and involved dealing with people. That she was good at.

She said yes with the best polite smile she could manage.

Neville didn't seem to notice. "You would work the check-out desk, ringing up the sales and wrapping the packages," he said, in a monotone so tightly controlled Marilyn wondered if he knew she was even in the room. "That leaves the salesmen free for more time on the floor. Sometimes, you'll deal the deck."

The deck? Marilyn looked puzzled.

"The deck is a stack of cards," Neville said. "It's how the floor manager keeps track of which customers are waiting and which salesmen are free."

"When do I start?" Marilyn said.

"This Saturday. Be there at nine. Ask for Mr. Wolfstone. He's the manager."

"I'll be there."

There was another long pause. Finally, Neville smiled ever-so-slightly.

"Don't you want to know what the job pays?"

"Oh. Yes, yes, of course," Marilyn stammered.

"Two ten an hour. Salesmen make two fifteen an hour or commission, whichever is the most. A lot of the floor girls become salesmen, but we don't have any sales openings right now."

Neville's face remained emotionless. He pulled some forms from a desk drawer.

"Fill these out and give them to Miss Gregory at the reception desk. If you have any questions, ask her. I'll call Mr. Wolfstone and tell him to expect you."

He reached across the desk and shook Marilyn's hand. His grip was firm, but cold and machine-like.

On the bus back to SPC, Marilyn turned things over in her mind. It had been so simple. After all that misery, she actually got a job in less than ten minutes. It seemed a bit surreal.

But a job! Not much of a job, but something, and it certainly sounded like an improvement over a lot of them she had seen. Neville made her uncomfortable; a cold fish, to say the least. On the other hand, he wasn't rude or vulgar. Business was business and he stuck to it. If he was typical of the people she would work for, she would do all right.

How long would the job last? Would it become permanent? Above all, would it pay enough to support her? She had no idea. But it was a job, the first step on the road to survival. She did some mental math. Two ten an hour, sixteen dollars and eighty cents a day, eighty four dollars a week, three hundred thirty six dollars a month. Not much. Her grandmother wouldn't charge her for room and board, but it would only be fair to contribute to food, say a hundred dollars a month. Transportation? Seventy cents a day, three fifty a week, fourteen dollars a month. Living expenses; soap, toothpaste and the like? Another ten dollars a month, if she was careful. It all came to about one hundred twenty dollars a month, about twenty five hundred a year.

A car? Maybe by the end of the year, probably later.

Money left over for a college fund? Could she ever save enough? How long would it take? She didn't know. A long time, certainly, and many things could happen along the way to derail her hopes. So this was her future.

The bus turned off of Dexter and into the ganglia of streets converging on the Fremont Bridge. It was overcast, the kind of late afternoon in Seattle when the sky seems a gray velvet curtain, erasing shadows, muffling sounds, turning one's thoughts inward.

So ended her college days, Marilyn thought. Seven months ago, her path seemed certain, her future bright.

She forced herself to harden her mind. Well, c'est le vie. Reality often forces people to change their plans and that's that.

What she would miss, however, was something she had not expected when she showed up on campus in September, 1964: The sense of community, the sense of identity, the sense of *us* that was the small college experience; people, young people, oh-so-young people, thrown together in a single place, in a singular moment in history, sharing a common destiny that defined itself as time moved on.

Marilyn sensed that destiny would be unique, for, certainly, remarkable events were happening at a remarkable rate. Each member of the class of '68 was responding to them in an individual way, and the sum of those ways would be something all its own. And whatever that something would end up being, she would not be part of it. She would be a floor girl at Nordstrom's; quarantined in the world of low pay, long hours and shoes. History would pass her by. A silent sob stuck in her throat.

Then she reached the bus stop at Brougham. The bus's diesel fumes battered her, and she began the long, dreary trudge up Bertona to Hill.

Chapter 28

"Politics?"

Elizabeth Fleming couldn't help but sound surprised. Had she heard her husband correctly?

"Yup. Skip Reinhardt asked me today," Layton Fleming said. "He said the republican party wants somebody like me, a guy with voter appeal."

"But you don't know anything about politics."

Layton seemed offended.

"I know this country needs talented leadership," he said. "I can certainly provide that."

Elizabeth was silent. Her look of disbelief remained.

"They're talking about me for state representative," he said. "It's not much of a job, but it could lead to big things, and I mean big. They're recruiting their next generation of candidates. Do you know what this means? In four years, the country will be ready for a republican administration. Then, who knows, we could even end up in Washington, D.C."

"I don't really think so. . . "

"There you go, being all negative and defensive," he said. "Don't you see? This is just the opportunity I've been looking for. Now is the time."

Elizabeth shook her head, unconvinced.

"Come on, we'd make a great team," he said.

"We?"

"You'll be in on this too, of course."

Elizabeth visualized herself as a politician's wife, standing in the background and smiling prettily. That much she knew she could do. Her father had paid a lot of money for those perfect white teeth. As for the rest. . . well, what exactly was the rest?

"Look, we're having some of them over tomorrow night, the real shakers and movers," he said. "I really need you to help me out here."

Oh well, what else is new, she thought. Coffee and hors d'oeuvres, smile and nod, let them check out your legs. Act gracious. And it would be an act, an act she was having more and more trouble look convincing. Gawd, how she was getting tired of it.

They arrived at 7 p.m. Skip Reinhardt came through the door with an imperious flourish, scanning the room as if on an inspection tour. Elizabeth said good evening. Reinhardt handed her his hat and coat without looking at her.

"Skip!" Layton gushed, bounding across the room. He took Reinhardt's hand in both of his and shook it eagerly; a bit too eagerly, Elizabeth thought. If Reinhardt thought so he didn't show it.

Just then, two other men came through the door. One was lean and spare, his face angular and hawk-like, his white hair parted in the middle, in the fashion of the nineteen twenties. He was wearing a starched, peaked handkerchief in the breast pocket of his worsted suit, another old-fashioned affectation.

The other man was stocky and bald, dark in the way of men with a permanent blue shadow on their jowls. His eyebrows nearly met. But his most prominent feature were his eyes; narrow slits, malevolent and porcine beneath a prominent brow ridge.

Both men handed her their coats. She stepped back to watch the introductions.

"Layton, I think you know Flashy Florence," Reinhardt said, gesturing to the white-haired man.

"Hey, everybody in town knows Flashy Florence!" Layton said, enveloping Florence's hand with both of his. Florence was Seattle's most prominent Rotarian – and Kiwanian, and Lion, and Toastmaster and chamber of commerce maven and just about everything else involved the mutual slapping of backs and bestowing of plaques.

"And this is John Ehrlichman," Reinhardt said, gesturing at the dark man.

Ehrlichman's expression remained somewhere between a scowl and a sneer. He grunted as Layton shook his hand.

"Oh, where are my manners?" Layton said. "This is my lovely wife Betts."

Elizabeth was still holding the coats, a nicotine-saturated pile that made her rock awkwardly on her heels. She felt like a fool. But she smiled and did her best to play the role – whatever that was.

It worked, in any case. The men smiled, except for Ehrlichman, and then got on with more important things. Elizabeth sensed it was time for her to fade into the woodwork. She carried the coats to the hall closet. As she walked past the living room, a man squeezed into a suit a size too small came through the front door. He was wearing a thin, garrot-like bow tie and was preternaturally red-faced, as if scraped raw by a razor. He sported a close-cropped crew cut with the hair in front pushed up like butch-waxed shingle, and was bug-eyed with forced joviality. The overall effect was that of a pimple about to burst. Elizabeth didn't catch his name. The men were headed for their chairs when Layton snapped his fingers and called out, "Betts! Coffee!"

She obeyed. She was used to obeying. Obedience was a virtue. Just try not to think about it while you are doing it. By the time she came in with the coffee pot, the men were already talking.

"Well, now that we're finally rid of that punk Kennedy, we can start doing something with this country," Skip Reinhardt was saying.

"Hey, I heard something from Bud Stanrud down at the chamber," Florence said. "Seems Jackie wants to remarry, but the pope won't let her."

"Hmm. I'm not surprised," Reinhardt said. "The pope's got that whole outfit under his thumb."

"I wish he could get control of Martin Luther Coon," the crew cut man said. The others chuckled. Elizabeth poured coffee and tried to act like she wasn't there.

"Now, don't get me wrong," crew cut continued. "I got nothing against niggers, just so long as they get a job and quit spending all their time popping out picaninnies and jumpin' around to that jungle music of theirs."

"What do you think, Layton?" Reinhardt said. The oral test had begun.

"Well, I think they should be able to vote," he said. "But trying to be equal to the rest of us; well, that's going to take time."

"That's right, that's right," the crew cut man said. "But, hell, they aren't trying very hard. Just last week, I saw some big, strapping buck at the grocery store, buying t-bone steaks and trying to pay for it with his welfare check! Can you believe it? Then he drove off in a purple Cadillac. I wanted to go up to him and say, 'Hey, you gotta earn it, just like the rest of us.'"

The rest nodded. Elizabeth retreated to the dining room. From there she could observe them without being seen.

"Yeah, well that sonuvabitch Johnson is just encouraging them," Florence said. "I heard that when he invited King to the White House, he sat him next to Luci, the cute one, not the big horsey one. Their knees were touching. Guess where his hand was all night."

More approving nods.

"To get back to the issues, where do you stand on integrated housing?" Ehrlichman said coldly, his eyes boring in on Layton.

"As I said, these things take time," Layton said. "In Seattle, at least, it doesn't seem that big an issue. They have their neighborhoods, we have ours. Most people seem happy enough with the arrangement."

"Yeah, but there are always a few," Reinhardt said. "The city council is talking about a new housing law – *fair* housing, they call it. Ha! Now, don't get me wrong. It's one thing if a Negro doctor or lawyer moves into the neighborhood, but how do I know they won't put some big old jigaboo with his fat mammy and a litter of porch monkeys next door? Have you seen how those people keep up their homes? They don't know what a lawnmower is used for."

He finished with a self-righteous frown. Then he held up his coffee cup Statue of Liberty style. Elizabeth obeyed.

"Thanks, sweetie," Reinhardt said, again without looking at her. Elizabeth considered pouring the steaming brew on his hand. That would liven up the evening.

Ehrlichman spoke again.

"Okay. Layton, we think the party is in a good position to build strength now. True, Goldwater lost, but he made an impact. And, southern democrats are starting to swing our way. So, we are trying to line up candidates at all levels. That's why we're interested in you for the state representative job in the thirty sixth. Our man

Heckson is retiring and the democrats have never been strong here. Skip tells me you're a pretty able guy."

"Thank you," Layton said humbly. "I try."

The "I try" made Elizabeth gag. She had always felt there was no dishonesty quite as disgusting as false modesty, and whatever else Layton was, he had never been modest – until now. And, the truly nauseating thing was, he made it convincing.

"One of the things we are looking at is the idea of people from outside the government moving into congress, bring fresh blood, new ideas and all that," Ehrlichman said.

"Yessir!" Florence spouted. "Time to start running this country like a business!"

Like a business? Elizabeth remembered the various jobs she'd had to work her way through college. At one, the owner was a drunk who came to the office hung over and then disappeared to lunch for three hours. At another, her supervisor managed his staff by picking out an employee, mercilessly ridiculing and harassing him for a month or so and then moving on to someone else. Even at nineteen years old, Elizabeth could see it was a tactic for drawing attention away from his own ineptitude. Fortunately, the summer ended before he could get to her. At yet another, the boss stayed in his office behind a locked door all day. Elizabeth never saw him leave, not once. His main contact with his staff was to send out the occasional memo bemoaning excessive paper clip usage.

And so it went. Some businesses were well-run, some were not. Some bosses were competent and humane, some were not. In all cases, it was the low-level employees like her who actually kept the operation functioning at some semblance of efficiency and they had no say in anything. Sit down, shut up and do what you are told; that was their function and they were reminded of it frequently. Run a country like that? Where? Fascist Italy came to mind.

Meanwhile, the discussion in the living room had moved on to other things. Vietnam came up, with crew cut pronouncing that we should just bomb 'em into the stone age and get it over with. Skip Reinhardt countered that the best thing to do was put all the Vietnamese on boats, then bulldoze the country flat – then sink the boats. That got big laughs.

They hated young people, particularly The Beatles and particularly their haircuts. Flashy Florence spoke glowingly of a school principal he read about who stood at the front door with a pair of scissors and wouldn't let any long hairs in until he whacked off their locks.

"They should do that here," he said. "Make all those little queers look like men, at least."

The assembled's views on labor issues was summed up by crew cut who said that back in the old days, Harry Bridges, leader of the west coast longshoreman's union, would have been hauled out and strung up from the nearest lamppost.

"Don't stop there," Reinhardt said. "Caldwell had the right idea back in '48 when he cleaned out all those reds over at the UW. Joe McCarthy was doing a pretty good job too until Murrow and the rest of those pinkos went after him."

And so it went, with crew cut and Florence getting increasingly red-faced and agitated while Reinhart leaned back, raised his chin and scowled imperiously. Ehrlichman said little, but his eyes saw much. They particularly settled on Layton and Layton knew it. An occasional word here, an occasional word there, the right expression and the right posture at the right time - he was so very good at it.

Elizabeth began to feel sick. She had heard conversations like this before, but never so much of it concentrated in one place. It was venomous. She wanted to run from the house. But where? This was the world Layton wanted. She would have to adapt.

So the men went on, fueled by their malevolence - and the coffee kept pouring and pouring and pouring.

In the end, Ehrlichman said he would get Layton a job on the state gambling commission. The commission didn't really do anything and it would give him some name recognition; the first step in what Ehrlichman hoped would be many.

Chapter 29

The onset of spring quarter is a singular feeling. It is in the air; new air, fresh air, warm and clear and bright. The rain-soaked wool that envelopes Seattle in winter has disappeared, and with it has gone a world of black mornings and wind-battered walks and wet feet and raincoats hanging from every wall and never quite getting dry.

In spring, the SPC campus is transformed. In winter, its huge trees are leafless and stark, forming dismal skeletons in the sodden gloom. In spring, they become wonders of emerald lace and dappled light and birds and squirrels and all the things of life.

By spring quarter, the freshmen who are left have come upon the realization they aren't flunking out, and probably won't unless they let themselves. They have survived. That awareness is a heady thing, much like inhaling the fresh air of spring.

Those who have flunked out are gone – you are allowed only one quarter of academic probation – and, cruelly perhaps, are quickly forgotten, much like the dead leaves of winter.

For spring is a time of new life, and on a college campus, that sense of awakening is palpable: Girls have boxed up their heavy, shapeless winter clothes and, with a great sense of relief, walk the campus in summer dresses, crisp cotton snapping with every step. Boys don short-sleeved shirts, their high, button-down collars framing clear-eyed faces sharpening into the planes of manhood. Impromptu picnics and string quartet recitals and Frisbee games suddenly start appearing on the lawn. Irises and roses and azaleas and tulips and daisies have finished clawing their way from beneath the earth and explode with color and fragrance that always seems a miracle no matter how many times you've seen it.

You hear laughter in the air.

Brewer was taking it all in from the roof over the first floor of the SUB. It was a balcony, actually, although few knew that and fewer still used it that way. Brewer spotted it while walking to the small recreation room at the end of the hall. He went there sometimes to study.

He passed an open door to the upstairs conference room where the student council met and noticed that the windows to the room were actually sliding doors. The doors led to the balcony and the balcony, he found, put him high amid the branches of the trees, a place free from the restraints of concrete and grit and gravity itself. This was the world of those who flew.

He took a chair from the conference room, propped it against the wall, opened a text book and took in the warmth and the light and the sights and the sounds of spring. His grades were good, his clothes were new, his apartment was pleasant and his car ran fine. A freshman, he decided, could ask for little more - except more female companionship, specifically more intimate female companionship. But wasn't that the way it always would be? Probably. At least from the balcony he could watch all the females he wanted. He could study them carefully and they didn't even know it. None thought to look his way.

Dale stuck his head out the door.

"Enjoying the view?"

"Indeed I am," Brewer said. "Join me?"

Dale pulled up a chair and took a deep breath.

"Ahhh, an afternoon on the veranda," he sighed languidly. "Care for a mint julep? Oh, I forgot, you are pure of body and mind."

"Not of mind," Brewer said. "Check out that little blonde in the pink dress."

"Ah, yes. An admirable exemplar of American femininity. I wonder if she likes it doggy style?"

"Go ask."

"Sir, we have not been properly introduced," Dale said with a diffident sniff. "What is it you are reading there?"

"A short story by Mark Twain, about his first try as a river pilot. It's funny as hell, actually. I go a couple of paragraphs and then I laugh so hard I lose my place."

"I can tell you how it ends."

"No need. I'm actually enjoying assigned reading. Go figure."

"Yes, yes, I know what you mean," Dale said. "If required reading isn't irksome, you aren't getting your money's worth. Education should be onerous."

Only Dale could use words like irksome and onerous and get away with it.

"Three months 'til summer break," Dale said. "Think you'll make it that far?"

"Looks like it."

"Me too. I even got a job lined up at Jay Jacobs. How about you?"

"I haven't checked yet," Brewer said. "But I think I can get my old job back bagging groceries at the QFC. I'll ask for half days so I can spend some time having a little fun."

"You can afford to do that?"

Brewer remembered that he'd never told Dale about the thirty thousand dollars. No need to now.

"Yeah, for a while at least," he said.

"So, you can go out and pick up hot chicks at Golden Gardens."

"You know, I wonder: Does that really happen?" Brewer said. "I mean, it's like the stories I heard about Parker's out on Aurora. It was supposed to be a place where girls would be all over you, but I went there and the music was so loud you couldn't even talk to them. I wonder if it's all just so much wishful thinking."

"Don't know if you don't try," Dale said.

"You've tried?"

"Uh, well, not exactly. . . "

Brewer laughed. So did Dale.

"Maybe it's one of those things were the idea is more fun than the reality," Dale said. "Kind of like fucking."

"I wouldn't say the expectation is better than the reality when it comes to that," Brewer said.

"I would," Dale said. "Perhaps I have programmed myself for predetermined disappointment."

"Huh?"

"I'm not sure what it means, either. But back to the subject at hand."

"Mark Twain?"

"No, dummy, the little blonde in the pink dress."

"She's gone."

"Ah, but not forgotten," Dale said. "How will I ever forget dear old whatshername."

Just then, Sally Huddleston stuck her head out the door.

"Hi there," she said.

"Care to join us?" Dale said.

"Will they let us?"

Dale shrugged.

Sally pulled out a chair and joined them.

"Hmmm. Nice view," she said. "Never seen the campus quite like this."

The three took in the warmth and the light of the day. None spoke. There was no need to. Brewer liked Sally a great deal, something about her unflappable calm, her seeming serenity. But he had no desire to ask her out, and the idea of trying to kiss her made him uncomfortable. It was more like she was his sister. Weren't guys supposed to be horny for every girl they met? Maybe there was something wrong with him. Or maybe. . . Aw, hell, it was what it was. If the past year had taught him anything, it was that lust, or attraction or relationships or whatever the hell you called it was incomprehensible at best and downright treacherous the rest of the time. To hell with it. To hell with it all. Enjoy the moment: a sunny day with friends.

"You got your summer figured out, Sally?" Dale said.

"My cousin got me job in the kitchen of a hotel up in Alberta. Never been there. I guess the scenery is nice."

"What then?" Dale said.

"One more year and I have my degree. Then I suppose I'll find a teaching job."

"Sounds clear-cut," Dale said.

"Oh, I don't know. I'd like to be a writer, maybe work on a newspaper. But it's tough to make a living that way. So I'll teach, for a while at least."

"Maybe you could teach in Samoa or some place," Brewer said.

Sally looked off into the distance, a wistful expression smoothing her freckled face.

"I've thought about that," she said. "They say you should take in adventures when you are young. But I have to make a living, too. And settle down, eventually."

"We read an essay about Emily Dickinson," Brewer said. "The writer said that even though she never left Amherst, her mind explored the cosmos."

"Wonder what would have happened if she moved out west, or something like that." Dale said.

"We'll never know," Sally said. "People like that do great things, but they hardly ever talk about what's on their minds when they do it. They don't seem to enjoy themselves much in the long run - not even Hemmingway, and he sure did try."

"Maybe Kerouac had the right idea," Dale said. "Just keep moving. It's not the destination, it's the movement itself that counts."

"Sounds kind of empty," Brewer said.

"Maybe adventure is just a myth," Sally said.

"Could be," Dale said. "But I'd like to find out for myself. Spend some time on the beach in Samoa. Tahiti would be even better."

The other two nodded.

Greg Lammermuir appeared at the door. He looked worried, with a furrowed brow and frightened eyes.

"What are you doing here?" he said, his voice high with fear.

"Sitting," Dale said.

That took Lammermuir aback. Nobody had ever sat on the roof like this. There must be a rule against it - somewhere. Even if there wasn't, there should be. It might upset the administration, and that presented scenarios so awful Lammermuir had to force them from his mind.

"But, but, you can't. . ." he said.

Dale fixed Lemmermuir a hard stare. Brewer had seen him do it before, a dark glower he used when he wanted to mess with people. Depending on the mettle of the person he used it on, it could be intimidating.

Brewer didn't want to confront Lammermuir or anybody else, not now, not in this place of warmth and friendship and dreams. But now that moment was lost. He felt sad.

Lammermuir took a step back.

"But, but . . ." he stammered.

"We're just leaving," Sally said.

Dale started to shoot her a look, then changed his mind. He gave Lammermuir one more glare, then stood and picked up his chair. He walked to the door and pushed past Lammermuir, making sure to give him a good jostle. He dropped the chair on the floor with a loud, rattling clonk. Brewer followed, then Sally.

As they walked down the hall, Dale muttered, "There's always somebody. There's always somebody."

Chapter 30

Sarah Gray looked over at her roommate. Shu Chen was, as always, hunched over a textbook, the light from a desk lamp reflecting off the lenses of her thick glasses. She was a chemistry major, a Chinese chemistry major, and she was at SPC thanks to some obscure scholarship fund for students from mission schools. There were a dozen or so like her on campus.

Sarah and Shu became roommates through the random selection process of freshman placement. The fact they had nothing in common didn't matter to said process and, truth be known, Sarah didn't particularly care. Shu was neat, clean and, above all, predictable. She went to breakfast 8 a.m., lunch at noon and dinner at 6 p.m. every day, no exceptions. She went to bed at 11 p.m. every night. Again, no exceptions. She never missed a class. The rest of her waking hours were spent studying.

Shu spoke English, but she rarely talked and, often as not, she responded to any conversation directed her way with an embarrassed giggle and the glazed expression of one who didn't understand what was happening around her.

But she was affable enough, if in a slightly confused way. There were worse qualifications for a roommate, Sarah decided.

Sarah felt no imperative to be friendly to Shu beyond common courtesy and, apparently, Shu felt more or less the same way, if for different reasons. Shu was, after all, ten thousand miles from home with a chance for a college education, and an American college education at that; a thing so rare as to be unknown in her world. Perhaps it was the consequences of failure – the sweat shop, the rice field, the street – that drove her so, Sarah thought. Or maybe books and studies were all she knew. Sarah suspected that was more likely. In any event, Shu spent all her days, every day, immersed in her toil.

They had just returned from dinner. One product of Shu's monk-like habits was that she often didn't notice if Sarah was in the room. And she certainly didn't keep track of Sarah's comings and goings.

"I'm going to the library," Sarah said.

Shu looked up briefly, smiled her typically uncomprehending smile and then went back to the replacement qualities of barium isotopes in colloidal electrolytic solutions.

At the sign-out desk, Sarah wrote "Library" on the sheet, checked the time – 7:10 p.m. – did some quick mental calculations and headed down the hill toward Weter Library.

On her way, she passed a few students who trudged by with the characteristic plod of undergraduates forcing their way through the ennui of the academic grind. They did not notice her.

When Sarah reached Weter, she kept going past it and walked down the stairs that led to Marston Hall. Rather than cross the street to the big, ugly dorm building, she turned left, went north, crossed Bertona Avenue and walked up Emerson Street.

She had waited for Tom Brewer to call. She had made a point of saying hello to him at the SUB. She thought he had dropped adequate hints. But he didn't seem to get the message.

Well then, she would take the direct approach. It was the pragmatic thing to do.

She felt calm, almost detached as she strolled on through the cool, misty night; alone, the way she preferred to be, complete within herself. Pragmatic

So this is what it's like, she thought. It seems like any other walk. But anticipation was there, too. Shouldn't you be trembling or something? she thought. Well, I'm not. I've made my decision. Pragmatic.

She barely made a sound as she climbed the stairs. She stopped and calmly knocked on the door to apartment 204. Tom Brewer opened it. He was dressed in a gray sweat shirt with the sleeves cut short, Levi's and moccasins. She had never seen him in grub clothes before. For some reason, they made him even more clean-scrubbed than usual. How did he manage it?

Brewer looked surprised.

"May I come in?" Sarah said.

"Yes, yes, or course," Brewer said, a slight stammer in his voice.

She put down her bag as he closed the door. When he turned to face her, she waited a beat, just enough for the moment to settle. Then she stepped forward, put her arms around his neck, pulled herself against his body and kissed him.

Later, after the wonderment that transpired between them was done, Brewer propped himself on his elbow and studied Sarah as she combed her hair in front of the mirror. She was slender, more girl-like than womanly, with her milky, nearly translucent skin gliding lightly over softly-defined muscle. She had a particular grace to her, especially now as she stood with her head tilted to one side, a leg bent back slightly so the tips of her toes brushed the floor. The fact she was naked, in the room of a boy she barely knew, seemed not to bother her at all; the antithesis of the awkward self-consciousness he had seen in other girls after they had shared their bodies with him – or at least parts of their bodies, to one degree or another.

It was the first time he had actually studied a naked woman in the light and looking at her in her quiet self-assurance, Brewer found himself contemplating the realities of femininity. It wasn't weak. It wasn't flighty. It wasn't the stuff of giggles and frills and pink curtains. It was, instead, a thing of power, a power like no other, altogether worthy of the awe that enveloped Brewer.

Sarah turned and faced him. He shoulders were straight, her neck long and graceful. Funny, he had never noticed that about her before. Her bush was black, thick and primal, such a contrast to the alabaster delicacy of her trim body. He wanted to have her again, the urge rising in him in a wave.

"Don't go," he said.

"I have to be back by 10. They lock the doors." She kissed him lightly on the lips.

"I want you to stay," he said.

Her gaze went downward.

"So I see," she said with an enigmatic smile.

"Consider it a compliment," he said.

"I do."

She kissed him again, again lightly. To Brewer it felt almost unbearably sweet.

"Can't control the clock," she said.

She dressed quickly.

"You were wonderful," she said as she headed for the door.
"So were you."

She smiled once more, that beautiful, inscrutable smile; her eyes soft, nearly serene, no shyness, no unease in them. Minutes earlier, this quiet girl, this delicate-looking girl, had been sweating and feral, grasping and moaning and pulling at him, demanding of him. Brewer found the dichotomy very disconcerting.

As Sarah walked back to Hill, she thought, so that's what it's like to lose one's virginity. I liked it. It wasn't the transcendent, ethereal, epiphany she had been told about long ago by a preacher diligently droning his way through a sermon titled, "Physical Expression in the Christian Marriage." Silly man. No magical melding of souls in Tom Brewer's apartment, with its concrete block book cases and football posters.

But neither was it the raw scraping and gouging she had been warned about in "Preparation for Womanhood," a Sunday school class she was forced to endure when she was thirteen. It's your duty, girls, so just lie still, think of Jesus and soon it will be over, the teacher had said. The neurotic old fool clearly hated sex. She probably hated men, too. She certainly hated the life force in them that always seemed on the verge of erupting in unpredictable directions. So many women fear it, Sarah thought. They view it as a disfigurement, something dark and unforgivable. Sarah liked it. She liked most everything about men. And why, she wondered rhetorically, shouldn't she? Man-hating was a silly cultural prejudice and those who ascribed to it were deliberately shutting themselves off from reality. The convictions of ignorance were far more comforting than the uncertainties of truth.

Now she had experienced a truth, an important truth. She found that losing one's virginity was. . . well, it was something all its own, a force all its own. The feel of his body, the taste of him, the warm essence of him inside her; she had imagined some of it and she had imagined it fairly accurately – but only to a point. The reality was considerably more than she expected.

Was this boy special? Different, certainly. And interesting. There was something about him; his clear, alert eyes, his presence, his, well, maleness; no different than many boys, in some ways, very different in others. And he seemed quite unaware of it. Yes, he was special.

But did she love him? Well, why should she have to love him? She wasn't even sure what love was. It was another of those concepts people constantly talked about but never defined, beyond assuring her, over and over, that it was terribly important and a necessary prerequisite to all kinds of terribly important things - including enjoyment of sex. A half hour ago, she had enjoyed sex just fine without it, so how important was it, really?

As she opened the door to the Hill lounge, Sarah decided her time with Tom Brewer proved what she already suspected: That much of what she had been told, what she had been taught, what she had been warned about in such dire terms, was a lot of pompous nonsense and, often as not, downright lies.

The thought gave Sarah pause. Reality is disquieting in its absence of familiar myth. But the truth indeed can set your free, she decided. There was more to be discovered.

She found herself very, very tired. The release of long pent-up tension, perhaps. Or maybe just the warm afterglow of a good fuck. She started at the word fuck. She had never used it before, not even in her silent conversations with herself. She whispered it out loud: "Fuck." She giggled. Better be careful, she thought, someone might think you're drunk. There was always someone watching for that sort of thing.

When Sarah got to her room, Shu was the same as she had left her: Hunched over her desk, working intently on the same chemistry problem. Shu glanced over her shoulder briefly and then went back to her drudgery. Fine with me, Sarah thought as she undressed. She might see that my vulva is all red and swollen. At least that's what those great minds back in sex ed class said it would be. She couldn't actually see it, so she didn't know. She touched herself lightly. No, it didn't feel swollen. It didn't feel sore. All things considered, it didn't feel any different than when she had left the dorm some two hours ago. Yet another myth conquered.

****

"Oh, you guyyys! You won't believe what I saw last night!"

The girls at the table winced. Whenever Terri Garstang said, "Oh, you guyyys!" they knew what to expect: A tale about something Terri found, in another of her favorite expressions, "Gurrrose!"

She found all kinds of things gurrrose: Boys with beards ("It's like things are crawling in there."); African students ("Their skin looks like the leather from an old billfold and the whites of their eyes are all yellow. Ickkkkk."); the appearance of a midget on campus ("I mean, those little bitty fingers and toes; it's soooo creepy.") and, of course, anything involving biology labs, the garbage cans behind Gwinn, the maintenance standards of campus restrooms and on and on. She was prone to elaborate on her revulsion while others were trying to eat.

Girls like Terri were a familiar fixture at most small colleges: Ignorant, dumb and loud about it. They wandered about campus in a perpetual state of incomprehension, babbling their imbecility to anyone who would listen, whether they wanted to or not. In short, they were nitwits.

Once in college, away from their protective cultural cocoons, the nitwits often found themselves confronted by a world that was less than sympathetic to their shtick. They ended up sitting alone through all three meals. They were never chosen as lab partners. They were never invited on road trips to basketball games. From time to time, another student might even tell them to shut the fuck up.

Even an amoeba responds to stimulus, eventually, and most of the nitwits learned, eventually, to keep their brainless twaddle to themselves – most of them, but not all. Terri was one of the ones who didn't. Now a junior, she still felt compelled to express her pre-pubescent cognition levels as frequently and obstreperously as possible.

She was doing so now, to a group of girls who, up to then, had been quietly eating breakfast together. They winced when they saw her approaching. As she sat down, they girded themselves for a ruined morning.

"Oh, you guyyyys! You won't believe what I saw last night!" Terri's voice had a distressed, nearly anguished tone.

The others either kept eating or made a point of staring off into space as if Terri wasn't there, hoping on hope that she would not continue. It was a vain hope.

Terri said, "I was out walking on Nickerson Street last night..."

"Oh, was it a good night for street walking?" Nancy Siegleman said sweetly. Nancy was a senior. Four years of observing girls like Terri brought out her fiendish side. Some of the other girls stifled guffaws. Terri did not notice. Her eyes gaped blankly in oblivion and her lower lip protruded as if she was trying to suppress a sob. What came next was sure to be especially gurrrose.

"I was going down Nickerson and it was dark and there was this apartment building and it had these, like, back stairs and then, you know what I saw?"

No one responded. They were too busy girding themselves for what was sure to be tedious, inane and long. Again, Terri did not notice.

"I saw this girl coming out of a door and just as she left she kissed this guy and then she started down the stairs and you know who it was?"

More silence. More failure to perceive any meaning in it.

"Why, it was Sarah Gray, the professor's daughter! And she had been in some guy's apartment and just think what they were doing. Gurrrose!"

Those who knew Sarah weren't surprised, little less shocked. It was just a matter of time before Sarah did it with somebody and, as one who prided herself on her nonconformity, she would probably do it in some flagrant way. Besides, most of them were doing It on a fairly regular basis themselves. They simply had the good sense not to be seen. The rest had accepted the reality that they would be doing it soon enough. Even the most upright knew, on an intuitive level, they were unlikely to wait until their wedding nights before sampling the sins of the flesh.

"I mean a professor's daughter going to some boy's apartment. Can you imagine? Oooooo, iccckkk!"

The rest continued their wall of silence, hoping Terri would run out of steam. She did, but she felt compelled to express her consternation just one more time.

"Well, it made me feel all barfy sick," she said, trailing off feebly.

"Are you sure it was her?" So said Thelma Jaeger, who was sitting at the next table. Thelma was a short, wiry girl with tight-cropped curly hair, squinty eyes and a hard, pursed mouth. Thelma was devout. Thelma was humorless. Thelma was perpetually angry at a world which did not measure up to her standards. She had known Sarah Gray most of her life: One of those first church girls who was so superior, the professor's daughter, the princess. Thought she was so smart. Thought she was so much better than everybody else.

"Oh, it was her, all right," Terri said, suddenly reenergized at the opportunity to be the center of attention again. "I followed her back to Hill and, you know what? She was walking funny, like her legs hurt or something. Gurrrrose! "

"Where was this apartment?" Thelma asked.

"Huh?" Terri was not used to having her train of vacuity interrupted.

"This apartment you saw her leaving. Where was it?" Thelma said.

"Oh, it was that brick one on the left side of the street, the one with the balconies, you know?"

"Good grief, who cares!" Nancy Siegleman had had enough. "Can't we just eat breakfast in peace?"

"But you guyyys . . ." Terri's lip was quivering now, as if she was about to break into tears. The scenario of a young woman spending time in a young man's apartment – *alone*, with the *door locked* – was clearly traumatizing to her.

"Did it have a yellow sign? 'The Canal View,' or something like that?" Thelma said.

"Uh, yeah, I mean I think so." Terri was disoriented by having to call upon her memory while, at the same time, leaning back and forth between Thelma's table and her own.

Tom Brewer, Thelma thought. She had met Tom Brewer only once, at the SUB. He had made a joke about Billy Graham. ("What do you call an evangelist with an accent? A Graham cracker.") It was tantamount to blaspheming God himself. Billy Graham was the greatest man of the Twentieth Century, possibly the greatest man of all time. Brewer thought it was funny. Thelma should have rebuked him, as was her duty as an anointed one of God. But she was too shocked to speak. However, she made a mental note to remember who he was. Later, she heard he got an apartment on Nickerson, with a name like "Canal View." Another mental note. Well, now we know what he had in mind for that, don't we, she thought. Tom Brewer, with his starched shirts and shined shoes. Thinks he's such hot stuff. She would show him.

Nancy Siegleman looked at Terri and then at Thelma. Her face was weary with contempt.

"Don't you people have something better to do?" she said. "Like almost anything at all?" Before Terri or Thelma could answer, she took her tray and moved to another table. Three other girls joined her.

Terri started to snivel. "But you guyyys . . ."

Thelma put her arm around her comfortingly.

****

"Chet, I'm holding you personally responsible!"

Hazel Rexler's eyes were afire, her lips like steel bands, her jaw jutting like the prow of a battle cruiser.

"What?" Chester Dalrymple said, his expression as blank as his mind.

"I'm holding you personally responsible!" Hazel snarled again, her finger pointing at him like a gnarled sycamore root. Dalrymple expected to see foam drip from her mouth at any moment.

He waited for her to continue. Instead, she silently glowered at him, her face a blast furnace of outrage.

Dalrymple had known Hazel Rexler for a long time. She was a campus fixture at SPC; part of a subculture of ex-missionaries, retired church secretaries, widows of dead ministers and the otherwise professionally devout. They were given jobs as house mothers, directors of minor programs and other menial tasks where they could do no particularly harm while lending their piety to the general atmosphere.

Dalrymple had hired one or two in his early years on the job, but he came to regret it. He found that in most of them there was a thin, twisted thread of the inquisitor and the hanging judge; an anger, a hate, a seething conviction that it was their right, their mission, their duty to root out deviation from the True Way – their way.

Not that Dalrymple cared about that per se. But people like Hazel Rexler were a pain to work with. Their prickly approach to almost everything caused problems. Chester Dalrymple did not like problems.

Anyway, here was Hazel at her most anointed, blaming him for some horrific aberration of which he, until now, was unaware. Dalrymple took a deep breath.

"Could you be more specific?" he said, trying hard not to sound disinterested.

"Animals! Animals! Some hip-wigging little tramp and some pimply degenerate rutting like pigs in their own filth! Right here! A block from campus! What's become of this place? What do you plan to do about it?"

Good grief. Dalrymple suddenly felt very, very tired.

"Well, we do have the Lifestyle Behavior Code and the Guidelines on Christian Intimacy," he said.

Both were official tomes on student behavior and both were, in effect, lists of rules, although they were carefully worded so they didn't sound like it. Buried in their primly obtuse prose was their true purpose: Students could be expelled for any of a long list of transgressions, including smoking, drinking, dancing, card-playing – and engaging in the procreative process.

"As if they do any good," Hazel snorted derisively.

She was quite right, of course; at least when it came to strictures against sins of the flesh. Those rules were rarely if ever enforced because proof was hard to come by. And, on a practical level, if the school expelled every kid who parked at Golden Gardens or Magnolia Bluff on a Friday night, the student body would become very small very fast.

But the policies were in print. They had dignitas. They had gravitas. They had the perfect mix of euphemism and glittering generality to make them sound high-minded. And hardly anybody could understand them, so they sounded learned; a triumph of policy-making if ever there was one. They were copyrighted.

Back to Hazel Rexler. Oh, what she had heard. When that wonderful Christian girl, Thelma Jaeger, had come to her with that vile, disgusting story; why the poor thing was nearly in tears, describing what her sweet, innocent friend had seen, how it traumatized her, how those other girls laughed at her – Hazel would deal with them later – how anyone could bear to witness such putridity. Hazel had listened stoically (she had to set an example, after all) and did her best to comfort the poor dear. She vowed to see what she could do.

When Thelma left, Hazel's calm façade cracked, them disintegrated. Fury washed over her, through her, focusing her mind in a jet of molten white hate. She had to act and she did, stalking across campus cloaked in wrath, looking neither left nor right, a puritan saber slashing her way through a noxious malignancy of lasciviousness, leaving a prop wash of righteous rage in her wake.

She had warned them! She had warned them! Them in their fancy suits and smooth smiles. First they let students own their own cars. Then they let girls stay out after 9 p.m. And now this. But they would not listen.

They would listen now.

"The girl was Sarah Gray," Hazel said.

Chester Dalrymple stared at her uncomprehendingly.

"Professor Herbert Gray's daughter."

Dalrymple was suddenly alert. A faculty member's daughter in trouble? That simply did not happen at SPC. If made public, it could defile the school's chaste image. President Dr. Donald A. Fotheringham Ph.D. would be displeased.

So that's why she came to me, Dalrymple thought.

He was partially right. True, Hazel had come to him because she knew he was obsessed with image and acceptance. But more importantly, she knew, intuitively, that he was weak and would not brush her off. Officially, student misbehavior was the prevue of the Dean of Students, but Hazel detested Layton Fleming. He epitomized the slick-talking know-it-alls that seemed to infest the campus these days. She could barely stand to be in his presence, little less actually talk to him. No, good old bumbling Chet was a better bet. So what if he was director of public relations and, according to organizational charts, had nothing to do with student affairs. Organizational charts mattered little at SPC. Gossip and rumor mattered a lot and this gossip would frighten him. Weak, frightened men could be manipulated.

Chester Dalrymple was indeed feeling the icy pangs of fear at the moment. Not only would he have to protect the school and its image, he dared not offend the faculty in any way. The faculty were a difficult lot, used to getting their own way, an extension of the conceit that they could flunk any eighteen-year-old who dared challenge their eminence.

Dalrymple began parsing the problem. Then he remembered Hazel was still in the room. He listened to her rant on for a while, carefully taking notes on the whos, whats, wheres and whens. Eventually, Hazel ran out of steam. Dalrymple assured her the incident would be duly investigated and she left.

Chester Dalrymple sighed with the weary resignation of a man used to being put upon. He took a long sip of coffee and collected his thoughts. He knew what to do, but he didn't want to do it. Up to now, his day had been well-arranged: Sign brochures until 11 a.m., lunch until 2 p.m. and the rest of the afternoon at the Cascade Club, where he could share tales of woe with other managerial minions enduring the injustices of weighty responsibility.

Well, someone has to do it, he thought. It's the price you pay for a cabinet-level job.

He turned to his typewriter. A half-hour later, he finished a memo detailing what he had heard. He read it over quickly, placed it in an envelope, sealed the envelope and addressed it, "Layton Fleming, Dean of Students. Confidential."

****

Chester Dalrymple's note sat in Layton Flemings in-box for two weeks.

Layton Fleming rarely looked at his mail. Instead, his secretary, Agnes Carswell, was assigned the task of sorting it; usually routing it to Fleming's assistant deans. Fleming explained this was necessary because he had to focus his gifts on the Big Picture, not the day-to-day trifles of lesser humans.

A bird-like, easily-frightened woman, Agnes Carswell not only obeyed without question, but lived in constant worry she might make some error in judgment that would trouble The Great Man.

So, an envelope marked "Confidential" posed a problem. If it had come from the President's office, it would have gone through immediately. Same with the Finance Director's office. But Public Relations? Chester Dalrymple was a campus joke. Even she knew that. She had heard Fleming say so many times.

Agnes Carswell fretted. Eventually, she decided to slip the envelope in the middle of the pile in Fleming's in-box. A small pile, that, but one whose contents stayed untouched for days at a time. Ideal. Eventually, Fleming would come across Dalrymple's note; soon enough that he couldn't accuse her of losing it, but sufficiently delayed that whatever news it contained would have cooled off a little. With Layton Fleming, he of the bold hauteur and thundering voice, urgency was not a good thing, particularly if you were a low-level secretary with the fortitude of a marsh tit.

Layton Fleming read his mail when he was bored or had nothing better to do. It amused him to scan over some impeccably-typed, earnestly-worded plea for his attention, then wad it up and toss it with a graceful free throw shot at the waste basket. So much for the aspirations of lower beings.

Things he actually had to act upon, he did, albeit as seldom as possible. Again, those assistant deans were invaluable.

So, it was unusual indeed that Fleming actually showed interest upon opening a letter in his in-box, especially one from a boob like Chester Dalrymple. Then he read it. A professor's daughter porking another student in his apartment on a week night? That had potential.

He saw the name Tom Brewer. Ah yes, Brewer. Had an apartment off-campus, did he? Not for long, he wouldn't. Fleming would enjoy settling with him.

A professor's daughter presented some potential problems. Such people had a certain amount of status in the culture of SPC and that tight little culture was extraordinarily stringent in maintaining delusions about itself.

On the other hand, the news was already out. That idiot Garstang kid had blabbed it in Gwinn, so any number of students knew. Hazel Rexler, the neurotic old crone, also knew. Chester Dalrymple knew. Sooner or later, the word would spread. It always did.

So Fleming would have to do something. He actually found himself looking forward to it.

Interrogating the little slut would be entertaining. She might reveal some information he could use. Or, he could extort her into becoming a snitch - "Snitch," such an ugly word, he thought. "Student Aide" sounded so much better.

When she arrived at his office, Fleming found Sarah Gray a bit of a surprise. Slender and dark-haired, she wore a serious, intelligent face and sat in the hardwood chair in front of his desk with the erect posture of cool confidence.

He looked her over carefully, searching for vulnerabilities. Sometimes, the confident ones were surprisingly easy to crack. They thought they were a lot smarter than they actually were, and when that was revealed to them they became lost and helpless. Well, we'll see, Fleming thought.

When asked why she thought she had been called to the dean's office, Sarah responded that she had no idea.

"Oh, I think you do," Fleming said with exaggerated sincerity.

"No, I don't," Sarah said.

"Yes you do," Fleming said, leaning forward as if trying to pry through the cracks of her self-assured façade. It's no use trying to lie your way out of it, sweetcakes. We know. You may as well tell us all about it.

"I'm sorry. I don't know what you are talking about." Sarah's voice wasn't quite as composed now; a slight, almost imperceptible tremor in it. Fleming sensed an opening.

"Look, it would be better for you if you just told us everything," Fleming said. "Otherwise, we won't be able to help you."

"I don't understand what you want," Sarah said, shifting slightly in her chair.

Fleming leaned back, and exhaled a breath as if he was very, very bored. He let the moment hang, all the while resting his eyes on Sarah with a resigned, jaded expression.

"Well, I'm sorry to be the one to do this," he said, carefully opening a drawer in his desk. He removed a letter and, with calculated languor, unfolded it panel by panel, making sure the paper snapped and crackled with appropriate dramatic effect.

He held it up in front of him, cleared his throat and ran his eyes over it slowly, doing his best to adopt an expression of weary resignation. Oh, how it pained him to have to read such things. Oh, how it saddened him to have to act on them.

"I'm afraid it's come to my attention, and to the attention of a number of other people on campus, that last week you had, shall we say, a meeting with a boy at his apartment over on Nickerson."

Sarah's eyes snapped with anger. "Who told you that?" she demanded.

"Look, I don't have spies out there," Fleming said. "And of course your private life is your business. But as you know, the school has standards. And ugly rumors don't help anybody. I want to help you, if I can."

"Help me? With what? I'm not asking for help with anything," Sarah said. "So, if you'll excuse me, I'll go now."

He had to hand it to her, the kid had backbone. As she rose from her chair, Fleming shot her a look, one he had spent years perfecting, a combination of concentration, contempt and cold fury. He had actually learned it from a movie where a sadistic Gestapo officer was interrogating Jimmy Cagney. It didn't work on Jimmy Cagney, but it worked just fine on eighteen-year-old coeds.

He saw Sarah hesitate ever so slightly.

"Sit down, young lady!" Fleming barked, in a voice that made Sarah jump. She sat down.

Fleming took a deep breath, as if to calm himself. He leaned back and smiled slightly.

"Sorry, got a little carried away there," he said reassuringly. "Now look, honey –" He knew girls hated being called honey. So he used it when he wanted to throw them off-balance. "– this does not have to ruin your life. Just tell me what happened and it won't go any further than this room. I won't even tell your father."

"My father?" Sarah froze.

She pictured her father walking across campus as he always did, slowly, with his head down as if immersed in thought. He was wearing his favorite tweed jacket, the one with the suede patches on the elbows. He was smiling; the patient, reassuring half-grin that he wore year after year as he gently guided legions of undergraduate through the intricacies of Thomas Aquinas and Kant. He told the same jokes and used the same droll homilies year after year, too; so much that they had become part of campus lore. Oddly, perhaps, students did not hold him in contempt for it. It was all part of his kindly, warmhearted approach, all part of the inherent goodness and decency that made the man.

Her father, the ever-loving presence who never failed to reassure her when she was sad, who never failed to encourage her when she was happy; the warm, dependable security in her life. She was his little girl. His adoration was complete. To harm him, to cause him humiliation . . .

What was she thinking? Fuck Tom Brewer because it seemed like a good idea, an expression of free choice that, based on rationality and logic, required no further explanation? Because it proved that she was a sophisticated woman of the world? Because it made her feel superior to the gaggles of cultural illiterates that infested SPC?

Because it felt good?

Well, it didn't feel good now. Memories of mixed sweat and mingled souls now seemed banal and repugnant. And that ethereal moment, her moment, when for such an exquisite briefness she seemed to float above the mere earth in a singular plane of exultation, a thing so far beyond the colorless muddle of everyday living . . .

What nonsense. She could do that for herself. She had heard Shu late at night, when she thought Sarah was asleep. If timid, clueless Shu could make herself climax, how hard could it be?

What a silly thing to think of at a time like this. I'm in trouble, real trouble.

She could be expelled. She could become the object of whispers and snickers. She could become the family's dirty little secret; never spoken about, of course, but known by all, expressed in the fake sincerity of every person who smiled at her at a Christmas party or Easter dinner.

Was it worth it?

Was it worth breaking your father's heart?

No.

What do I do now?

Fleming saw it all in her eyes. He had her. Now to use her.

"Just tell me what happened," Fleming said.

Sarah struggled to catch her breath. Finally she succeeded and began.

"I went over to his apartment. He didn't know I was coming. He let me in and then we . . . you know."

"No, I don't know. Tell me."

Sarah's face reddened. She squirmed in her chair, unable to speak. Fleming watched coldly, measuring the moment. Oh, how he loved his job.

Finally he said, "Who was it?"

"Do I have to tell you?"

"I'm afraid so," Fleming said, spreading his hands as if he was helpless to do anything else.

"I don't even know him that well," Sarah said. "There's just something about him. He's very nice, really. I don't want anything to happen to him."

"Don't worry," Fleming said. "I'm not here to judge. I'm here to help." It was one of his favorite pat sayings. It always made him chuckle inwardly.

"His name is Tom Brewer," Sarah said.

Gotcha Brewer, you conniving little maggot, Fleming thought.

"And where is his apartment?" Fleming said, in as mild a tone as he could manage.

Sarah was staring to choke.

"It's the Canal View Apartments, Room 204," she rasped in a near whisper.

"Okay, okay you're fine," Fleming said comfortingly. "Now don't worry about a thing."

"You won't tell my father?"

"No, but I can't guarantee he won't hear the rumor," Fleming said.

A trace of a tear ran down Sarah's cheek.

"And my record?"

"I'm not recommending any action be taken against you," Fleming said. "But, well, we did have this meeting, so I'll have to put a note about it in your file."

"What will it say?" Sarah was genuinely frightened now.

"Oh, don't you worry about it," Fleming purred. "Nobody ever reads those things. You trust me and I'll trust you."

Sarah knew what he meant. He had her. He would use her. And there was nothing she could do about it.

Chapter 31

"Pool?"

"Pool. That's what the man said." Agnes Carswell was nervous. Layton Fleming did not like surprises. And this definitely constituted a surprise.

"Where are they now?" Fleming said.

"Downstairs by the back door."

Indeed they were. Two workmen were rolling a large crate through the door on a dolly.

"What's going on here?" Fleming demanded.

"Delivery from Northwest Sporting Goods," one of the men said. They continued to carefully roll the crate through the door.

"Wait a minute. Hold up. We didn't order anything from Northwest Sporting Goods," Fleming said.

The men stopped. The one who spoke went out to a large moving van parked on Bertona. He returned a moment later with a clipboard. He thumbed through the papers until he came to a blue sheet.

"Here it is," he said. "Two pool tables to the Student Union Building, Seattle Pacific College. Install in basement."

"Let me see that," Fleming said.

The order said exactly what man had recited. Fleming flipped a few more pages. He found the sales invoice. Two Brunswick pool tables, Lassiter Model, $516.14 each. Payment by check. Signed off by Thomas F. Cowen, Treasurer, Associated Students of Seattle Pacific College.

"What the he. . ." Fleming caught himself. "What the heck?"

He paused to collect his thoughts.

"Take them back," he told the delivery man.

"Can't," the delivery man said. "We're just the delivery company. You'd have to call Northwest Sporting Goods. Besides, we already have one downstairs. I think they have it set up already."

"What?!" Fleming gasped.

"Like I said, we just deliver 'em," the man said.

"Well, don't take that one down," Fleming said.

"You want us to leave it in the doorway?"

Fleming looked around. There was no other place to put it in the SUB - except the basement. Good grief.

"All right, all right. Take it down, but don't unpack it."

The man shrugged and went back to pushing the dolly. Just then, another deliveryman came up the stairs from the basement.

"Lou, we got the first one installed," he said "You need help with that one?"

"No, we got it," the other man said. "Just clean up the cardboard. And hurry up if you can. We're running kinda late this morning."

Layton Fleming felt lost. What in the world was going on?

Back upstairs, Fleming watched the moving van drive away. He told Agnes Carswell to get Greg Lammermuir. Fifteen minutes later Lammermuir was standing in front of Fleming's desk. The office door was closed.

"What in the Sam Hill is going on here?" Fleming demanded.

"Uh, sir?" Lammermuir said, confused. Or maybe he was just being wimpy. Lammermuir was terminally wimpy which, up to now, had always suited Fleming just fine.

"Pool tables!" Fleming roared. "Whose bright idea was it to buy pool tables? And you'd better have a good explanation!"

"Uh, well, the student council approved it last month. We had a budget surplus and entertained a number of proposals. I had reservations about the pool tables myself. . ."

"I don't care about your reservations," Fleming said, sneering sarcastically at the word reservations. "I said, whose bright idea was this fiasco?"

"I believe the proposal came from Nancy Siegleman, the senior class representative," Lammermuir said carefully, in as low and evenly modulated a tone as he could manage so as not to aggravate Fleming all the more. "It seems the idea was suggested to her by some freshman. I believe his name was Brewer. . ."

Fleming's attention immediately snapped awake. Lammermuir kept on droning - something about the vote count or some such drivel – but Fleming ignored him. Brewer, 'ey? Well, well, well.

Lammermuir prattled on. Fleming glowered at him like he cared, but his thoughts were elsewhere.

Finally he barked, "I've heard enough. Get out of my office. You haven't heard the last of this." Lammermuir slinked away.

Fleming considered. There will be a flap about it, of course. Pool at SPC? He laughed inwardly at the absurdity of it. You would think that after four years at this place, those twits on the student council would know better than even to think it. But what do you expect of undergraduates.

Anyway, now he had something on Brewer. Fleming had been trying for two years to get enough on McLean to get rid of him, but he never could and decided that McLean was too cagey to justify expending energy on him. Same with Weldon. And Parris, well, except for his attempts at editing the Falcon, he essentially was a nobody, so who cared. But, to successfully draw attention away from himself as the origin of the disorder fomenting in the SPC continuum, Fleming would have to pillory somebody. So, he could start a tab on Brewer. Yes, yes, a very good idea indeed.

Meanwhile, there were two pool tables in the SUB basement. Someone would have to do something about them, successfully or otherwise, which conjured scenarios of meeting with the student council, listening to their gibberish, contacting the company that sold the table, arranging to have them removed, getting the Finance Department to revoke the check and on and on; a morass of the kind of managerial drudgery that Fleming had spent a lifetime strenuously avoiding.

It would be far easier just to leave the tables where they were. He could even use them for leverage; an example of where the college was headed if permissiveness was given free rein, like what was happening with the Falcon. Time to crack down.

Yes, he could make that work.

Meanwhile, someone would have to take the blame for the mess. That would be easy.

****

"Pool!"

Layton Fleming's face was dark with anger. He gripped the arms of his chair as if to keep himself from rocketing to the ceiling with rage.

When Chester Dalrymple had been called to the office of Dr. Donald A. Fotheringham, Ph.D., he had no idea what to expect. But he certainly didn't expect to see the dean of students in the initial stages of apoplectic seizure.

"Pool?" Chester said, bewildered.

Fleming slapped his forehead in exasperation.

"Pool in the basement of the SUB! They want to turn the SUB into a pool hall! What next, whores and cigars?" Fleming pointed an accusatory finger at Chester. "And the director of public relations hasn't done a thing about it!" Fleming was panting loudly, the very picture of righteous outrage.

Dr. Donald A. Fotheringham, Ph.D., stood with his hands clasped behind his back, gazing with weighty contemplation out the big plate glass window on the east wall of his richly carpeted office; east so he could draw inspiration from the rising sun each morning.

"Now, now, let's not be too hasty here, Layton," Fotheringham intoned in the slow, deep, oh-so-dignified voice that was his trademark. "Let's hear Chet's explanation for this situation."

"Yeah, Chet, what do you plan to do about it?" Fleming sneered, with just the right tone of contempt to seal the certainty of Chester Dalrymple's malfeasance.

Pool tables in the SUB basement? Chester Dalrymple could barely believe it himself. Up to now, it had never occurred to him that SPC students even knew what pool was. But, of course, the pool tables and whatever controversy they precipitated were not the issue. Who to blame for it; that's what mattered. And at the moment that who was him.

He understood what Fleming was doing. Say the same thing over and over again, say it loudly and with unwavering conviction and it will be accepted as truth, or at least something resembling the appearance of it enough to shift blame. Chester Dalrymple used the tactic himself sometimes. It was surprisingly effective, usually because the people on the receiving end of it became rattled and tried to respond to it directly. That just made them look all the more guilty.

"The student council voted on this?" Chester said. "Don't they meet next door to your office, Layton?"

Fleming was unphased. He knew how to play the game, too.

"Oh, you just pass the buck, you just pass the buck!" he bellowed. "Typical, typical! No wonder Public Relations is a campus joke!"

"Layton and I were at the Cascade Club that afternoon," Fotheringham said. "I was speaking there and I wanted to introduce him to some of the members."

Chester knew what that meant. Layton Fleming was a Young Man on the Way Up. Everyone said so. There even were rumors he had been approached by the local Republican Party committee.

"Aren't the student council and the SUB the responsibility of the dean of students?" Chester said weakly.

Dr. Donald A. Fotheringham, Ph.D., visibly jerked in surprise. For a heart-stopping moment, an existential moment, the world of the infallibility of the president and his institutional cronies, went off the track with a loud, unnatural screech. Chester Dalrymple - who definitely was not a member of Fotheringham's inner circle - was daring to challenge Layton Fleming - who very definitely was. Oh no, that would not do.

"Now, now, Chet, let's not muddy the situation with a lot of parsing," Fotheringham said. "I'm sure none of this was deliberate on your part. Sometimes things happen. It seems to me you should be grateful to Layton for bringing it to your attention the way he has."

Layton Fleming looked on, his chin lifted regally.

"But I must say and am a little disappointed in you, Chet," Fotheringham declared solemnly. "Why just last week, I saw two students in a car on Cremona, next to Hill and they were. ." his brow furrowed in disapproval "ahem, necking, only two blocks from my home."

Fleming smirked.

"Chet, I want you to stay on top of things a bit more," Fotheringham intoned. "And let's find some positive public relations implications for this."

Chester Dalrymple's mind was swimming, like food coloring squeezed into a whirlpool of cold oil. It made no headway against the tide. Dr. Donald A. Fotheringham, Ph.D., was a Dynamic Leader, a man who expected Results, who urged his staff To Think Outside the Box and use Innovative Approaches, a visionary who epitomized all things Cutting Edge.

Chester knew these things because he had seen to it that every brochure, news release, alumni magazine and anything else printed that came out of Seattle Pacific College said so.

Oh, well. He knew what to do next.

****

"Pool?"

Paul Trimble spoke as if he couldn't believe what he had just heard.

Chester Dalrymple did not appreciate the déjà vu. Once down this road was enough. He took a deep breath, partly to calm his nerves and partly to make it look like he was exasperated with Trimble's impertinence.

"Paul, if you can't see the importance of this, I'm worried that you are out of touch with the SPC ethos," Dalrymple said.

Ethos? What the hell did that mean? Trimble wondered. It was one of those learned-sounding words you heard around college campuses, the kind no one ever took the trouble to define. Tenet was another one. So was credo. Something to do with the place's customs and traditions, but at a higher, more cerebral plane. They were Greco-Latin words, after all. That proved it.

Who gives a flying fuck, Trimble thought. The administration, that's who. It was a hierarchy that broached no challenge to its authority, or the appearance thereof, no matter how slight. Democracy, with all its indecorous noise and squabbling, was something distinctly sinister to the apparatchiks who occupied the dark hallways of the administration building.

So maybe Dalrymple was right. He did not understand the SPC "ethos."

But for now, he had to act like he did, or at least like he did give a flying fuck.

"How exactly is this a public relations matter?" Trimble said. "The students wanted the tables and were willing to spend their own money on them. They voted on them in an open meeting and, as I understand it, no one opposed the idea. Pool is a just game. Who cares?"

The moment Trimble said "Who Cares?" he knew he had made a mistake.

"Who cares?!" Dalrymple said with a dumbfounded look. "Is that all you have to say? The alumni care, the community cares, the entire country will care when it finds out that one of the few remaining pillars of wholesome Christian education has been taken over by pool halls . . ."

"Wait a minute," Trimble interrupted. "Two tables in the basement of the Student Union Building don't constitute being taken over by pool halls. You have to go down a flight of stairs to get to them and the stairwell is by the door to the dumpster. I've never even seen the fool things. Have you?"

Chester Dalrymple had not. No matter. Trimble had backed him into a rhetorical corner. What to do, what to do?. . . Then he remembered: When faced with a question you can't turn to your advantage, simply change the subject.

"Paul, you're a professional," he said with exaggerated weariness. "I expect solutions, not negativity. I have to say I'm worried about you."

It was then that Trimble realized he was in danger. The whole mess was being dumped in his lap. He had not caused it, he had very little knowledge of what had happened or why it was a scandal and he had no authority to do anything about it. But shit rolled down hill and he was at the bottom of the institutional heap. If he wanted to keep his job - *you need the money, you need the money* - then it was up to him to solve the Great Pool Table Crisis.

His mind moved very fast. First, he would have to throw Dalrymple off-balance to gain some time.

"Okay, so what do we do?" Trimble said in a reasonable tone, as if he was brainstorming courses of action. "A news release? What would it say? That the student council pulled a fast one right under the nose of the administration? That the college has been invaded by pool hustlers and doesn't know what to do? That . . ."

"Again that negativity," Dalrymple grunted. "This is no laughing matter."

"Okay, how about this," Trimble said. "The college is experimenting with changes - no, make that 'adjustments' - to its student conduct code - with the introduction of pool tables - no, make that 'billiards' tables - on a temporary - no, make that 'probationary' - basis in the school's Student Union Building. 'The time has come to trust in SPC students' maturity and responsibility,' said whoever we use as a spokesman. 'We hope - no, make that we 'trust' - we can depend on them.'"

Trimble wanted to go rinse out his mouth with Lysol. Instead, he gave Dalrymple his best sincere smile.

Chester Dalrymple looked back at him with the expression of incomprehension that was his trademark. After a few awkward seconds, Trimble's words finally seemed to penetrate his psyche.

"But why would we want to adjust our student conduct code?" he said, still clearly confused.

"Because the Student Council voted on it," Trimble said. "Surely, as concerned, enlightened leaders, we want to be responsive to the opinions of the student body."

Dalrymple nodded vacantly.

"That's your best recommendation?" he said.

"My best recommendation is simply to ignore the whole thing," Trimble said. "I seriously doubt anyone beyond the campus borders care, or that very many people within its borders care, for that matter. I haven't seen any protesters marching around The Loop."

"But. . . "Dalrymple started.

"But you see it differently," Trimble said. "I respect that. . . "

Like a bucket full of walrus pus, I respect it, you retarded douchenozzle. God, I need a drink.

". . . so, I would suggest the best way to put a positive spin on this is to promote our status as a modern, forward-looking institution with. . . "

. . . here comes the broadside from the battleship . . .

". . . innovative approaches to student growth opportunities."

And if that doesn't get us laughed off the manure pile, I can't imagine what would.

Dalrymple looked thoughtful. After a minute or two, he said, "But if it's a test, that would indicate it has some specified duration. Or that we might shut the tables down some time in the future."

"Possibly. But after six months – a year, tops – everyone will have forgotten about them anyway. Then we can shut them down or, and I still consider this the best option, simply ignore them and no one will notice," Trimble said.

Hmmm, that actually sounded pretty good. Maybe I am cut out for this line of work after all, like I'm cut out for buggering wildebeests or emptying buckets at the guillotine. A drink! A drink! My kingdom for a drink!

Trimble watched Dalrymple's face, searching for a hint of how his eloquent little soliloquy had gone over. Whether or not it worked as public relations didn't particularly matter. Whether it saved his ass did. How it fit into the intricate calculus of status, jealousy, paranoia, and scores of other unarticulated delvings that constituted Chester Dalrymple's decision-making process; that was the most important part of all.

For Trimble knew that although Chester Dalrymple wasn't the sprightliest daisy in the chain, he had a certain low, Neolithic cunning you had to respect, in the same way you respected a Gila Monster in the second day of its menstrual period and out of cigarettes.

Dalrymple thought some more. His face was a blank. Finally, he spoke.

"I'm holding you personally responsible for all this, you know."

"For the pool tables?" Trimble said.

"Pool tables in the SUB and the director of press relations doesn't know a thing about it," Dalrymple said. "I'm disappointed, to say the least."

Chester Dalrymple took a stack of brochures and started signing them, one-by-one. It was as if Trimble was not in the room.

Trimble started to speak. Dalrymple raised his hand to stop him.

What is reality, really? Trimble wondered. *Whatever your mind makes it in order to suit your purpose? In this place, in this moment in time, evidence had no meaning. Words had no meaning. Reasoned thought had no meaning. Lewis Carroll and Joseph Heller didn't write fantasies. They knew more about reality* than anyone imagined. Other people just didn't see it. Instead they laughed; the laughter of the mad. The world truly was an exercise in psychosis.

For now, however, stay focused, he thought, you have to stay focused. Somehow he forced himself.

"What about the news release?" Trimble said.

Dalrymple continued to diligently sign the brochures, one-by-one, as if Trimble was not in the room.

After about three minutes, Trimble tried again.

"The news release. Should I write it up and send it out?" he said.

Dalrymple looked up, apparently surprised to see Trimble there.

"Huh?" he mumbled. "Whatever."

Then he went back to signing.

Paul Trimble's urge for the consumption of alcohol became almost unbearable; strong alcohol in large quantities, the stronger and larger the better. But first, he had to write up a news release. It would be done in record time, assuming anyone recorded the times for such things. This is Chris Schenkel reporting from the Tokyo Olympics, where American Paul The Sleazemeister Trimble has just ground out 422 words of putrid drek in fourteen minutes and thirty two seconds of what some are calling the most amazing example of dung-shoveling ever seen in international competition. So how do you feel about your victory, Paul?

Like I want to stick a long, pointed object through my right eye, piercing my brain and leaving me in a permanent vegetative state, Chris.

Well, thanks Paul. I'm sure your parents must be very proud.

Yes, Chris, they've changed their names, undergone extensive plastic surgery and moved to a cave in northern Saskatchewan. Say, you wouldn't happen to have ice pick handy, would you, Chris?

Alcohol. Must have alcohol.

****

In the end, Layton Fleming and even Dr. Donald A. Fotheringham, Ph.D. had to bow to reality. The money already had been spent and the tables already had been lifted and hauled and pushed and pulled down the basement stairs. They had been set up with much grunting and sweating and cursing. At roughly 450 pounds apiece, they weren't going anywhere. Fleming went downstairs, took one look at them and knew he was stuck.

Fotheringham did his best to underplay the whole business but, inevitably, the Board of Regents found out. A few of them did indeed fume with righteous wrath, even repeating, nearly word for word, Layton Fleming's observation that pool would lead to a campus infested with John Barleycorn and scarlet women.

Fotheringham said nothing. He knew the puritans on the board would save the pool table debacle as a sword slowly swinging by a thread over his head. No telling when it might come in handy.

Fotheringham knew that sometimes you just have to accept bad outcomes. Well, maybe somebody had to, but not him, not a nationally-recognized Leader Of Christian High Education. Whoever was responsible for it - Layton Fleming, the Student Council, whoever it was who suggested it to the council in the first place - whoever it was, they would pay. Fortheringham didn't know how and he didn't know when, but someone would find out what it meant to besmirch the prestige of Donald A. Fotheringham, Ph.D.

All these things happened over a period of one week, two days and roughly three hours in March, 1965 in Seattle, Washington. They happened because one college freshman, a certain Tom Brewer, made a casual suggestion to one college senior, a certain Nancy Siegleman, while drinking coffee between classes in the Student Union Building; a benign exercise, they thought. The possibility that it might result in any kind of conflict never crossed their minds.

Chapter 32

The University of Washington is a closed place, both physically and metaphorically. Some would argue that, as a secular, state-supported institution in an obscure corner of the continent, it also is closed intellectually, but its list of Nobel Prizes, Pulitzer Prizes, ground-breaking developments in medicine, physics, engineering and other fields would evidence otherwise, as would its thousands of alumni who, thanks to their education, have gone on to eminence in their chosen callings.

Anyway, physically, it is closed by its borders. On the east, it is bordered by a high cliff that drops down to Mountlake Boulevard, which is a major thoroughfare in that part of Seattle. To the south, there is Pacific Street, another thoroughfare, a particularly congested and unpleasant one; so busy it can only be crossed safely on pedestrian overpasses which lead to the university's medical school. South of the med school there is the Lake Washington Ship Canal and Portage Bay.

To the north runs Northeast 45th Street, yet another busy thoroughfare. The western border is 15th Avenue Northeast. Like many streets in Seattle, it had to be cut across the side of the hill, which means large sections of its eastern bank are shored up by high concrete walls. Along with the rest of the university's borders they effectively cut off the campus from the rest of the world. Therefore, the university is, for the most part, all but invisible when viewed from the outside ~ which means that, aside from occasional glimpses, the majority of people in Seattle have never actually seen this institution which dictates the lives of the forty thousand souls who attend it, not to mention the rest of the state.

Metaphorically, the university's inhospitable mien is more difficult to quantify, but no less real to those who experience it. The UW is big, with more than five hundred buildings sprawled across seven hundred acres of sloping plateau. The buildings are often big, too and the best of them, built in the Gothic style with high arches, leaded windows, gargoyles and the like, are imposing to the point of foreboding. The campus plan, if there is one, is chaotic and difficult to navigate, even if you know where you are going. Few people take leisurely strolls across the UW campus.

Then there is the rain. No place suffers Seattle rain quite like the UW. All the university's features, both physical and metaphorical, combine to make walking the campus in the rain an experience in dreariness like no other.

Beyond all that, the UW epitomizes The Establishment. It doesn't mean to. Its goals of learning and enlightenment are, by any standard, noble. But it is a place many want to attend, few are accepted and, if you are a student there, you are reminded of that fact on a daily basis. The people who man its front desk bureaucracy generally treat undergraduates as something between a necessary evil and a nuisance. It is a convenient way to vent their quiet desperation at being stuck in jobs they hate. Students have no defense against them.

And the university is big. And intimidating. And closed.

All of this was very much evident to Brewer as he made his way across 15th Northeast, then up the low hill at the UW's Northeast 42nd Street entrance, and finally onto the campus proper. He was greeted by the backsides of buildings. The fronts faced inward toward the center of the campus which, (here comes another metaphor), tells you a lot about the UW's definition of welcome.

Brewer made his way down the campus's tree-lined main boulevard, passing students along the way. Most looked about the same as SPC students, although there was a somewhat larger contingent of young men with unkempt beards and young women with unshaven legs. More dark-skinned people, too, although not many.

Brewer was careful to avoid eye contact. There was a chance he might meet someone he knew from high school and the idea made him squirm. They might ask why he was there, which would involve a long explanation about how he was attending SPC because his parents forced him to, how he wanted to transfer ~ and on and on. Tedious. Boring. And, besides, he was uncomfortable in general. The bureaucracy of higher education, with its endless labyrinth of forms, questionnaires, signatures, deadlines and the like, grated on him. The fact that he was asking to be accepted to this place was tantamount to begging, which, in his mind, meant he was, by definition, vulnerable - and in an unfamiliar and hostile place.

He knew where Suzzallo Library was. The Administration Building was next door to it.

He found the admin building oppressive, even by UW standards; granite gray with tall, narrow windows, almost a caricature of ominous castles, something Walt Disney would draw for an evil queen. Its most prominent feature was a high, rectangular bell tower. On the top corners of the tower were four spike-like spires, the sorts of things Henry VIII used to display the crania of those who had displeased him.

Or so it all seemed to Brewer. He had to concede he was not in the most receptive of moods at the moment. He wanted to pick up the necessary paperwork, get the hell out of there and that would be that.

Those papers were on a large, battered yellow oak table in the main foyer. Brewer looked through them to make sure he had everything he needed - application for admission, housing request, financial statement - checked other papers to see if he needed anything more, then left. Nobody had seemed to notice he was even there, which suited him just fine.

He felt a palpable sense of relief as he went out the door and into the fresh air. He had taken the first step. He still had to fill out the papers, order copies of his transcripts from SPC and drop the whole collection in the mail. Then he would have to wait. How long until the UW made up its mind? He had no idea. But things would happen, one way or the other, things he had initiated. He was moving into a new future, one where he could finally live his life the way he wanted to.

It would not be idyllic, of course. On the way back to his car, Brewer passed more students. They seemed a distinctly grim-faced lot. College life could be hard and lonely, and at a place like the UW there was no camouflaging it. But Brewer found himself liking the idea. Reality with no predetermined agenda, no sales job, no demands that one conform, conform, conform. Where would it lead?

****

Marilyn Pennell was hurrying down the stairs from the second floor of Peterson, bumping, squeezing past and excusing herself. God, how I wish I was invisible, she thought. If ever there was a time I did not want to be noticed, this was it.

But she had little choice. The bus arrived on Nickerson at 1:10 p.m. Sometimes it was early and she didn't dare miss it. Mr. Wolfstone, the manager at the Northgate Nordstrom's, spent much of his day checking his watch, convinced his staff was chronically late or deliberately skulking; anything to defraud the company out of an honest day's work. She didn't want to get on his S list. Everyone else at the store called it the shit list, but the vulgarism made her uncomfortable, even if she was only thinking it.

She trotted across campus as quickly as decorum would allow. Freshmen coeds with hair-sprayed coifs, nylons and sling-back pumps did not run. It looked tacky. But, again, she had little choice.

She reached the bus stop at 1:07 p.m. and stood there, catching her breath through lips parted as slightly as possible. Bad enough she had to run. To pant like a dog was beyond déclassé.

Déclassé? She smiled wryly. You can take the girl out of the country club, but not the country club out of the girl...

Well, her country club days definitely were behind her now, and they weren't coming back. No use thinking about it now.

The thought was interrupted by the sight of the bus rounding the turn on the hill from the Ballard Bridge. It wheezed and smoked its way to her stop.

Marilyn was the only one waiting. Good. She didn't want to talk about why she was there or where she was going. There was an easy explanation: "I have a job." College students respected that. But she hadn't told anyone she had a job because she would be leaving school in June. Better to disappear quietly, fading from memory over the summer until, by September, most would not remember what she looked like.

Perhaps her fortunes were something out of Dickens; the pure-hearted protagonist done low by a corrupt, pitiless world, cast out to fend for herself on the barren moors of fate. She considered. Well, first of all, you aren't all that pure-hearted, she thought. And unlike the world of Dickens, there will be no kindly aristocrat emerging in the final chapter to save you. Better to go gentle into that good night.

She smiled again. Careful, you're mixing your literary allusions. Sloppy analysis. But then, soon the world of intellectual analysis will be far behind anyway.

Meanwhile, she was still in school and, although the rattles and jolts of a Metro bus did not constitute an ideal environment for study, she was determined to complete the year with the best grades she could manage. In addition, an open book and intent expression was a good way the keep busborne flora and fauna at bay.

Her last class on Monday was Anthropology 203, cultural anthropology. For two weeks, they had been studying the Iroquois Indians of upstate New York and southern Ontario. Among other things, she had learned they called themselves the Haudenosaunee, although even the instructor couldn't pronounce it correctly, so he stuck to Iroquois. Marilyn made a point of memorizing the name anyway. It probably would show up on a test.

The class was studying the Iroquois because they were a matriarchal society, a cultural rarity in which bloodlines were traced and family names passed down through wives and mothers. Women also owned and controlled the real property - corn fields, longhouses and the like - and had the job of appointing clan leaders. They could initiate divorce and often did.

As a woman, Marilyn thought it all sounded quite refreshing. Perhaps a woman's touch would combat the dunderheadedness typical of male-dominated societies.

Then she found the Iroquois were vicious, murdering thugs. Understanding their religion, politics and cultural mentality was difficult at best. Throwing matriarchy into the equation just made the whole business all the more confusing.

Oh, well. She opened the textbook. She had to read with one eye cocked so she wouldn't miss her stop at Third and Stewart. There she would wait on the cold, dirty concrete until the first bus for Northgate arrived. The wait always made her nervous, the specter of Mr. Wolfstone lurking in her mind.

The ride out to Northgate was long and tedious. Marilyn forced herself to read some more. Among other things, Iroquois women often were the chief torturers in the village. They enjoyed it more, were far more ingenious at it and were particularly talented at prolonging the merrymaking – a much admired skill. Their victims always were men, preferably handsome young men. The Iroquois rarely if ever tortured women. Their inherent status in the matriarchal world view made them too prestigious for such frivolity.

Marilyn memorized the words and organized the concepts, etching them on her memory circuits she could successfully regurgitate them on the next test. But try as she may, she could not form any sense of the Iroquois mind. Learning was one thing, understanding was quite another.

The bus reached its stop at east side of Northgate, across the street from an ugly, sprawling parking lot.

Again Marilyn ran – if you wanted to call it that – trotting through the basement of the Northgate Bon Marche, hopping on an escalator and, again, catching her breath through pursed lips so she wouldn't look flustered when she arrived for her shift.

As she walked through the store's main entrance, she checked carefully to see where Mr. Wolfstone was. If she was lucky, he would be far across the room and looking the other way. But not today. As usual, he was in the middle of the sales floor, eying her with a suspicious glare and hiking up his cuff to check his watch.

Some of the other staff had told her to ignore him, he did it to everybody. That is, the ones who talked to her told her that. Most did not talk to her. She was the new girl, the kid, the lowest of the low on the pecking order.

It was an interesting pecking order. Mr. Wolfstone was at the top, of course. His main job was to walk the floor, alternately glowering at his staff like Cotton Mather or toadying to customers like a puppy dog.

Every Saturday morning, he presided over the weekly staff meeting, which consisted of reports on last week's sales, updates on incoming stock and the like, followed by a few words from his assistant managers. There were two. Mr. Stenslund was a sullen, expressionless man who rarely spoke because, apparently, completing an intelligible English sentence was a challenge he had not yet mastered. How he was ever promoted to management was a subject of much speculation among the staff. Mr. Stenslund's usual contribution to the staff meeting was to declare, once a week, "ththgrmbslgnpldyshldi." Translation: "The stock room is looking pretty shoddy." At least, that's what Marilyn thought it meant. She wasn't sure. No one was sure.

The second assistant manager was Mr. Thorndyke, who ran the men's shoe department.

Mr. Thorndyke had been at it twenty years and had seen it all. Everyone knew this because Mr. Thorndyke reminded them frequently throughout the day.

Mr. Thorndyke's contribution to the Saturday staff meeting was the weekly motivational presentation. Marilyn's favorite was when Mr. Thorndyke told the assembled a great way to start the morning was to stand in a corner, put your hands on your knees, shake your head and go, "Blblblblblblblbblblbl, I'mmmm enthusiastic! Blblblblblblblbblblbl, I'mmmm enthusiastic!" It was optimal to do it three times, he assured them. No one laughed, or even showed signs of suppressing a grin. The store pecking order was iron.

Then it was on to work. Marilyn's job, the cashier desk, was to box the shoes the salesmen had just sold, ring up the sale, place box and receipt in a big bag and seal it with a taped handle. She had learned to do it neatly and fast, too fast to suit the full-time cashier, one Lena St. Germain.

Lena St. Germain was an older woman, well into her forties, and she looked even older thanks to over-tanned skin and hair bleached nearly white. However, she had a stunning physique for a woman of any age, with bulging breasts and jutting rear end she emphasized by wearing the tightest clothes she could squeeze into.

She smoked seemingly all the time, giving her voice a throaty growl which would be attractive if she spoke in a civil tone. She rarely did.

"You're finally here, huh?" Lena grunted as Marilyn began wrapping a pair of newly-sold shoes in tissue paper.

Lena lit another Virginia Slim. She too was in the process of ringing up a sale, but she did it with deliberate languor, all the while a disdainful sneer creasing her once pretty face. The doings of menials like Marilyn were beneath her dignity. Such was a privilege bestowed upon her for being an Old Hand, a place on the pecking order just below assistant manager. This afternoon, she was being particularly sluggish.

"A customer is waiting," a young salesman said, tapping his foot impatiently. Lena did not look up from her torpor.

"Things are tough all over, honey," she sighed, turning her head to hiss a long cloud of smoke with well-honed contempt. It was one of her favorite responses.

Marilyn did her best to ignore Lena. The salesmen did not. Marilyn would watch them try to make nice to Lena of the tight blouse and short, short skirts and promise of dark eroticism. For her part, Lena enjoyed excoriating the salesmen's manhood. She had developed venom into a fine art, always ready with a sneer, a turned shoulder, a practiced grunt of disgust.

The salesmen kept trying anyway. Male hope sprang eternal, Marilyn knew, but wasn't there a line between hope and absurdity? If there was, the young men didn't seem to know it.

And young they were; most under twenty five; many of them college drop outs, all in a great rush all of the time, hustling from floor to stock room at a near run. Once in the stock room, they rushed aisle to aisle, throwing out goddamns and fucks and shits to no one in particular, especially when a size or style they needed wasn't there. Then, with three boxes under their arms – a required company policy – they were back on the floor, all smiles and fawning for the women waiting in the comfortable chairs.

The women rarely smiled. After observing them for a while, Marilyn noticed some common themes. The women were not at all inhibited about reciting their personal problems loudly and in public. Sore feet, hot days, fading looks, husbands not sufficiently sensitive to one's moods: All were acceptable cause for taking out one's unhappiness on people who couldn't fight back, particularly if they were male, particularly if they were young and particularly if they were trying to sell shoes.

Marilyn wondered: Was the torturing of young men a cultural animus, as with the Iroquois? Or was it simply human nature? Young men were the ones sent off to die in wars or to work at especially dangerous jobs and no one seemed to find anything wrong with it, including the young men.

Marilyn looked out onto the sales floor. A stringy, sour-visaged woman had just thrown a shoe in a salesman's face in righteous outrage. Another had her blubbery hand on the back of her four-year-old boy's head, grinding his face into a mirror and shouting, "See the bad boy?! See the bad boy?!"

Still another, a young woman with bulging, watery eyes, a receding chin and a distinctly vacant expression was whining loudly about the selection the salesman had proffered for her discernment. Marilyn counted fourteen opened boxes surrounding the young woman's feet. The salesman kept trying. Mr. Wolfstone was watching.

It made Marilyn ashamed of her gender. All the clichés about girls as cute flirty little coquettes with an inherent right to caprice rang sour when she saw the reality of foolishness, weakness and thinly veiled cruelty. The women customers seemed to expect a perfect world - smaller feet, perfect fit, styles suited exactly to their whim of the moment - and it was up to someone else to provide it. The women themselves did not even have to articulate their wants and needs. That was up to someone else, too.

Marilyn decided she was lucky. Work at the cashier's desk might be tedious and repetitive but, Lena aside, she generally wasn't on the receiving end of the lower malignities of human nature.

It was all such a contradiction. The more Marilyn wrapped and boxed the shoes themselves, the more they impressed her: Their graceful lines, their workmanship, the scent and feel of new leather. They were fine things. And the store was lovely, with tastefully coordinated carpets and wallpaper, carefully-arranged displays of shoes; all of it bright and inviting.

But then there was the reality, where appreciation of beauty and good taste was secondary - if rated at all - to tawdry narcissism and hustle, hustle, hustle.

So on this, as on many nights and Saturdays, Marilyn did her job quietly and efficiently, smiling at her coworkers from time-to-time ~ out of politeness, if not to make friends ~ and good-naturedly fending off the occasional expression of interest from the salesmen. Male hope sprang eternal. . .

When her shift finally ended, it was back on the bus for the long ride downtown, then the transfer on Stewart Street - a particularly unpleasant wait after the late shift when she got off at nine thirty - then another long ride out to SPC, where she faced an hour or two of weary study before falling asleep, often at her desk in the clothes she was wearing. She did not dream.

****

Paul Trimble was worn out and he couldn't ignore it anymore. He had been cloistered in his windowless office for ten hours straight, with no let-ups save bathroom breaks. The accumulated dust, stale air and fluorescent light had mummified his skin to sticky parchment and glazed his eyeballs with something that felt like dried-on soy sauce. He needed light. He needed air. He needed to feel the world beyond his small, small corner of it.

There was no one left in the office when he left. All the better, he thought. He did not feel like bidding cheerful good byes. He did not feel cheerful - or pleasant or even civil. Mostly, he felt dirty, inside and out. He was fed up with his life.

Outside, the evening air was soft and clean and new. He inhaled deeply and exhaled hard to clear the crud from his lungs. Then he did it again. He could feel the difference. He wanted to watch the sunset. From where? He thought. He wondered about the view from the Aurora Bridge. Quite a Bridge: About a half-mile long and 167 feet above the Lake Washington Ship Canal at mid span.

Trimble had driven over it a number of times, but with traffic chronically bad and the bridge chronically narrow, he couldn't risk turning his head east or west. With nothing to block the view, the sunset, from 167 feet straight up, should be interesting. He was curious. Well, why not. Let's go take a look.

Trimble drove to Fremont and parked his car on North 41st Street just east of Linden Avenue. He climbed the steps of the old concrete pedestrian overpass on Aurora Avenue. He had always liked that overpass; a humble thing, old by Seattle standards. It was supposed to keep kids safe on their way to school. How many kids had walked over it, he wondered; small people, with their little coats and lunchboxes, their parents' adored ones, back and forth, back and forth to rooms with tall windows and children's crayon drawings on bulletin boards, drawings made with small hands, earnest and innocent.

He stopped at the middle of the overpass and watched the traffic streaming north on Aurora Avenue from downtown; a plasma of machines, some red, some black, some beige, moving almost as one, almost as a singular living organism. Trimble took it in for a full five minutes; the slipstreams and noise buffeting him, cleansing him.

He went back the way he came, then down the stairs and started his walk toward the Aurora Bridge.

It was not easy. Trimble had to hop over a series of curbs and concrete dividers at the 39th Street entrance, all the while keeping a careful eye out for cars that could not see him until it was too late. Once on the bridge, he found the walkway quite narrow. Fortunately, it was raised a couple of feet above the roadbed, offering some safety. The cars continued to stream by, close now, but he didn't notice them anymore. Funny how quickly you can get used to a thing, he thought.

The northwest shore of Lake Union, and with it the entrance to the ship canal, was surrounded by steep hills, nearly cliffs. You wouldn't notice them so much from the ground, but from up here, with an occasional building jutting out like a villa along the Mediterranean or a castle in the Alps, it all looked like something from a *National Geographic* pictorial. Trimble felt better with each step.

At mid-span, he stopped. The ship canal stretched on to the west, broadening at Fisherman's terminal, broadening more at Salmon Bay and then finally forming a flat, meandering delta at Shilshole Bay. It shown metallic in the evening light, a river of mercury and ink as it spread into Puget Sound and then disappeared into the sunset blackened foothills of the Olympic Mountains. The mountains themselves were blue now, a tenuous Prussian blue silhouetted against the neon fuchsia and orange bands of the sunset. No clouds tonight, just light wisps of rapidly cooling air; a world of shimmers and shadows, of light shifting minute by minute, of colors now bright, now muted; all so very subtle yet so very grand.

God, how I love Seattle, Trimble thought; the shape of it, with its dark hills inexorably blending into the water, all melding together without plan. Nature did not use straight lines or right angles. This part of Seattle he particularly liked; workshops and piers and docks studded with fishing boats, a place of rough hands and dark ropes and oil and fish stink, a place of pushing and pulling and muscle and sweat, all of it on the water, the deep, clean water, the dark jade that drew people to this place a hundred years ago.

He drank in the elusive qualities of the evening light and basked in the hint of sea air wafting in from the west. Too bad Carl Sandburg never saw it, for here too was a place of broad shoulders – and faces lined by the sun and work clothes stained with the grime of toil, and muscles sore from a day of hard work, day after day, year after year, generation after generation as the people who lived in the humble wooden houses on the ordinary streets that led to the canal and the bays played out their hopes and joys and griefs and loves; the stuff of the world, the stuff you could smell and feel.

He thought again of children on their morning walks to school, so small, so earnest, so wondrous. He wanted to fill his mind with good things, as many good things as he could. And he did.

I think I'll miss Black and White Scotch whisky the most, he thought; that first magical sip of it. Then he put his hands on the bridge's railing, hoisted himself up and jumped.

Chapter 33

Chester Dalrymple was sifting through his morning mail. Dalrymple's secretary was supposed to sort his mail, but she was out with the flu ~ or so she said. The hired help is always trying to shirk an honest day's work, Dalrymple thought irritably. That's why they're the hired help, as opposed to a member of the president's cabinet.

Chester Dalrymple did not like to read. So, as mornings go, this one definitely had started on a sour note.

Then Skip Reinhardt came in unannounced.

"Well, Chet, looks like good old Whatshisname, over in publications, really did it this time." Reinhardt said, his lower lip protruding in a caricature of smugness. It was an expression he practiced in the mirror twice a week.

Dalrymple had no idea what Reinhardt was talking about, other than he was denigrating another member of the staff, something he did on and off all the time. It was his right as a tough, no-nonsense businessman and distinguished community leader. Dalrymple's mind was still flummoxed over having to read. He stared blankly at Reinhardt's supercilious simper.

"Yessir, old dumdum definitely screwed the pooch," Reinhardt said, clucking his tongue loudly. He waited for Dalrymple to respond. The wait stretched on, with Dalrymple's expression becoming more vacant all the time, like a lemur watching a Three Stooges movie. The envelope in his hand stayed there, half-opened.

Sensing that his supervisor may need counsel, Reinhardt finally said, "Trimble. He jumped the Aurora Bridge last night."

"Who?" Dalrymple said.

"Trimble."

Trimble? Innocuous. Easily manipulated. Unimportant. Why should I care about anything he does? Dalrymple thought.

Wait a minute.

"What about him?" Dalrymple said.

"He's dead," Reinhardt said.
"Dead? What do you mean, dead?"
"He died."

Dalrymple continued to gawk uncomprehendingly, his mouth ajar. Finally, he said, "Wait. What about last night?"

"Trimble died last night. He jumped off the Aurora Bridge."

Dalrymple finally got it. He slapped the envelope down on his desk in exasperation.

"Why wasn't I told about this?!" he said, his voice rising. "My staff is supposed to keep me abreast of these things!"

"Yeah, it's getting harder and harder to find good help these days," Reinhardt said ruefully. "Back in my day, I would have fired the lot of them. I remember this one time when one of the secretaries starting taking extended coffee breaks. . ."

"He jumped off the Aurora Bridge?" Dalrymple said.

"They found him floating under a dock on Westlake about two hours ago," Reinhardt said. "A reporter from the P-I called."

Dalrymple barely heard him. His mind was on the publications schedule. Only Trimble really understood it; what was completed, what needed to be done, when things were due to and from the printer. Someone would have to straighten it all out. That someone might end up being Chester Dalrymple. Damn Trimble, damn him for doing this to me . . .

Then he remembered.

"A reporter?" he said.

"From the P-I," Reinhardt said. "I told him we would call him back."

Another confounded problem to deal with. Dalrymple was hoping for his typical daily routine. Why would a reporter care about Paul Trimble? He looked up at Reinhardt, spread his palms and shook his head in aggravation.

Who would call the reporter back? Reinhardt? He would simply refuse, secure in the knowledge that, with his Rotary memberships and Kiwanis memberships and Lions memberships and Chamber of Commerce memberships and. . . well, the list went on for quite a while; a curriculum vitae of Babbitry that effectively safeguarded him from the petty scutwork of ordinary menials.

Dalrymple quickly went down his staff list. None could be relied upon to dodge questions and mouth vacuous platitudes effectively. That left him

"And the president wants to see you," Reinhardt said.

Dalrymple cringed. It was the stuff of his worst nightmares.

As he climbed the steps to the third floor, Dalrymple considered his options. Maybe he should disavow Trimble. He would say Trimble was a problem employee, that they were getting ready to fire him. Maybe even say they already had fired him.

No, that might sound like he jumped because he got fired. Think, think . . .

Maybe paint him as a deeply troubled young man. We all tried to help him, oh how we tried, but we couldn't seem to reach him. No, that wasn't good, either. SPC was a college, after all; full of people with degrees in psychology. And we have a counseling center . . . Or do we? Dalrymple wondered. He had never heard of one. The fact the college did not would not play well in the papers. And the alumni? The SPC of their rose-colored memories did not employ "troubled young men." In a proper environment, no one was troubled.

When Dalrymple reached for the door at the top of the stairwell, a phrase passed through his mind, a rare phrase, rather out of date, but somehow perfect for the moment: "A prince of a fellow." Yes that was it. Trimble would be a prince of a fellow: Bright, cheerful, with impeccable manners; the sort who would lend a helping hand without being asked and never ask anything in return. Trustworthy, loyal, friendly, courteous . . . beloved by all, a young man with a bright future ahead of him. Such a tragedy. If only there had been some sign, if only we could have helped.

And here's the kicker, Dalrymple thought, the beautiful, perfect kicker: "There's a lesson in this for us all." Even the brightest and the best of us can have hidden pain, hidden suffering. But there is hope, hope in God and in his son, Jesus Christ! Yes, that would work. It always did. You could turn almost anything into a sermon lesson and people would believe it. It was, after all, what they wanted to believe in the first place.

Dalrymple checked himself. Concentrate, concentrate. You have to see the president. Have your spiel ready. Say it over and over in your head so when you say it out loud, it will sound spontaneous and natural.

Elva Shrofe was the president's secretary. A nervous woman with a nearsighted squint and perpetually pursed lips, she guarded the door to his office like a sentry at Fort Knox. No one got to see Dr. Donald A. Fotheringham, Ph.D., unless they had a darned good reason, and even then Elva would inspect them suspiciously as they passed through the hallowed portal.

On this particular morning, however, she barely gave Chester Dalrymple a nod. That's when Dalrymple knew he was in real trouble.

The office of Dr. Donald A. Fotheringham, Ph.D., was a shrine to status. The seal of the college was displayed in a velvet-lined box in a glass case on an altar near the door. Behind it, on the wall, hung the school's original charter, handwritten on properly-yellowed parchment. A few old photographs – graduating classes of young women in shirt-waists and young men with their hair parted in the middle – added to the sense of weighty heritage.

Fotheringham's own credentials, his various diplomas, were framed in polished rosewood and fastidiously matted in the appropriate school colors: Blue with tasteful orange piping for Wheaton, purple for Northwestern and, of course, crimson for Harvard. Harvard's was written in Latin, just to remind everyone how important it was. In all, the display did a first rate job of certifying Dr. Donald A. Fotheringham Ph.D.'s divine right of caste entitlement while carefully cloaking it in the trappings of meritocracy.

At the moment, Dr. Donald A. Fotheringham, Ph.D. was, as he often was, staring out the window, his hands clasped behind his back, deep in thought.

"Chet, close the door," Fotheringham said with practiced solemnity. "And have a chair."

The chair, a plain straight-back, was in distinct contrast to the president's Circassian walnut desk; the biggest desk on campus, a desk with no in-box or out-box, no souvenirs or other accouterments, only a photograph of his wife and two children – another polished rosewood frame – a pen set and a telephone. Lesser humans else took care of the petty details in the life of Dr. Donald A. Fotheringham, Ph.D.

Fotheringham turned around. His jaw was set, his face was grim.

"I suppose you've heard about this business with Trimble," he said icily.

"Yes."

"How did it happen?"

"We don't really have the details yet, but . . ."

"That's not what I meant," Fotheringham said, his voice deep with affected, theatrical menace. He let the moment sink in.

"Nothing like this has ever happened here before," Fotheringham went on. "I have to speak at the Chamber of Commerce today. What am I going to tell them? Have you thought of that?"

Fotheringham was glowering at Dalrymple with the best glare he could manage. But it was forced, almost an act. Dalrymple had seen it before; the expression of weak men trying to act tough. It was his cue.

"He was a prince of a fellow," Dalrymple said, doing his best to sound like a man bereaved. "So bright, so friendly; the sort who lend a helping hand without being asked and never ask anything in return. Everybody loved him. He had such a bright future. Such a tragedy. If only we had some kind of sign."

Fotheringham relaxed ever so slightly.

"If it were me," Dalrymple said, "That's what I would tell the chamber; that there's a lesson in this for us all, that even the best among us can have hidden pain, hidden suffering. But I like to think there is hope, there is always hope, through Christian faith."

Dalrymple was going to say "hope in God and in his son, Jesus Christ" but it sounded a bit too obvious, the sort of thing that freshmen YFC twits were prone to babble at inappropriate moments. In any case, it was the best spiel Dalrymple had. He waited to see how it took.

It took.

"Yes, yes, a tragedy," Fotheringham said, looking off into the distance and stroking his chin. "A prince of a fellow, a prince of a fellow . . . Did he belong to any church groups or volunteer organizations?"

"We're still checking on that," Dalrymple said, suddenly realizing he knew next to nothing about Trimble; where he lived, where his family lived, what church he went to – if indeed Trimble went to church at all. Dalrymple could not even remember the sound of his voice. There was no reason he should.

"Hmmm, yes, yes . . ." Fotheringham said contemplatively. "Well, let me know what you find out." Then his voice hardened again. "I'm still holding you responsible."

Dalrymple took that as a signal to leave. As he went down the stairs, he felt his chest untighten. True, the president was still angry with him, but he was a lot less angry than he was ten minutes ago. With a little luck, his anger would be gone after he used A Prince of a Fellow on the Chamber of Commerce. So things were off to a reasonably good start.

Now, what to do about the publications schedule. Well, blame it on Trimble, of course. ("Such a prince of a fellow, but well, heh-heh, a little disorganized. You know how it is . . .") But the actual writing, photographing, printing and mailing? Dalrymple would have to find a way to dump it on someone. But who? He wracked his brain. When he reached the second floor, he remembered. There was that lummox, the ex-basketball star. They'd given him a job as a resident assistant in Moyer, as a reward for a 16.4 ppg average. What was his name anyway? No matter. He had been hinting he wanted Trimble's job. Considered himself quite the wordsmith. The fact he had no experience beyond writing term papers didn't matter. He was a former big man on campus and the job is his just due. Fine, fine, Dalrymple thought. Hiring him will ingratiate me to the toadying rabble. If he complains about the mess I dump on him, I'll give him the usual speech about how he's a professional now, about how managers work with what's given them, about that's The Way Things Are In The Real World. They always fall for that.

By the time he got to his office, Chester Dalrymple was feeling better about life. He might make it to that afternoon golf game after all.

****

Later that same morning, Layton Fleming set out to nail Brewer.

He could, of course, merely expel the two-bit little wise-ass. School policies gave him the power to do so, no evidence necessary. But Brewer was friends with Parris and McLean. They would put it in the Falcon and that would generate all the kinds of publicity Fleming didn't want.

He also thought about using Sarah Gray: Threaten to tell her father, begin formal disciplinary hearings against her, that sort of thing; all with the goal of making her go to Brewer and beg him into leaving school. Fleming relished the scene in his mind. But, pragmatically, it involved a lot of uncertainty and a lot of time. Sigh. It would have been such fun. Maybe later. Meanwhile, he could add it to Brewer's file. One more straw on the camel's back.

Ultimately, Fleming decided on going through the proper channels. That meant finding out for certain that Brewer had an apartment. That and the fact Brewer was forcing acts of unspeakable filth on innocent, unblemished young maidens in his den of depravity - "Who knows what else his sick mind can conceive!" - should do it. Brewer also was known to frequent pool halls, just in case Fleming needed more. And, of course, there were those libels in The Falcon. The accumulated dossier made Layton Fleming feel very much a man walking in righteousness.

The proper channels first meant calling Brewer's parents. Fleming assigned that task to Agnes Carswell. She had done it before. The school regularly called the homes of off-campus students on a random basis to make sure they lived where they said they lived.

When Agnes called, a deep male voice answered the phone.

"Is this the Brewer residence?" Carswell said.

"Yes," Orrin Brewer said. Probably a salesman of some kind, he thought. He would listen through the first sentence, say, "No thanks." and hit the receiver button before the salesman could say another word.

"This is Mrs. Carswell from the Dean of Students office at Seattle Pacific."

"Yes?"

"Mr. Brewer, we are checking our records as part of an ongoing auditing process and according to the information in our files, your son Thomas says his home is at 6475 52nd Avenue Northeast. Is that correct?"

She thinks I'm Dad, Orrin thought. His instincts told him something about this call wasn't quite right. So let her think I'm Dad. This could be interesting.

"Yes." Orrin said. Again the monotone.

"And is he living there now?"

Why the hell do you care, Orrin wondered. Then he remembered what Tom had told him about SPC, that is was a tightassed place, oddly obsessed with its students' private lives. Tom found it all rather amusing. But the unusual tone of Carswell's voice, the hint of fear beneath the practiced officialese, told Orrin something serious might be involved.

"Yes," Orrin said.

"With you and his mother?" Carswell said.

Orrin smiled. He wasn't responsible for the wording of her questions.

"Yes."

"And he has lived there, ever since fall quarter?"

"Yes."

There was a pause. Orrin sensed that the prissy-sounding woman at the other end of the line was wracking her brain for more questions. Fine. He would continue to respond in monosyllabic grunts.

Then, for a moment, a tide of anger rose in Orrin Brewer.

Leave My Brother <u>Alone!</u>

Whoa, keep calm, keep calm, a wiser voice said. Silence is the best tactic.

"Well, that's about it," Carswell finally said. "Thank you for your time."

"You're welcome." Orrin's finger hit the receiver button before Carswell could speak again.

He had no idea what the college was up to; probably nothing, probably just routine. But he was still suspicious. He would tell Tom the next time he saw him.

Back at the dean's office, Carswell reported the conversation to Fleming. Fleming was displeased.

What now? Fleming huffed and gently clapped his hands together under his chin. Time for another official channel. He ordered Agnes Carswell to type up a letter ordering Brewer to appear before the Dean of Students on a disciplinary matter. Put it in writing on official letterhead. That should do it.

****

Jeff Killeen was one of Fleming's assistant deans. He was a former shortstop on the baseball team, served as senior class vice president and generally fit the model of the all-around nice guy/achiever/conformist that Fleming liked to hire as assistant deans. They could be depended on to do what they were told and not think too much. They usually lasted two years, sometimes three. Killeen was in his first year and, therefore, still properly obedient.

When Fleming told him about his special assignment, parking his car in the lot at the Canal View apartments and watching for Tom Brewer, Killeen was confused. What in the world was the purpose of that? he wondered. Fleming told him that Brewer might be involved in illegal drugs. Killeen didn't believe it. Despite Fleming's impression of him as Mr. Clean, Killeen knew the realities of life at SPC - who used booze, where girls went to get birth control pills, who bought and sold term papers and the like. Drugs? A few people talked about smoking pot, mostly Free Methodist preachers' kids trying to show how rebellious they were. Killeen doubted many of them actually did it. In any case, Brewer was not part of their peer group. Even if he was, Killeen didn't care. Live and let live.

On the other hand, an assignment was an assignment and Killeen tried to be conscientious at whatever job he was given. So, on Wednesday afternoon, he parked his car within sight of apartment 204 and settled down for the work of surveillance. He surveilled for two hours. No sign of Brewer. He surveilled for three hours. No sign of Brewer. When the hands on his watch hit 6 o'clock, Killeen had enough. Screw this, he thought. I didn't sweat four years of college to sit around in a parking lot and get a sore ass. I'm going home.

The next day, he reported to Fleming he had seen no sign of Brewer. Fleming ordered him back for more surveillance. Killeen nodded obediently and then drove off to see a movie.

The next day he did the same. And the next day after that. He was becoming quite the film buff.

"Hmmm. Maybe we should ask the landlord if he lives there," Fleming said.

Sure, you bet, like hell I will, Killeen thought. But he kept his obedient expression intact. Then he went to see another movie.

When Killeen reported back that the landlord refused to give out the names of tenants, Fleming was visibly annoyed.

"Okay then," he growled in frustration. "Go back and check the mail boxes."

Enough, Killeen thought.

"Can't," he said.

Fleming started. Nobody said no to him.

"What?" he said in surprise as much as anger.

"Tampering with the mail is a federal offense," Killeen said.

Fleming looked flustered.

"Jeff, Jeff," he said condescendingly, "You're being melodramatic. I'm not asking you to tamper with anything. Just kind of, like, look at it, you know?"

"It goes in locked boxes," Killeen said. "How am I going to look it over without tampering with it?"

"Oh, I'm sure you'll come up with something," Fleming said breezily. "That's why I hired you!" He waved Killeen out of his office.

As Killeen walked back to his cubicle, he analyzed his conversation with Fleming. It didn't take long.

I'll do it in July, he thought. Not much happening on campus then. Hardly anyone will notice. And it will give them to September to find somebody else. No point in burning bridges if I don't have to. I can work at my dad's hardware store while I look for something else.

College life had been fun while it lasted, but I let it last a little too long.

****

Sometimes God is kind.

Grace Hollebeck had been at SPC for sixteen years, thirteen of them as Registrar, the person in charge of student records.

She was born Grace Schuman in Cottonwood Falls, Kansas, the daughter of the local farm implements dealer. As a child she often accompanied her father on his trips to deliver machines to farmers or to help repair the ones he had sold them. He never charged for such repair work, or even thought to. He simply considered it part of his responsibilities to his neighbors.

Grace saw calves born, hogs butchered and various species of livestock copulating on a more or less daily basis and, by age eight, had reached a stage of life where very little, if anything, shocked her.

Meanwhile, she had learned from her father the importance of forthrightness, honesty and that a person's word was her bond. Her father did not teach these lessons through instruction, but through his own unwavering, good-natured example.

The lessons took. By the time she was eighteen, Grace faced the world calmly, head-on and without fear.

Came time for college. Grace went to Kansas State Teachers College in nearby Emporia where, after her freshman year, she decided she had no interest in teaching. So she enrolled in the business school, where she majored in organizational management with a minor in accounting. At the end of her sophomore year, she spent the summer managing the office at her father's dealership. Within a month Grace had it running like the proverbial well-oiled machine. All orders and bills were processed the day they arrived and all invoices, receipts, delivery slips, tax records, repair orders and payroll files were organized in a system so flawless that any document could be retrieved in less than two minutes.

Grace Schuman had found her calling.

However, she wanted more out of life than could be found in Cottonwood Falls, Kansas, so when at a dance she met a handsome young flight instructor from the Naval Air Station in Olathe, she was distinctly interested.

So was he.

Grace Schuman received her Bachelor of Arts degree in business, with honors, on June 8, 1944. On June 12, 1944, she became the wife of Lieutenant (junior grade) Robert Andrew Hollebeck.

A few weeks later, Lieutenant (junior grade) Hollebeck was transferred to Naval Air Station, Seattle, where Grace got a job in administrative record keeping.

Her efficiency and ingenuity impressed her superiors and within six months she was in charge of the entire section.

Then the war ended.

Grace was not the least bit surprised when she couldn't find a comparable job in private business. Women just didn't. It did not make her angry. It did not make her resentful. It's simply the way things were.

Grace was one of those rare human beings who had no illusions. What is is, she liked to say and she based her view of the world on what she experienced and what she observed. She knew what she knew and was confident in that knowledge with steady, farm girl common sense.

In short, she knew bullshit when she saw it, and no amount of slick talk or convincing appearances could fool her into thinking it was anything else.

Grace's skills and attitude served her well at SPC, where she got a job in the Registrar's office and, within three years, worked her way up to director. There was much bullshit at SPC, but Grace didn't particularly care. She had a job to do, she did it, and that was that.

Then came Layton Fleming. It was dislike at first sight. Fleming was loud, flashy and obnoxious. In Grace's experience, such characteristics were more than surface traits. They usually betrayed inherent character flaws, foremost among them dishonesty and conceit.

As a result, she scrupulously ignored Layton Fleming. If there was a faculty luncheon, Grace made sure she took a table as far from Fleming as possible. If by chance they actually ran into each other, Grace was excruciatingly correct, with such icily perfect conversational etiquette that Fleming usually retreated as soon as he could.

So, when Agnes Carswell called on behalf of Layton Fleming, Dean of Students, asking for the class schedule of one freshman Tom Brewer, Grace Hollebeck knew what to say.

"No."

Sometimes God is kind.

****

"What?!" Layton Fleming roared.

"That's what Mrs. Hollebeck said," Agnes whimpered quiveringly. "Such records are private unless there is a family emergency. It's department policy."

"Like fun it is!" Fleming grabbed the telephone, took a deep breath to calm himself and then dialed the Registrar's office.

"Grace Hollebeck, please."

"This is she."

"Grace, this is Layton Fleming."

"Good afternoon, Mr. Fleming. How may we be of service?"

"I have a problem and I need your help." Fleming said it with a mixture of fatigue and sincerity he had developed through devoted practice.

"And what might this problem be?" Grace's voice would have done Emily Post proud.

"We need to find one of our students, a freshman named Tom Brewer."

"Is he lost?"

"Oh, no, nothing like that. He's just gotten himself into a little bit of trouble; nothing serious, but we want to call him in for a some counseling, see if we can help."

"How very considerate."

"If we could get a look at his class schedule, it would be a great help."

"Oh, how unfortunate," Grace said. "You see, such records are private unless there is a family emergency."

"But. . ."

"I'm so sorry we could not be of more assistance, Mr. Fleming. Good day."

Click.

Fleming glared into the receiver. Mentally flailing in a turbid glycerol of chagrin and frustration, he began dialing the president's office. When he reached the fourth number, he stopped. Even in the heat of rage, Layton Fleming's logical mind told him to take a moment and consider the consequences. Dr. Donald A. Fotheringham, Ph.D., did not like to be bothered with the trivialities of underlings. More importantly, complaining about Grace Hollebeck, a long time and well-liked campus fixture, might make Fleming look like a rocker of institutional boats. Worse, she was a woman. It would make him look weak.

Fleming cursed under his breath and waited for his blood pressure to subside. Finally, he pushed the button on the intercom.

"Agnes, send Killeen to my office."

Fleming was still puffing a little when Jeff Killeen came through the door. Killeen sat down without being bidden, a breach of hierarchical protocol. Fleming noticed but decided to let it pass.

"Jeff, we have to do something about this clown Brewer," Fleming said. "You dropped the ball the first time around, but I want to give you a second chance. Go find him and tell him to get his trouble-making butt to this office immediately."

"How shall I find him?" Killeen asked. "I never did see him at his apartment."

"Well, you know what he looks like. Keep an eye out for him around campus," Fleming said.

Actually, Killeen had no idea what Brewer looked like.

"Seems a little hit and miss," Killeen said.

"Hmmm, yes, yes." Fleming's brow furrowed in thought. "I know: He has to go to chapel. Try waiting for him there."

"Sure thing!" Killeen said brightly and left Fleming's office with the best imitation of a jaunty step he could muster.

Killeen was glad for the assignment. When the bell rang for chapel each morning, he drove over to the Copper Clock Café on Northlake Way. There, he drank coffee, watched the passing parade and flirted with an aggressively-chested fortysomething waitress named Mavis. They were developing quite the relationship. After an hour or so, he drove back to campus, walked in front of McKinley so he would be seen and then returned to his office, where he spent the rest of the day shuffling official paper.

Fleming asked if he had spotted Brewer.

"Not yet," Killeen said. "Maybe he's slipping out the back way or something."

"Well, you'd better start patrolling there," Fleming said. "Say, have you thought about grabbing him while they are taking their seats?"

"I have," Killeen said. "But it might create a scene. Bad for the image."

"Hmmm, yes, yes, of course," Fleming said in the tones of a great commander contemplating global strategy. Killeen struggled to keep from smiling.

"Well, keep up the surveillance," Fleming said. "Something's bound to break."

Yeah, Killeen thought, with a little luck I'll break into Mavis, so to speak. And I'll be doing it on SPC's dime. A career in academia has so many supplemental benefits.

Chapter 34

Brewer was in the SUB, enjoying his Friday afternoon coffee. It was a ritual he observed once a week. Classes were over, a whole evening with nothing to do, no worries until Monday, one week closer to surviving the quarter. He gazed out the window, casually watching students strolling by the Loop in the slanting sunlight. Life seemed breezy and serene.

Nancy Siegleman sat down.

"Good afternoon," Brewer said jovially.

Nancy managed a tight smile, but no more.

"Tom. . ." she said. She stopped to collect her thoughts.

"Tom, I have something to tell you."

She took a long breath, started to speak, then stopped again. She fidgeted. Finally, she said, "Oh, to heck with it. Look, you've got trouble. Jeff Killeen told me."

"Who?"

"One of the assistant dean of students. He's a good guy, actually."

"Never heard of him," Brewer said.

Nancy shook her head.

"No, no, that doesn't matter. Just listen, okay? This girl named Thelma Jaeger went to Hazel Rexler, who went to Chester Dalrymple who sent a note to Fleming. . ."

"Who are these people? I don't know any of them."

Nancy shook her head again.

"This dingbat, this idiot named Terry Garstang, said she saw Sarah Gray coming out of an apartment on Nickerson one night. Blabbed all about it at breakfast. I don't know how many people heard her.

"Anyway, she saw Sarah kiss some guy before she walked back to campus. When Thelma heard about it, she decided to do something. She's one of those Free Methodist idiots who believes it's her sacred duty to tell other people how to live their lives. And I hear she has a grudge of some kind against Sarah. Anyway, she told

Rexler, that old bat they have as house mother in Hill. Eventually the word got back to Fleming. Fleming called Sarah in and gave her the third degree."

Nancy stopped and stared at the ceiling in embarrassment for a moment.

"She said the guy was you."

Brewer felt a tinge of fear. But he also was a bit baffled.

"She's a professor's daughter and you have an off-campus apartment," Nancy continued. "They won't tolerate that kind of thing."

Brewer was irritated. "Kind of thing? What kind of thing? I'm not the only guy on campus who fu. . . uh, who hooks up with the opposite sex."

"There's more to it," Nancy said. "There's the interview with Fleming."

"What about it? Everything that went in the paper was true, word for word."

"That doesn't matter! You questioned authority."

"We didn't question it very much," Brewer said. "And he didn't say anything particularly interesting."

"Like I said, it doesn't matter. Then there's the pool tables."

Brewer knew the pool tables had caused a stir, but it was a minor one at best and it didn't last long. Most people laughed it off.

"Wait a minute," Brewer said. "I only suggested them. The student council approved the idea – the student council as in you."

Nancy's face drooped in an expression of weary resignation.

"Yes we did," she sighed. "But we're all seniors. Or YFC members. Or we have rich parents. Get the picture? And even if the administration did come after us, it would end up in The Falcon, and they don't want that.

"Meanwhile, the idea of pool tables in their pious little world has the alumni upset."

"Why?" Brewer said.

"I dunno. Ninety nine percent of them don't know about it and don't care. The one percent who do are like Thelma Jaeger: Bigoted and vindictive. You have to understand: These people never give up. In a way, you can't blame the administration for being afraid of them."

Nancy took another long breath.

"So, Fleming is out to get you," she said. "'I thought you'd want to know."

Brewer tried to take it all in.

"But I haven't done anything, at least nothing important," he said. "*I'm* not important. I'm not a rebel. I just want to be left alone."

"Maybe they respect that somewhere else, but not here," Nancy said.

"Good grief," Brewer said. "Don't these people have better things to do with their lives than fixate on me?"

"No, they don't," Nancy said. "Look, SPC is a world onto itself. The people who run it, the power structure, have a vision of it. We're all supposed to be bright Little Mary Sunshines skipping around campus, adoring our professors, worshipping our administrators, cheerfully dedicating ourselves to Christian service – and all that hogwash."

"But it isn't like that at all," Brewer said. "I'm only a freshman and even I can see that."

"They probably see it too. They just don't want to believe it. If the place is imperfect, then they are imperfect. And they sure as heck aren't about to admit that."

"How do you know all this?" Brewer said. Despite the seriousness of his predicament, Nancy's words made him curious. There was something else here, something beyond just him.

"It took me a while." She said. "I kind of suspected it all along, but it finally became clear last year, when I ran for student council. I had to meet with Fleming and some of the others. I saw what they were right away. Funny how obvious it was. I wondered why I hadn't seen it earlier. Probably because I didn't want to see it."

"So why did you run?"

"Seemed like the thing to do at the time. And, yeah, there was the status thing, too. Now I know what a waste that is."

"How so?"

"Well, your status is determined by other people's approval. So, if you are seeking it, the way I did, what you really are doing is playing the other guy's game. You're denying your individuality to put on a show to suit someone else. You're letting them dictate your life."

Brewer had never heard the whole business summed up quite so succinctly.

"That's heavy," he said.

"Yeah, it is. But I'm glad I figured it out now, rather than wasting ten years, or twenty years or whatever before it hit me in the face. Or maybe it never would have hit me at all. There's a scary thought. Anyway, another quarter and I'm out of here - with student body officer on my resume and faculty recommendations in my pocket. So I can't really complain."

"What about a recommendation from Fleming?"

"Not gonna happen, thanks to you."

"Sorry."

Nancy chuckled. "Don't be. Nobody cares. He's just a silly little man with a silly little job at a school most people never heard of. But enough. Back to your problem."

"Any suggestions? Brewer said.

"Not really. Transfer to the U Dub, I guess."

"I'm working on that."

"Hmmm. Good. Other than that, just lay low."

"Getting layed is what got me in trouble," Brewer said. He instantly regretted the vulgarity.

Nancy blushed. She looked at Brewer and for a moment she thought, maybe I should have paid more attention to him. Okay, he's only a freshman, but he's bright and really quite nice once you get to know him. And there's nothing wrong with the way he looks. . .

"It seems to have a way of getting most of us in trouble at one time or another," she said. It was a pointless statement, a space filler with no real meaning. But it deflected the moment.

"Well, thanks, I guess," Brewer said.

"You're welcome. If I hear anything more, I'll let you know."

****

Brewer was scared. He wasn't sad, he wasn't angry, he wasn't confused. He was scared. He could be expelled, and he had no reason to doubt that's exactly what Fleming would do if he could. Expulsion would send him to the netherworld of flunk-outs and dropouts and failures who would spend the rest of their lives making excuses for why they never finished college. The fear went to Brewer's core.

Would it be like a court of law, where you are innocent until proven guilty and it's up to the accuser to prove it? Brewer doubted it. Oh, they might go through the motions, although they probably wouldn't even do that. This was SPC, a hierarchical place where authority is what counted trumped all other considerations.

Then there was the draft. If he got kicked out before finals, Spring Quarter wouldn't count. That would put him behind his class. That meant he would get drafted. He could think of no solution to that conundrum. He would just have to hope for the best, and even at his young age, Brewer knew that trusting hope was forlorn foolishness.

The only practical course of action Brewer could think of was to make himself as inconspicuous as possible.

****

"What?!"

Agnes Carswell flinched. She always approached Layton Fleming with the greatest possible deference. He was a great man and she was a mere secretary, a prole, an anonymous functionary in the wondrous organizational symphony that was Christian higher education. To invoke Fleming's displeasure was to subvert the perfection of the cosmos.

"We put the letter in the campus mail last Tuesday," Agnes said, her head bowed, her body tense, nearly trembling.

"And it's been stuck in the mail every since?" Fleming snarled.

"Yes."

"And why is that, Mrs. Carswell?"

"It's in his mail box," Agnes said in a tremulous voice. "Apparently he hasn't checked his mail in a long time."

"'Apparently'? Don't you know?"

"All I know is that I saw the letter in his box," Agnes said in a near whisper. "The mail lady wouldn't discuss it or let us in the mail room. She said federal law doesn't allow it."

"And just who is this 'mail lady'?" Fleming sneered.

"Her name is Maria. Maria Black. She's a student on work-study."

"A student, huh? Let's just see how well she likes the idea of not being a student anymore," Fleming said. "Get her for me. Now."

Agnes backed out of Fleming's office. She was shaking visibly.

Maria Black was a tall, slender young woman with eyes the color of glacial runoff and an expression to match.

"What's this hogwash about not letting my secretary in the mail room?" Fleming demanded.

"Those are the rules," Maria Black said in a flat, indifferent tone.

"Whose rules?"

"The United States Postal Service."

"Ohhh, the United States Postal Service," Fleming sneered. "You know all about it, huh?"

Maria Black looked straight ahead. No symptom of emotion betrayed her pristine features.

"Did it ever occur to you that you work for this college?" Fleming said.

"Actually, I don't," Maria Black said. "The college has a contract with the postal service. I'm a postal service employee."

Fleming was momentarily stunned. A student working on campus who was beyond his control? That could not be.

"Oh. Oh, well, we'll see. . ." his lips fumbled on the words. "We'll just see about that!"

Maria Black continued to gaze into the distance, unmoved. Well, when in doubt, attack, Fleming decided.

"So what do you have to say for yourself?" he demanded. It was one of his favorite unanswerable rhetorical questions, all but guaranteed to disorient even the most imperturbable recipient.

"What would you like me to say?" Maria Black replied.

"That you're going to do something about this problem! That you show a little cooperation!"

Maria Black remained silent, her face as immutable as permafrost. She did not shrug a shoulder, tap a foot or even take a breath; no indication whatsoever that she cared she was being addressed by the Dean of Students Himself. After a long period of silence, Fleming said, "Are you reading me?"

"Would you like me to repeat our conversation?" Maria Black said.

"I would like you to show a little cooperation!"

"I know. You already said that."

Fleming felt an urge to jump out of his chair, wrap his hands around Maria Black's straight, slender neck and squeeze it until ice water came out. Instead, he inhaled deeply, tried to think of something to say and couldn't. He waved his hand dismissively for Maria Black to leave. She did. Her footsteps made no sound.

****

Brewer carefully mapped out his movements. From his apartment on Nickerson, he could cut through alleys and back yards to Bertona and then dodge over to Fifth Avenue West behind Marston; not ideal, but it involved the shortest distances and the best cover he could think of. Few people went there.

He had classes in Moyer, Adelaide and the basement of Marston. From Marston, he could continue on to the path behind Moyer and Alexander. The distances between them were short. If he used them when other classes were in session there would be few people around. Then, of course, there were the various men's rooms in the buildings; good temporary hiding places.

Would they follow him to class? Possibly, but he doubted it. To do that, they would have to know his class schedule, which meant going through a lot of records, and then actually showing up at the right place at the right time, which meant a lot more trouble than they had time for. At least that's what Brewer hoped.

The SUB? That was the first place they would look for him. He would miss that place of friendship and possibilities. He sighed. It had been fun while it lasted.

He dressed in the most drab clothes he could find. He walked with his head down, never making eye contact; a hunched, silent figure, prowling the back roads, keeping in the shadows. In class, he sat in the rear of the room, far from any windows. He never spoke except when asked a question, and then in as few words as he could muster. No one noticed him, except his friends, whom he rarely saw.

He never relaxed. If there were cars on Bertona and he couldn't cross, he dodged behind some shrubs or stepped behind a tree. If he saw a teacher or administrator or anyone who resembled an authority figure, he turned into the nearest side path or stairwell or whatever else was nearby, anything to avoid recognition.

The fear never left him. So this is what it feels like to be a nonconformist, he thought; not a poser, not a hipster, not any of those things that pass for nonconformity but actually are ways to call attention to yourself. No. This is how it feels to be with the world against you and little you could do about it except hide and hope.

On Fridays, after dark, he would go to McLean's, but he found little comfort there. McLean wasn't throwing parties anymore and Pam was more sullen than ever.

And McLean didn't seem to like having him around. Finally, he just said it: "You're my friend, man, but what you're into is scary. It raises stuff I don't want to be part of."

"You mean it takes all your rebel without a cause crap and makes it face reality," Brewer said.

Brewer thought that would make McLean angry. It did not.

"Yeah, I guess so," McLean said with a sigh. "It all sounds so good when you are drinking wine and there are good-looking chicks listening to you. But now there are real consequences. Shit, maybe we're all just jerking off."

Brewer nodded. He didn't resent McLean and his angry young man act. So it wasn't reality, but what was? Reality is what you make it - well, some of the time. Brewer didn't create the reality he was experiencing now, not deliberately, in any case. He had a lot of risks and few choices; that was his reality.

Came finals. For Brewer, they were an act of will. He locked himself in his room and crammed. It was hard. The fear and loneliness kept him in a continual state of distraction. He was always waiting for a knock on the door, a fatal knock.

He forced himself to read, to write notes, to somehow jam the information into his brain. He did so all afternoon and every night. After all, he couldn't go out.

The tests themselves were finals; this was Brewer's third round of them and he knew what to expect. Once they were underway and he had questions to respond to and essays to write, his fear would disappear – at least for an hour or so.

At the end of his second day of finals, Brewer decided to check his mail box. He went to the SUB at 7:30 p.m., a half hour before it closed and dark enough to offer some cover. The lights in the upstairs offices were off.

Brewer went in the north entrance, the back way, which was just a few steps from the wall of mailboxes.

He opened his box quickly. There was a letter from the dean's office. He didn't touch it. There was another letter, with the return address in purple ink. Brewer pulled it out.

"Office of Admissions. The University of Washington."

Brewer jammed the letter into the breast pocket of his coat and walked away. He walked fast, across Bertona, through the alleys and backyards to his apartment. He checked the parking lot for suspicious cars.

For a moment, he wondered what, exactly a "suspicious" car would look like. Sinister, low-slung and black, with engine rumbling ominously? Jesus, this is nuts, he thought. I'm living a goddamned spy movie, and a bad one at that.

He hurried to his apartment.

Once there, he closed the door and locked it – yet another precaution – and opened the letter.

```
Dear Mr. Brewer;
We are pleased to announce that you
have been accepted to the University of
Washington for Fall Quarter, 1965.
```

It went on to say more, about where to register, what the deadlines were and, of course, the costs of tuition. And other stuff. Brewer didn't care. His last final was tomorrow morning. When it was done, he would hurry to the UW's Admissions Office, sign whatever had to be signed, make whatever arrangements had to be made and then... and then...

And then he would be a free man.

Brewer let the thought sink in for a moment and then he threw back his head and laughed. In his mind's eye he went over the past two weeks – the hiding, the sneaking, the fear – and it all came back to him like a Bugs Bunny cartoon: Dashing from bush to bush with zipping sounds, peeking out from behind rocks, all the while being pursued around campus by Elmer Fudd, he of the big shoes and speech impediment. What an absurd way to live, all because of somebody else's rules and their obsession for imposing them. And Brewer laughed and laughed and laughed.

Chapter 35

"Hat and gloves?"

"Hat and gloves."

"You're kidding."

"'Fraid not." Judy Thorson took a long sip from her wine glass. "It's required. And she'll check."

Elizabeth Fleming studied her friend's face carefully, searching for a trace of a joke. Judy wasn't joking.

"I don't even own a hat," Elizabeth said.

"Neither did I. I dug up my old Girl Scout beanie and used that."

"Didn't she notice?"

"Sure. But I was already on the shit list. It didn't matter."

Elizabeth shook her head in a mixture of amusement and admiration. Judy she liked. She was a rare individualist in the subculture of faculty wives. She could get away with it because she was married to Dick Thorson, Professor of Chemistry and Biology. He had a Ph.D. in biochemistry, the only one on campus. Dick held full tenure and, perhaps more importantly, was the brother of Bill Thorson, who owned the largest Chevrolet dealership in four states, along with extensive real estate holdings in Seattle's burgeoning suburbs east of Lake Washington. Bill was the frequent recipient of visits from supplicants from of SPC's fund-raising department.

Dick himself was the most amiable of men, content to teach the intricacies of hydro carbon interactions and to immerse himself in research projects so abstruse that nobody outside the world of theoretical biochemistry – and few within it – understood what he was talking about.

He and Judy were a perfect match, the good-natured absent-minded professor and the resident campus flake. Judy dressed however she wanted, said whatever she thought ~ including advocacy for such things as FDR liberalism and free love ~ and did whatever she damned well pleased. Unlike many supposed individualists, she didn't flaunt her heresies in order to attract attention. She honestly didn't care whether other people approved of her or not.

And she drank wine. She did it at her home, with the doors closed. This was SPC, after all, and to be seen with a glass in your hand could get you in genuine trouble. But she drank it when Elizabeth came over. Elizabeth she trusted.

And Elizabeth trusted her, which was why she was in Judy's living room.

Elizabeth had received an invitation to the Spring Wives Tea held by the president's wife, Margaret. She had managed to evade most such functions, but this one was special. The invitation came from highest of the high herself. As much as Elizabeth disliked politics, she recognized their necessity. She would have to put in an appearance.

And not just any appearance. She had heard there was a dress code and specific rules of behavior for Margaret Fotheringham's gatherings, but she was afraid to ask about specifics lest she make herself vulnerable. Hence her visit with Judy.

"So what kind of hat?" she asked. "Like Jackie Kennedy?"

"Maybe. But be careful. If it hints of anything avant-garde, you could be in trouble. Care for some chardonnay?"

"No thanks. Jackie Kennedy is too avant-garde?"

"For Margaret Fotheringham she is. Think about the sorts of hats Mamie Eisenhower used to wear."

"Do they still make those?"

"Beats me. Who said any of this is connected to reality."

How will I ever fit in? Elizabeth wondered. She didn't know many faculty wives. They were a distinctly bland lot for the most part and Elizabeth saw no particular reason to be chummy. A whole room full of them? For two hours? She would have to make conversation. She would have to act liked she cared. In short, she would have to put on the same act she had been required to put on for on most of her life.

But the time had come. She'd had enough. She simply wanted to be herself. Problem was, she wasn't quite sure who that was. But she seriously doubted she would find out at the Spring Wives Tea.

And Margaret Fotheringham? Elizabeth had seen the woman but, despite Layton's urgings, had never spoken to her. From a distance, Margaret Fotheringham appeared imperious; very much the president's wife and don't you forget it. Elizabeth certainly did not want to attend a tea hosted by her. But here it was. Elizabeth shuddered.

"Hemlines," Judy said.

"Hemlines?"

"Yeah, she's obsessed with them. They have to be below the knee, at least three inches."

Elizabeth did a quick mental inventory of her wardrobe. All her skirts and dresses were knee-length or a little higher, as was the fashion — and as had been the fashion throughout the western world for five years.

"Remember Grace Kelly in Rear Window?" Judy said. "That's kinda what she likes. But don't look as good in it as Grace Kelly. That might be a problem for you."

"Grace Kelly wore full skirts in that one. I don't own any full skirts."

"Uh-oh."

"Now what?"

"With a shape like yours, a form-fitting dress is definitely suspect."

"Good grief. I'll have that glass of wine after all," Elizabeth said.

"And gloves."

"Hmmm. Well, I have the mittens my mother knitted for me in fourth grade," Elizabeth said. "They're attached to each other with a string."

Judy laughed. "An interesting fashion statement, certainly."

"What will the gathering itself be like?" Elizabeth said.

"Don't know. I didn't hang around long enough to find out. But I would think the uniform regulations should give you a pretty good idea."

"This can't be real," Elizabeth said with a resigned sigh.

"Ah, but it is," Judy said. "Does it surprise you?"

No it didn't. That was the hell of it. Elizabeth joked with Judy some more, finished her wine and headed home. Layton was already there, watching the afternoon news.

"Hey, gorgeous. Where ya been?"

"Over to see Judy Thorson. I wanted her opinion on something."

"Oh! What?"

"Margaret Fotheringham's Spring Wives Tea. I've been invited."

"Great!" Latyon beamed. "I'm sure you'll be a hit."

There was a long silence. Latyon looked puzzled.

"What is it?" he said.

"I don't want to go. I think I'll be out of place."

Layton's expression changed instantly, like a finger snap.

"You what?"

"It's just not me," Elizabeth said. "She seems like a nice woman and all, but the whole business doesn't sound right."

Layton rose quickly from his chair and stalked across the room to face her. His jaw was set and his eyes were hard. No, not just hard, something else; a vague hint of panic, liked a cornered animal preparing to make its last stand. He took her by the shoulders, something he had never done before. His fingers squeezed hard.

"You're going," he said, his voice a near-hiss. "And you will like it and you will make a good impression. You got that?"

She had seen Layton angry before but, again, this was something different. For the first time since she had met him, Elizabeth Fleming was actually afraid of her husband.

"But it sounds awful," Elizabeth said. "It's everything that I hate about this place."

"Hate about this place?" Layton snarled. "This place is where I'm laying the foundation for my career. You are *not* going to foul it up."

"It's just one silly little social," Elizabeth said. She tried to keep the fear out of her voice, but it kept creeping in. "I won't be missed."

"Yes you will and you know it," Layton said. "What are you trying to do to me anyway?"

"Nothing, nothing. . ."

"That's right, nothing. You actually have a chance to do something important and you whine like a spoiled nine-year-old because it doesn't quite suit you."

"That's not it. It's..."

"I know what it is and I don't care. You're going, understand? And you will make a good impression, understand?"

"But..."

"And I don't want to hear any more about it." He stalked back to his chair and resumed watching television. Elizabeth tried to speak, but he cut her off.

"Get me my dinner!" Layton barked and Elizabeth realized he was struggling to contain his rage, a special rage, something she had never seen before. What was going on?

"I said dinner!" His body twitched as if he was going to jump up.

Elizabeth hung her head and went to the kitchen.

****

Brewer's last final, in Anthropology, was on a Thursday afternoon. It went well. He was done with his freshman year.

The next morning, he drove to the QFC in University Village to see about his old job. Mr. Sperling, the manager was still in charge. He was as affable and direct as ever. A good man. A good boss.

"Well, I can't hire you full-time. All those jobs are filled. But I can sign you on for half days; sometimes the day shift, sometimes the night shift. You would start next week. Interested?"

Brewer was.

On his way home, Brewer decided to check his campus mail box one more time. It was 2 p.m. on a bright day and this time he didn't sneak in through the back door. Instead, he parked on Third West, strode the fifty yards or so to the east door of the SUB and ambled casually down the hall, all but challenging Fleming to confront him. But he knew Fleming would not. He knew whatever had happened was over now. He was in a different realm, a realm of sunny days and a good future. He could feel it. He knew.

His mailbox was empty except for the letter from Fleming's office. Brewer smiled and turned away.

He decided to go out the front door. As he passed the coffee shop, he looked in. A straggle of a dozen or so students were scattered about the room, reading newspapers, sipping cokes, staring blankly off into space.

Some things will never change, Brewer thought, and he was glad for that. As he walked back to his car, he stopped for one last look at the SUB, this humble place where so much had happened, this cynosure of so much of his life.

A year ago, he didn't even know it existed. But here he had learned more than he ever expected; about people, about ideas, about himself. For a moment, a distilled essence of the experience, the richness of it with all its petty cruelties and all its silent beauty, the beauty of the ordinary, imploded on him and, for a moment, he knew what it all meant.

He had come far. In nine months, his mind had been razored down from a collection of inarticulate musings to an analytical tool for facing the world forthrightly and with confidence. He had a way to go, oh yes he certainly did, but now he knew he was capable of doing it, of becoming an educated man.

Already, he had learned the power of the English language. Already he had learned there was a world beyond his own experience. Study Joan of Arc? He certainly wouldn't have volunteered. But he studied it nonetheless and in doing so came to understand her and her world, a world like none that existed now.

Sociology? Hard to stay awake in that class. No one droned on like good old Prof. McClosky. But Brewer forced himself and he learned that group dynamics have reasons and patterns, often elusive reasons and patterns, but they are there if you know how to look for them. And now Brewer did.

Philosophy? Thank you Ralph Waldo Emerson and Rene Descartes and John Locke. For they had shown him ways to find the truth of things. And such truth was real. Brewer thought about the legions of dolts who, when the subject of philosophy came up would recite such profundities as "Well, that and a quarter will get you a cup of coffee." And now he knew he could give them the finger with confidence.

And so it went in his mind; the tedious lectures, the long, long nights hunched over books, the weekends spent sweating out papers on subjects which, when he began the papers, held no interest for him. But when he was done, they did. His mind had opened.

All thanks to this small collection of people and buildings on the north slope of Queen Anne Hill, a neighborhood few cared about in a city few knew about in a corner of the continent few ever visited.

He had learned about people; some good some bad, some indifferent. People could be intelligent and decent and interesting or they could be obtuse, venal and so dull you wondered if they were a form of plant life. Sometimes you could tell when you first saw them, but generally not. In any case, they were complex and valuable. Yes, valuable. Brewer remembered the worlds to an old cowboy song:

And so my friend
I bid adieu
I'm a better man
For just the knowin' of you

There had been Dale and Nancy and Morrison, who he only seen that one time, and McLean who, for all his hipster bullshit, had done Brewer a kindness when he needed it most. And damnit, McLean was fun.

And there had been Marilyn.

The vision of her, in a mist, like frosted crystal, so beautiful it made him ache; it was settled in his depths and it would not go away. Oh, if only. . .

He tried to shake the feeling. But he could not. He knew it would remain in him, always there, always haunting.

Then he thought of his parents and the money and the girls and the harridan at the bus station and Fleming conniving to destroy him for. . . for what? For wanting to live? When you have something, even something as simple as independence, people want to take it from you. Brewer had learned that lesson; oh how he had learned that lesson.

And, if they have power, even a small amount of power, people will always try to impose their will on you. It was a certainty as sure as the sun rising in the east and water flowing downhill. But why? Brewer could only guess the specific reasons. They varied a lot depending on the person and the situation. But he knew the most important one, the all-encompassing one: Because they *could*.

And don't you ever forget it, Brewer thought. Not ever.

As he unlocked the door to his tan Pontiac, he took one more look at SPC. He was coming out better than he went in. He was leaving with honor.

****

Hillford House, the home of the President of Seattle Pacific College, was perched atop a peak-like hill near the intersection of 6th Avenue West and West Dravus Street. In the middle of a particularly tangled jumble of streets and slopes, it was hard to get to. Parking was all but non-existent. Maybe that was on purpose, Elizabeth thought as she trudged up 6th West. *It keeps the lower orders at a proper distance. Well, no point in being bitter about it now. You're going to the spring wives tea and you are going to like it – or at least endure it with whatever good grace you can manage.*

She had the requisite hat and gloves. She couldn't find a Mamie Eisenhower skull plate, so she had to settle on a Jackie Kennedy pillbox. If that constituted a faux pas, so be it.

The gloves. . . ah, the gloves. Frederick and Nelson had all kinds. She toyed with the idea of long black ones, like Audrey Hepburn in Breakfast at Tiffany's. Or maybe even longer white ones like Natalie Wood in Gypsy. Then she could take them off, coyly, finger by finger, spin them around and toss them to the crowd. Gypsy Rose Lee at Hillford House; there was a thought.

But of course she did not. Simple white wrist length. She did indulge the shocking detail of a single pearl fastening button on each glove. Maybe somebody would notice and be properly scandalized. One could hope.

Oh, knock it off, Elizabeth thought. *You have a role to act out and you will act it.*

When she reached the crest of 6th West, she did a quick mental inspection. Makeup fresh, hat in place, gloves on – and buttoned – white shoes (plain pumps, a modest two-inch heel) new and unscuffed. Dress a straight-line yellow silk shift (Don't show off those curves, girl), yoke-necked and sleeveless ~ and hemmed at mid-knee. Blast it all, she was not going to look ten years out of date to suit the president's wife or anyone else.

Yes, you're a real rebel all right. Now stand up straight, smile prettily and take proper lady-like short strides.

A maid greeted her at the door, a real life maid in a black dress, lace tiara and frilly apron. Elizabeth had never seen a maid before.

"May I announce you?" the maid said.

"Elizabeth Fleming."

The maid checked a list.

"Would that be Mrs. Layton Fleming?"

"Yes."

The maid turned. In a soft voice, but one that carried across the room, she announced that Mrs. Layton Fleming was present.

The room was spacious, with the sort of angular, almost over-simplified furniture called "modern" a few years earlier. The colors were all pastel, neutral and forgettable.

About two dozen women were gathered, the faculty wives. What surprised Elizabeth about them was their homogeneity. She expected they would be similar, but not this similar: All in pale dresses of the same sort of shapeless generic cut; all with nondescript features – or pretty features they did their best to make nondescript; all smiling the same small, contented half-smile. They were circulating; not walking, really, more like drifting with slow, waltz-like semi-pirouettes; moving to an inner assonance of unconscious intuition.

Well, don't take too much time analyzing it all, Elizabeth thought. You look like a totem pole. You're here to mingle. So mingle.

She joined the waltz. It was surprisingly easy. Smile and nod, smile and nod. Move from covey to covey, act like you are interested, smile and nod, smile and nod. Step, step, twirl, twirl. When she came to the refreshments table, she looked over the cucumber and watercress sandwiches, fussed as if she couldn't decide (ladies at teas were supposed to do that, play the role, play the role), then chose what was close. One bite. She didn't notice the flavor.

Smile and nod, step, step, twirl, twirl, act like you are interested. She said little, listened as much as she had to and kept moving.

Eventually, Elizabeth reached the far side of the room. There, she found Margaret Fotheringham. The president's wife was ensconced on a simple, straight backed wood chair. Except it wasn't simple. The legs and frame were mahogany carved in delicate motifs and the seat and back were upholstered in patterned ivory silk.

Her back was to the large plate glass window that looked out upon the campus and, further away, the ship canal and the hills of Fremont and Wallingford; a sweeping view, bright, almost glaring in the afternoon sun. It framed Margaret Fotheringham like a backdrop in a Hollywood set.

Her chin was raised so she looked downward at the gathering regally. Her ankles were primly crossed, her hands folded on her lap. There was a small leather notebook under her hands.

Two faculty wives were talking to her, one on either side so they would not impede her view. They bent at the waist slightly so she could hear them. Margaret was nodding serenely at their obsequicies.

Well, now or never, Elizabeth decided. She drifted gracefully until she was in Margaret Fotheringham's orbit. The other two women – one Janet Porter, wife of Dr. Andrew Porter, associate professor of sociology and Diane Pluchino, wife of Keith Pluchino, MA, assistant professor of history – smiled at Elizabeth, again that the same small, contented half-smile, and initiated chit chat about the weather ("What a perfect day for tea.") and how happy they were to be there. Margaret Fotheringham nodded without breaking her imperial countenance, all the while her eyes firmly fixed on Elizabeth.

Elizabeth smiled and thanked her for such a lovely gathering. Margaret Fotheringham did not respond.

"My husband admires the way the president plays tennis," Elizabeth said.

Margaret Fotheringham did not respond.

"I've heard that Layton is quite the ace," Janet Porter said, a little nervously.

"He tries," Elizabeth said, as gaily as she could.

Margaret Fotheringham remained motionless.

"Do you play?" Diane Pluchino said, also a bit nervously.

"I used to, but not much anymore," Elizabeth said. "So much to do, you know."

"And you?" Diane said to Margaret Fotheringham. The president's wife raised one eyebrow slightly and gently shook her head a single time.

The three faculty wives looked at each other nervously. The conversation had been going well until Elizabeth arrived. Why had Margaret Fotheringham frozen up?

"Coffee?" Diane said to Elizabeth.

"Yes, sounds good." Then she spoke to Margaret Fotheringham. "Thank you again for such a lovely gathering."

The corners of Margaret Fotheringham's mouthed twitched slightly, vey slightly. Then her eyes went straight forward, as if Elizabeth wasn't there.

On the other side of the room, Elizabeth poured herself coffee from the urn. She took it black. She started to thank Diane for rescuing her, but Diane nodded and returned to the waltz without a word.

What in the world? Elizabeth wondered. Then she noticed Margaret Fotheringham was doing something. Carefully, so as to look as graceful as possible, she was opening the small leather notebook on her lap. She took a pencil from it and made some notes. Then, with superb decorousness, inserted the pencil back in its loop, closed the notebook, slipped it under her folded hands and returned to her regal mien.

Elizabeth sensed the president's wife was writing about her. But why? Had she said something to offend her? No, she had said next to nothing at all. What then?

Elizabeth looked around the room, studying it and the people in it. Was she prettier than the other women? *Oh no, not that again.* Perhaps, but not overtly so. Was she somehow different than the norm? She studied some more. Then she noticed. She was the only one wearing a sleeveless dress. And her dress was yellow, a fairly bright yellow, certainly nothing that would give Van Gogh pause, but bright. And yellow. And silk. And an inch shorter than everyone else's.

It must be something else, Elizabeth thought. She studied some more. No, that was it: A sleeveless yellow dress that dared to show an inch of human patella. Scandalous stuff? That wasn't the point. It was merely different. It was not the norm according to Margaret Fotheringham. It drew attention, no matter how slight, away from the sanctity of the conclave. The wife of the president of Seattle Pacific College could not brook such heterodoxy, certainly not in her own home. Elizabeth Fleming's sedition had been noted. It would not be forgotten.

    Elizabeth took a long draw of coffee. It was strong and very hot, so hot it should have made her gag and cough. But it did not. She savored the burn and the acid as it went down her throat. It focused her. Clarity came.

    So this was it, the world for which she was destined. Elizabeth snorted. (Unladylike, but she couldn't help it.) She should have known. Well, let's see how good an actor you can be, she thought.

    She started the waltz again, smile and nod, smile and nod, but this time she drifted gradually toward the door. Smile and nod, smile and nod. Eventually she made it. She waited until the maid wasn't looking and Margaret Fotheringham wasn't looking. Then quickly, more quickly than she thought she could move in heels, she slipped out the door and into the soft glory of a spring evening in Seattle. She did not stop to catch her breath or otherwise take stock of her situation. She walked. She walked as she fast as she could, her bearing erect, her eyes clear and focused. She should have felt angry ~ or hurt, or disappointed or something. But mostly she just felt sad. Why must things be like this, she wondered. Why must people be like this? There is kindness and goodness in the world if people were to choose it. But more often than not, they do not.

    Elizabeth walked down 6th West to Gwinn Commons, then down the small hill to 5th West, past Marston and Moyer Halls and to the main campus. With no place else to go, she headed for the donut shop across from the Loop on 3rd West.

    The donut shop was a humble hole in the wall left over from a time when Seattle was a city of nooks and crannies and idiosyncratic shops tucked away on unassuming streets real estate developers had not yet discovered. It was far from the world of hats and white gloves and cucumber sandwiches and, therefore, it seemed like a good place to hide for a while and contemplate this latest chapter in one's existence.

    Elizabeth ordered coffee and a chocolate cake donut, the kind her mother always warned her about.

The view out the window offered no solace. The campus; a place she had seen hundreds of times. The times all seemed the same. At least on this particular time, the leaves were green and the sky was bright and clear.

A man came through the door.

Elizabeth barely noticed him beyond the fact he was wearing a cheap suit in some discordant pattern of electric blue and pea green.

"I know you!" the man exclaimed, beaming at Elizabeth. "Mrs. Fleming, Layton's wife, right?" His smile was broad, his round face an archetype of joviality straight from the Saturday Evening Post.

Elizabeth tried to generate a nod and a smile and failed. The man pulled a chair over to her table, sat down and held out his hand.

"Bud Gafney!" he announced. "Heard so much about you! Always wanted to meet you!"

Elizabeth shook his hand. She didn't know what else to do.

"Boy, whatta day, huh?" Gafney said gesturing out the window. "Makes ya glad to be alive, doesn't it?"

If I finish my doughnut fast, maybe I can leave before he gets settled in, Elizabeth thought.

"Yes sir," Gafney said. "Glad to be alive." He paused for a moment to study her. "Say, you seem to be a little down in the dumps. Is everything okay?"

"Yes, fine. Just kind of a long day."

"I know how that is," Gafney said. "But maybe it can still work out for the best."

He seemed like a nice enough man, if a bit pushy. Right now, anything pleasant would do, even a person she barely knew. But something wasn't quite right about him, as if his good nature was a façade with something else behind it. Oh well, he was an improvement over Margaret Fotheringham.

The chocolate donut tasted rich and sweet and decadent. Elizabeth bit away half of it in one chomp. Most unladylike. She didn't care.

"Layton tells me you have a degree in English lit," Gafney said.

"Yes," Elizabeth said. American lit, actually. She couldn't relate to English writers and their world of elaborate etiquette and never saying what you actually mean. In view of what just happened at Hillford maybe she should have studied British affectation more closely.

"Always wished I taken more courses in that," Gafney said. "Turned out marketing was more my style."

"There's not a big call for English majors in the job market," Elizabeth said.

"Hmmm, maybe, maybe. But what if I were to tell you that you can make that work for you," Gafney said.

Elizabeth didn't really want to talk about it - or much of anything else. But she felt obligated to say, "How?"

"By harnessing the power within *you*," Gafney said, pointing his finger at her.

Elizabeth did not answer. But she couldn't help herself. She was curious. It showed.

"Look, I grew up on a little farm in Illinois," Gafney said. "Closest town was a place you never heard of. We were so broke, all I had in my lunchbox were the soybeans I picked the day before. The other kids teased me about it. There wasn't much I could do except take it."

"Sounds rough," Elizabeth said.

"That's what I thought. All my life it seemed like everyone doubted me; the poor kid from nowhereville. Then I got to college. I had to work part-time to pay for it, so I missed out on a lot of the fun the other kids had. It used to get to me."

This was going awfully fast, Elizabeth thought. One minute she's chewing on a donut and trying to get her head together, the next minute a man she doesn't know is telling her his life story. Odd. Again, she realized Gafney had finished his statement in such a way she had to ask a question.

"What did you do?" she said.

"Well, one day it came to me: People didn't see inside of me. *I* didn't see inside of me."

Elizabeth gestured that she didn't understand.

"What I learned is that there is power inside you," Gafney said. "Only you can harness that power."

I could certainly use some power right about now, Elizabeth thought.

"How?" she said.

"By believing in that power," Gafney said. "Look, I'm guessing, but it looks to me like you're looking for something."

You got that right.

"Whatever it is, you already have it," Gafney said. It's right there, inside you." He looked at Elizabeth straight in the eye. It disconcerted her.

"And whatever it is, you can make it work for *you*. Greatness is yours."

Elizabeth started to speak. Gafney didn't notice.

"Now I'm not selling you anything – except a better everything," he said. "See, I found that through Greatness is Yours, I could find happiness, fulfillment and," he winked knowingly, "no small amount of good old fashioned samolians. How about that, huh?"

Before Elizabeth could answer, he leaned closer to her, smiled even more broadly than before and said, "Greatness is Yours was founded a few years ago by Guy W. Fabb, just an ordinary fella, the kind people ignore, just like you and me. Now he's a multi-millionaire, with an empire that's growing all the time. And you know how he did it?"

Elizabeth couldn't help but shake her head in curiosity.

"Chick pea oil. Yup, something as simple as chick pea oil. Why, they throw the stuff away at canneries. But Guy W. Fabb knew there was something there. He believed in his own power and he made it work for him.

"Now he markets cosmetics with a chick pea oil base around the world. And they are the greatest, the most wonderful products to hit the cosmetics market for . . . well, forever. So, what do you say?"

"What do I say to what?" Elizabeth asked. She was confused and she knew it and she didn't know what to do about it.

"I want to help you out," Gafney said. "So I'm going to let you in on a secret. Guy W. Fabb is about to expand his empire, and I mean expand it worldwide. I can help you get in on it."

"But. . ."

"Look, you can't wait. If you want to get in on the ground floor, you have to do it now. Tell you what: I'll send you thirty cases of Fabb cosmetics. You can sell them to your friends. Better still, you can set them up to sell them too. That would make you a distributor and part of the Fabb team. It's all yours – for just a minor startup fee, of course. And then the sky's the limit. And it's not just the money, either. The top sellers can even win free trips. This quarter it's the Grand Ole Opry. That's in Nashville Tennessee! Such a deal, huh?"

Gafney was beaming in expectation of her acceptance.

Elizabeth felt herself recoiling, like when she was a child wading in the creek and an eel slithered along her leg. But she had been raised to be polite. It bound her.

"I don't know. . ."

"Hey, I understand your reluctance," Gafney said. "The first step is always the hardest. But, you know, I bet it would make old Layton proud to see a wife of his stepping up like this. Say, how about I give him a call? Yessir, it would make him proud. No question about it. I'll call him tonight."

No, not that. For god's sake, not that. Elizabeth ran the scenario through her mind. She didn't want to sell. She couldn't sell, even if she did want to. She would end up with a garage full of junk and no idea what to do with it. What was happening here? Where in all of this was Elizabeth Fleming, whoever that was. Was her function on this earth merely to be used by others?

Did anyone care about *her*?

"I'm sorry, I just don't think it's for me. . ." Elizabeth said haltingly.

Gafney's expression changed to one of deep hurt, as if she was being cruel to him.

"But why not?" he said in disbelief.

"It's just not for me. I. . . I. . ."

"I'm so sorry. So sorry," Gafney said. "I was only trying to help." He hung his head.

"I know," Elizabeth said. "But I can't. I mean I'm not in a position. . ."

"Hey. It's okay," Gafney said, the reassuring tone in his voice deep and sincere. "So, let's do this. I'll send you one case, thirty percent off the regular price. I bet you'll find it will sell out before you know it. So, what address should I deliver it to?'

"No, please. . ."

"Oh gosh, I'm sorry. I didn't mean to rush you. How about we do this: I send you Guy W. Fabb's book, 'Greatness is Yours.' How's that for a title, huh? It has the answers you're looking for. I read it every night. It's like the Bible, I tell ya, the Bible! Read that, then I'll give you a call, say on Tuesday?"

"No." Elizabeth thought she might start to cry. Before Gafney could say more, she got up and headed for the door, nearly knocking over her chair in her haste. She could hear Gafney saying something, a pleading sound in his voice, but she kept going. Home was three blocks away. With luck, no one would see her. No one would see the tears trickling down her face.

****

Marilyn Pennell ran to the bus stop at Fifth Northeast as fast as she could.

The bus, if it arrived on time, was due at 9:41 p.m. Nordstrom's closed at 9 p.m. and the staff had to stay until everything was properly put away. That could take anywhere from fifteen minutes to a half hour depending how messy things were, how fast the salesmen tallied up their day's sales and, above all, how Lena St. Germaine felt about filing them.

On this particular night, Lena was especially languorous, her Virginia Slim drooping from her lip precipitously and she sighed loudly from time to time as if she was terribly put upon. She occasionally stopped what she was doing to shoot Marilyn a dirty look, as if her grueling tribulations were all Marilyn's fault. The clock read 9:30. If Marilyn missed her bus, another one wouldn't come until 10:15.

Time dragged on. Finally, Lena tossed the stack of sales receipts in Marilyn's general direction and sashayed for the door in regal cadence.

Marilyn straightened up the receipts as fast as she could, ran up the stairs, put the stack in Mr. Wolfstone's in-basket, ran back down and out the door.

She was getting tired of it, the constant dashing to and fro to meet schedules determined by someone else. She had little choice, of course, and she kept telling herself that such things actually constituted challenges one met with as much grace as possible, a test of character, if you will. But as she lurched and stumbled across the parking lot behind the Bon Marche - why can't they make skirts you can actually run in? - she was less than convinced.

She spotted the bus at the stop light a block up the street. How long had it been there? If the light changed could she make it in time? There were cars cruising through the parking lot. Did they see her? She kept an eye on them - for god's sake, don't trip over something! - and... and...

Good grief, why are things like this always happening to me?!

She reached the street. There was traffic on it; not much but enough that, again, she would have to watch carefully as she ran for the bus stop.

The stop light turned green and the bus began to move. A '57 Chev screeched its brakes and blared its horn as Marilyn dodged in front of it. She wanted to shout at the driver but she wasn't the type who shouted.

She waved at the bus, hoping the driver would spot her. Apparently, he did. The bus stopped just as Marilyn reached it.

Marilyn found a seat and caught her breath. Two teenagers who felt that public transit was an ideal place for conducting expressions of physical affection - particularly ardent expressions of the prolonged variety, interspersed with bouts of giggling - sat in front. Nearby, a sour-faced old woman scowled at the lewd goings-on, her jaw grinding, her eyes glistening and feverish. Marilyn moved to the back of the bus, as far away as she could get.

For all that, the ride was better than when she was still in school. No transfers. It went straight to a stop two blocks from her grandmother's house on Capitol Hill. It gave her time to think, when she was in the mood for thinking, which she was now.

She arrived at work early and left late every day. It was either that or Mr. Wolfstone would suspect her of being was a chronic malingerer, embezzler and sneak thief. Based on such his suspicions - he didn't waste his time with proof - she would lose her job.

So, she spent about ten hours a day at the store, sometimes more.

The commute was roughly forty five minutes each way. Add the time she spent waiting at the stop and the time walking to and from the store and it came to about two and a half hours a day.

So, roughly twelve hours a day – half her life – were dictated by the mechanics of making a living.

That living paid $2.12 an hour for an eight-hour day. The other hour and a half at the store was, as Mr. Wolfstone once told her, a demonstration of her loyalty to her employer – to whom she should be eternally grateful for giving her any job at all.

Her expenses? Five dollars a week for transportation. Taxes took – what? Twelve percent or so? And, of course, she was required to contribute a dollar a week to United Way. All the store's employees did, otherwise Mr. Wolfstone wouldn't get a plaque for his office wall each year. To complain about it, or to even bring the subject up, was cause for termination of your employment with Nordstrom Inc.

Soap, shampoo, hairspray, tampons and the like came to another ten dollars or so a month.

Fortunately, her grandmother did not charge her rent. She didn't ask for food money either, but Marilyn felt she should contribute. Another $20 a month.

What did that leave? Not much. Marilyn put as much as she could in the bank. Maybe someday, she would have enough to buy a car. And maybe she could even scrape together enough to return to school – but at the rate things were going, that was a very distant hope indeed. She tried not to think about it. Meanwhile, she mended the clothes she had brought with her to school back in September – it seemed much longer ago – and took her shoes to the cobbler's shop on Broadway. Cheaper than buying new shoes, although repairs cost too.

The bus stopped at Roosevelt Way and Northeast 65th. The two kids got off, their hands all over each other, squirming like eels. In view of her own love life – what love life? – Marilyn wondered if perhaps she should envy them. But she did not. Catching such things when you can, where you can – Wednesday night on a Metro bus, for example – was sad, an act of desperation, even if the people committing it didn't think so.

Desperation? Looked in the mirror lately, kiddo?

Marilyn moved to the front of the bus so she could see her stop coming. That put her in the sights of the old woman, who now scowled at her, her face a caricature of cold hatred. Marilyn nodded at her politely. The old woman's expression did not change. What did I ever do to you? Marilyn wondered. Do you hate me because I'm young, or do you simply hate everybody? Or are you just another bus ride whacko? In any case, I wish you would leave me alone. I wish the world would leave me alone.

The bus rolled on, the old woman continued to scowl. Outside, there was the city, a place Marilyn once considered magical. Now, with bus's overhead light cancelling out all other illumination, Marilyn could not see the city beyond the slag gray outlines of the sidewalks and the occasional street sign.

The old woman reminded Marilyn of so many members of her parents' generation; all the burned out souls who manned counters, or pumped gas, or hauled unkempt, unwilling children around the local Gov-Mart.

In her mind, Marilyn saw them smiling at her with smug cruelty. Well, well, well, get a load of the princess. Boo-hoo. Now it's your turn to lose your life, your hope, your dreams to The Real World. Now you can be just like us, defeated and narrow and mean.

The idea settled deep in Marilyn's consciousness and would not go away.

Finally, the bus stopped at 15th and Thomas and Marilyn got off. The old woman watched Marilyn out the window, her scowl frozen in malignity as the bus wheezed into the darkness.

****

When Elizabeth Fleming got home, she ran to the upstairs bathroom, washed off her makeup and changed into jeans and a pullover. As she was checking herself in the mirror, she heard Layton come through the front door. He trotted up the stairs to their bedroom.

"Hey, babe, got everything ready for the rap session tonight?" he said.

"Tonight?"

"I told you last week. Did you forget?"

"Layton, I. . . it's been a tough day. I. . ."

"A tough day?" There was an edge in Layton's voice. "You went to the tea, didn't you?"

"Yes, of course."

"So how was that rough?"

Elizabeth took a deep breath. "Margaret Fotheringham doesn't seem to like me. I felt unwelcome."

"Doesn't seem to like you?" Layton said warily.

"She wouldn't talk to me."

"Why not?"

"I don't know, I..."

"You 'don't know?' There must have been a reason. What was it?"

"Maybe it was the way I dressed..."

"What did you wear?"

"That new yellow dress, the one..."

"New yellow dress? I don't remember you telling me about any new yellow dress."

"I didn't think it was that important..."

"Well, clearly it was. Didn't you think to ask me about it?"

"I can choose my own clothes."

"Apparently not," Layton said. "So now you go off and buy some tacky gee-gaw and the president's wife thinks you're some kind of tramp..."

"Hey, wait a minute," Elizabeth said, her voice rising.

"Oh, excuse me," Layton said sarcastically. "Permit me to rephrase: Some kind of Ozark trailer trash. Do you have any idea what this will do to my career?"

"Have you even seen the dress?" Elizabeth said, and immediately realized she had made a mistake.

"Well, no. Thanks to you, I guess I haven't," Layton said. "Doesn't make much difference now, does it? The damage is done."

Elizabeth could think of nothing to say. Layton folded his arms and looked down his nose at her condescendingly.

"Think you can put something together for the rap session? Or is that beyond your capacity?" he said.

"But..."

"They'll be here in fifteen minutes. Are you going to disgrace me in front of them, too?"

Without waiting for Elizabeth to respond, he turned on his heel and walked out of the room. His posture was erect with righteous indignation.

Elizabeth stood for a moment, trying to catch her breath and clear her mind. But she could not. The boys would be arriving soon and the idea of causing an awkward scene, even at something as unimportant as the rap session, clutched at her and choked her in embarrassment. Mechanically, she went to the kitchen and checked the pantry. There was little to serve in the way of hors d'oeuvres. Finally she found a bag of popcorn. It would have to do. She put the big skillet on the stove, poured in some oil and tuned on the heat. Then she ran to the garage, found two six-packs of coke and shoved them to the back of the refrigerator, the coldest part.

She had just finished the first batch of popcorn when the boys began to arrive. Even from the kitchen, she could tell that they were louder than the ones who usually came to Layton's gatherings. She peeked out the door.

Where in the world did he find these?

There was a fat boy, sloppy with greasy, uncombed hair. His glasses were too small for his face, which exaggerated a permanent, pout-like grin. As he moved around the room, he bumped into the furniture. When he collided with the walnut table Elizabeth's mother had given her, the table with the exquisite porcelain vase her brother had sent from Japan, Elizabeth winced. The vase rocked, but did not tip over. The boy didn't notice and plopped himself down hard on the couch; so hard, Elizabeth feared the springs would break.

Another boy, with a pointy chin, squinty eyes and face red with severe acne, was wheezing and gurgling like an asthmatic ferret at some joke Layton had just told.

Still another was staring blankly around the room, his eyes wide and uncomprehending, his mouth pulled back in a chimp-like grimace. It was as if he was an illustration next to the word "brainless" in the dictionary.

These must be the ones left after all the good ones had already been invited, Elizabeth thought. She did not want them in her home.

Wait a minute, you are being a snob, she thought. Well, maybe. . . No. Even snobs have a point sometimes. An idiot is an idiot. Feeling guilty for identifying him as such is prissy self-delusion.

Well, Layton had chosen them and she could see why. They laughed uproariously at his jokes and joined enthusiastically in the macho joshing and repartee. But even Layton had to be a little disgusted by the way they couldn't keep their hands off each other; pushing, prodding and poking like four-year-olds, all the while emitting grunts and giggles and guffaws. Or by the way they wiped their noses on their sleeves. Or scratched their crotches. Or bit their nails. Or. . .

The first batch of popcorn was done. Elizabeth dumped it in a big bowl, poured on the butter and salt and grabbed three rolls of paper towels. She made a point of tossing the rolls to the boys, in hopes they would take the hint and keep their butter-coated hands off the upholstery.

Then she put two unopened six packs of coke on the coffee table and headed back to the kitchen. She did not smile, she did not say hello. Two more bowls of popcorn, one more six pack and her hostess duties were done, as far as she was concerned. Layton gave her a dirty look when she delivered the last bowl.

Well, so be it.

Elizabeth made herself some coffee, sat down at the kitchen table and read the Seattle Post Intelligencer for the rest of the evening. About an hour into the festivities, she heard the telephone ring. She started to get up, but then it stopped. Layton must have picked it up in the living room.

So she continued sipping and reading. She had just finished Mr. Abernathy on the comics page when she heard the boys starting to leave. Finally. It had been two and a half hours.

Before Elizabeth could leave the table, Layton came through the kitchen door.

"And what was that all about?" he demanded.

"I fed them and gave them drinks. They seemed satisfied."

"I expect you to be a proper hostess."

"Layton, I'm really tired. I doubt they even noticed I was there. Look, I have to clean up. Then I just want to go to bed, okay?"

He stood blocking the door, his feet apart and planted.

"I got a phone call," he said.

"Yes, I heard." Elizabeth started for the door.

"It was from Bud Gafney. Seems like you two had quite the little conversation this afternoon."

"I stopped at the donut shop. He sat down and we chatted for a few minutes. That's all."

"Oh? He tells me you're all hot to sell Fabway. Just can't wait to get your first shipment."

"What?!"

"So that's how you want to spend your time, eh? Not enough to do around here for you?"

"No, no, you've got it all wrong," Elizabeth said. "He asked me if I wanted to and I said no. I don't want to do anything like that."

"But you don't want to help me with my career either, do you? I ask you, just once I ask you to make a favorable impression on Margaret Fotheringham and instead you insult her and make a fool of yourself."

"I did not insult her!" Elizabeth said, her voice starting to crack. "She insulted me!"

"The wife of the president does not insult people."

"What? What makes you think that?"

"She is the wife of the president," Layton said with finality. "Who else do you call into question? Billy Graham?"

Elizabeth found herself at a loss for words.

"I think this Fabway thing sounds like a fine idea," Layton said. "Maybe it will teach you some sense of responsibility. Time for you to start paying your way around here."

"No, for god's sake, Layton no! I can't be like those people."

"Like what people?"

People like Bud Gafney; ignorant, vulgar and smug. Cheap people in cheap suits, with cheap, tawdry lives, pointless lives. People whose awareness ran a sixteenth of an inch deep, if that. People not very much unlike the man who was eyeing her from across the room with a superior smirk.

"Layton, I. . ."

He held up his hand to silence her, the condescending gesture of one who expects underlings to acquiesce with proper humility.

"I told Gafney to send over four crates. You'll work off the cost with sales. He said it should only take a month or so. That shouldn't be too tough, should it?"

Again a question she was compelled to answer, yet another tool of the cheap people in their endless quest to pull the rest of the world down to their level.

But Elizabeth did not answer. Instead she headed to the door, pushing her way past Layton, who gave way in surprise. She was out to the driveway and closing the car door before he could respond. She saw him standing in the doorway as she drove away.

****

As she walked to the door to the basement at the back of her grandmother's house, Marilyn Pennell found herself slouching, an unforgiveable breach of self-respect. She forced herself to stand straight. But the fatigue deep within her did not go away.

Her bedroom, such as it was, was in the corner of the basement, on the other side of the room from the furnace. The furnace was off tonight. When it ran, Marilyn found its steady hum comforting, nearly hypnotic, an ideal way to go to sleep every night.

She carefully hung her clothes on a piece of pipe she had rigged with bent coat hangers to suspend from the upstairs floor joists. Such was her closet. A single bed, a laundry hamper and an old chest of drawers with a clock, a radio and a lamp on it, completed the arrangement. Marilyn was thinking about putting up some curtains or maybe even buying a small portable television set. But no. Save your money, girl, save your money.

She lied on her bed and stared at the ceiling for a long time. Her daily grind was dictated by the fear of destitution, a very real fear and justified. What did that leave for her? Was she merely a forgotten fragment in the events that dictated her existence? The available evidence certainly seemed to suggest it. She had to make a living. It was the one reality she could not ignore.

Marilyn went to the small table that served as her desk, sat down on the scuffed wooden chair and turned on the radio. A young man with a nasal voice was singing. Something about his voice, the raw, unrefined quality of it, made her listen.

He was singing about a girl, a former rich girl, apparently, who was out on the streets, alone, with no direction. She used to be snug and proud. Now she was scrounging for a meal.

That sounds familiar, Marilyn thought. Too familiar. She had to hear more.

The young man sang on, his voice grating, like sandpaper against skin. No one would call it pleasant. But something about it was honest, as honest a thing as Marilyn had ever heard. How does it *feel?* the young man demanded.

Good grief, was he singing to *her?* To her and her alone? The reality of Marilyn's world shifted a little. How does it feel? How does it *feel?*

Not good. But bad? No, not that, either. Her life had a feel to it all its own, something beyond easy measure, but something real nonetheless.

How does it feel, when you have nothing to lose, when you can't hide your secrets anymore?

Hide my secrets? I have no secrets at all, Marilyn thought, not anymore.

The words and the music and the singer's nasal twang combined into a challenge: Can you take it? Can you, princess?

How does it *feel?*

The music settled into her. It was fearless, facing the world head-on with no gentleness, no apologies.

It feels, it feels. . .

It feels *clean.*

I may be broke, I may be alone, I may be a failure, but *I Am Here;* my feet on this floor, my hands touching the arms of this chair, that which is me solid and existent. It will be here another sixty years or so, so what does the rest matter. The rest will change and shift and go away from my sphere of existence. Whatever I am will remain.

What will happen next?

The young man with the nasal voice did not answer. Then he was done. Marilyn did not know his name. A song by the Beatles came on. It was called, "I'll Follow the Sun." Marilyn had heard it before and never paid much attention to it. But she was in a different place now.

The music was light, oddly subtle, like the scent of tea, just enough to convey the message and no more. And the message was. . .

There is a world out there, a different one than you feel you are forced to live in. There is movement and imaginings, there is creating one's own reality, not simply being subjugated to the one others have created. So follow the sun.

Such was the current permeating the air in the spring of 1965; air filled with music like nothing from any other time. Many who lived it, and there were many, would never forget the feel of it.

If you seek it, if you pay attention to it, life is a wonderment, Marilyn thought. Her job? Her situation? Her job was a way to make money, nothing more. Her situation was what it was, mostly the result of things beyond her control and, therefore, why get unduly upset about it? She was responding to it as best she could, and that was nothing to be ashamed of. Ultimately, it was a small thing, for beyond it was another world, a world of infinite possibilities; deep and clear and free.

Before Marilyn could complete her thought, another song came on, this one by a group she had never heard before, a group led by an alto with a clean, bell-like voice.

Leave me alone, Marilyn thought. I'm trying to think...

The alto sang on, her voice ringing clear. The last stanza of the song, the one Marilyn would never forget, spoke to her as if the song, the singer, the music was more than mere sound. It personified something she had known all along, something she had tried to suppress. But it would not be suppressed.

"*I know I'll never find another you.*"

It is rare in life, and for most people it never happens at all. But now it happened to Marilyn Pennell: A veil was lifted and she experienced reality; clear uncluttered reality.

She was transfigured. And now she knew what she would do. She knew it was time.

****

Elizabeth Fleming drove into the night, the endless night, without borders, an infinity, balmy and still in the warmth of late May. Driving, driving. To where? She did not know and did not care. The world was huge, full of places she had never seen, possibilities she had never imagined. Driving, driving, driving...

She wound her way through the streets of East Queen Anne and soon found herself speeding southbound on Aurora. The cars were fast, the night was clear, she was alone and in motion. She felt free. The lights and the movement exhilarated her.

She would leave the bastard, yes she would. Let him sell his Fabway crap. Let him kiss the president's ass. Let him entertain the freaks that blundered around her home like drunk hippos. Let him, let him. She would be free.

Elizabeth passed through the Battery Street Tunnel and on to the Alaska Way Viaduct. Elliott Bay spread out toward the west, the endless west, toward a world open and unconstrained.

****

"Hello?" Tom Brewer's voice sounded slightly apprehensive. Apparently, he didn't get many phone calls.

"Tom, it's Marilyn."

"Hello." His voice was neutral, in the way of people who aren't sure what's coming next and are waiting cautiously to find out.

"Tom, I wanted to tell you. . ." Marilyn choked. She paused to catch her breath.

"Are you all right?" Brewer said, genuinely concerned.

Yes, yes, I'm fine. Who cares?! She paused nervously.

It was time. It was time. Say it!

"I want to see you," she said.

Marilyn paused again to catch her breath. It almost turned into a sob. Her chest felt full, her throat was cramped.

"I'd like to see you too," Brewer said politely.

No, no, he's missing it. Don't let him get away. Do something. . .

Marilyn stopped analyzing. She stopped choosing her words carefully. She stopped thinking about the impression she would make. She no longer cared about what she had once been. She would say whatever came to her.

"The first time I saw you, something in me stopped," she said. "It was like I wasn't there. I, I . . ."

She took another deep breath.

"I tried to refuse, but I couldn't. It never went away."

Marilyn stopped again. She felt a tear forming. She wiped it away.

She continued, "I don't understand it, I don't know why, but I know it is real. I know it is good. I have to see you. Please come over, please."

Her voice left her, but she had to say it, she had to. She forced the air from her lungs.

"Tom . . ."

"It wouldn't work,' Brewer said softly. "I . . . "

"I don't care."

". . . we're so different . . ."

"I don't care."

"The future; I don't know where things are going," Brewer said.

Marilyn could hear Brewer stop to catch his breath.

"I don't care," she said. "It's all been so bad. But you were there; always you, only you. This is our time; now. It's what we have, all we have. Come to me, my love. Oh, god, come to me."

There was a long silence. Finally, Brewer spoke.

"Marilyn," he said, his voice reverent. "Oh, Marilyn."

A silence passed between them, a silence that said everything, a silence like nothing either had ever experienced.

Finally, Brewer said, "I'm on my way."

And for that moment, all was well in Marilyn Pennell's world. All was what it was; singular and certain and right.

Chapter 36

The adrenaline in Elizabeth Fleming's blood had subsided and she decided it was time to stop and think a little. She picked up the Spokane Street Viaduct and headed for West Seattle. There, she pulled up the car at Duwamish Head, parked, turned off the engine and looked out at the city across the bay. Street lights bathed its skyscrapers in an art deco glow and the Space Needle stood alone in the night sky, always graceful, always beautiful.

Elizabeth took it in for a while. Gradually, the beauty of the scene stopped affecting her. True, she could describe what she saw in lovely terms, but the truth was, she didn't feel it. She tried again. But again, no sensation. It was merely a scene, a place. Maybe music would change her mood. She turned on the radio. KJR was playing music by The Beatles. So was KOL. Elizabeth listened, but it meant nothing to her. She knew that critics called the new music from England bright and fresh and unlike anything before it, and it probably was. But for her it was only empty sound. After five minutes, she turned it off.

She looked out across the bay for a long time.

Seattle, her home. The lights and the beauty camouflaged a mundane place, a place of petty people grubbing and moiling with no purpose, no direction, people like Layton and Gafney and the women at the tea and the boys at the rap session. Theirs was not a world of horizons, but a world of small things, meaningless things. It was as far as they would ever go. And they didn't even know it.

She sat in silence some more, for an hour, perhaps longer. Gradually, reality, in the form of practicalities, started to settle in.

Escape into the night? Just where would she go? Her parents were dead. Her brother was in Germany with the Army, on the second year of a four year tour and with a family to support on a captain's pay. Whatever other relatives she had were in Wisconsin and she barely knew them. Other than Judy, she had no real friends here. Judy might put her up for a while, but only for a while. Then what?

Get a job? With an English degree that was eight years old? She had no teaching certificate. She could type and answer phones, probably, but did that pay enough to live on?

Get a divorce? How? She didn't know any lawyers. And she had no money for a lawyer anyway.

Where would she even go tonight? She had six dollars in her purse.

And so was that Elizabeth Fleming, like so many before her, came to understand, with sickening finality, that she was stuck in the life she had.

She had no power. She was not rich. She was not a member of an elite. She had nothing with which to exert herself on the rest of the world. Logic? It didn't work with Layton and never had. Why should it? He could rock back on his heels and laugh at her impotent rage because she could do anything about it.

It didn't matter if you were right or wrong or even why you were right or wrong. It didn't matter what was done, only who did it. Margaret Fotheringham had taught her that.

So this was life, Elizabeth thought; the life lived by the majority of humanity. She couldn't dodge it any more. She would continue on in a marriage she hated, doing a job she hated, stuck in a subculture she hated because there was, try as she may to find one, no way out of it.

Elizabeth knew she probably never would accept it completely. Instead she would spend years fantasizing about something better – but never finding the wherewithal to do it. Again, just like the majority of humanity.

Elizabeth did not cry. There would be no point to it. After a while, she started the car and headed home. Layton would be angry, but enough time had passed that he also would be worried. She could probably calm him down by lowering her chin and looking up at him with big, soulful eyes. When they got to bed, she might even take him in her mouth. He had certainly asked her enough times. The practice revolted her, but it might pacify him for a day or two. You do what you have to do.

She drove on and after a few minutes, her mind became blank. There was nothing left to think about.

****

So this guy decides he needs to make a few bucks, see, so he puts up a sign: "Boil Sucker. No job too big, no job too small." Next day, this bitch shows up; big, fat, ugly old pig. She says, "Gotta boil on my uss. Can you suck it?" So he takes a look and here's this humungous boil, all red and purple with green crust around the edges. And the guy says, sure, five bucks. So she pays and he starts suckin' away, and the boil pops a little and he gets some pus on his face, and he keeps on a-sucking, and gets some more pus, 'cept this pus is kinda green and it runs all over the place, gets in his mustache, one loogie even hits him in the eye. But he keeps on a-suckin' and wipin' away the pus and finally, the whole boil pops. Blows up out like a goddamned volcano, I tell ya! So, he spits out the pus out and starts wipin' it off his face and just then the bitch lets out a great big fart. I'm tellin' ya, a fuckin' thunderclap! And the guy looks up and says, "Jesus, lady, what are you tryin' to do, make me sick?"

"Heeheeheehee!" Max Dritt giggled between lips loosely holding a drooping Lucky Strike. The guys at the Chelan loved that one. They had loved all his jokes. He had been the master of the evening. As he turned on to Highway 99 northbound, he smiled at the memory.

Pussy is nature's survival kit. You can eat it, you can fuck it and when it rains, you can stretch it out and pull it over your head.

"Heeheehee – grrrrgh." Max choked back a cough. Then he carefully took his cigarette from his lips, put his tongue to his teeth and gently spit a fleck of tobacco out the window. He always liked that gesture. It made him feel very masculine.

Max Drittt usually spent his Wednesday nights at the Chelan. It was the watering hole for the men from the Harbor Island ship yards, where Max worked – rather, where he was *employed*. For he did as little actual work as possible.

Max had learned that if you moved around a lot, talked a lot and made raunchy references to as many things as possible, you could get away with doing very little. It helped that his boss, good old Bob, was a weak and rather unintelligent man whose main qualification for a supervisor's job was the fact he dressed like one: Always in the same gray work uniform ordered from the Sears Roebuck catalog (a new one once a year); always with a tape measure holstered in a specially made belt; always scowling, his brow furrowed at the difficulty of thought.

Max giggled. Good old Bob. Today he had fucked with Bob, confusing him with lewd references to kippered snacks and the licking thereof. Bob didn't get it, but thought he should and spent most of the day trying to turn it over in his mind. A confused Bob was good. It meant Max could get away with doing even less work than usual.

"Fuck 'em all, fuck 'em all, the long and the short and the tall." Max hummed the tune. That's my motto, he thought. To Max, shirking had become one long, ongoing game. If he couldn't actually escape a job, he could do it slowly. That involved things like dropping tools, then taking his time in picking them up, all the while leering at Bob - or whoever else happened to be nearby - with a conspiratorial grin, as if he were letting him in on some joke. Or he would trip or bump into things and say ouch and flex his arm or wiggle his leg or whatever like he was hurt. You could eat up a lot of time that way and, just as important, draw attention away from the job at hand.

Machines that wouldn't run quite right, or vises that wouldn't grip quite right, or a light bulb that blew out, or any kind of mechanical or technical glitch, offered perhaps the best opportunities. Max could take a long time setting them straight - making sure it took two or three tries - all the while grinning his moronic grin and giggling his moronic giggle.

Occasionally, someone would call him on it, particularly Sessue, the squat, humorless Japanese machinist who worked steadily, quietly and seemingly all the time; immersing himself in the big, dirty machines that made the shop go. Once, during lunch, Max noticed Sessue was eating some sort of Japanese concoction made of fish.

"Ummmm, I can smell that from here," Max said. "You gonna eat it or just put it between two slices of warm liver and fuck it?"

Sessue frowned. "I put in a day's work for a day's pay," he said haltingly. Sessue was not good with words.

But Max was. He laughed. A day's work for a day's pay. Sheeeit.

This night at the Chelan had been a particularly good one. Guys like Bob and Sessue didn't show up there, so Max has free to regale his fellow literati with jokes about getting your teeth cleaned by the barber, or one's turn in the barrel, or the old woman and the hot buttered corn.

"Heeheeheehee!"

Yeah, I've got a million of 'em, Max thought as he passed over the Alaskan Way viaduct. The view from the viaduct; the silver pepper of the stars, the timeless arc of Elliot Bay, unchanging, year after year, century after century, heedless of the petty works of men, was lost on him. He was too busy enjoying being the hip, the with it, the oh so smarter than thou Max Dritt. Fuck 'em all, fuck 'em all, the long and the short and the tall. . .

His car entered the Battery Street tunnel. In twenty minutes Max would be home, to the small shake house in Lake City, the house with the peeling paint and curling shingles and a lawn he mowed only when he got tired of his wife nagging him.

She would be nagging him tonight, standing at the door in her frayed, colorless house coat; her flat, bunioned feet in the same heelless slippers she'd had for five years. She would sniff the alcohol on his breath and ask why he was so late again. She'd had it in for him ever since he tried to slip it up her ass a couple months ago. She yelped and jumped out of bed and demanded to know just who did he think he was.

Max snorted. Hell, he was doing her a favor, her with her cottage cheese legs and tits hanging down like wet beanbags. He could have any woman he wanted. Hell, no secret to knowing what women wanted. Just show them how you can lick your own eyebrows.

"Heeheeheehee!"

The ash from his cigarette fell onto Max's shirt. Damn! He brushed at it, hoping there wasn't a spark that would leave a hole. Damn!

Max fumbled for the package of Lucky Strikes on the passenger's seat. His hand knocked the pack to the floor. Damn! Maybe he did have one too many beers. But hell, he could hold his liquor. He was Max Dritt. Fuck 'em all, fuck 'em all, the long and the short and the tall. . .

"Heeheehee!"

He bent sideways to reach the cigarettes, but he couldn't find them. He tried again, but this time his hand slipped on the steering wheel. The car jerked over the center line. Max pulled the wheel back and sat up. Whew, no harm done. He didn't even see the tan 1960 Pontiac coming the other way, the tan 1960 Pontiac that swerved to miss him, then skidded, then spun off the road.

No, Max Dritt didn't see that. He was too busy thinking about the joke that got the most laughs at the Chelan, the one about the guy who goes to the park with this bitch on a dark night, so dark that after a while the bitch says, "You know that's the grass you've been lickin' for the past half hour. . ."

****

Elizabeth Fleming came out the Battery Street Tunnel and was about a quarter mile from the Aurora Bridge when she saw flashing lights up ahead, on the shoulder of the south bound lane. She slowed with traffic and found herself passing the scene of a wreck. A tan Pontiac had gone off the road and hit a tree head on. The front of the car was crushed back to the windshield. Next to it, an ambulance crew was pushing a gurney. There was a figure on it covered head to toe in a sheet.

So sad, Elizabeth thought. But, well, that's life, it happens all the time. No use getting upset about it. And she drove on, home to her husband.

Epilogue

These things happened many years ago. Some who were there have died, that which was them unraveling into threadbare sunsets. Others have forgotten the reality; recalling only soft tableaus of daisy-colored sunshine and the songs of The Beatles on long ago April afternoons.

But others remember truly, and when they do, their throats tighten and their hearts skip. And they remember and remember and remember.

The End

Meet our author

Doug Margeson

Gazing at the Distant Lights is Doug Margeson's first novel.

Margeson's fiction short stories have been published in The Chaffin Journal, The MacGuffin, 580 Split, Straylight, Worcester Review , The Homestead Review, SNReview, Soundings East and New Millennium Writings magazines. His creative nonfiction has been published in The Palo Alto Review and The Santa Clara Review. His story "Gold Star Buckle" was nominated for the 2011 Pushcart Prize. His story "Barton's Pipe" was chosen for the anthology Best Indie Lit New England, Vol. 2, 2015.

A former newspaper reporter, Margeson won 184 regional and 28 national journalism awards; 212 in all. He was nominated for a Pulitzer Prize in investigative reporting in 1985.

Margeson has taught as a guest lecturer at the University of Washington and for the Pacific Northwest Writers Conference, the Washington Journalism Educators Association and the Washington Press Association.

He served on the boards of directors of the Washington Press Association and the Western Washington Chapter of the Society of Professional Journalists, Sigma Delta Chi. In 1983, he was presented the press association's Superior Performance Award for his work with the state's student press.

He lives in Woodinville, Washington.

CPSIA information can be obtained
at www.ICGtesting.com
Printed in the USA
FSHW021355091219
64897FS